Delicious Housewives!

An Erotic Parody
of the Popular TV Series

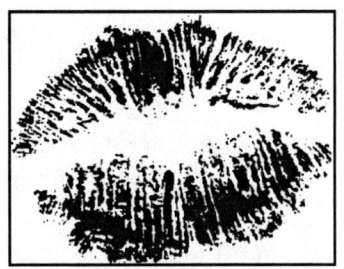

A Novel

by

Tamarias Tyree

Original Publication Copyright MMVI

© MMVI RSVP Press
Revised RSVP Press
Electronic Book Division

© MMVI RSVP Press
ISBN # 0-930865-79-0
978-0-930865-79-5
Digital: 0-930865-81-2
MobiPocket: 0-930865-80-4

This book is a work of fiction.
All rights reserved by the publisher.

No part of this book may be reproduced
without written permission of the publisher.

Please direct all inquiries Via email to:
RSVPPress@RSVPBooks.com
http://RSVPBooks.com

Cover design by the author.

All paper versions of this book were
manufactured in the United States of America.

Dedication

*To the one I love
who loves me
like no one else ever could...
fantasies and all!*

Acknowledgment

A special thanks to the editor, *EB*, who helped shape the manuscript (for ***Delicious Housewives!***) and to the staff of **Professional Editorial** for the final touches.

Lyrics for songs by ***Diet Dr. Creeper*** and ***Sex On the Beach*** used by permission of **C1 Records**. Mp3s available on *MSN Music, Rhapsody, eCast,* and other online music services.

"There are no good girls gone wrong, just bad girls found out!"

- Mae West

"Ever notice that 'what the hell' is always the right decision?"

- Marilyn Monroe

Tamarias Tyree

Other Books by the author include:

**Sex You Up! - Erotic Fantasies
Sizzling Hot Erotica**
(*Volumes I & II*)

Titles Above are Best-selling Digital Ebooks
from Firefly Publications & Media
(www.fireflyerotica.com)

Available at Amazon.com, Powells.com,
ebookmall.com, Mobipocket.com
and other fine booksellers.

Prologue

Welcome to Erotica Lane

Welcome to Erotica Lane. My name is Mary Lynn Young. I used to live here not so long before that fateful day when I made a distasteful discovery I would never be able to get over, no matter how hard I tried. It was truly a life-changing discovery, enlightening but devastating. At that point, I knew why my husband no longer touched me and why we no longer made love. Why we no longer looked forward to making love on Saturday night twice a month. That explained why I spent Saturday nights curled up with Mary Higgins Clark or James Patterson while Paul pretended to watch TV, surfing through what seemed like a million channels, watching only snippets here and there.

Foolishly, I thought he must be really exhausted (and he may have been!) from work or that he had erectile dysfunction. I even thought about suggesting he see our family physician to get a prescription for Viagra, Cialis, Levitra ... or ... something ... I saw those ads on TV. So the products must work, I thought, and the side effects were modest, something about a thirty-seven hour erection. That would be plenty of time for intercourse, I decided. We might even have a chance to do it twice...for once!

I wondered why we didn't have sex every other Saturday night, why he was always tired, and why he spent so much time in the yard even though I never saw him doing anything. That was, until the day I followed him into the side yard, through a hole in the fence (damn Mrs. Hoover's dog!) and watched as he entered Mrs. Hoover's back door. What was he doing? I wondered.

Later I remember wishing that I had just finished baking my apple cobbler rather than following my husband on his sordid little adventure. I remember thinking my family would not have dessert after dinner that evening. But then, once I decided to kill myself, it didn't seem all that important. But I'm getting ahead of myself a bit....

I crept closer for a peek. Looking in the kitchen window, I nearly fainted where I stood. There was my husband riding the elderly Mrs. Hoover like a flea on a monkey in a wind storm!

I couldn't believe what I saw and was tempted to pluck my own eyes out! Literally! Then, turning away from the unpleasant scene, I felt light headed and more than a little nauseous I felt as if I should cry, but no tears would come. Maybe I was just too shocked – or maybe it was the fact that the scene I had witnessed was forever burned into my retinas! I'd never be able to erase that image from my mind.

Embarrassed, humiliated and shocked by what I'd discovered, I stumbled back to the fence, through the hole and managed to make it back inside my home. There, in my dining room I put my husband's pistol to my head and pulled the trigger...funny thing is even in the afterlife I can still see their naked bodies on that rickety old island....

Yes, there truly is a hell!

1

An Apple a Day...

After Mary Lynn's funeral, the ladies who lived on the cul-de-sac at the end of Erotica Lane met for coffee at SueAnn's house. They crowded around SueAnn's cramped breakfast nook and watched while she poured freshly-brewed coffee and said nothing. It was as if they were waiting for someone to speak, to break the silence that had hung in the air since the funeral.

"It was a good service, I thought," Wynette spoke up, unable to bear the silence. Then she took a quick sip of her coffee. Wynette, an often harried wife and mother of three, was a tall woman, slim with attractive–if somewhat angular–short, straight dirty-blonde hair and friendly, intelligent eyes. "A really good service."

"Yes, it was fine," SueAnn said absentmindedly and sat a cup of coffee she'd just poured in front of Giji. Tall, lanky but undeniably female, SueAnn was a fair-skinned beauty, with raven-black hair, a fresh-scrubbed face and a warm, genuine smile. Although she looked barely old enough to be out of high school, SueAnn was the divorced mother of a teenage daughter.

After an awkward pause in the conversation, Giji nodded her curly mop of platinum blonde tresses in agreement and said, "As good as a funeral can be, I suppose."

Giji was also a divorcee–although she would never confirm or deny that she'd ever been married! She had been divorced longer than she cared to admit or recall. Often labeled a sexpot by people who knew her and especially by those who didn't, Giji seemed to do everything possible to live up to her reputation. Truthfully, the only thing Giji liked more than having fun was men, and she wasn't ashamed to admit it. In fact, Giji wasn't ashamed of anything, really. If that made her a sexpot or worse, then Giji wasn't about to apologize.

Giji looked down at the coffee and then raised her head to look at SueAnn. "Did you forget?" Giji said with a bit of sarcasm. "I said no thanks when you asked if I wanted a cup of coffee?"

"Oh I forgot," SueAnn said, quickly retrieving the cup and setting it aside, then taking a seat between Connie and Wynette.

"SueAnn, are you okay?" Wynette asked, looking directly at her.

SueAnn shrugged. "Yes. I'm just glad Julie is visiting her father for the summer and isn't here to see what's happening. Really I'm fine, it's just...you know...everything..."

Wynette reached across the table and patted SueAnn's hand. "I know. It's been hard on all of us, losing a friend…to suicide."

Connie sat perfectly with her back straight, her make-up perfect, every hair in place. She moved with the sleek grace of a cat. Like a cat, she had mysterious, green eyes that gave the impression she could see right through you and into your soul. That was not the only misleading thing about Connie. She wanted everyone to believe she was the perfect wife, the perfect mother and the perfect woman. Perfect. That was the impression Connie tried to convey and the illusion that her life was seamlessly perfect. Somehow she believed that if she could keep up appearances, it would somehow be enough. It never was, though, she fought to maintain the illusion of perfection because that was easier than admitting the truth that her life was far from perfect. She couldn't even admit the truth to herself.

"I miss her," Connie said quietly.

"We all do," Ariella agreed. The youngest of the wives and almost a newlywed, Ariella was a slender, dark-haired Latina beauty, with an olive complexion and dark, deep, fiery brown eyes that sparkled with a passion that smoldered just beneath the surface.

SueAnn looked up at Wynette and then around to each of her friends that were seated around the table. "I just keep wondering why a woman would decide to kill herself in the middle of baking an apple cobbler?"

Giji started top open her mouth.

"Don't say it, Giji!" Ariella warned quickly.

"Okay, while you're all sitting around here feeling sorry for yourselves," Giji said. "FYI my house just sold. For me it's almost a record to sell a house in less than a week, and I'm proud of the fact as a real estate agent. However, I'm unhappy because I didn't have a chance to find a new house before the sale. Now I'm –"

"Homeless?" Ariella asked.

"How did this get to be about you?" Wynette asked, her voice betraying a note of annoyance.

"It's pretty simple," Giji said bluntly. "I need a place to stay. Hint, hint..."

"Well, most of us have kids," Connie reminded her.

"What does that matter? What do I look like?" Giji asked. "A pedophile?"

Unable to control herself Ariella laughed, then tried to suppress any further laughter by putting her hand in front of her lips.

Giji gave her a stern look. "Do you find this funny, Ariella?"

Ariella shrugged. "I wouldn't say funny," she answered. "You might say mildly amusing or comically tragic. Take your pick!"

Giji threw up her hands in frustration. "Come on people," she said in a tight voice. "What would our good friend Mary Lynn do? Huh?"

"Well, she might drive you to the nearest homeless shelter," Wynette said bluntly. "I can assure you that she would never take you into her home."

"Well, big surprise," Giji erupted. "She always stopped just short of calling me the neighborhood tramp!"

"I'm sure she meant that in the nicest way," Connie said, trying to hide the faintest of smiles.

Giji stared at her blankly. "Oh, Connie, there's no nice way to say 'Hey, I think you're a slut!' Besides, she said you were the coldest, snobbiest person she'd ever met!"

"She did not!" Connie snapped back indignantly.

"She did, too," Giji shot back like a small child arguing with a sibling. "She said you never allowed your kids to play with all the neighborhood mall rats! Just the ones from the more prominent families!"

Connie looked at Giji, a sobering, level eye-to-eye glare, and for a moment she could have sworn she were sitting across the table from her mother. "Well, we don't let the children of people we frown upon play with our children," she said, "after all, poor breeding doesn't skip a generation!"

"You would know," Giji said with a smile. "Mary Lynn felt you were too concerned about where the parents of those other kids shopped."

"Mary Lynn was entitled to her opinion," Connie said crisply. "I don't really care what she said. After all, if her life was so perfect, she wouldn't have killed herself, now would she?"

"You could try to be a little warmer," Giji suggested, "less of a snob."

"Your only warmth," Connie erupted, "is between your legs!"

"There you go!" Giji gasped. "Hands down that makes me warmer than you!"

"Guys, please, you sound like foul-mouthed kids," Wynette protested.

"And as for Mary Lynn, she wasn't little miss perfect herself," Connie said, a note of anger still evident in her voice. "I could tell you –"

"We don't need to go there, Connie," Wynette begged.

"Mary Lynn was a wonderful person," SueAnn said, "and I won't sit here and let her be maligned. Mary Lynn did wonderful things for each one of us."

"Speak for yourself." Giji said under her breath.

"I am speaking for myself," SueAnn said, remembering, "when my marriage ended, Mary Lynn was there for me, supported me and helped me see that Scott's affair wasn't my fault. She helped me through it, and I'll always be grateful for that. No matter what anyone says Mary Lynn was a very caring person."

"Yeah," Ariella said quietly, "when Marco and I moved into the neighborhood, Mary Lynn was the first one to welcome us."

"Several years ago when I was addicted to soaps and they took over my life," Wynette recalled, "Mary Lynn staged an intervention that really opened my eyes."

"Hey, like I said, she was always calling me a tramp. At least, she was thinking it. I saw the look in her eyes every time we talked and I knew what she was thinking…" Giji paused for effect. "Tramp!"

"Well, you certainly didn't change any opinions at the service," SueAnn said.

"Yeah," Ariella chimed in, "what were you doing in the closet with that mortician?"

Giji sighed with a wicked glint in her eyes. "Well, isn't it obvious? I'm really, really hot and he needed to get warm – fast! He was a cute guy, but he was a real stiff, if you know what I mean!" She giggled playfully, and continued, "But, not where it really counts! I have to say that his cold hands felt really good on my –"

"Giji!" SueAnn gasped. "We were at the funeral service of one of our friends. Show some respect!"

"Yes, Mother," Giji said with a touch of sarcasm, then playfully added, "I'll be good, but I have to say that when he kissed my neck, even his breath was cold."

Ariella laughed softly, but stopped quickly when no one else joined in.

SueAnn looked as if something had just occurred to her. "Paul seemed so unemotional at the service," she said quietly, "kind of detached."

"Cold?" Giji asked and rolled her eyes toward Connie.

"Well," Wynette said, frowning at Giji, "he could just be emotionally drained after losing his wife that way."

"Or, he could just not care," Giji says, then, when everyone looked at her. "I'm just saying what we're all thinking!"

"He's probably devastated," Ariella said softly, "Sometimes people don't grieve until weeks or months after they lose someone. It could be that they can't believe that the person is actually gone."

"Or, he drove her to kill herself," Giji added, "and doesn't care."

Connie sighed heavily. "Giji, please give it a rest," she said, standing. "I don't know about the rest of you, but I have to get home, make dinner...."

The other wives followed and SueAnn stood alone at the window of her dining room as her friends returned to their homes. *Life goes on,* she thought, thinking of Mary Lynn, *even when you're not here...*

***

Wynette shed her clothes, sank into the warm bath and settled back to relax in the warm soapy water. She closed her eyes and placed a warm, damp washcloth over her face. So much of the tension drained from her body, right away, the warm water going to work immediately to soothe and relax her tense muscles. The last week had been so stressful. Losing a dear friend like Mary

Lynn was devastating, and not knowing why she took her own life added to the sense of loss.

Forcing herself to think of more pleasant topics, Wynette thought of her husband Steven's homecoming. Steven, a marketing representative for an insurance company, was on one of his frequent business trips. Usually he was away two weeks at a time most months. Occasionally he was away three weeks out of the month if he had an unusually high number of clients to visit. That was common when the company had a new product they wanted to push. Fortunately, for her especially, most of Steven's trips were two weeks at a time.

He would be home tomorrow night, and she felt her anticipation growing as she thought about him being home, in her bed and in her arms! She was looking forward to their lovemaking, but she was looking forward to Steven even more. She looked forward to having him home, enjoying his company, his smile, his laughter, his touch, his warmth, his closeness, his smell (she had grown accustomed to a smell no man could match). His deeply passionate kisses, which were still hot after nearly twelve years of marriage were another thing she looked forward to as the warm water caressed her body.

Wynette fantasized about Steven's homecoming and touched herself. Her hands caressed her sudsy, wet breasts. She used one hand to fondle her breasts and pinch her hardened nipples. At the same time, she dropped the other hand beneath the warm, soapy water and began to touch and finger her pussy. She felt the warm water flow into her pussy when she pushed three and then four fingers inside herself. Once her fingers were deep in her pussy, she started to rub her clit, gently at first, then harder and harder with a growing sense of urgency.

While her hands explored and pleasured her body, her mind wandered, thinking of Steven, imagining he were touching her, his hands doing amazing, wonderful things to her body. Her fantasy began by imagining Steven's homecoming, a perfect reunion…

After a tough day of running after the boys and making sure they weren't killing each other, literally, she would straighten the house. Then she would bathe the boys and tuck them into their beds for a sound sleep. Once she had a chance to catch her breath, she would soak in a warm lavender scented bath. After her bath, she would dress in her sexy silky pajamas, without the bottoms. She would wear the button up top but would leave a few of the top buttons open to show just enough cleavage to get Steven's attention.

The scene played out in her mind. She would meet Steven at the door, opening the door open as he held his bag and fumbled for his key. He would have that familiar dog-tired look from the long trip, as if he could drop were he stood. But at the sight of her, he would become rejuvenated, giving her his biggest smile, his eyes twinkling with excitement as he caressed her with his eyes. Dropping his bag just inside the door, he would push the door and take her into his arms, holding her so close that she could hardly breathe. For the briefest of seconds, he would look deeply, lovingly into his eyes, then he would press his lips to hers. They would share a long, lingering kiss that gave a promise of what was yet to come.

As usual, when he returned from a business trip, she would offer him something to eat, but he would say he had a bite on the plane. He would ask how the boys are and if they were a handful while he was away. "They were wonderful," she would lie. Then she would tell him a little story about something the boys had done while he was away. Maybe they gave each other haircuts or climbed over the back fence and fell into one of those muddy holes Mrs. Hoover's dog dug before it disappeared.

They would share a quick laugh while she unbuttoned his shirt in an eager gesture to indicate what she wanted. "Hon, I'm exhausted," would be his frustrated words, but he would give her a quick kiss when she was a few buttons away from having his shirt off.

"I know, sweetheart," she would say as her bottom lip began

to show that slight pout when she didn't get what she wanted, "but it's been so long."

He would smile through his exhaustion, pleased at her interest, her eagerness and desire for him.

"I can't promise anything, hon," he would say, "we'll see. I'm just so tired after the long flight. Let's just take it easy and see where things go, okay?"

She would nod with a faint smile, knowing he would move heaven and earth to satisfy her tonight.

They would turn out the lights, stand close in the dark for a few seconds, listening to each other breathing and whispering to each other about how much they'd missed each other. He would wrap his arm around her shoulders, pulling her close to his warm chest and they would walk up the stairs, quietly, careful not to make any noise that would awaken the kids. She would stand in the doorway while he went into their sons' room, giving each of their beautiful, sleeping angels a soft peck on their foreheads as they slept.

Closing the door quietly behind them, they would walk a few steps down the hall and enter their own bedroom. There they would rekindle the passion that gave off sparks earlier. He would finish unbuttoning his shirt and take it off in one sweeping motion before she pushed his T-shirt up and over his head to reveal his somewhat muscular chest. She would place a quick kiss on his chest, just a brush of her lips, because it was one of the little things she did. One of the things he'd found cute when they were younger, and she continued because it was something she'd done in the early days of their relationship when they were younger, life was simpler and they'd enjoyed each other every time they got the chance.

It had been two long weeks since she felt his kiss, his touch and it seemed like an eternity! Oh, how she wanted him, and she could see in his eyes that he wanted her, too. She longed for a deep passionate kiss that lingered forever, with their tongues touching, exploring each other's mouths. He would kiss her earlobe, gently nibbling her lobe before he kissed her neck and made his way to her breasts. He would lick and kiss her breasts, then suck her nipples, first one and then the other, until she was climbing the walls with anticipation. She wanted to feel their naked bodies close, touching. With an overwhelming longing for his touch, she wanted to feel his hands all over her body, wanted to feel his strong hands massaging her breasts and pinching her erect nipples.

Wynette fantasized about Steven making love to her all over their bedroom, on the bed, on the floor, on the chaise lounge, and finally in their bathroom, against the cool tile on the floor, then in the shower while cool water rained down on them, as she pumped her fingers in and out of her wet pussy and rubbed her clit wildly. He would lift her against the wet tile and shove his cock deeper and deeper inside her until she moaned so loudly, she was afraid she would wake the kids.

As she was about to cum, a thought broke her concentration and shattered the fantasy. Sex, she thought, and suddenly her fantasy was crushed and she was brought back to the moment. She removed the damp cloth from her face and washed her breasts, dripping water down her stomach. Ever since it came up at SueAnn's after the funeral, she had thought about her intervention. Mary Lynn had been so wonderful, so understanding, so caring....

***

When the doorbell rang, Wynette was well into her daily ritual of marathon viewing of the daytime soaps (she even taped them to watch again on the weekend), her day punctuated only by commercials that allowed her just enough time to grab a quick snack from the fridge, check on her son's play in the back yard, or make a mad dash to the bathroom for a two-flush pee! Unable to do anything but get the door, Wynette hurried, trying to get back to the TV before Jack proposed to Mrs. Chancellor.

Wynette raised her eye to the peephole. Her friends stood on her small porch, looking straight ahead with serious expressions on their solemn faces. Seeing them at her door sent a shock wave through her. She was concerned that something was wrong and they'd come together to break the news to her. Her first thought was that Steven had been in an accident or worse....

Wynette opened the door, her heart raced. "What is it? Is something wrong?"

"Hon, this is an intervention," Mary Lynn announced. "You're addicted to soaps, sweetie."

Without another word, Mary Lynn walked past Wynette into the house.

Wynette looked after her then at the other wives standing just outside the door, trying to decide what to do. Finally, without a word to anyone, she turned, left the door open, followed Mary Lynn into the living room and she sank onto the sofa, already defeated.

Mary Lynn stood over her while SueAnn, Connie and Ariella stood just inside the living room, watching, grateful they were in their shoe's–and not Wynette's.

Wynette clutched the remote close to her body as if it protecting it from her friend's words. "I thought Sheridan and Luis would finally get together, but no, Sheridan was carried off by a really big bird, a pterodactyl, I think and it's all Tabitha's fault! If only she'd learn how to cast a decent spell!"

The other wives just watched, listened and hoped they could just stand nearby and offer support.

"Hon, you talk about these people as if they're real," Mary Lynn placed a comforting hand on her friend's shoulder. "You need to spend less time watching imaginary people on those soaps and more time with real people."

Wynette looked at Mary Lynn through pathetic eyes, filled with unshed tears. "I'm not addicted, I swear," she uttered these words, but couldn't tear her eyes away from the TV screen. "I just watch them to see how people in other cities live, what fashions are in, and if Stephanie pushed Brooke off the ledge!" She paused, looked away from the TV, then added, "Oh, God, I am addicted!"

Mary Lynn sat beside Wynette and reached for the remote, but Wynette held it just out of reach. Suddenly, she aimed the remote and raced frantically through the channels one after another.

"What are you doing?" SueAnn asked.

"I have to find 'Guiding Light,' " Wynette told her in a serious voice. "I have to see if Reva confronted her stalker and if Phillip's sex-change was a success!"

Connie stepped in front of the television. "Don't you see what this behavior is doing to you? My God woman, you're out of control!"

"Yeah," Ariella said and frowned, "why you couldn't you become addicted to porn like normal people?"

Wynette placed her face in her hands as if she were sobbing. "I can quit any time I want," she mumbled, "as soon as I find out if Nikki's amnesia is hereditary and if Victor's still on life-support."

"No," Mary Lynn spoke firmly and wrestled the remote from her hands. "You have to stop watching soaps. You have to stop, now. Not tomorrow and not next week. That's the only way you can beat this thing."

Wynette looked at Mary Lynn, a serious look on her face. "I'm not sure I can," she admitted finally.

Mary Lynn knew this was the breakthrough she'd been waiting for. "Sure you can," she said soothingly, "and all of us are here to help you. Together we'll help you beat this thing. Soon you won't care if Nikki's sex change took or if Victor ran off with the chamber maid!"

Mary Lynn was right. Wynette got over her addiction to soaps. Her friends helped her, supported her, shared hundreds of cups of coffee with her while she stopped wondering what was going on in Pine Valley, Genoa City and even Springfield....

The only problem was that when she beat her soap addiction, Wynette had almost immediately found another...*sex*.

***

Mrs. Hoover sat at the small table in her dark, dated kitchen, sipping a cup of freshly-brewed coffee while flipping through her diary. *Diary,* she repeated to herself, yet it was so much more than that and so much more important.... It's more like a lifeline, she told herself. Oh, the secrets that were hidden between the covers!

All mine, all my tasty little secrets about the unsavory side of suburban life, valuable and powerful, but their power lies in keeping them secret... She thought of Giji. She would have to make sure that Giji Brickhouse did not discover any of her valuable little secrets.

Oh Giji, Mrs. Hoover hoped she wasn't making a huge mistake letting that trampy vixen move in with her. It could be wonderful, she decided, or disastrous. The one moment she actually felt a bit of compassion for someone else, why did it have to be Giji Brickhouse! If only she had held her ground and said no when Giji hinted about moving in. She would have been stronger, she knew, except for one detail Giji mentioned, the other wives had refused to offer shelter in her time of need. That did it. Martha Hoover finally had a chance to one up the other wives by taking in the very undesirable Giji Brickhouse! Even so, it wasn't her smartest move and she had to be very careful while Giji was under her roof. If she wasn't extremely careful, chances were, she would pay–and pay dearly!

Mrs. Hoover closed her diary and patted the red faux leather cover lovingly. Her little secrets had paid off handsomely over the years. These secrets afforded her extra monies and other fringe benefits. If it weren't for them, she would probably be homeless herself, just like Giji. Her late husband, Earl, certainly had not left her well off. Earl, hadn't been good for much, not even a good provider, she sighed to herself. (He wasn't even especially good in bed, but she didn't know that until after he died.) If she had had to depend on the little monies he'd left her, she'd actually have to eat her own casseroles, she decided, or worse! There had been so many bills, Earl's life insurance had been spent before the check arrived. She shared a certain empathy with Giji, even if she wouldn't admit it to anyone except herself.

Yep, Earl had left her nearly penniless, she remembered. Poor pathetic Earl, he had not been especially lucky in life...or even in death. He died of pneumonia or something similar the doctor had told her, but in the back of her mind Martha knew full well it could have been food poisoning from the potato and cod casserole she'd inadvertently left out on the counter two nights straight–and in the middle of summer. Good thing she hadn't eaten much of it herself, Martha thought. Earl, God rest his soul, had consumed the casserole like food was about to be rationed. There had just been a tiny bit left in the bottom of the casserole dish. Well, Martha let out a deep sigh, like she'd told herself so many times over the years–it was probably the pneumonia that killed him!

After Earl's death, the Reverend Daley took up the slack. He made his move here in her modest kitchen shortly after Earl's demise. The Reverend came over to express his sincerest condolences for her loss and to see if he could be of help in her time of grief. She'd been about to pour him a cup of freshly-brewed coffee, when the Reverend embraced her, she got a feel of the Reverend like she had never felt his presence before. His hardness pressed firmly and thickly against her black satin mourning dress. It was then that she knew: The Reverend wanted a muffin with his coffee! That had been the start of many wonderful afternoons of passionate lovemaking with the good Reverend Daley, who filled a void for intimacy in her life, a void her late husband had never fully satisfied–even when he was alive! No, she had never missed Earl, she told herself, despite his untimely death....

Thinking of death, she suddenly thought of Mary Lynn Young. Truthfully, she never cared for the woman. Over the years at church gatherings, community get-togethers, and other social events, she noticed that Mary Lynn would never touch her signature dish, her beloved casseroles. From the way Mary Lynn frowned at her casseroles over the years it was like the woman felt these dishes were beneath her. In essence that summed up how Mary Lynn Young felt about others. Mary Lynn was one of those people who felt she was easily superior to others. In fact, she wouldn't have been surprised if that was what lead to Mary Lynn's downfall, her sudden suicide, something happened to put the holier-than-thou Mary Lynn Young in her place and her fake façade was shattered once and for all.

Martha wondered what it could have been as she took a slow sip of her coffee. It briefly crossed her mind that Mary Lynn might have discovered the truth. No, she quickly dismissed the idea. Mary Lynn had no idea of Martha's involvement with her husband, Paul. Neither did Mary Lynn know about Paul and the church treasurer, Tawny Daley, the Reverend Daley's daughter. Martha had noticed Paul and Tawny making eyes across the pews, but Mary Lynn would never have noticed that since she was too focused on doing the right thing. Such a do-gooder, Martha thought cynically. Yes, that's probably what contributed to her suicide. Mary Lynn was probably so distraught when she finally learned that most people aren't concerned with doing the right thing, they just do what suits them personally, financially, politically–or any combination of those things. Poor Mary Lynn! Martha thought, she was unable to deal with the truth and unable to go on....

Her thoughts were interrupted by a most unpleasant sound. "Yoo hoo, Martha!" Giji called. "I'm back."

"I'm in the kitchen," Mrs. Hoover called to her.

Giji came through the door with the biggest, most annoying smile that Mrs. Hoover had ever seen in her life.

"What's that?" Giji asked, looking down at Mrs. Hoover's little red book.

Mrs. Hoover smiled and pushed her little red book aside.

"Are we keeping secrets?" Giji teased lightheartedly, breathing heavily from carrying another load of her things. "A diary, at your age, how very *Red Shoe!*"

"It's nothing of importance," Mrs. Hoover said in a tight, uncomfortable voice. "How would you like to take a break from moving to join me for a quick cup of coffee?"

"That'd be great," Giji said. "I like mine black with a little sweetener." She paused briefly, then she smiled that annoying, saccharin smile again, the one that grated on Martha Hoover's very last nerve. "You know what they say, I don't need the added sugar, I'm already sweet enough!"

"I'll bet you are," Mrs. Hoover said, her face a combination of a forced smile with an unavoidable frown, as if something had left a bad taste in her mouth. "If you were any sweeter, you'd be a diabetic!"

After a light chuckle between them, Mrs. Hoover went about getting Giji a cup of coffee. While Mrs. Hoover had her back turned, Giji reached for the little red book and was about to open it when Mrs. Hoover turned back around.

"Ah - ah - ahhh!" Mrs. Hoover said, catching her new houseguest in the act. "We wouldn't want to wear out our welcome so soon, would we?"

***

In her lilac and tan living room with rose accents, Martha Hoover held the phone and stood so she could peer through the blinds to watch her front walk way. She wanted a clear view just in case Giji returned from her house with another load of her god-awful belongings.

Giji had worked all morning like a ditzy worker bee bringing over one load of her ghastly belongings after another, each one seeming more gaudy and cheap than the last. Martha had never seen so much crap in her life. It even occurred to her that Giji might be turning her spare bedroom into a replica of the showroom at the local Goodwill. How could one person have so much uncoordinated garbage? God forbid they should have a fire, all that cheap leopard print fabric and pink vinyl would go up like a torch!

"Yes, Gladys," Martha Hoover was saying, sounding almost cryptic, "you heard correctly. Trailer trash Barbie is moving in with me."

"Oh, I hope you haven't made a big mistake, Martha," her longest and dearest friend's concern was obvious in her tone. "I worry about you taking in strays like her."

"I know, dear," Martha sounded as if saving the down trodden was her life's calling. "I know. But what else could I do? She doesn't have any place else to go. God knows her high-falutin family didn't want her."

"Well, maybe she could find a place to rent," Gladys suggested. "She could get an emergency rental or something, after all, she is a real estate agent."

"Some real estate agent!" Martha Hoover told her friend. "She sold her house before she had another place to live!"

"She did not!" Gladys repeated incredulously. "Really?"

"Oh, she did," Martha assured her, relishing the moment and the disclosure. "I kid you not. I suppose the quick sale is a testament to her ability as a real estate agent–or maybe just dumb luck, Giji is a blonde so who knows?"

"Wow, Martha, you saved her," Gladys sounded genuinely impressed. "She could have been homeless living under a bridge somewhere if it wasn't for your kindness. That is so nice of you. It makes me proud to know you and call you my friend. You're a hero, Martha, a true hero."

"Well, I don't know about hero," Martha said, rolling her eyes heavenward, but she had to admit that she was enjoying the spotlight her friend cast upon her. "Let's just agree I saved some nice Christian family from the shock of seeing that living under a bridge." She chuckled at her words, but stopped short of laughing when Gladys didn't join her. "Just my good deed for the day. I guess you could say I saved Giji, God bless her sordid little soul."

She paused mid chuckle as a thought occurred to her. "I suppose Giji is worth saving."

"Of course, she is," Gladys assured her. "All God's children are worth saving Martha, no matter how blonde they may be."

"You're probably right, Glad," Martha reluctantly agreed, letting out a deep sigh. "I just hope I don't live to regret my own generosity. Giji hasn't been much of a neighbor, she could be an even worse houseguest."

"Well, I warned you," Gladys said, recalling her earlier comments about Giji. "She could turn out to be the houseguest from hell, and I'm not a swearing woman, dammit!"

Martha rolled her eyes at Glady's last comment. "Would you believe she's driving a gaudy pink Cadillac, she said her father gave it to her at her high school graduation. With all the pink surrounding Giji, it looks like she was run over by a Mary Kay representative!" she said and caught a movement through the blind. "Oh, Gladys, here comes Miss Congeniality now! She's wearing vintage Daisy Dukes and dragging the last of her tacky pink vinyl luggage. God only knows where she got that!"

"Probably at a Barbie swap meet!" Glad snickered.

"Good one, Glad!" After an exchange of hearty laughter, Martha heard the door opening and said quietly, "The little bitch is here, I have to go."

"What?" Gladys said loudly in Martha's ear.

"Giji's here," Martha Hoover said loudly, forgetting that Glad was sometimes hard of hearing. "I'll fill you in on everything later, hon. Bye."

Martha was putting down the phone as Giji entered. She turned to face her new houseguest. "I wish I could help you, dear," she spoke softly, feebly, "but the doctor doesn't want me lifting anything chea ummm - heavy!"

"Was that Gladys?" Giji asked, breathing hard, winded from dragging the luggage.

"Yes." Martha smiled. "I told her how much I'm going to enjoy having you here!"

Giji glanced down proudly. "How do you like my luggage?" she asked like a kid showing off a new toy to a friend. "I just got it a couple of weeks ago over on Rodeo Drive."

"You mean Rodeo Drive," Martha corrected her. "It's pronounced Ro-DAY-oh!"

"No, it's Rodeo Drive over near the mall," Giji told her matter-of-factly. "You've probably seen their ads on TV during the 'Filthy Rich: Cattle Drive.' They sell western wear!"

"Ummm, how nice," Martha Hoover said and smiled. "It - it's my ... ah...my favorite color!"

2

Like a Virgin...

Giji lay on Mrs. Hoover's lumpy old sofa after their first meal together. Her head was swimming and it seemed to be traveling down somehow to her stomach, stopping just sort of nausea.

Mrs. Hoover had made one of her infamous casseroles, one she claimed was her husband's favorite, a special potato and codfish casserole. Giji didn't know why the dish would have been Mrs. Hoover's late husband's favorite, it wasn't especially tasty, in fact, it seemed unusually fishy. Giji had to hold her breath and try to force down the mixture of flaky fish and mushy potatoes.

At one point during the meal, she felt as if the meal would make a return visit. It paused half way down and wouldn't go any farther. Almost gagging, she'd grabbed her glass of watered-down tea and gulped until the fish and potatoes were dislodged and slid down her throat.

After dinner, Giji didn't feel well, but Mrs. Hoover assured her it was probably exhaustion from moving all her things earlier in the day. Giji felt pretty sure it was because of the meal they shared. She didn't say anything, since Mrs. Hoover was especially nice, even offering to do the dishes so Giji could lie down for a while.

Giji drifted into a restful sleep when she heard glasses clinking together and she looked up to see Mrs. Hoover standing over her. "Sit up," Mrs. Hoover boomed.

Reluctantly Giji swung her legs off the edge of the sofa and moved to a sitting position.

"A little wine before bedtime and you'll sleep fine!" Mrs. Hoover announced, smiling brightly. "At least, it always works for me and it'll make you feel better. Besides, we have to celebrate our first night together."

Giji rolled her eyes suspiciously. "Are you trying to liquor me up, Martha?" she asked, trying to tease her hostess.

"I thought we could share a little toddy," Mrs. Hoover said, "especially since this is our first night as roommates."

"As long as that's all we share..." Giji said under her breath, still feeling the effects of the casserole dinner.

"What'd you say?" Mrs. Hoover asked, putting two wine glasses on the table in front of the sofa.

"Share and share alike!" Giji lied. "You're such a sharing person!"

"Speaking of sharing," Mrs. Hoover said and glanced at Giji as she seated herself and began unscrewing the cap on the wine. "I haven't gotten your share of the rent for the first month."

Giji gave Mrs. Hoover her sweetest smile. "Didn't I tell you?" she asked coyly. "It's in the mail." She chuckled as her dinner threatened to come back up.

"Well, if it doesn't get here soon," Mrs. Hoover commented, pouring the wine, "we may have to think of another way to settle up."

"I have a feeling my share will be arriving at your door, first thing in the morning!" Giji assured her, smiling, uneasy about the meaning behind Mrs. Hoover's words. "It may even get here sooner!"

"Now there's something worth drinking to," Mrs. Hoover said

and smiled her own saccharin smile.

Giji looked at the huge bottle of discount wine. "Wow! You really splurged."

Mrs. Hoover paused, smiled at her, and said, "No, silly. It was on sale." She handed Giji a glass. "To being roomies!" She touched her glass to Giji's, then paused with a smirk on her face. "Bottom's up!"

"Salute!" Giji said and they clinked glasses. Giji took a big sip and almost gagged. She had to fight to keep the wine in her mouth. She was sure there were tears in her eyes. "Gee," she said, her lips slightly puckered. "This stuff is powerful!"

Mrs. Hoover had a pleased twinkle in her eyes. "Isn't it great? Oh, I just knew you'd like it," she said, thinking yep, it's cheap, Giji, just like you!

After her second glass, Giji noticed the wine suddenly tasted a lot better. It occurred to her that it was probably because her taste buds had adjusted to the tartness of the wine–or the concoction had totally burned out her taste buds! Either way, the cheap wine was more tolerable and was giving her the nicest buzz she'd had in a while. It almost made Mrs. Hoover seem like a human being, Giji thought. Wow! This stuff really is powerful!

Mrs. Hoover kept refilling their glasses and laughing occasionally like a demented dingo. Somehow, Giji thought, it seemed appropriate. In fact, she realized that she liked Mrs. Hoover like this instead of her usual self.

Then Mrs. Hoover "accidentally on purpose" touched one of Giji's boobs, and there was an awkward drunken moment when things seemed weirdly wrong but Giji wasn't sure what was wrong. Suddenly, they both laughed uncontrollably and it didn't seem to matter anymore… After that, there was only the blur of hands, arms, legs and other body parts. Even in her advanced state of inebriation, Giji remembered thinking something just didn't seem right….

***

Giji awoke the next morning curled in the fetal position on Mrs. Hoover's lumpy old sofa, where she apparently slept all night. Rolling over on her back, she felt tired and stiff, then she tried to sit up and fell back onto the sofa. She put one hand to her throbbing head and the other on her unsettled stomach. Her head hurt so bad she could hardly think. Then she remembered the night before, she and Mrs. Hoover drinking the discount wine.

She noticed the most horrendous smell that seemed to be wafting from the kitchen. Whatever it was, it was as unbearable as the pain in her head and stomach.

Suddenly Mrs. Hoover appeared in the doorway. "I see her royal highness is awake," she observed. "It's about time. Breakfast is almost ready."

"What is that smell?" Giji asked, thinking it smelled like a heady mixture of codfish and bile.

Mrs. Hoover smiled. "Oh, it's breakfast, sweetie," she answered, pleased that Giji had noticed. "I'm reheating the leftover casserole from last night. Nothing like leftover codfish to get your day started right!"

Giji's stomach started to churn, and she realized she might hurl any minute. With that unpleasant thought in mind, she swung her legs off the sofa and sat up. "I think I'll pass," she said weakly. "I seem to have plenty leftover from last night!"

"You have no idea what you're missing!" Mrs. Hoover told her in a bright, sing-songy voice.

Oh, yes, I do, Giji thought, putting her head in her hands and trying to fight the nausea, she wondered why Mrs. Hoover wasn't hung over. Then a thought occurred to her. The old bat had probably drunk so much cheap, discount wine from the esteemed vineyards of Toledo, Ohio, that her body had built up a resistance to the stuff and its powerful after effects. If anyone could become immune to the effects associated with drinking wine so cheap that was probably made from imitation grapes, it was Martha Hoover!

Glancing down through her partially closed eyes, Giji noticed that the word *Naughty!* was on the front of her sweatpants when it should have been in back. Giji looked up just as Mrs. Hoover was about to go back into the kitchen. "Did we do something?" she asked, puzzled.

Mrs. Hoover paused and smiled. "No, of course not," she answered, then with a knowing look in her eyes, added, "at least nothing you weren't willing to do!"

Giji tried to frown but it hurt. She winced, her whole face hurt, and her eyes, even her lips! "What's that supposed to mean?" Giji wanted to know.

Mrs. Hoover sighed. "Well, you were willing for the most part!" she admitted coyly. "Although, I did have to pry your legs open at one point." She paused and then added, "Bet that's never happened to you before!"

Giji put her head back in her hands and wondered what she'd gotten herself into, but she quickly realized there was nothing she could do about it now. All her things were here, and she had no place else to go. She would have to be more careful–and stay away from discount wine. Forever!

"Oh, sweetie, we had so much fun last night," Martha gushed. "Like that Madonna song, we were like two virgins touched for the very first time! Except with you the term virgin probably never really applied!" She smiled and licked her lips. "You were so sweet and tasty! Very juicy, very ripe!"

Giji couldn't believe what she was hearing and spoke before she could think better of it. "Mrs. Hoover, you are very, very sick!" She then heard how loud her voice was to her own ears and raised her hands to her head.

"Oh, come on, Giji," Mrs. Hoover said in a light, almost playful voice now. "I'm only teasing you! You know that nothing happened last night. After we finished the bottle of wine, you passed out on the sofa. I covered you. End of story."

Giji smiled through her pain. She wanted to believe that, but the thought that something had happened still nagged at her. Yet she had already decided, there was nothing she could do. Besides with the worse hang over of her life, she had no strength to do anything about it. She thought it would be good to call the office to let the receptionist know she wouldn't be in. Good thing she didn't have any appointments set up for the day because Mrs. Hoover's casserole of lingering death and cheap wine was so strong she wasn't sure she could even stand on her own two feet.

This wine is so strong, it could short out your nervous system! Giji thought. She put a hand to her throbbing head and tried to block out the sound coming from the kitchen.

"*Like a virgin,*" Mrs. Hoover sang in a wistful voice as she returned to the kitchen. "*being touched for the very first timmmmmmmmmmme!*"

***

After the kids left for school and Lex headed to the hospital, Connie sat on a bar stool at her kitchen counter and settled into her second cup of coffee. This was the time she allowed herself to catch her breath, to really enjoy a cup of coffee, and decide what she would do during the day. Each day there were certain chores that needed to be done that day. This was laundry day, the most dreaded day of the week. Doing laundry seemed so solitary, although in truth it was anymore solitary than her other weekly chores, like cleaning the oven or mopping the kitchen floor. It just seemed more lonely, Connie decided, but she didn't know why. Maybe because it was a chore that required sorting, washing, drying, then sorting again, this time by item and by owner, and finally putting away each garment.

Taking a sip of coffee, Connie decided it was better if she didn't think about it. Her daily chores went more smoothly if she didn't think too much and just did them. They weren't that challenging, she reminded herself, and did not require a lot of thought. Often without realizing, she was on autopilot to get through the mind-numbing dusting, wiping, scrubbing and soaking that was her daily life.

Housework, she sighed heavily, this wasn't exactly how she'd envisioned her life, her perfect domestic existence. It was supposed to be so much more, so much more than the unfulfilling existence her mother endured.

Connie wasn't sure when she decided her life could never mirror her mother's, that her life would be perfect. It might have been when she realized how desperately unhappy her mother was, but she wasn't sure. At some time in her transition from girl to woman, she'd decided her life would be perfect. She would have the perfect husband, the perfect family. In high school, she'd set her sights on the perfect catch: Lex Vanderkellen. He was from the wealthiest family in their small hometown and she tried everything to make him notice her, but nothing had worked. One day Connie decided that the quickest way to a guy's heart was through his friends, so she became friends with two of the guys Lex hung around with. They introduced her to Lex; a year later they were dating. She encouraged Lex to follow his parents' wish that he become a doctor instead of pursuing his dream to play professional baseball. Underneath the surface, she felt Lex resented her involvement in the decision, but it was all a part of her plan. Nothing could be more perfect than being married to a doctor, at least that is what she thought back then. Connie was so excited when she thought about telling her mother that she was going to marry a doctor! She could almost see the pride in her mother's eyes and even hear the pleased tone in her mother's voice. But, when she told her mother the news in the small apartment they shared after her father's heart attack and subsequent death, her mother stared at her through cold, resentful eyes and continued to take deep drags on another cigarette in her daily ritual of chain-smoking. Connie expected her mother to be proud of her daughter's prospective good fortune in life, but she had not been prepared for her mother's bitter displeasure that her daughter would think that she could do better in life than her mother had.

"I'm happy for you, darling," her mother had said between

puffs, but it was obvious from her tone and expression that she didn't mean it.

They never discussed her mother's obvious resentment, although Connie always wondered if they might have, if her mother hadn't become sick and died of lung cancer two short years after Connie's marriage to Lex.

The perfect life, she repeated to herself, realizing this should probably come under things to be labeled "Be Careful What You Wish For!"

Enough of that, she thought and reached for the phone on the wall, but hesitated and drew her hand back as if she had touched a hot stove. What was she doing? She closed her eyes and realized she was about to call Mary Lynn to see if they could chat later. I can't do that anymore, she told herself, I have to get used to the fact that Mary Lynn is gone…forever. It shouldn't be so easy to forget, especially after her funeral.

Connie took a last sip of her coffee and went around the counter to the sink. She rinsed out the cup and placed it in the sink to wash later.

For a moment she wondered if the reason Mary Lynn killed herself was because of the monotony of being a housewife; the long hours, days of mindless chores, the meals, being supportive, and so often being unappreciated. Never even a "Thank you," Connie thought. No, Mary Lynn wasn't like that, she decided, Mary Lynn was the kind of woman who enjoyed being a housewife and mother, she thrived on it, and seemed completely fulfilled. So, why would she commit suicide?

Shaking the cobwebs from her head, Connie went down the hallway into the laundry room and lifted the laundry basket full of dirty clothes and dumped the contents onto the sorting table. She had only sorted a few colors from the whites when her hand touched something that was out of place. She lifted the rigid, thin plastic item as if it were dangerous, alien, and as if it might sting her.

She looked at it for a minute before it dawned on her that it was a condom. When was the last time she saw a condom? It has been since…well…since she and Lex were dating. But, now there was a shiny, bright orange wrapper, a latex condom ribbed for added pleasure in her dirty laundry.

Suddenly, she realized it had to be her son Andrew's! How could it be? Connie grabbed the side of the washing machine as she tried to overcome her initial shock. He was only sixteen. Andrew…her baby was having sex. It seemed like only yesterday she and Lex brought him home from the hospital, newborn, fresh, unspoiled. She just couldn't wrap her mind around the fact that her baby son was having sex. Gradually, she realized her son wasn't a baby any longer, he was growing up, faster than she'd realized…

For some reason, finding the condom in the laundry brought back memories of a day from her childhood. Maybe it was because the day of the incident, without saying a word, a piece of her innocence was stolen…

She had walked upstairs to put her school books away and she passed the door to her parents' bedroom. When she passed the door, she heard noises, then she noticed the door was opened slightly. She crept closer. Inside she saw her mom sitting on top of some big, hairy bald guy. Her mom's back was to the door, but it was obvious she was completely naked and she was sitting below the man's waist. Why was her mom groaning and why was the man breathing heavy and moaning?

At first, Connie didn't recognize the man, then she got a good look at his face when he turned toward the door with a knowing gleam in his eyes. Suddenly, her eyes met his and locked for a second before she quickly turned away, shaken by what she'd seen. The man was her father's best friend, Uncle Roy.

Connie moved away from the door quietly. She crept downstairs and sat on the couch, unsure of what she should do, then she realized her school books were still in her hands.

"Connie, sweetie," her mom's voice called from the top of the stairs, "you're home. Can you put your books down and do mommy a favor?" Without waiting for a response, she added, "Go out back and check on Bunny. He didn't eat when I fed him earlier. I think he misses you."

Twenty minutes later, Connie returned to the house and Uncle Roy was gone and they never spoke of what had happened that day.

***

From the window of her dining room, SueAnn could see the new neighbor carrying his belongings from his pickup truck into the house. When he came out of the house to get another load, it occurred to SueAnn that if she had noticed the new neighbor, someone else may have, too. Someone like Giji Brickhouse!

After all, Giji had sold him the house, and she might know when he planned to move in. Giji said his name was Nick and that he was single, but what she had neglected to say, intentionally, was that he was absolutely gorgeous! Good ole Giji, true to form as usual, always looking out for herself! SueAnn almost couldn't blame her, but maybe she could. Especially when the man was a drop dead gorgeous hunk–and Giji was interested in keeping him all to herself.

Glancing at herself in the mirror over the buffet, SueAnn decided she looked good enough for a meeting with her potential Mr. Right and she felt her heart skip a beat with her growing excitement.

Her dark hair was down around her shoulders. She decided her hair was almost flowing and for once she was wearing a decent outfit, a button up pink cotton blouse and matching pink shorts that fit rather snuggly, almost form-fitting (good thing no one knew they were her daughter's!) This was instead of the old ratty bathrobe she usually wore while she sat at her computer tapping on the keys, trying to finish the latest book in her children's picture book series **Hank the Hungry Hippo**. (They were selling only slightly less than Madonna's **The English Roses**. Maybe slightly less was an overstatement. But, her books were selling…a little here and there… enough to make ends meet, at least.)

SueAnn took one last glance at herself in the mirror. Not bad. Not bad at all. Go get him, hot stuff! She told herself, then frowned at her own self-flattery.

As she started out the door, she glanced in the side window panel beside the door and saw someone else making a move. *Oh no!* she thought. *Giji!* With that, she flung open the door and started quickly across her lawn. She almost sprinted through Mrs. Hoover's thorny roses, directly at the most handsome man she'd seen since George Clooney left "ER"!

Apparently, Giji saw her as well because Giji was also walking quickly to the handsome newcomer. Damn Giji, she was like a heat-seeking (make that man-seeking!) missile in her skin-tight Daisy Dukes and a Ace bandage that doubled as a tube top! Didn't the woman own any real clothes?

SueAnn walked toward her new neighbor, smiling and extending her hand, but not looking where she stepped. She stepped into a hole dug by Mrs. Hoover's mutt, Jasper. Thank goodness Jasper had run away, she thought, too bad he left so many reminders of himself behind.

SueAnn fell almost flat on her face, luckily her entire body broke her fall. As she started to sit up, she saw grass stains on her shorts, and her hand caught in the front of her blouse as she was extending it to greet the new neighbor and ripped the buttons off half way down. Her breasts were spilling out of her blouse. Why hadn't she worn a bra! At least then she would have had some coverage. Instead, she was pretty much exposed. She put her hands in font of her chest and pulled the blouse around her to cover he breasts as best she could.

Giji laughed her fluffy-light laugh, pleased that her neighbor had taken a spill until she noticed what else had taken a spill! It was apparent from the sour look on her face that Giji wasn't pleased after all. In fact, she had a sneaky suspicion that SueAnn planned the incident to garner instant sympathy and attention for herself and to display her assets for their handsome new neighbor. That would be just like her, Giji thought, sneaky, freaky, always trying to win at any cost. Giji rolled her eyes, I loathe any woman more cut-throat than I am!

"Are you okay?" Nick asked, a concerned look in his bright clear blue eyes.

SueAnn attempted to nod while struggling to hold her shirt tightly across her breasts. "I-I'm fine, I think," she answered in a small voice. "I just took a spill."

"Apparently, that's not all that took a spill," Giji commented, dropping her eyes drop to SueAnn's breasts.

"I must look a mess," SueAnn chose to ignore Giji's curt remark. "I'm sorry –"

"No need to apologize," Nick said quickly, drinking in her beauty despite her unkempt appearance. "You look fine. Nice... everything!"

SueAnn managed a smile. "Thanks," she said, beginning to feel better. "I'm SueAnn Day."

"I'm Nick Delfino," he smiled back at her and extended his hand. "I'm your newest neighbor in case Giji hasn't told you, and as you can see on the side of my trusty pickup truck, I'm a plumber by trade."

"Oh, Giji told me almost everything, I'm sure," SueAnn said and hesitated before taking her hand from her blouse. She managed to hold her blouse together with one hand and placed her other hand in his. His touch was cool but warmed up quickly and sent little shivers up and down her spine. "It's great to meet you, Nick. I hope to see you around."

"I hope to see more of you, too," Nick said, letting go of her hand.

Giji rolled her eyes. "If you look, you can see more of her now," she said under her breath.

"Did you say something, Giji?" Nick asked.

"I was just thinking out loud. You know, after I sold my house, I was almost homeless," Giji said in her most pathetic voice with just a hint of flirtiness. "I'll have to kick myself later. I could have moved in with you."

I wish I could kick you now, SueAnn thought as she listened to Giji's shameless flirting. After giving Giji a knowing look, SueAnn started slowly back toward her house, limping slightly.

"SueAnn, do you need some help?" Nick asked, noticing the way she was walking. "I'll be glad –"

"Oh, let me," Giji volunteered, taking SueAnn by the arm. "I'm headed that way anyway."

"Thanks, Giji," Nick said and smiled, pleased. "I'll see you both later."

"Sure, Nick," SueAnn said as she frowned at Giji.

"See ya, Nick," Giji called over her shoulder, then looked back at SueAnn. "Way to steal the show!"

"Well, it's not like I planned it," SueAnn told her.

"Really?" Giji asked, not convinced. "Oh, I'll just bet you tripped over yourself just so Nick would shower you with all his attention."

"I did not," SueAnn assured her, pulling away. "I'm genuinely injured."

"Sure you are," Giji still sounded skeptical. "I'm surprised you didn't strip naked and attack the guy right there on his lawn!"

SueAnn looked her directly in the eye. "That," she said with a determined tone, "would be more your style."

Giji grinned. "Touché!" she agreed. "Besides I saw him first!"

Thinking two could play this little game of words, SueAnn said, "Big deal. He saw more of me!"

"I can't argue with that, can I?" Giji laughed, as if her mood were lightening. "You didn't even say thank you for my help!"

"Gee, thanks, Giji," SueAnn said in a mocking voice. "I couldn't have taken those three steps without you."

Giji ignored the sarcasm in SueAnn's comment and was about to leave when she paused and said, "You'll be pleased to know I'm no longer homeless. Martha Hoover is letting me use her spare bedroom until I find my own place."

She glanced over her shoulder toward Nick's house, then back at SueAnn. "Who knows? I have already found the prefect place!"

"I wouldn't count on that just yet," SueAnn told her.

"Well, let the best woman win," Giji challenged.

SueAnn stuck out her tongue.

"Real mature, SueAnn," Giji taunted. "I expected more than that from you!"

And you'll get more, SueAnn thought as she limped across her lawn. *You're in for the fight of your life, Giji! As soon as I'm able to fight, that is!*

***

SueAnn stepped from her hot bath and slowly dried herself with a soft, Pale blue bath towel. She had hoped the hot soak would relieve the pain she experienced since her fall earlier when she met her new neighbor. The warm water might also help alleviate some of the pain she was sure she would feel later and especially in the morning.

After she finished drying herself, she hung her towel on the towel rod to dry and tip-toed naked across the narrow hallway to her bedroom. She slipped the sheer gown she'd laid out earlier over her head and was about to slip into bed when the phone rang. Sitting on the side of the bed, she picked up the receiver. "Hello?"

"Hello," Wynette greeted her, "I just called to see how you are."

"I'm fine," SueAnn told her. "I soaked in a hot tub for a while. That should help."

"That was a good idea," Wynette agreed. "You're sure Giji didn't push you or trip you trying to get to Nick first?" her friend teased.

"I wouldn't put it past her," SueAnn said lightly, "but no. I tripped when I stepped into one of the many holes Mrs. Hoover's dog dug before he ran off."

"Okay, as long as you're sure," Wynette said.

"I'm sure," SueAnn said, her voice took on an edge of excitement which made her sound like a giddy schoolgirl, "and despite my unhappy spill, I'm glad I met Nick this afternoon. He is so handsome, and he seems really nice and sweet."

"Well, you just met the guy," Wynette reminded her. "You can't get to now much about a person or what they're really like in such a short time."

"I know," SueAnn admitted, drowsily, "but I have a feeling about Nick, that he's really special."

"I just don't want to see you get disappointed," Wynette worried.

"I know," SueAnn agreed. "So, when is Steven getting home?"

"Soon," Wynette sighed, impatiently. "Tomorrow I hope."

"What do you mean, you hope?"

"Well, he'll be home tomorrow unless something comes up," Wynette explained. "If he doesn't finish his appointments on schedule that could mean an extra day on the road."

"Oh," SueAnn yawned loudly. "I hope everything goes as planned and he gets home tomorrow."

"Thanks, sweetie," Wynette said, "Listen, you sound tired. I'll let you go so you can get some rest. Goodnight."

" 'Night," SueAnn said sleepily and put down the phone. She slipped between the covers, wincing at the sharp pain as she lay back in bed. Although she was sore almost all over from her fall, she was glad she had gone over to meet Nick.

The last thing SueAnn thought of as she drifted off to sleep was Nick Delfino.

3

Secrets, Surprises & Seduction!

Ariella admired herself in the mirror over the console table while she waited patiently for her husband, Marco, to get home from work. Tonight they were going to dinner at one of her favorite restaurants, maybe *La Maison* or *Casa del Sole Aumentante* or the newer, sexier *Chez Paradise*. It was eat out or do without as Ariella always said, she wasn't about to cook! In the three years she and Marco had been married, she had not cooked one meal, not even breakfast, and she wasn't going to start now. Marco knew when he married her that there were certain things she would not do, cooking and domestic work in general were primary on her list. That's why she had insisted that they have a maid. Once Marco saw how meals weren't cooked, dirty laundry piled up around the house, and their sex life suffered because of the disorder and dirt, he agreed wholeheartedly! The next day he called around to placement agencies and had several maids sent over for Ariella to interview. After Ariella had rejected all but the last candidate, they had hired the small Asian woman named Sun Li. For Ariella and Sun Li, it had been instant dislike, but Ariella needed someone to do all the work she was not willing to do and Sun Li needed employment, so a match made in hell seemed tolerable.

Striking a pose reminiscent of her modeling days, Ariella viewed herself in the mirror from different angles and was pleased with what she saw. She wore her slinky, low-cut red dress – her husband's favorite – because it showed her assets to their best advantage. The low neckline gave a preview of her full, firm breasts while not revealing too much. The tight waist showed off her flat stomach and ample rear. When she wore the dress, Marco's eyes were always filled with desire, which made her feel sexy, wanted, and of equal importance, she felt powerful!

Ariella thought about how her relationship with Marco started. It was during her brief modeling career. Maybe, career wasn't the right word. She modeled in a few print ads and a few television commercials (she'd almost been the douche girl for the Ever-Fresh Feminine Hygiene campaign, but as often happens they went with a big-chested Pamela Anderson clone instead). She actually made a little money, almost enough to survive, but not enough to get above the poverty level or enough to eat three square meals a day. Good thing she was a model. She realized early in her modeling stint, that she didn't need to eat much.

Her agent, the late Bernie Sleigel, got her a television commercial audition for a used car dealership, *Fluentes Fine Cars*. During the audition she caught the owner's eye. There was a whirl wind courtship with Marco Fluentes that led to their marriage–a very short courtship.

She never finished the commercial; Marco didn't want his future bride doing cheesy TV spots (even if they were for the business his father had started). She wasn't sure that she wanted to marry Marco, but her agent informed her that there were few modeling jobs on the horizon–maybe a cat food ad here, an occasional feminine hygiene product there. The younger models got the best jobs - Bernie told her while he puffed on the stinky cigar she loathed. Once her agent spelled it out for her, she decided. marriage sounded like a good gig– for a while, at least. During their courtship and after their wedding, Marco's top salesmen, referred to her repeatedly as Marco's spokeswhore. When she went to her husband and complained, Marco fired the guy on the spot. At that moment Marco reeked of power and Ariella was attracted to him as she had never been attracted to another man. It was then that she knew she had made the right decision. Nothing was sexier than power, she'd decided. But, as time passed, the sense of power wore thin and Ariella looked elsewhere for her excitement. She found it again and again, although short-lived, with one man after another.

She turned away from the mirror and looked at her reflection over her shoulder, admiring the curves of her ass, down to her long, slender legs. Just as she was about to sit on the sofa and wait for his arrival, Marco came through the door, loosening his tie. She could tell from the lively expression on his handsome face that he was in a good mood.

After a quick kiss, she pulled away from Marco. "What's with the happy face?" there was a suspicious, tone in her voice, "Something you want to tell me?"

"Ah," he tried to sound hurt, "can't a man come home after a great day to his lovely home and absolutely gorgeous wife without enduring the third degree?"

Ariella pouted. "No," she said matter-of-factly, "now 'fess up! What's going on with you?" She paused, giving him a tiny smile and added, hopeful, "Did you sell the dealership or what?"

"No, nothing like that," he took her hand in his and lead her to the sofa. "It was an amazing day," he said when they were seated.

"Don't keep me in suspense," Ariella said impatiently, "Tell me already!"

"I sold five cars today!" he announced. "That's a record for one day. Everyone was so happy and excited at the dealership. I just wish Pop had lived to see this."

Ariella nodded. "Well, congratulations, sweetheart," she said softly, "I'm proud of you."

Marco turned and looked directly in her eye. "Are you?" he sounded skeptical.

"Of course, I am," Ariella tried to sound genuine.

Marco smiled suddenly. "I know, babe," he said, pleased, "Today was just so damned good. Let's go upstairs and celebrate!"

"Celebrate?" she repeated, uncertainly.

"Yeah, babe, let's have sex," Marco said in a deep, seductive voice. "I have some unspent energy I'd love to spend on my special lady."

Ariella took a fashion magazine from the large leather ottoman in front of the sofa and began flipping aimlessly through the pages. "Hon, I'm not feeling it, my energy is all spent. I had a rotten day, Sun Li was acting up and she refused to wash my unmentionables by hand. I finally had to do it myself, and I broke a nail. Then I could not get an appointment to have my nails done until mid-week. It's been such a trying day, you understand, don't you?"

Marco sighed heavily, a disappointed expression on his dark, handsome face. "Yeah," the enthusiasm suddenly drained from him, "I guess so." He paused, then suddenly smiled when an idea occurred to him. "Would you like to eat in tonight?"

Ariella looked up from her magazine. "Sun Li has probably already eaten everything," she sounded bored. "I don't know what she does with the food after I send her to the grocery. Before she leaves for the day she must be hiding steaks in her underwear!"

He gave her the same amorous look he showed when he came home. "Well, I have something else in mind," he spoke with a deep, seductive voice.

She closed her magazine. "We're going to order delivery. We can order steaks. No, surf and turf, maybe oysters…"

Marco started kissing her arm and worked his way up to her shoulder. "Who needs oysters?" he asked, looking deeply into her eyes.

Ariella shivered. She had to admit that he was getting to her, no matter how hard she tried to fight him. He made her body respond no matter how hard her brain fought it.

She wanted to give in, but her "look" took so long to achieve and she wanted to enjoy it until her next appointment. He should understand since her looks brought them together in the beginning. She'd been a model. Hell, she'd probably have been a super model by now, if she hadn't met him... She tried to wiggle her shoulder away from his warm, wet, seductive lips, but he resisted. He was moving in for a big, wet kiss. *Not the lips,* she thought to herself. *No!* she screamed to herself. *Not the lips!* She turned away at the last possible second.

"You're not making this easy," he complained and kissed her shoulder again, like a man who knew the affect it had on her resistance.

"Well," she said, "My mom did not raise me to be easy."

"I know," he agreed, "but playing hard to get is no fun especially when I've already got you!"

That comment made her Latina blood boil. She hated that some Latino men felt they owned their girlfriends and wives as if they were mere possessions or beautiful trophies. But, she had to admit she played along with Marco because she enjoyed being beautiful, turning men's heads and seducing men. That was her security in knowing that Marco did not really own her... because there were other men. She gave herself to others in ways she never would with her husband because he felt entitled...

While Ariella tried to block out what was happening, Marco slid down in front of her and put his head in her lap and looked up at her with the brightest, puppy dog eyes. "Come on, babe," Marco pleaded, "Don't make me beg. I had a wonderful day, let's make it a wonderful night, too."

Ariella didn't say anything and she was determined to resist him, but Marco eased himself between her legs and pushed up her dress. As usual, Ariella wasn't wearing panties, Marco placed his face between her legs and let his nose and tongue slide between her tight pussy lips. He started licking her folds slowly, then more aggressively. Marco started to lick deeper and deeper into Ariella's pussy. He could already taste her sweet pussy juices.

"Ahhh," Ariella moaned loudly as she placed her hands on the back of Marco's head and held his face tight against her pussy, "That feels so good, baby. Don't stop, just keep going!"

Marco licked gently around her clit first and gradually he became more aggressive with his tongue as Ariella moaned louder and louder. Eventually, Ariella couldn't resist anymore and her pussy started to quiver as she enjoyed a series of mini-orgasms that gradually led her to a huge orgasmic peak!

After he licked her clean, Marco lay back on the sofa beside her, exhausted. Through half-closed eyes, Ariella looked over at him, satisfaction written all over her face. "That was wonderful, darling," Ariella purred softly, then her eyes slid to the enormous bulge in his slacks.

"Thanks, babe," Marco glanced down, "aren't you going to return the favor?"

"Oh, Marco," Ariella began, "I'm drained. Besides, we still have to go out for dinner and you wouldn't want me to ruin my make-up on that!"

Marco sighed. This was getting old, he thought. Wondering why she was punishing him this time, Marco said, "All right, hon, as long as you take care of me when we get back from dinner."

"You got it, sweetie," Ariella said, leaning in to give him the smallest of pecks on the mouth, their lips barely touching. I'll still be too tired then, Ariella thought selfishly, but at least I'll have had a good meal!

***

Connie stood in her laundry room and sorted clothes as she looked through the window into the backyard. She thought about how hard it had been these last few months, with Mary Lynn's death and having to pretend her world wasn't on the verge of falling apart. She folded all of the socks and took the laundry into the various rooms to put it away. Maybe she had time to do one more load before starting dinner. She grabbed a dirty load from the laundry table and started to load the washer.

She turned around and her foot slid across the floor, almost knocking her to the ground. Luckily only her elbow collided with the washer as she righted herself.

"I wonder what the hell that was?" she said out loud, and looked under her tennis shoe.

It was a square piece of foil. She bent down and picked it up. Turning it over in her hand she stopped cold and stared. It was...another...condom, this one was in a bright metallic wrapper.

Andrew, she thought.

At that moment the phone rang.

"Hello?" Connie held the condom in her hand, rolling the green foil between her fingers as she listened.

"Hi, sweetheart, it's me. I wanted to let you know I'll be working late tonight. I have a consultation scheduled late and I can't get out of it. Sorry, save me a plate, okay?"

"Lex, we have to talk. I found another condom. I believe it belongs to Andrew." She paused as if letting what she'd just said sink in. "You need to talk to him."

"Where did you find it?" he wanted to know.

"I was doing laundry and slid on it. It was on the floor. A condom in a bright foil wrapper."

The other end of the phone went strangely silent.

"Lex... Lex, are you there?"

"Yeah, I'm here. Look, don't fly off the handle with the boy; I'm sure there's some explanation. I guess we should consider ourselves lucky that he's using protection."

"But Lex-"

"Look, I've got to go, babe, don't talk to him until I get home, okay?"

"Okay, just come home as soon as you can."

Dinner was awkward. Connie pushed her food around on her plate and started to say something to Andrew several times, but would stop short and get a glass of milk, another roll, anything to avoid eye contact with him.

"What have I done?" Andrew finally asked.

"We're not going to talk about this now," Connie avoided the question, relieved that Danielle was spending the evening studying at a friend's house and wouldn't home until later.

"No, tell me what you think I did."

"Andrew, go up to your room. Your father and I will be up to talk to you about this later."

"No, Mom. I'm not a child and I want you to tell me what's wrong."

"Very well, young man, since you're so grown up, maybe you can explain this?" Connie whipped the condom from the pocket of her dress as though it were a magic trick.

"What's that?"

"Don't play dumb with me, mister. What do you need a condom for?"

Andrew leaned back and set down his fork.

"You know very well what a condom is for, Mother. What you need to ask is who's this one is. My condoms come in a red and black wrapper. Check my bedside table if you don't believe me." He looked at her defiantly.

"Then who's is this?" Connie didn't know what else to say. She was quiet for a minute, then looked at him, horrified.

"Danielle? She's only fourteen."

"Oh Mom, do you really think miss bookworm is having sex?" Andrew threw down his fork and stood up. "I'll go to my room, but I bet you and dad don't come up to talk to me. You had better face some facts, Mother." He turned and left her sitting alone.

Gradually it dawned on Connie as she sat alone at the dinner table with a forkful of fish with her perfect hair and clean house. Who schedules a consultation at 8 o'clock at night?

***

The clock ticked on as Connie waited in the dark for Lex. Finally, around midnight the door opened quietly and Lex came into the living room, taking off his jacket as he walked in. Connie snapped on the light.

"You're right, we should be grateful that he's using protection. But, since you're a doctor, I don't have to tell you that sometimes those things don't work." It came out clipped and cold, just the way Connie had spent the last four hours practicing it.

Lex looked down.

"Tell me, Lex, who schedules a consultation for eight o'clock at night and then let's it go on for four hours?"

"I guess you already talked to Andrew," Lex said.

"I guess I did," Connie said quietly, "was she pretty?"

"I was working late at the hospital…" Lex started.

"Is it someone I know?" Connie went on, "A female doctor? A male doctor? One of the nurses? Deanna? Janine?"

"We're not having this conversation," Lex said.

"Well that's fine," Connie told him in the voice she'd been rehearsing. "Go ahead and have your little indiscretions. Just make sure your whores know one thing. I will not give you a divorce."

"I'm not asking for one," Lex assured her, his relief was obvious in his voice.

"Good. I'd rather see you dead first!"

"Is that a threat?" Lex looked at her, surprised.

"Call it whatever you'd like, just don't think of calling a divorce lawyer. I've got the upper hand because of your adultery! I'll take everything." Connie stormed out of the room, leaving Lex on the couch. He sighed and put his head in his hands.

Connie started upstairs, and saw both Andrew and Danielle on the landing. Andrew looked tired, bored, like he was only there for Danielle, who cried and leaned against him for support.

"Mom, what happened?" Danielle asked, sobbing.

"Your father and I were just having a little discussion, that's all. Everything's fine."

"It didn't sound fine, and you've been crying. Where's Dad?"

Connie handled the situation the only way she knew how. After her father had discovered her mother's affair, her childhood had ended overnight; her life had never been the same. Although her parents reconciled shortly before her father's death, things were never the same between them, and her mother never seemed happy again.

"Nothing is happening. Everything is fine. Now go up to your rooms and go to bed." Connie told her children. "But Mom …"

"I said now!" Connie slammed her fist against the banister. Danielle turned and went into her room. Andrew lingered at the top of the stairs, looking at his mother who was scared and disgusted, he slowly turned away.

***

Wynette met Steven in college where they both majored in business management. Two mutual friends played matchmaker and set them up on a blind date in their junior year. It had been loathing at first sight; they hated each other immediately, and the date seemed like one big mistake–until Steven drove her to the small apartment she shared with two other girls.

Steven insisted on walking her up when they reached her building, after all, it was dark and he wanted to make sure she got to her apartment safely. Reluctantly she'd agreed, touched because he cared about her well being.

She didn't expect a goodnight handshake at the door, but her roommates were out so she asked Steven in, as a good will gesture for his earlier kind gesture.

She had bought the new Van Halen album, *1984*, earlier in the day and it lay on the coffee table where she placed it. Steven said he liked Van Halen, too. Finally, they had something in common! She'd put on the album and things were a lot more relaxed.

Before they knew what was happening, they started talking about music and laughing. At some point in the evening they ended up making out to "Jump."

She offered him a glass of wine, and after a couple of glasses of cheap wine, they shed their clothes and made love on the soiled orange carpet. *Those were the days,* Wynette thought, suddenly brought back to the present. *Spontaneous and free...how they had changed....*

Steven would be home tonight, but Wynette was exhausted. She stood in front of the bathroom mirror after getting the boys off to bed with food in her hair from the boys throwing it at dinner. Staring at herself in the mirror, she felt less than sexy.

She needed to feel wanted. Even with their phone conversations every other day, she missed him and looked forward to him coming home. She longed for him to hold her, to look into her eyes and to feel his hands all over her body...

Wynette started the water for a quick shower before he came home, when she felt his arms around her waist. Steven had come in through the back porch and crept up the stairs behind her.

"You nearly scared me to death!" she jumped at his touch. "But I'm glad you're home, I missed you. You're home earlier than you said you'd be, I'm a mess, I wanted to take a shower before you got here."

"You look wonderful to me," he said and ran a finger along her neck and licked the finger tip, "and you taste great, too. Is that peach cobbler?"

"Well, I've heard it called that before, but I wouldn't swear to it," she tried to sound light, despite feeling and looking so hopelessly domestic, "Speaking of food, have you eaten?"

"Ah," he spoke softly against her ear, "There's only one meal I've been missing, sweetheart."

"Have you been drinking?" Wynette teased; behind his back she frowned, wishing he were a little less crude.

"Are you okay, hon?" His voice was serious now, concerned. "I mean since Mary Lynn's death, are you okay?"

"I told you on the phone, I'm holding up," she reminded him.

"I know," he said, "but talking on the phone isn't the same as being here with you. I just wanted to make sure you got through the service that everything went okay and you're fine."

"I am fine, sweetheart," she assured him, touched that he cared. "It's been hard on everyone. I'm really concerned about SueAnn because she's alone for the summer while Julie's with her father, but she seems to be managing okay."

"Good, babe. Since the shower's still on, whaddaya say we get clean together?" he slipped off his pants and began to unbutton his shirt. Wynette stepped into the shower before him and began to wash the cobbler from her hair. While the boys slept, their parents closed out everything else when they closed the door to the shower. Steven took Wynette in his arms just the way she had thought about in her own bath the other night, and pressed her up against the wall of the shower. She grabbed the railing across the top of the stall door and he took her from behind, bracing his legs against hers. She had never felt better, with the warm water showering over her and the steam all around them. Her husband grabbed her breasts and squeezed her nipples lightly while he held on to the railing, placing his hands over hers.

After they made love, they dried each other off and lay in bed together.

"So, you still sleep with my boxers under your pillow while I'm away?" Steven said as he pulled the covers up closer.

"I do not!" Wynette lied.

"Remember when you had that foot and sock fetish and had to smell my feet after a hard day's work?"

Wynette frowned, "When you say it like that, it sounds even worse than I remember. I wasn't addicted; I just like your masculine scent."

"Well, you're going to be smelling my masculine scent around the house a lot more often since the boss has decided I don't need to travel so much any more. It'll be fun to hang out at home on weekends and help with the boys at night."

"Oh, Steven, you mean it?" Her eyes shone in anticipation.

"That's what the man said. Speaking of scents, remember when you refused to shave your armpits and looked like a hairy ape with a bra on?"

Wynette threw her pillow at him, "Enough! You loved it, admit it!"

He grinned. "Okay, I admit it; it was kind of sexy, kind of wild, and kind of free."

She snuggled close to him again and laid her head on his chest.

"Where did it all go?" she raised her head and looked at him.

"You shaved, sweetheart."

"Not that, silly. Where did those two starry eyed young kids who were hell bent on being free go?"

"They grew up, had kids and got a hell of a lot of responsibility."

"I guess so," she said sadly, laying her head back down.

Wynette enjoyed the sex but didn't feel especially satisfied. Steven started to snore soon after their conversation and Wynette now lay in the dark, thinking of her fantasy of their perfect reunion. Wynette wished there had been more intimacy. She tried to roll Steven onto his side.

"Not, anymore tonight, honey," he mumbled, "I'm tired."

"Okay, big boy," Wynette said quietly. *One disappointment per night is enough!* she thought and turned her back on him.

***

Marco leaned back in his worn leather chair and stared out the window of the car dealership. He watched the young couple pause to inspect the Ford Taurus and then walk off, hand in hand. He sighed and thought of the last few months with Ariella, about how he got what was coming to him for marrying a gold digger.

The office door was open and he could see Tia going about her work, moving from the file cabinet to her desk and back again, leaning down to file something in the bottom drawer. He could see her tight little ass straining against the fabric of her skirt, and without thinking, he rubbed his cock through his slacks. If he hadn't married Ariella, he might have married Tia.

Tia stood up and started to cross the room, but noticed Marco looking at her through the office door. She came into his office and closed the door behind her. Marco moved away from behind the desk but was still seated in his leather chair. He noticed she wasn't wearing a bra, her nipples stood erect through her blouse. He felt himself getting harder.

"What's with that?" said Tia, looking at his lap.

"It's just, Ariella...ah... you know..."

"I do know," said Tia. She sat on the edge of his desk, legs parted slightly against his knees. "I can help you, Marco." Her voice dropped and in a seductive tone she asked. 'do you want me to help you?"

Marco was so hard that he couldn't answer. He just looked up at her and nodded. Tia slid onto his lap and rubbed against him. Sliding her hand between them, she unzipped his slacks. He reached between her legs and was pleased to find she wasn't wearing any panties. As soon as he was inside her, she leaned back and unbuttoned her blouse to expose her bare breasts.

"Lick them, Marco. Nibble on them as much as you want."

He took one of her breasts in his mouth and she rocked faster and harder on his cock. He moaned. She stood and took his hand.

"I don't want you to cum so fast; let's move to the couch." Her skirt was hiked up over her hips and she sat on the couch, her dripping pussy exposed to him. Marco took his slacks off and she pushed him down in front of her.

"You know what to do, baby, lick me all over," Tia winked at him and leaned back against the couch. Marco knelt in front of her and soon she was so wet they couldn't stand it anymore. He pulled her down on top of him and they rocked furiously until they both exploded.

After they were both satisfied, Tia repositioned her skirt and went back to work. Marco sat in his leather chair and watched out the window of the car dealership. He thought of Ariella, but only briefly and realized that he didn't feel guilty...he didn't feel guilty at all. It was nice to be satisfied...for a change.

"Tia, could you come in here a moment, please?" Marco called through the open door. He stood out of her sight and waited for her to come in. When she came through the door, he closed it behind her. He turned her to face him, pushed her against the closed door and kissed her deeply, running his large hand over her breast through her blouse and reached the other hand under her skirt.

"Let's do it again," he whispered in her ear.

"Of course, Marco, anytime you want," she breathed back. Behind his head and out of his view, she smiled. This fling could be the beginning of something that would lead to a different world for her, away from typing and filing, and at least he was handsome.

She unbuttoned his slacks and slid them down around his ankles as he groped for her pussy under the skirt. He was full hard on excited and she helped him remove her skirt. She made a mental note to buy a couple more skirts that were alluring and could be removed easily, maybe with only one hand. As they collapsed onto the expensive rug he entered her by grabbing her shoulders and pulling her to him with such force that they both cried out. They pumped furiously and Tia's head laid back with her tongue between her teeth as she tried to muffle the sounds so they wouldn't attract attention from outside the office.

Marco couldn't believe that he felt alive again and more like a man than he had felt in all the time he had been married to Ariella. He slid out of Tia and ran his tongue down her neck and onto her nipples, flicking them with his tongue and sucking on each one in turn. Finally, he couldn't take it anymore and pushed his way back into her, it was easy because Tia was so wet and tight. He knew he was going to try to do this every day. His mind reeled with the possibilities, maybe they could get a room during the lunch hour and maybe she could come with him on the next business trip. Come with him... he smiled at the many possibilities for those words.

Tia pushed him off of her and rolled him over, getting on top.

She rocked on him, moaned. Shifting her body slightly, she positioned her firm, jiggly breasts so that they were right in to Marco's face. He alternately sucked and flicked them, grinding against her.

After they were both dressed again, Marco asked Tia if she would come with him on his next out of town trip.

"How would we justify that?" asked Tia.

"Let me worry about that," he said.

She smoothed her skirt and picked up her notebook, pausing at the mirror over the small wash basin in Marco's office to fix her hair and retouch her make up.

"You realize this is very chancy, with my father being one of your old friends and since you're married."

"I'll handle that as well, just don't say no," he said.

"Oh, I wouldn't do that," Tia smiled at him as she shut the door.

On the other side of the door Tia continued to smile, but it was the smile of a woman who knew she was about to get what she wanted.

***

Connie sat on the edge of her bed crying, but she didn't want the children to hear her. Her mind wandered back to how it used to be, when they were first married. *Maybe it would be good to get away for a couple of days,* she thought. A little bed and breakfast along the river in her mother's hometown might be just what she needed.

She wiped her eyes and rummaged through the closet for the blue suitcase. It was her favorite because it wasn't too big or too small, but just the right size for a weekend getaway. In the back of the closet she saw an old costume, and smiled as a naughty idea hit her. Maybe she wouldn't go away for the weekend after all; maybe she would do something else. After all, Lex was always trying to get her to be more spontaneous. For once, she grinned to herself, she was going to take him up on his challenge!

She left the blue suit case in the closet took the nurse's costume and her long coat out. With a grin on her face, she put the nurse's uniform on and covered it with her long mohair coat and walked out of their bedroom.

She leaned into Andrew's room and said, "I'm going out for a little while, please tell your sister I'll be home in time for dinner."

"Yep," was the only answer she got.

Looking in the mirror, she checked her make-up. Although it took a few tries to get a look she could stand, she was wearing a bit more make-up than normal. She couldn't help thinking that she looked more like a hooker pretending to be a nurse than an actual nurse, but she hoped it would add to Lex's fantasy. It was an attempt to be sexier and more appealing to her husband, but most importantly, she needed to prove to him that she could be adventurous, playful and most of all spontaneous! It hurt to know that Lex thought she was as starched as the crisp, white nurse's uniform she was wearing, but today he would see a different side of her. Sexy and alive!

Connie remembered how hot Lex had been for her the last time she wore that costume, even as she handed out candy he came up behind her, grabbing her ass and telling her how hot she looked. When the last of the trick or treaters were gone, she turned out the porch light and Lex gave her a treat. She sighed as she drove and remembered how hot he got seeing her in that uniform, how hard he had been, and how she had told him not to rip the costume off of her, because she might want to use it again. At that time she didn't have any idea she would use it to seduce her husband back from the arms
of (at least one) other woman.

Lex will get the surprise of his life! Connie decided as she pulled her sedan into the parking lot at Willow Ridge Hospital. She stepped out of her car and pulled her long coat close to conceal the nurse's uniform, making sure the uniform was well hidden. Glancing down to make sure the belt was secure she noticed the stark white shoes. She hadn't thought about the white nurse's sneakers! It might have been better to wear a pair of flats or low heels and she could have stashed her nurse's shoes in a shopping bag and then changed them in Lex's office. People probably wouldn't give her shoes a second look, she decided as she walked toward the hospital entrance, since it was a hospital!

Once she got inside, she headed for the elevators. An older couple and a lanky teenage boy were inside the elevator.

"Hold the door!" Connie called.

The teenager stuck his foot between the doors as they started to close and stopped them.

"Thank you," Connie said to him as she got on the elevator.

"No problem." The teenage boy leaned against the wall of the elevator and looked her over. "So, you're a nurse?" he asked, chewing a huge wad of gum that was almost too big for his mouth.

Connie smiled and nodded. "Uh-hum," she said quietly, not wanting to draw too much attention to herself.

"Cool," he said and loudly popped a bubble. He gave her another slower look, from her white nurse's shoes to her face. With a knowing look in the eyes, he licked his lower lip with his tongue. "Mmm."

Pervert! Connie thought and turned away from the kid just as the elevator door opened on the second floor. She stepped off quickly without looking back and walked down the hall to Lex's office. The receptionist was away from her desk, so Connie could slip into Lex's office unseen. She hoped that the receptionist had gone home for the day. Connie slid her key into the lock and the door opened. It dawned on her that he must not be carrying on his affair at the office since she still had a key, that works.

Connie entered Lex's office and closed the door behind her. Feeling for a light switch beside the door, she turned on the lights. She felt like a sexy female spy on a deadly mission of seduction! For once, she didn't even try to deny the damp excitement she felt.

Taking off her coat, Connie hung it on the coat rack in the corner. She smoothed her outfit, noticing it wasn't exactly traditional nurses' wear. It was shorter than normal, showed quite a length of thigh, with small slits on either side that showed even more flesh. But perhaps most noticeable of all was the low-cut neckline; it showed more cleavage than she thought that she had!

Connie needed to focus on what she was doing, without over thinking all the sordid details that might get in the way of the pure enjoyment of the adventure that laid ahead. She might even be able to truly enjoy making Lex's fantasy come true! At least, that's what she hoped....

Connie unclasped the pearl barrette that held her hair swept up in a tight bun, and let her flowing, thick mane of red hair fall across her shoulders. Taking her compact from her purse, she flipped it open and looked at her face in the mirror. Her make-up still looked good and her hair, which was her best asset, looked fabulous. As she closed her compact, she caught a glimpse of her cleavage in the mirror and paused looking at her full, firm breasts. Her breasts were a close second when it came to her best features. Nice. Lex was going to enjoy those, she almost giggled out loud, feeling more naughty than she ever imagined she could. *Yep,* she decided, *if she allowed herself, she could really enjoy this...if she didn't think about it too much!*

She checked the lights and turned them low. The backlight in the ceiling provided the slight, partially eerie and partially romantic glow she wanted. Connie tried different positions on the desk, and after trying a few poses she came up with a naughty position on his desk. She placed one leg on his char, showing him when he walked in that she wasn't wearing any panties.

Connie sat in Lex's office with the muted lights and thought about other times she had been with her husband. Their honeymoon, when he taken her in the water on the shore in Honolulu, with the stars twinkling overhead and the waves washing over them as they played and swam and ultimately made love with more passion than they ever had before...and probably ever since, Connie thought as she repositioned her leg.

What the hell was taking him so long? He usually got to his office after rounds to make a few notes before going home. In the past she had surprised him with plates of dinner late often when he had first got the cardiologist position and had worked late on so many occasions, building his practice and providing for her and the new babies. She repositioned her legs again and sighed.

There was a noise in the outer office. Footsteps came closer to the door and she draped herself across desk. The office door opened. Connie could only see his silhouette against the light from the outer office.

"Come on in," she said in her most seductive, slow and breathy voice. "I've been waiting for you. I'm Nurse Goodbody and I'm waiting for Dr. Feelgood!"

The door closed and he walked to her without a word. They started to kiss deeply and more passionately than Connie could ever remember! She knew they were definitely off to a good start, but she couldn't over think it or analyze it while it was happening because that would spoil the moment. Besides, she could analyze the hell out of it later–if she wanted!

"That's it," she cooed. "I'll make your fantasy a reality!"

He kissed her neck, skillfully working his way down to her breasts...

"Suck my tits, Doctor," she said urgently, enjoying the sensation of his mouth on her soft flesh. "Show me your bedside manner!" Connie continued as she remembered the lines from the one porno movie she'd ever seen. "I need you, sweetheart as I never have before!" She suppressed a giggle before it became a full-fledged laugh that would kill the mood. "Show me some intensive care!"

He pushed himself onto the desk and on top of her. That's when she realized he had taken his manhood...er cock...out of his pants. He was like a wild man... and she was excited to realize she really liked it.

"You like the doctor and nurse fantasy, darling?" Connie

asked quietly.

"Uh-hmmm," He grunted with his mouth firmly pressed to and surrounding her nipple.

His shaft seemed thicker than she remembered as he pushed his rock-hard cock inside her pussy lips, then he dove deeper and deeper into her juicy cunt.

Yep, she thought, *I should have taken that damned plant off the desk!*

Just as Connie was nearing orgasm, her hands traveled up his back. Wow, he was so muscular, she wondered if he had been working out at the gym without her knowledge. Her hands rested for a few seconds on his broad shoulders, then she slid her hands up the back of his neck to his hair. She loved to let her fingers run through his hair when they made love. Her fingers had barely touched his hair when Connie realized something was definitely not right! Lex did not have curly hair. This wasn't Lex!

Connie started trying to push the man off of her, but her body was hit with a series of one deep orgasmic wave after another each more pleasurable than the last! Shaken by the after effects of her shattering climax, and the finding out she had just had sex been with a total stranger (and she liked it), Connie pushed the man away, and turned on the desk light.

Connie went into her housewife-slash-cleaning machine mode, returning the items she removed from Lex's desk. Then she knelt down and busily swept up the loose dirt from the plant with an old file folder from the garbage. She periodically dumped the soil she swept up with her hand into the trash can. Between sweeping she snuck glances at the young man who had just made love to her.

He stood there with a stunned, but satisfied look on his handsome face for a while, then he turned away from her and zipped himself up. He was handsome, but shorter than Lex and he had curly hair. All of a sudden, Connie remembered he knocked lightly before coming into the room.

"Oh, my god," she mumbled. "Who are you?" Connie asked

after he'd turned to face her again.

"I'm Jimmy Landis," he answered in a breathless voice. "I'm an intern. I came by to consult with Dr. Vanderkellen about a patient. He must have forgotten about our meeting and headed home." He paused and then posed a question of his own. "Who are you?"

"I'm Dr. Vanderkellen's wife," she said coolly. "I was hoping to surprise my husband."

"Looks like I got the surprise!" the handsome young intern blurted out, the realized his mistake when the woman who had been so hot moments earlier gave him a look that chilled him to the soul. "Sorry," he apologized uneasily.

"I thought you were my husband," said Connie, cleaning herself up and straightening the skirt of the crumpled nurse's uniform, "I guess we'd better keep this to ourselves."

"Well, when can I see you again?"

"You didn't see me the first time, if you remember. I thought you were my husband, it was an honest mistake."

"I should go," he said as he backed into the door.

"Well, don't run off quite yet," she said. "We'll never–do you understand–never do this again, but as long as we're here…" She pushed him against the door with one hand and ripped the blouse of the uniform with the other. He took her breast in his hand and put his other hand between her legs, fingering her and rubbing her clit. She reveled in the incredible feeling as he massaged her clit and fingered her dripping wet pussy.

Well, Lex, Connie thought as she started to cum again, it doesn't get more spontaneous than this! She wondered how she could ever explain this to Lex–or if she would. It occurred to her that she had no reason to feel any guilt, she should only feel satisfied. After all, Lex had cheated on her and this had been an accident. Well, the first time was an accident. She had not planned to seduce the handsome young intern and certainly not twice…in her husband's office.

4

The Sexual Psychic Sees All

It was time for the girl's monthly get together at SueAnn's house, and as they all filed in and found comfortable places in the living room, SueAnn brought out a large plastic shopping bag.

"Look, I bought us matching journals!" she announced as she dumped the bag on the coffee table, "I thought it might help for us to keep journals after, you know, what happened to Mary Lynn."

Giji frowned; SueAnn's saccharin sweet smile really annoyed her, it seemed a few less shakes than sincere. She secretly wondered what SueAnn's motive was behind this. "What are we, back in junior high school?" asked Giji with obvious sarcasm. It was clear to everyone that Giji did not trust the idea of matching journals.

"Yeah," Wynette found herself agreeing with Giji for the first time…ever. "It's like we're suddenly the Ya-Ya sisterhood or something!"

"It seems that way to me, too," Ariella chimed in, glancing over at Connie for validation. Connie said nothing and seemed to be listening intently, "Remember that book club you insisted we start? You couldn't get past chapter one! You chose that book about nuns, and we read some of it–the most boring book ever– and then you lost interest!"

"I couldn't get past the blurb on the back cover," admitted Giji.

SueAnn looked at Giji but said nothing. She didn't bother reminding them that her book club idea had lead to her reading at the local nursing home once a month. Besides, that didn't seem to be a good argument at the present.

"We seem to be getting off topic, let SueAnn speak," said Wynette.

SueAnn drew herself up and looked at all of them, maybe they weren't friends, but neighbors who had shared a very sad experience together.

"Well, after what happened to Mary Lynn, I felt we needed a way to share our feelings or at least have an outlet to record them. We could even read excerpts from our journals at these monthly get toget-"

"Like hell we will!" Connie suddenly interrupted. The thought of having to expose her less than perfect marriage and maybe even the tryst with the intern in Lex's office... But she pulled herself together immediately, appearances were everything, after all. "I mean... I'm sorry, but I'm not comfortable sharing the deepest details of my life, that's all."

"I just thought that–" SueAnn started.

"Well that's your problem, isn't it? You just think too much," Connie erupted again, which was out of character for her.

"Hey, Connie, calm down," said Giji. "You're certainly in no position to tell anyone how to talk about feelings, least of all SueAnn. You're wound tight with secrets, and because it's so important to you to put on appearances, maybe you should keep a journal, just to keep all of your secrets straight."

"How dare you!" Connie looked as though she couldn't decide whether to throw coffee on Giji or cry.

"At least with me, what you see is what you get," Giji said.

"And for a cheap rate, too," Wynette mumbled.

"What did you say?" Giji turned to Wynette.

"I said, Tom is a cheap skate, too," said Wynette, then quickly to SueAnn. "I think it's very nice that you bought us all matching journals. I thought it was a good idea, why don't we all just try them for one month, and when we meet back here, we can decide whether we want to read excerpts or not."

"Well, I'm not," said Connie. She got up and went into the kitchen, poured what was left of her coffee in the sink and headed for the door. She let it slam on the way out, which triggered the other women to start moving. One by one they apologized to SueAnn, and left, leaving the matching cloth covered books in a little heap on the coffee table.

Wynette was the last to leave.

She gave SueAnn a little non committal sideways hug and tried to console her as best she could.

"We're just not that into sharing our personal lives, especially with each other, you know what this neighborhood is really like, SueAnn. Secrets everywhere and everyone is tearing around trying to make this street look like something out of a *Good Housekeeping* magazine. No one wants to write that stuff down and no one wants to talk about it out loud, ever. Look at Connie; she tries so hard to keep up that perfect veneer. Can you imagine what would happen to her if she had to let it all out?"

"She'd crack?" asked SueAnn. "Like Mary Lynn cracked?"

"It was a good idea," Wynette avoided the question. "You could give 'em to the battered women's shelter. They could use them; I'll bet they'd really appreciate that."

"I suppose so," SueAnn agreed, "at least someone will get some use out of them."

Wynette patted her on the shoulder and started to leave, and then she turned around and took one of the journals from the table.

"You never know," she said as she left.

***

Martha Hoover parked her car and picked her way across the cracked asphalt to the west side of the strip mall. When she had first opened her business there had been beautiful, flowers in pots lining the walkways and fresh paint had shouted to customers on the street. Now it was a run down strip mall, abandoned by shoppers for the new 400 hundred stores and Cineplex mall on the other side of town. The only businesses that remained were her small shop, an ABC Package store, a fish market and the Sexual Psychic. Today the Sexual Psychic had a new sign in the window.

The Sexual Psychic Professional
Psychic since 1999 Predicts
Future and Love
Sex Dream Interpretation
Sex Therapist
Celebrity Gossip!

   I must have paid for that new sign, Martha thought, it seems like I'm the only one that comes in here! The smell of fish from the market next door doesn't help, she was sure, but she didn't find the smell all that offensive.

   The Sexual Psychic was a wiry little Asian woman named Kimiko who could be a little abrupt at times, but she was fiercely accurate and provided Martha with information which she used to turn a tidy profit. Martha didn't particularly like Kimiko but found her oddly appealing and even arousing with her small frame and breasts like lotus buds.

   More importantly, Kimiko's information kept Martha's little red book full for the past few years. It was Kimiko who told her about Paul Young embezzling money from the brokerage firm where he worked, and that Steven Harris was having sex with his secretary and almost twenty hot young ladies he screwed on his business travels – all of which he met on the internet. Kimiko was pretty sure Steven would eventually die of a disease he would contract from these escapades, but Martha didn't think so. He must have been very careful, or his pretty little wife would've noticed something by now.

Kimiko's cards also told about Lex Vanderkellen's little perversion of liking kinky sex along with being tied up and spanked. Martha made a good profit on that piece of information.

A little bell jangled softly as Mrs. Hoover opened the door to the shop. The room was very small with hardly any space to move around in and there was a curtain leading to the back room with two chairs on either side of a small marble table. The walls were red, with old gold inlay–making the shop look less like an Asian tarot reader's and more like a Chinese restaurant throwback, but it had a kind of ancient charm that Martha had found relaxing and even comforting over the years.

The first room with the one table was the waiting room. The marble table had a small ceramic teapot on it with two empty cups; guests could pour hot tea for themselves while waiting their turn to shuffle the cards. Martha didn't like tea, and opened a roll of Life Savers as she waited.

Presently, she heard shuffling from the back room, and Kimiko poked her head through the curtain.

"Oh, you, nosy lady who like gossip about friends, okay I see you, come on back."

"Kimiko, you know my name is Martha, we've known each other for years."

"We have business relationship for years. You come to my house? I go to yours? No. You ask questions about neighbors, that's all I know. Sit down."

Martha took a seat opposite Kimiko in the next room, which was much larger than the entrance room, but was still decorated with the same red and gold wallpaper and a worn Tibetan carpet under her feet. The table where she sat was much larger than the first, round table and made from dark wood, with scratches and marks in it that appeared to be as old as her. There were a few chairs that appeared to have been part of an old dining set, spread about the room and an old sofa covered with what appeared to be a worn, faded tapestry.

Kimiko laid all the cards out one by one, face up, and then gathered them up and shuffled them sideways, so that they would all be face up when she read the future. Martha had seen her do this every time she came to visit. By shuffling the cards sideways instead of the traditional way of end to end as most cards are shuffled, she kept all the cards facing the same direction, which would mean that an inverted–or upside down–card would have a much stronger meaning. Shuffling them end to end would ensure that at least half the cards would come out inverted, and where was the mystery in that?

Gossip aside, Kimiko considered herself a professional and she operated her business in a professional manner. She was refined, quiet, and methodical while she lay out her cards, unlabored and regal, her movements like her mother and grandmother before her. She could see much deeper into the future than who was screwing who, but Americans cared nothing for the truly supernatural, wanting only to sit like lard on their couches, watching half naked people in reality shows and going to the local church to play bingo every Tuesday. They disgusted Kimiko, but they were willing to pay good money to hear gossip, and so that's what Kimiko provided, and she provided it well. Occasionally, to select clients, namely those willing to pay, she provided her extracurricular activities under the guise of a sex therapist.

When she finished what she called "clearing" the cards, Kimiko pushed them across the table toward Martha, who shuffled them sideways as she'd been taught during her first visits to the Sexual Psychic. She cut them three times and slid them back across the table where Kimiko laid them out, one by one.

"You ask future of neighbors again, yes?"

"Yes, anything new? Anything about the wives?" asked

Martha as she sucked on her Life Saver.

"Six of swords, a journey across water; Swords are words, gossip, and hurtful gossip. You will be found out."

"Not if I keep being as careful as I am," Martha said, "go on."

Kimiko hesitated at the next card.

"Oh, the chariot!" Martha sounded excited. "That means something good, huh? Like a trip?"

"Umm, it's the dea-uh-life card," she lied, "Much travel."

"What do you see–am I going on a trip?"

"You could say that."

"Really! Some place warm, like San Diego?"

"Even warmer."

"Oh, Charleston! I've always wanted to visit that city. I hear it's like stepping back in time, with all the antebellum plantations, I'll feel just like Scarlet O"Hara!"

"Farther South."

"Mexico?"

Kimiko shrugged, "No, we say Charleston. Close enough."

"That is just wonderful," Mrs. Hoover gushed, pleased. "Okay, now about the people who live in my neighborhood...the wives. No. What about SueAnn?"

"No, almost pure as virgin snow," Kimiko answered.

"Did you say almost?"

"No dirty underwear on her!"

"You mean dirty laundry, Kimiko," Mrs. Hoover corrected, disappointed. "How about the husbands?"

"Hmm...tall, dark and handsome sells cars, did it with his pretty secretary."

"Marco?"

Kimiko shrugged and sat back.

Martha could hardly believe what she was hearing, she had waited so long to get some dirt on that handsome Latin hunk! she thought as she opened her purse, took out her wallet and fished out a twenty.

Kimiko sighed audibly and pointed to another new sign. This

one read Psychic Readings, $50.

"Oh, dear, I should've stopped by the bank. I'll have to catch up next time."

"I take credit card."

"Kimiko, as long as we've known each other you'd think you could cut me some slack," she said as she pulled out her bank book. She hurriedly wrote a check and handed it over as she gathered her bag.

"This business. We not friends."

Mrs. Hoover stopped and turned, looking hurt. "How can you say that?"

"Because, my dear woman," said Kimiko in perfect English, "you have never once asked me about my family or my life."

Martha Hoover's mouth dropped open.

"And furthermore," Kimiko said, glancing into Mrs. Hoover's handbag. "You never offered me a Lifesaver!"

"Yeah, okay," Mrs. Hoover said, clearly irritated.

"Enjoy your trip," Kimiko called as Mrs. Hoover left in a huff, "bitch!"

***

Standing on the small porch, Giji waited for her clients, an older couple, to arrive for a showing of the house, a two-story red brick colonial that had just come on the market and located a block over from Mrs. Hoover's house,. She almost wished she were buying the house herself. *As if I could afford it!* she thought. But she knew she would eventually find a place that was right for her, a small house or a condominium that would be right for her – and affordable. Although she appreciated Mrs. Hoover letting her crash at her house, she was ready to have her own place and get back to living her own life in her own space.

Yep, I'm definitely ready to be in my own home away from Mrs. Hoover's horrible casserole concoctions, she thought as she watched each vehicle that went by, finally a small red sports car slowed down and turned into the semi-circular driveway. When they got out the woman waved to her and smiled.

"Hope you didn't have to wait for us long," she said as she came up the steps, "I'm Valerie–call me Val–and this is my husband Dave."

"Nice to meet you in person," said Giji shaking their hands.

Giji looked the couple over, unimpressed. Val was a small, slender woman with limp, almost severely straight blonde hair, too much makeup, and a shapely figure that gave her the appearance of a much younger woman. In contrast, her husband was a large man, tall, with dark hair flecked with silver-gray. He had lively eyes and an easy, warm smile, but his most obvious feature was a beer belly that hung over the top of his worn jeans and enormous, tarnished silver belt buckle that read "Texas."

"Thanks for coming, let me just show you the inside," said Giji as she unlocked the front door. Val went in first, followed by her husband, who smiled and looked at Giji a little too long for her comfort, making her feel awkward in her short skirt.

"Well, here's the entry way, you'll see the inside has been freshly painted, and this part of the ceiling has just been tiled, oh about two years ago. The owners wanted to brighten up the entranceway so they had the cream and blue tiles installed. It really lightens the place up."

"Oh, yes, very nice," said Val, "can we see the upstairs?"

"Of course, the stairs are right this way."

Giji led the couple through the living room and into the hallway, pointing out the house's finer changes the owners had made over the years along the way. When they got to the stairs leading to the second floor, Val rushed ahead in front of her.

"After you," Dave said pleasantly.

Giji climbed the stairs to the second level with the distinct feeling that Dave was watching her ass the entire time. The couple looked at the master bedroom and adjacent bath, the second, smaller bedroom and the stained glass half window at the top of the landing. Giji explained that the owner's wife had picked it out when they first moved in, and could hardly bear to part with it, and the couple paused to admire it.

"Oh, look!" Val said, looking through the clear center of the window. "There's a hot tub in the backyard!"

"It's only a couple of years old and will stay with the house," said Giji quickly.

"Well, I'd like a closer look at that backyard!" Dave started back down the stairs, then got an idea and paused.

"Babe, why don't you go check out the kitchen while Miss Giji shows me the backyard?"

"Ooh! Great idea!" Val said with a bit too much enthusiasm.

Val walked into the kitchen and Giji slid open the sliding glass door which led to the backyard. The hot tub was at the far end by the fence.

"Does it work?" Dave asked.

"Oh, it works very well," answered Giji. "It was installed on a separate circuit, so it's always on. You have to shut it off at the breaker box. It was installed like that so the owners could get into it as soon as they got home from work without waiting for it to heat up."

"I'm starting to heat up right now," Dave said.

"Oh...uh...excuse me?" Surely, she heard him wrong.

"I'll make you a deal, Giji. We'll buy the house if you climb in the hot tub with me."

"Wouldn't your wife be pissed?" That was all Giji could think to say.

"No, she'll get a kick out of it, I promise," Dave said as he started to unbutton his shirt. "She's never gets mad if she can join in."

Giji only hesitated a minute.

"Anything to close the deal!" she said as she slipped off her skirt and climbed in with him.

He sat at the far end of the hot tub and motioned for her to join him. Crossing her arms Giji took off her top and threw it over the side. She slid over to Dave while he masturbated under the water.

"You are so pretty, so hot," he whispered as she positioned herself on his lap. She faced away from him, and slid his surprisingly huge cock inside of her. She didn't want to face him so she wouldn't have to kiss him. That was one part of this whole scene she just wasn't willing to do, but he didn't seem to mind and he grabbed her hips as she leaned forward.

He controlled the whole episode, pumping her hips up and down as she braced herself by holding the cedar rails of the tub. Harder and harder, Giji began to enjoy it, after all, she didn't have to kiss him and he felt good inside her. *What a big cock for an old man!* she thought, I'm gonna have to remember to get me some more of this.

At last he came, holding her hips as hard as he could to keep her pushed down on top of him, and then with a little moan he let go, just as Val came out of the house.

"You naughty children! Starting without me!" she said as she made her way across the backyard. She unzipped her pants and took them off, and then undid her blouse.

"Help me off with this, will you dear?" she said to Giji as she leaned over the edge of the tub. The steam and splashes from Dave soaked the cotton top and Giji could see her nipples standing erect through the fabric. Feeling oddly turned on, she helped Val into the hot tub and squared her shoulders as Val began to suck on her breasts.

She knew what women liked, and kissed and pinched Giji's nipples until Giji threw her head back and put her tongue between her teeth. Out of the corner of her eye she could see Dave touching himself again under the water and before she knew it he had come over to their side of the hot tub and was fucking his wife from behind.

Val was moaning and sucking Giji so Giji moved her hand between Val's thighs to help Dave massage her clit. Val almost screamed with pleasure and ran two fingers into Giji's pussy, moving them back and forth and side to side. Giji began to sway with the rhythm of them all enjoying each other, and then switched places with Val so she could get another taste of Dave's big cock. They took turns with each other for at least an hour. It was the best time Giji had ever had selling a house!

***

Martha Hoover let herself in to the house and left her bag on the entry way table. There was a note from Giji scrawled across a slip of paper, "Had an early morning appointment, see you later, don't wait up!" Perfect, thought Martha, she won't be back to interrupt what may turn out to be a hot afternoon.

She dialed Marco's number and waited as the phone rang once, twice, on the third ring Marco answered the phone. Thankfully, Ariella didn't answer, so she asked him to come over for a few minutes–there was an urgent matter that she needed to discuss with him, and she put down the phone to wait. Occasionally, she peeped through the blinds, trying to catch a glimpse of any movement outside. She could already feel the excitement stirring in the pit of her stomach; she hoped the meeting would not be too uncomfortable.

On the drive home from the Sexual Psychic she had formulated a plan. Mrs. Hoover had been attracted to Marco since the couple first moved in, and although the money she could blackmail him with by using Kimiko's information would pay a generous portion on her upcoming trip. She thought that her chance to have him would come with his refusal to pay. *Cash or cock,* she giggled on the way home. She could imagine enjoying the sexual pleasures she could have instead, and Marco was a most appealing man. A hot Latin hunk with dark skin and she imagined he had a fiery passion.

She opened the door on the first knock and smiled into the dark handsome face of her neighbor, Marco Fluentes. He smiled back at her, unaware of what lay ahead of him.

"What did you say?" Marco asked, hoping he had misunderstood what he thought he'd heard.

"Cash or cock! I know you're sleeping with your secretary and so will your beautiful, spoiled wife. You have a choice to make, Marco, cash or cock," repeated Mrs. Hoover.

"Oh, I don't think you can prove that," Marco stalled.

"Do you deny it?"

"How much cash do you want?" Marco sighed.

"Hmmm," Mrs. Hoover looked thoughtful for a minute, "A few thousand."

"Once…"

"A month," Mrs. Hoover finished for him. She turned away and pretended to study the talk show on TV. She'd heard Latin men were great lovers. Secretly she hoped that he'd feel cash was out of the question and choose the alternative. She unconsciously licked her lips in anticipation.

"Let me think," Marco said as he began to pace. His thoughts were a jumble. He felt his penis shrivel at the thought of any kind of sex with Mrs. Hoover–even oral. He'd just as soon bang his mother's toothless friend Alita! He sighed again. Ariella was high maintenance with expensive tastes and daily shopping sprees. With that and the monthly mortgage payments, Marco was tapped. He didn't have much in the way of choices and he mulled the possibilities as he continued to pace the floor. Of course, there was a third choice that Mrs. Hoover hadn't thought of, he could strangle the old bitch right here in her den. As appealing as that was, he couldn't see it as a reasonable option. He would end up getting arrested; god knew she had probably taken precautions so if anything happened to her, his secret would get out… well, the secret and her murder. One thing was sure; he couldn't keep stalling, so Marco did the only thing he could.

Mrs. Hoover waited patiently, and then as she turned to hurry Marco along, she saw it. Long, thick, and hard–the biggest cock she had seen in her life! It was sticking out of his unzipped fly, right in her face. She drew in a sharp breath.

"I see you've made up your mind," she said.

"I have," he said in a voice that sounded like a man destined for the gallows. He moved to the couch and she kneeled on the floor in front of him, making little purring noises about her first Latin lover. He was more than a little disgusted and felt drained even as she took his cock in her mouth. Unable to close his eyes, Marco watched as she let her lips give the tip of his cock a light touch, almost like a kiss, softer than Ariella ever had, even softer than Tia had handled him the first few times.

Once she was working on his cock with all her concentration, he had to admit that the nasty, blackmailing old bitch was pretty good at giving head; she was born to suck cock. He lay back against the armrest of the couch and closed his eyes. It felt great, warm and wet, wonderful. He began to imagine Ariella sucking him, but for some reason, possibly because of the circumstances, that was just too weird, so he imagined a porn star sucking him off. Damn!

Mrs. Hoover was good–like a vacuum cleaner with lips and a crazy tongue that was everywhere at once. Marco thrust forward and moaned. This seemed to excite Mrs. Hoover very much, and she began sucking harder, moving her tongue faster in circles around the shaft of his cock. Finally after what seemed like forever, Marco exploded into her mouth. She sucked even harder while he came in her mouth, swallowing everything he forced into her.

Mrs. Hoover could feel how wet she was, *I could learn to like this,* she thought, *like a forbidden delicacy. Well, it's my delicacy now!* She leaned back and wiped her mouth on the back of her hand, stood up and went into the kitchen, leaving Marco drained and uncomfortable on the couch. When she came back in, he had zipped up his fly and was making for the door.

"I take it we're squared away," he said without looking at her.

"Until next month," she smiled as she let him out.

***

Ariella froze. "Did you hear that?" she asked, listening intently.

"No, baby, I didn't hear anything. Roll over onto your knees; I want to take you from behind," the gardener said as he ran his tongue down Ariella's stomach.

"John, shut up. Did you hear something? Oh god, I think Marco is home early. Get off of me!"

Ariella shoved her gardener off the bed and struggled to her feet. Opening the closet door she motioned to him. "Hurry up! Get in there!"

"I'm not hiding in the fu-"

"Now or you're fired!"

John had been putting on his clothes; he was dressed except for his shoes. His cock was still hard, and this bitch tease had been trying to hump him since the day they'd met, so why was she making up this shit now about her husband coming home? For weeks she had found a reason to be in the garden when he was there, wearing practically nothing, leaning close when he asked a question, touching his arm and smiling, stroking his back as she bent over to pretend to be interested in what he was saying.

Ariella grabbed his arm and tugged. "Now!"

John allowed himself to be shoved in the bedroom closet, narrowly escaping the fact that Marco was coming up the stairs. No one noticed that he had left his shoes just under the edge of the bed.

"Hi, baby," Marco said as he came in the room. He took off his coat and threw it across the chair. "Taking a nap?"

Ariella realized she was naked and the bed was messed up. "Hmm, yes, I was just getting up to take a long bath. Why are you home so soon?"

"Can't a guy surprise his wife once in awhile?"

You don't know the half of it, Ariella thought. She smiled at him and tried to move past him into the bathroom, hoping he would follow her and John might have a chance to escape the closet. Instead he reached out to her as she tried to get past him.

"Hey, what do you say you wait a while before taking that bath?"

Ariella started to protest, but realized the idea of having sex with her husband while another lover was in the closet was just too much for her. She smiled up at him and let him lead her back to the bed; she was already hot and naked, wet and ready, so why shouldn't she let Marco make her cum? She almost came on her own; thinking about John huddled in the closet next to her fur coat, with his sweaty body and dirty Levis. He was a blue collar boy and she was ready to take him anyway he wanted her before Marco came home and ruined it. But, she might get some fun out of the afternoon, after all.

Ariella lay on the bed and watched Marco get undressed. It was so exciting she touched herself while he took off his shirt. She pulled her knees up to her chin and began to rub her clit, lightly at first and then harder and faster. Then she noticed the crack in the closet door. John could see her! She winked toward the door and rubbed herself harder. A little moan escaped her, when Marco looked up from removing his shirt he was more than a little surprised.

"Wow, baby, you feeling a little hot today?"

Marco's cock was rock hard by now. Ariella's pussy was glistening and he could smell her, he climbed on top of her and rammed her so hard she moaned.

John shifted position in the closet. Damn, she would have the audacity to do this right in front of me, he thought. He peeped out through the crack in the French door and watched Marco thrust in and out of Ariella while she wrapped her legs around his waist. He felt his cock start to harden inside the jeans and scrambled to unbutton the tight fitting Levis that had attracted Ariella ever since he had come to work for her. As he watched Marco slip in and out of her, John realized he hadn't even gotten any, he was just about to roll the rich bitch over and pump her like a dog when her old man showed up.

He reached inside his jeans and squeezed his cock, and as he did he saw Ariella looking at him from over Marco's shoulder. She smiled and licked her lips at him, just as Marco leaned down and took her right nipple in his mouth. She moaned and threw her head back, but not before catching John's eye through the crack in the door.

John began to masturbate furiously, as hard as he could and still be quiet. Ariella looked so hot and he could see Marco start to grind on top of her, which he found oddly arousing.

He came in his hand and looked around for something to wipe it on. He would be damned before he wiped it on his jeans, and the floor of the closet was hardwood, which wouldn't get all of it. He looked around the closet while Marco and Ariella continued to go at it, and then his eyes fell on the perfect material to wipe cum on. He wasn't sure it was real mink, but he guessed it probably was. *That'll teach her, I got cum all over her fur,* he thought as he put away his cock and crouched, ready to bolt at the first opportunity.

Ariella reached behind her head and took hold of the headboard. She used it as leverage and pushed as hard as she could against Marco, who was coming so hard he was shuddering. He pulled out and flipped her over on her stomach, and getting behind her, reached over her back and grabbed the headboard himself. Grinding and throbbing, he finally came again, and Ariella collapsed beneath him.

He pulled out and she turned over, but when she started to get up, he pushed her back down and knelt between her legs. He gently licked her pussy, a little at a time, flicking his tongue over her clit, swirling around her opening and darting in and out. He tickled her clit again with his tongue, knowing she liked that best, and buried his face in her pussy sucking as hard as he could. Ariella grabbed his face and held it there, quivering and smiling at the closet door. She jerked her head toward the door to the bedroom and mouthed the word "Go!"

"Oh Marco, I love it! I love it!" she whispered to cover the sound of the closet opening. "Oh no, baby, don't stop, please don't stop," she said as John came out, his jeans half buttoned and Ariella's fur in one hand. He dropped the coat on the floor and picked up his shoes in one motion. Ariella knew immediately what had happened to her fur but as she tried to make a face Marco hit a spectacular spot with his tongue, and she could only moan as the orgasm hit her. John blew her a kiss and was half way down the stairs as Marco came up for air.

5

Queer Eye for Mrs. Hoover

While Mrs. Martha Hoover was watering her roses while her friend Gladys watched, a moving van pulled up, followed by a Ford Expedition and stopped in front of the house across the street. The house had sold a little over a week ago. Martha had been so relieved when those Jesus killers, the Jew family had put their house on the market. In the five years, that family had lived across the street, she'd pretty much ignored them. It started when they returned her Christmas card with a picture showing a manger scene with baby Jesus in the hay! How dare they be so rude, so sacrilegious! Well, she'd let that one pass and decided to make a goodwill gesture on New Year's by taking over a dish she'd made from a recipe by that hunky Emeril Lagasse! Well, once they had literally refused her pork and wiener casserole that was the final straw! How insulting! Imagine turning down fresh pork and Ballpark franks!

The guys in the moving van started unloading the van while the black family got out of the SUV and watched.

"Ugh, Archie Bunker was right," Martha commented, rolling

her eyes toward the new neighbors across the street, "you let one family in, and the whole neighborhood starts changing colors. Several white families have moved out in the last month!"

"I blame Jesse Jackson and his so-called Rainbow Coalition!" Gladys said with a deep sigh. "Before you know it, those queers will be the next ones to move into the neighborhood."

"Oh, they already have!" Martha told her, trying to concentrate on her watering. "A white guy and a black guy with a bi-racial child and a Dalmatian puppy moved one block over just last week!"

"Oh no!" Gladys gasped. "A Dalmatian!"

"Well, now that we have our own A. Bunker in the white house, we'll see how far they get!" Martha hesitated. "Speaking of queers, hon," Martha spoke quietly, just loud enough for Gladys to hear her over the sound of the spray of water, "I was watching that 'Queer Eye for the Straight' Guy the other night." She glanced up at her friend quickly, then continued, "I thought it was a rally put on by the evangelical Christians for the conservatives, of course."

"Of course," Gladys agreed.

"Well, that program is filth, pure filth. I never saw so much inappropriate touching in my life!"

Gladys's eyes grew wide. "Really?"

"Oh, yes," Martha assured her. "Hon, they were touching each other's most private places!"

"Oh no!" Gladys could not hide her shock—or her interest.

"Yes!" Martha continued. "One guy was actually touching another guy's—"

"No!" Gladys gasped, wondering if the show was on TV that night.

"Yes!" Martha looked her in the eye. "He had his hand on another guy's knee!"

"That's so hard to believe," Gladys said quietly, trying to hide her disappointment.

"Shameful! I tell you!"

"What did you say the program is called?" Gladys wanted to know, glancing at the driveway next door as Wynette parked her mini van with the sticker that read *Soccer Mom on Ritalin*.

" 'Queer Eye for the Straight Guy'!" Martha said rather loudly, remembering that Gladys was sometimes hard of hearing.

"Oh," Wynette said as she and her boys climbed out of the mini van, "if you like that show, you'll love 'Queer as Folk'! It's no longer on TV, but you can buy the DVD set."

"Did you say 'Queer as Fuck'?" Gladys asked quickly after the kids scampered away. Making a mental note to check eBay later for a deal on the DVDs, she waved to the younger woman and smiled.

Martha continued watering her roses while ignoring Wynette and giving her friend a hard glare. "Nosy bitch," Martha mumbled under her breath.

***

The phone rang in Mrs. Hoover's kitchen. Giji was the only one home so she answered it.

"Giji? Giji, this is Val, we bought a house recently? Remember us, Val and Dave?"

"Yes, Val," Giji said, remembering. "How are you? I hope everything is fine with the house?"

"We're fine, thanks," Val assured her, "and the house is wonderful. The reason I'm calling is we'd like you to come over for a minute, if you could." She paused, then added, "We have a surprise for you and we'd love it if you could drop by."

"A surprise?" Giji repeated uncertainly. "For me? That's so nice. When did…?"

"Now," Val said quickly, "if you come over now, it'd be great."

"Okay," Giji agreed. "I'll be right over."

Giji hung up the phone and pulled the door behind her as she left. It was a short walk over to the house she had recently sold to the Harper's. She was so excited and genuinely surprised, she could hardly wait to see what the swinging old couple had in store for her.

Dave answered the door. "Come in Giji, come in." He smiled. "We're so happy you could make it."

"Close your eyes!" Val said as she came around the corner from the kitchen. Giji closed her eyes and Val got behind her. Giji thought she was going to cover her eyes from behind but was surprised to feel Val's hands on her breasts. Giji shrugged and was led to the small room door on the first floor of the house that the previous owners had used as an office.

"Are your eyes still closed?" asked Val.

"Yes, dear, they are," Dave answered for her. He pushed open the door to the room and Giji felt herself pushed gently into the room.

"Okay, you can open your eyes now," said Val.

Giji opened her eyes to a freshly painted pink room. Everything in it was a shade of pink.

It was a nursery.

"I don't understand, this is for me? What do you want me to do, be a surrogate mother?" *That could mean a lot of money,* she thought to her self, but she wasn't sure she was comfortable with the idea.

Val and Dave laughed. Dave stood just inside the door, leaning against the frame; Val came into the room and put her arm around Giji.

"We want you to be our little girl," she smiled, "Isn't it lovely? Pink and frilly, so girly, just like our sweet Giji!"

"I do like pink," said Giji uncomfortably.

"Our special little girl," Dave cooed behind her.

"We bought you toys!" said Val, heading for the closet. She took out a poofy dress with pink bows, in the style of a baby doll dress, but Giji's size, "Isn't this one beautiful?"

Dave pointed to a toy box on the other side of the room. "Now you can be a kid again. There's a catholic schoolgirl outfit with fishnet stockings and peek-a-boo panties." He drew in his breath sharply. "I'd like you to wear that one first."

Giji shivered, this was a little too weird, even for her. She took the pink frilly dress from Val and held it up to her. "Wow, this is a very cute outfit, I always pictured my daughter–or very effeminate son – wearing dresses like this, if I'd had kids and all…"

"Well it's a good thing you never did, and neither did we, so you can relive your entire childhood with us. We will dote on you and buy you everything a little girl could want," said Val.

"Everything an especially sweet little girl could want," Dave added, winking at Giji.

"Like a second childhood," added his wife.

"Knowing everything you know now, of course," Dave patted her on the behind, "There will be many perks for you, dear Giji."

"Like what?" Giji couldn't believe that she had just said that, but was curious just the same. She wondered how far these people would take their little game.

"You will be pampered, fed, bathed–I get to do that–all your needs will be taken care of as long as you're here."

"More than that," Val interrupted, "you'll always have a room here in our home and we promise to always be available to see that your sexual needs are taken care of as well."

"What do I have to do, just out of curiosity?" asked Giji.

"All you have to do is call us Mom and Dad."

"Daddy's little girl can have anything she wants," Dave said with a smile Giji could only think of as leering.

"Wow, what an offer, I'll have to think it over," stammered Giji. *It might be a step up from being molested in my sleep by Mrs. Hoover,* she thought. *Or – maybe not!*

"Well, while you're trying to make up your mind, my baby, why don't you try on one of those dresses?"

"The schoolgirl one, please," Dave said, still grinning, his eyes bright with excitement. "We'll be in the kitchen fixing lunch. You will stay for lunch, won't you?"

"Sure, what the hell," said Giji, "I'll change and be right out."

The couple left the door open and went down the hall toward the kitchen. Giji shut the door after them and walked slowly over to the closet, half expecting to see something jump out at her. When nothing did, she took the catholic schoolgirl outfit down from its hook and began squeezing into it. The uniform was a good fit; they had certainly done their homework. She thought about how much better it might be here than at Mrs. Hoover's, while she tried to figure out what she was going to do with the rest of her life. To be honest, it wouldn't be the first time she had lived in strange circumstances or traded sex for shelter. It might be just the thing while she decided if she was going to use the money from the sale of her house to leave the state and maybe start over again somewhere else. Then again, she would need to stop running sometime, and this situation was definitely a little weirder than things from other times in her life. She sighed and pulled the fishnets up over her thigh, and then went into the kitchen. Val and Dave were just sitting down to lunch.

"There's our good girl!" Val said. Dave patted his lap and Giji dutifully went over and pretended to climb up on it. Dave slid his hands around her waist and held her there. She wriggled around a little, thinking that's what he would like, and then slid down and into her seat, across from Val. Val put hot tomato soup, a grilled cheese sandwich, and a glass of milk in front of her and they began to eat.

Giji took a bite of her sandwich and followed it with some soup. She slurped the hot soup from the spoon and caught both of them looking at her.

"We do not slurp our soup here," said the old man.

"Oh, sorry, I–"

"Come here, little lady, you'll need a spanking for that," Dave rose to come over to Giji's side of the table and that's when it hit her. This was definitely just too weird.

"Hey, you're not going to spank–hey! That hurts!" Dave had a hold of her arm, and was squeezing too hard.

"That does it! That is enough. I'm outta here!" Giji threw down her napkin and headed for the door. "Screw you and your baby doll fetish!" she said as she passed Dave.

"Take all the time you need, dear, you'll be back!" She heard as she slammed the door behind her.

Giji ran down the street and toward Mrs. Hoover's house. She wasn't crying, but she felt that she had humiliated herself. It was true that she liked sex as much as the next girl, probably more than most, but the idea that she might actually had gone for the Harper's game made her queasy. What had she been about to do?

Giji slammed the door behind her and started up the stairs to her room when she heard a cough. She stopped on the stairs and looked into the living room. Mrs. Hoover sat on the couch watching her soaps.

"Well, now, don't you look nice," she said.

It was only then that Giji realized she was still wearing the Catholic school girl outfit. "Where have you been?" Martha Hoover asked curiously and chuckled. "The prom?"

"Worse, it was a costume party," Giji lied. "More like a freak show!"

"And you're back so soon?" Mrs. Hoover snapped, amused.

Giji shrugged, disinterested in continuing the conversation and having to explain the whole sordid mess to Mrs. Hoover.

Martha Hoover took a quick of her iced tea. "Come here and sit beside me," she said as she put a handful of potato chips in her mouth. She winked.

"Arrgh!," said Giji.

Upstairs Giji stripped and changed into jeans and a T-shirt. She grabbed her bag and went down the back stairs and outside, heading for the peace and quiet of the Java Hut.

***

The sky became overcast and rain pattered lightly on the sidewalk as Giji opened the doors to the Java Hut. She brought one of her favorite books and ordered a vanilla latte, so she could pretend to read while she checked out the hot guys who came into the Java Hut! That would take her mind off her humiliation, if only for a little while.

Ariella was at the counter, ordering her usual, a mocha latte, and Giji came up behind her.

"Hey."

Ariella turned, surprised to see her neighbor. "Oh, hi, Giji, want to share a table?"

Giji looked at her book and sighed, "Sure."

"Hey, I don't mean to cramp your style, if you'd rather be alone…"

"No, it's just that, well, yeah–I do kind of need to talk."

"Okay, get your coffee and meet me at the table," Ariella paid and picked up her cup.

Giji took her latte and went to sit with Ariella. They both sipped in silence for a moment, and then Ariella spoke. "I like to come here," she said. "It's a cool place to chill for a while – and the coffee's not bad, either!"

"I'm not a huge coffee drinker," Giji admitted. "I usually hang out here to guy watch. There are so many hot guys who hang out here."

"I know," Ariella agreed, tossing her dark hair as she took a quick look around at the guys in the crowded coffeehouse. "Lots of cute guys in and out of here all the time. And they do make a mean latte!"

"I usually get the Double Mocha Latte, too," Giji told her, seeming surprised that they had things in common they'd never noticed or appreciated when they were in a group setting with the other wives. "Today I just felt like having a plain vanilla latte."

"So what's wrong?" Ariella asked, sipping her coffee.

Giji relayed the entire story, from the day in the hot tub when she sold the Harpers the house a few blocks over to that afternoon, when she had left them and walked back to Martha's in the catholic school girl outfit, only to be leered at by Mrs. Hoover when she got there.

"This has given you insight to your obviously poor choice of lovers?" Ariella wanted to know.

"They wanted me to dress up like their little girl and call them Mommy and Daddy!"

Ariella rolled her eyes, "A fantasy obviously, I mean you, a little girl?"

Giji ignored her sarcasm. "It just didn't feel right. I got a totally strange vibe that just weirded me out, I mean first they wanted me to pretend to be their daughter and they where going to teach me about sex, and then he wanted to spank me…"

"More than sick, that's clueless," Ariella said. "They were going to teach you about sex? Ha!"

Giji smiled, "I know, that is insulting. I'll bet I could teach them a thing or two about sex! Imagine they wanted to… how disgusting!"

"You get that a lot, don't you?" Ariella observed, "Being molested, I mean. Mrs. Hoover, god knows who was before her and now a couple you decided to sleep with! Oh, where does the insanity end?"

"It ended today with the Harpers." Giji drank the last of her coffee. "From now on I'll be much more careful where I lay my head. If the Harpers want to molest someone, I suggest they molest each other!"

"You'd better be careful where you lay your head or your face will end up in Mrs. Hoover's lap!" Ariella teased. "Speaking of Mrs. Hoover, are you still eating those god awful casseroles she makes?"

"Almost every night," Giji answered. "Last night it was bratwurst and sweet potato! It's like living in *casserole hell*. I think her secret ingredient is laxative!"

"Eeww, that's disgusting!" Ariella stood up and they carried their empty cups to the café's sideboard. "I'm waiting for the one where her secret ingredient is marijuana!"

"That would be worth waiting for," Giji agreed, "but that'll never happen. Mrs. Hoover is too cheap for that."

"Too bad." Ariella frowned. "It's something to hope for, though. That's the only casserole that Mrs. Hoover could ever make that I might be willing to try!"

Giji nodded. "Well, if you ever see me running down the street toward your house with a casserole dish, hurry and open the door," Giji quipped, laughing, "That'll be the one!"

Ariella laughed, remembering something she'd wanted to ask Giji for quite a while. "Her perfume is also yuck. That fragrance she wears is overpowering. What's the name of it?"

"She says it's some sort of old fashioned Eau de Toilette called *My Sin* that she wore as a school girl in Sheboygan. It smells like a mixture of witch hazel and *Ben Gay*!"

"Or, witch hazel and a hint of alcohol?"

"That's her breath, she's always sipping something, it seems."

"I saw her the other day coming out of the ABC Package store in the strip mall," Ariella recalled. "I figured she was getting something to sip on to get her nip on!"

"Probably picked up something for her tea, she's almost always sipping her infamous iced tea spiked with bourbon. Hey, we can pick up with that topic next time!" Giji pushed through the door and out into the light rain.

"Agreed!" said Ariella as she made her way to her car. "Feeling better?"

"A little," Giji called as she made a dash for her pink caddy.

6

Beauty & the Beast

SueAnn heard the noise and laughter as she walked up the drive to the community pool and cabana area. She bought a new white dress for the occasion. It was made of a soft linen material and was short, very risky for her. She thought it looked great when she had tried it on in the store.

As she turned the corner, she saw Nick standing by the barbeque pit and she walked over to talk with him. It looked like he had his hands full with Giji hanging all over him. She showed up in a tight red outfit, looking like a hooker on steroids! SueAnn smirked behind her hand and set down the six pack of beer she brought. When he saw her he gently disentangled himself from Giji and walked over.

Before SueAnn could even say "Hi," Wynette's brats began pulling her, trying to get her to play with them, or so she thought at first. It became clear the older child was more interested in looking up her new, short dress than he was in playing tag.

"Now, boys, I just got here, give me a minute and we'll play volleyball or something," SueAnn tried to sound kind. What she really wanted to do was smack them both…hard.

"Guys, you heard SueAnn, let her get settled in," Wynette called from across the courtyard.

Nick came over. "Hi, SueAnn, I'm glad to see you." He smiled and handed her a beer.

"I'm glad you could make it, too. It's hard being the new kid on the block, isn't it?"

"Not when I have such accommodating neighbors," he smiled down at her. He'd been in the pool and his hair was slicked back. He put his shirt back on but his shorts were still wet, SueAnn could see the nice package he had. Just as she started to say something witty to Nick, Wynette's monsters came over and started pulling on her again.

"Come on, you said you'd play with us!" they cackled as they pushed her along. She smiled at Nick who shrugged and as she turned, she felt the little demon's hands on the small of her back. The last thing she remembered before hitting the water was that she was sure the older one pinched her ass.

SueAnn made a huge splach as she went under the water, sinking almost to the bottom of the pool. She came up, thrashed about, then went under again. Finally she resurfaced, still thrashing around.

"Again SuSu has to have all the attention on her!" Giji complained. "She;s such an attention whore!"

"Attention my ass," Mrs. Hoover said, "I think the little bitch is drowning!"

"Yeah," Ariella agreed. "I wasn't counting, I believe she's going down for the third time!"

SueAnn thrashed around as she made her way to the edge of the pool

Standing by the edge of the pool, Nick reached a hand down and helped her up. SueAnn thought that she could get to the edge and then jump the rest of the way but Nick ended up dragging her out. The result was that the thin linen caused the dress to ride up her thighs as she came out of the pool. Her bare ass hugged the string of her thong, hung out for a second for the entire party to see.

She was mortified and pulled the dress down over her wet thighs as fast as she could. Then she saw Nick's eyes get wide as he tore off his shirt and covered her with it. As he wrapped the shirt around her shoulders, she realized her ass wasn't the only thing that everyone could see. The light dress had gotten wet and it became completely see through! It was basically invisible, she grabbed Nick's shirt as laughter floated across the cabana.

"Nice tits!" called someone. Later, SueAnn would bet it had been Giji. She thought she would die of embarrassment as the laughter continued and some people pointed. (She imagined they were pointing since she was afraid to look.) Wynette had the decency to call her monsters over immediately and SueAnn thought she heard Wynette scolding them. But, she wasn't sure since everything was hazy, as if it was coming from very far away.

Nick saw the perfectly round, firm shape of SueAnn's breasts, her nipples erect pressed against the thin (and now sheer) fabric of her dress. As his eyes went down her body, Nick could see that her stomach was flat and sculpted like he might imagine a goddesses was... chiseled from stone. Her thong was white and he could see the wet mound of her pussy and even her labia as he pulled her out. It was soft and pink and he looked away quickly because he could feel himself getting hard just looking at her and the cows had gotten enough of a peep show for one day.

He drew in his breath sharply as he covered her up, realizing that if he could see how wet and hot she was, so could everyone else, including those brats who pushed her in the pool. In the back of his mind he figured the older one pushed her to see how see how clear her dress would become. He silently thanked him for pushing her in the water.

SueAnn tried to speak but no words would come. She made a gesture to thank him but the shirt started to slip when she moved her arm. Nick caught the shirt and placed it back up over her shoulders.

"It will be okay," he whispered. SueAnn looked at him helplessly and clutched the shirt around herself. It was only then that she saw how sexy he was, standing there tan and strong in the sun.

"Ohh!" said Giji, eyeing him from the other side of the pool.

Ariella sat next to her, well into her third beer. "Yeah, too bad you didn't take a spill."

"Yeah," Giji agreed and laughed, "but he can keep his shirt, I'd rather he wrap his body around mine!"

"Giji, I hope your attitude isn't the reason Nick's standing over there with SueAnn and not over here with you."

Giji rolled her eyes, "Yuck! SueAnn's a mess," she said flatly, "She takes more spills than a circus tent full of drunken monkeys! How can any man find that attractive?"

Ariella shrugged.

SueAnn was coming past them, on her way to the cooler.

"Always have to steal the show," said Giji when she was close enough to hear. SueAnn stopped before she opened the cooler and looked blankly at Giji, "You don't really believe..." She turned and ran, still clutching Nick's shirt around her.

Giji shook her head and looked up just in time to see Nick run after SueAnn.

***

Nick caught up with SueAnn at the edge of the driveway. "Hey, you don't have anything to be embarrassed about, you know."

"I'm naked!"

"You were the hottest woman at the party. All the guys were looking at you...before you fell in the pool."

"I feel so bad, Giji said something..."

"Well, I wouldn't take anything she says seriously."

"Hey, I've known Giji for a long time; she sees things other people don't. Maybe I did buy this dress for some ulterior motive.

Maybe I was trying to…"

"You're beautiful," Nick said. "Can I walk you home?"

"Yes, I guess so."

"You did look incredibly sexy, you know."

"Little good it does right now, I just exposed myself to the entire neighborhood!"

He smiled at her warmly. "I know what I saw, and I felt a little jealous that the other guys could see the same thing."

As they walked along SueAnn's dress began to dry in the sun. Eventually she took off Nick's shirt and handed it back to him. Much to her secret delight, he threw it over his shoulder instead of putting it back on.

"My daughter Julie is with my ex and his new wife for the summer," she blurted out, immediately feeling sheepish. "I guess I'm feeling a little sorry for myself, a little lonely…"

Nick winked when he said, "Well, then I can come in and get something to drink."

They walked up the steps to SueAnn's rambler and paused at the front door.

"Do you feel okay about this?" He leaned toward her.

"I do right now," SueAnn replied as she inserted the key.

They were barely inside with the door shut behind them when he pulled her close. SueAnn was hot, she felt her pussy starting the get wet and kissed him harder, letting her tongue roam around his mouth. His breathing changed, it was short and heavy and she felt weak when he lifted the dress over her head and let it fall to the floor. She was as beautiful naked as she was with the wet dress clinging to the sensuous curves of her body.

Nick pulled her down on top of him on the couch, and clawed at his jeans, lifting her hips as he got his jeans to his knees. He was so hard and big! SueAnn couldn't wait. Nick tried to kiss her breasts but she pulled away and wiggled to allow him to slide inside her with little effort. She moaned and slid her hips forward so the base of his cock pressed against her clit. They rocked, moaning and Nick got one of her firm, pink nipples into his mouth.

"Stop, Stop, I don't want you to cum yet," she whispered in his ear.

She got off of him and knelt before him, taking it into her mouth in one movement. Nick moaned again and tried not to shove his entire member down her throat, she sucked him, flicking her tongue over the head of his cock and ran it down the shaft. She reached between her legs and began to finger herself. Nick's eyes had been closed, but when he felt her move, he looked down to see the marble goddess rubbing her clit with her thumb.

"Let me do that," he breathed and moved with her to the floor into the sixty-nine position. SueAnn was on the bottom, sucking him and thrusting her hips as he ate her out. His mouth was heaven, and SueAnn came twice before he flipped her over and rammed his cock as far as he could into her drenched pussy. It only took a minute after that–he was ready to explode anyway–and they collapsed together on the carpet, Nick on his back with SueAnn curled up on his chest.

When SueAnn awoke she realized it had gotten dark out, and she nudged Nick gently. "Hey, you gotta be somewhere?"

"Hmm? No, sugar, I don't," he said sleepily.

"Wow, you sure took it out of me," SueAnn nuzzled him again, "You want to stay?"

"Yes, I do," Nick grinned.

"Well, do you want to take a shower? Maybe I could make you something to eat?"

"Let's order Chinese," Nick said, picking up her phone. SueAnn loved it immediately that he felt at home.

"What do you like?" he asked, dialing.

"Whatever you want will be fine," SueAnn started to say, and then she remembered that this co-dependant attitude was part of what she had been working on after the divorce.

"I like Mooshoo Pork," she squared her shoulders unconsciously.

Nick laughed. An easy laugh, not directed at her, and kept dialing. He placed the order and raised his eyes and asked her for the address. She told him and when he repeated it into the phone it sounded so comfortable, like he'd lived there his whole life. SueAnn sighed and smiled to herself.

When Nick was finished ordering the Chinese food, she suggested that they take a shower while they waited. Nick thought that it was a great idea and they went upstairs and were soon going at it again in the small shower in the bathroom across the hall from SueAnn's master bedroom.

SueAnn felt very safe with this guy, he was strong and kind, lathering her up and kissing her. It wasn't so much about the sex, but it seemed to be about the steam, the closeness, and his powerful arms. SueAnn felt sure that Nick was "the guy". At one point she simply laid her head on his chest and he held her while the water washed over them both, and she was happy for the first time in a long time.

While eating Chinese food naked on her bed, Nick gestured with his chopsticks,

"So, tell me about yourself," he said.

"Not much to tell. I went to school a few towns away from here, I married my high school sweetheart because…well, because he was my first love. We had our daughter Julie and then he left me for a young thing from his job. Same old story for divorced women my age, I guess."

"Biggest mistake he ever made," Nick gestured with his chopsticks again.

"Now tell me something about you," said SueAnn.

"I think you are the most beautiful woman I've ever seen," Nick said immediately.

"Thank you, but that doesn't answer my question." she leaned forward and took another egg roll. She put the tip in her mouth, nibbled on the end, then sucked out the filling.

"I like the way you eat egg rolls," said Nick.

"That's not an answer, either."

"Not much to tell on my end, either. I was born in Jersey, came out here to make my fortune when I was about twenty and stayed."

"Ever married?"

"No." Nick didn't offer any further comment.

"Why not?"

"I don't know," Nick said with a shrug. "Guess I just never found the right woman." He started to gather up the empty cartons. "Now that you've eaten, my goddess, do you have your strength back?"

SueAnn didn't like that he changed the subject, but how important was it really? She didn't need to know everything about this guy…yet. She smiled up at him, let him put her to bed, and she happily laid there and watched him turn off the lights before he joined her.

***

Those kids are going to be the death of me yet Wynette thought as she scrubbed crayon marks from the appliances and walls; it's a daily chore with these budding Picassos. Between scrubbing, Wynette occasionally stopped to catch her breath and glance out the kitchen window to the backyard to make sure the boys weren't killing each other; she had ominous visions of them burying each other alive. Right now her little darlings were playing hide and seek, but she knew they'd find a way to destroy the lawn furniture and seriously injure each other.

Moving to the living room, Wynette picked up pillows and put them back on the couch. She glanced out the window and saw a repair man climbing the telephone pole across the street. Mmm, that's a *sweet package,* she thought, *I wonder if he needs a glass of water?*

Scolding herself, she knew Steven would be home more often now and maybe she wouldn't be so horny anymore. But why did she constantly think about other guys? She could hear Mary Lynn in her head, reminding her that she was addicted. Releasing a deep sigh, she went back to scrubbing her kitchen.

Suddenly the doorbell rang. Wynette took off her rubber gloves and dropped them in the kitchen sink on the way to the front door. Through the peephole saw a person who appeared to be a salesman at the door. Wow, He is damned cute! Or maybe I'm just way too horny, or Mary Lynn was right and I'm addicted. But, she felt the place between her legs become wet almost immediately. Wynette smiled to herself as she opened the door.

He was short, stout, and had a smile like an overweight leprechaun. *Ooh, a young Fabio!* Wynette thought, excited.

"Yes?"

"Good afternoon, ma'am, I have a great deal for you…"

"Yes, yes, I see, a vacuum cleaner salesman. Well, you'll do in a pinch," she said.

"I don't…"

"Get in here, buddy, today's your lucky day, but hurry, we have to be quick. My kids are in the backyard."

Wynette pulled the salesman into the living room.

"Go ahead and start it up, it will cover the sound," she said.

"Well, this little beauty here…" The salesman began his boring sales pitch.

"Are you stupid?" She shook her head and gestured to his crotch. "Take off your pants."

The salesman looked so surprised Wynette had to laugh, then she whipped his pants down to his ankles and hiked up her skirt. They had to hurry, the boys could be in any minute.

"Turn it on," she nodded to the vacuum, "Then you can turn me on."

"Uh… I'm Stan."

"Nice to meet you, Stan, now get to work."

He switched on the vacuum and leaned it against the couch. Wynette lay on the carpet and pulled him down on top of her. It didn't take any time at all for him to get hard and soon the vacuum cleaner was sucking while Stan was thrusting. Wynette stared at the ceiling while he pumped into her quivering and rocking pussy. She noticed a crack in the ceiling and hoped now that since Steven would be home more often that he could fix a few things around the house. It also occurred to her that she should stop fucking strange guys that showed up at her door. Various salesman that happened by, the meter readers (electricity and city utilities) and others. She felt a twinge of guilt, coupled by the thought of her three young sons entering the house and getting an eye full. Then they would spill the beans to their father no matter how much she tried to bribe them. But, the feelings of guilt were overpowered by the vibration of the vacuum on the carpet… or maybe it was Stan, who had cum in one loud moan, a shudder ad then he collapsed on her.

"So what did you think?" said Stan, gesturing toward the vacuum cleaner, which was still running next to him.

"Hmmm," Wynette pretended to think, watching the repair man on the telephone pole outside the window. He was tall, ruggedly built with a tight T-shirt and jeans that hugged all the right places, "you were pretty good, if a little quick. The vacuum cleaner, I'm not impressed."

And with that she shoved Stan and the vacuum onto the porch just as the boys came barreling into the house, soaking wet. Apparently, Mrs. Hoover turned the hose on them again.

***

Giji watched the guy on the Harley through her rearview mirror. A seemingly endless string of bad experiences with her car had suddenly turned into quite an adventure. When her car broke down on the side of the highway she was pissed, but it looked as though she would be saved, and by a good looking biker no less!

"I'm a mechanic," was all he said when she rolled down her window. He was tall and lean, with tight blue jeans and black jack boots. Giji decided what the hell, she might as well go for it.

"Maybe you could rotate my tires sometime?" she teased,

reading the name Bruno on the name patch sewn on his work shirt.

"I could certainly take you for a spin," he played along.

Giji looked him up and down and then directly in the eye. "When?"

"Oh, any minute now," he put his hands on his hips so she could see the rise in the crotch of his tight jeans. Ohhh yeah, thought Giji, this should be fun.

She got out of the car and they both looked around. Deserted road. Nowhere to fuck. Rocks on the ground. "Have and idea," he finally said. "Let's do it in the trunk."

"I'm game," said Giji, pushing her body against him.

The trunk was roomy and they climbed in. Giji removed her thin shirt and her lacey push up bra. The biker, whose name was… Bruno, started to lick her nipples, and she pulled him down on top of her. Giji was hot, the guy was hot and she knew she was in for the time of her life when Bruno started tickling her. In her excitement, she got her heel caught in the seam of the underside of the trunk lid. With one well placed tickle, she jerked her foot. The lid slammed down on top of them both.

"See what you did!" she said loudly. Her voice sounded even louder in the tight confines of the trunk.

"Me?" he questioned. "Hey, hot stuff, I ain't the one wearing spike heels!"

It began to get hot in the tight space. Although Giji's trunk was big enough for them to screw, it wasn't comfortable, and she wriggled out of her remaining clothes. *Good thing I wore a skirt today,* she thought.

"Hey, what are you doing?" Bruno asked.

"Well, we're not going anywhere just yet. This is even better since no one can see us in here, so I figured…"

"You're quite a woman," he pulled down his jeans.

They squirmed until they were both naked. There wasn't very much room for foreplay, so Bruno laid on the floor of the cramped trunk as best as he could with Giji positioned on top of him. She worked her way over his hips and moved her hand between them, helping to put him inside of her. As his cock slid into her wet pussy, they both shuddered and she tried to move.

"No, just stay still," whispered Bruno.

"How can you expect me to do that?" Giji whispered back.

"It's an old Kama Sutra position," he answered, "just stay still. You'll get off, I promise."

"How does somebody like you know about Kama Sutra?"

"Look, hot stuff. We're not all uneducated grease monkeys, you know. I went to college, where I read a lot of books."

Giji couldn't believe how horny she got by not being able to move, and she tried not to contract her pussy muscles. It was nearly impossible, but she felt so good that she made a mental note to try this position–a lot, when she had another chance outside of the trunk of her car!

When it was over and they had both cum (twice for Giji) she fumbled around for her purse, which she kept in the trunk, just in case she forgot it when she went in somewhere, and she finally found her cell phone.

"Who should I call... the cops?"

Bruno struggled to pull his jeans up, "Naw, I have... um... unpaid tickets."

Giji decided to call the only other person she could think of who got into similarly embarrassing situations–SueAnn. She flipped open the phone and went to "contacts." They squirmed into a new position while they got dressed and Bruno was between Giji's legs. She hadn't bothered to pull her skirt up and as SueAnn's phone rang she felt Bruno's hand tickle her clit.

"Get your greasy hands off..." Giji's voice trailed off as she felt Bruno's big mouth slide up into her wet, hot pussy. "Oh," she moaned, "Yeah, baby, that's the spot! Don't stop, big boy! Drive me so crazzy!"

Those were the words that SueAnn heard when she answered her phone. "Who the hell is this?"

"Oh, no, not you... SueAnn. It's me, Giji. I'm in kind of a

pickle here and I need your help."

"Where are you?"

"Locked in my trunk on the side of the highway," Giji moaned as Bruno hit the spot.

"How the hell did that happen? Who's in there with you?"

"It's complicated," Giji said. "Can you come let us out?"

"How the hell am I supposed to get into your trunk?" SueAnn was incredulous that Giji locked herself locked in the trunk because she tried to fuck some stranger in the middle of the road. But, she had to admit that it was kind of funny.

"I have a spare key hidden in the ashtray," Giji told her.

"You know cars are made with emergency release handles in the trunk, in case kids get in there or you get kidnapped," said SueAnn.

"I'll take that into consideration next time I buy a car, now could you please hurry?"

SueAnn sighed. "Where are you?"

After Giji gave SueAnn directions, stressing the location of the unpaved road, she hung up and shoved her hips as far into Bruno's face as she could in the cramped quarters.

"Ooh," she moaned, "That feels sooo good! Lick that spot again, baby! Yeah, baby, hit me one more time! Ummmm, that's the spot Britney Spears sung about!"

"Is someone on their way?" Bruno looked up.

"Yeah, baby, but don't stop now!"

Bruno shrugged and lowered his face to Giji's pussy. He flicked his tongue and licked her full face, which made her moan loudly. Bruno smiled as he thought about the look on any state patrol's face as they walked up to the seemingly abandoned car to ticket it. He decided to make her call out his name and placed his mouth over her entire pussy area, tongue flat against her clit, and didn't move.

"Hey, oh god, hey, are you dead down there?" Giji moaned. Bruno began to hum. Giji went wild, moaning and gyrating as hard as she could. She was just about to climax again when the trunk flew open.

"Well, look what we have here, beauty and the beast!"

"Hey!" the biker said, sounding offended.

"Don't worry, Bruno," Giji told him. "I'm sure when she mentioned the beast, she was referring to me!"

"Yep," SueAnn agreed and smiled knowingly. "Looks like I'm not the only one who's prone to freaky accidents–or did you plan this ahead of time? I wouldn't put it past you!"

"Okay, I deserve that," Giji said, trying to climb out of the trunk. She held out her hand. "Would you help me, please?"

SueAnn took Giji's hand and helped her from the trunk. The biker leapt out behind her.

Giji looked at Bruno. "Well, Bruno, it's been… well… what can I say? It's over, big guy. Have a good life!"

"Sure thing, hot stuff," Bruno started toward his bike, buttoning his fly and tucking in his shirt. Giji watched him saunter away and she turned to SueAnn.

"I'd appreciate it if you didn't mention this to anyone. I have a reputation to protect."

"Giji, I don't think you have to worry," SueAnn assured her. "Your reputation is still intact. You'll always be a hopeless slut!"

"What can I say?" Giji grinned, "Isn't it wonderful!"

7

Rent-A-Hubby

SueAnn put down *Home Beautiful* magazine when she heard knocking at the door, three knocks and then the doorbell. *Someone wants to sell me something,* she thought as she turned the knob. Wynette stood on the porch with a sheepish look on her face.

"I just wanted to apologize for the boys' behavior the other day at the pool, and I wanted to say how sorry I am that I didn't defend you with Giji. She can be so catty and sometimes I get pulled into it. Please forgive me." Wynette said this all in one breath and SueAnn realized that she had probably been rehearsing it.

"Come in," she held the door open. Wynette came in and perched on the edge of the couch, still looking self-conscious.

"Forget about it," said SueAnn, "It was humiliating but there was a positive side, too. When Nick walked me home, he stayed."

"All night?" gasped Wynette.

"Yes."

"So?" Wynette leaned forward, "Details woman! I want

details!"

"Well," she began as Wynette relaxed into the couch. No longer self conscious, she wanted to hear all the details of SueAnn's night of passion, "It was magical. He was so gentle and caring. He seemed to really like me and he asked me all sorts of questions about myself and listened to the answers. It wasn't like he was just being polite because we were sleeping together," she paused. "You ever wonder if the guy you ended up with wasn't the right one, after all. That maybe by some stroke of luck the perfect guy will come along and you might…"

"Have another chance at happiness?" Wynette broke in.

"I would like to know more about him," she said. "He seems… so mysterious. I couldn't really get him to tell me anything about himself."

"They all do at first," said Wynette. "Sometimes it's best not to know. That air of mystery can be alluring. What else happened?"

"We took a shower and ordered Chinese food, and then we spent the night together."

"Well, that sounds like a fine start," Wynette stood to leave. "I have to get back now, there are a million things I have to attend to. Steven will be traveling less so he plans to fix a bunch of stuff around the house, but he never gets to it all on his days off. You know, pushing helpless women into a pool isn't all the boys do. They've done so much damage to the house! Maybe, I should just hire someone to do all the work."

"You could always rent a hubby," SueAnn suggested.

"What's that?"

"Rent-a-Hubby. You call and give a list of all the repairs that need to be done and they match you up with a guy that knows how to do it. You pay; they come over and fix stuff."

Wynette felt herself quiver just a little thinking about a big, rugged repair man working while she watched. "Is that all they can fix?" she said.

"Oh, you," SueAnn laughed, then copied down a number and

handed it to her. "Just call, I'm sure you'll find what you're looking for."

I'm sure I will, thought Wynette as she left.

***

Wynette called Rent-A-Hubby as soon as she got home from SueAnn's. She listed the items that needed to be repaired and made an appointment with the woman on the other end of the phone. They could get someone out right away and she was feeling pretty good about SueAnn's advice when she answered the door.

The repair man was big, strong looking and very cute. He said that he name was Greg and shook her hand. Wynette showed him the damaged paint on the doors, the cracked tiles, and some other places that needed repair. He nodded and made notes on his pad, he was professional all the way. When they reached the small bathroom on the second level, she leaned into him, brushing her breast against him and causing him to drop his clipboard.

"Oh, sorry, let me get that... Greg," she said as she bent over. Her jeans were especially tight and she felt herself getting ready to be bad again. She accidentally, on purpose slipped and Greg caught her just before she landed. "Oh, thank you."

"Ma'am, it seems as though your blouse has come undone," he said, trying to look away.

"Well, I guess it has! Could you help me with it, please?" Wynette reached her arms up with a little smirk. Greg the repair man looked at her for a full half a minute before dutifully helping her.

"I like it on the cool, tile floor," she whispered in his ear.

"Whatever you want, ma'am," said Greg.

He helped her to the floor, where she lay on her back looking up at him. She wriggled out of her tight jeans and pulled down her red panties. Greg whipped off his Dickies and was on top of her in a heartbeat, pumping and grunting. No foreplay, no kissing on the mouth.

Wynette was hot and wet. She played out a fake rape scene in her head while Greg pumped her and became so excited at the picture in her mind that she came twice before he was done.

Ohhh, I'm cleaning the bathroom when I hear a noise outside the door. There's no one home, who could it be? I open the door to the bathroom to find a guy going through my jewelry box in the bedroom. He hears me and turns around, He's cute, but I'm still scared.

"There's no need to be scared, ma'am," he says.

But, he comes over and pushes me down onto the cold tile anyway. He's rough, and covers my mouth so I won't scream. He rips off my blouse, tears at my pants, and is inside me before I can think of what to do. He's huge. Not long, but thick and— OHHHH!

Wynette came again. Greg started to get off of her and she wrestled him onto his back, where she began to give him head furiously, trying to get him hard again.

He forces me to give him head, pushing my face into his cock. When he's hard again, he rolls me over and onto my knees. He enters me from behind, all the while grabbing at my breasts and pinching my nipples. He's so thick! I grab hold of the side of the bathtub, pushing back against him as he thrusts into me..."

"Lady, I'm done. If you want, I can eat you out."

"What? Oh, no, that's okay; you can put your pants back on now."

Greg the repair man stood up and zipped his Dickies, then went into the bedroom, looking around like he didn't know what had hit him. Wynette felt satisfied, but dammmit! She'd done it again! This guy won't do, I'll be jumping him every time he comes over! I'll have to call back and request someone that I won't be attracted to.

Buttoning up her blouse as she entered the bedroom, she told Greg that it just wasn't going to work out.

"Was it something I did?" asked Greg.

"No, buddy, I just can't be jumping you every time you come over. You'll never get any work done. At least you can feel good that I can't employ you because you're so cute! Rest assured that your performance was one of the best, and I will convey that when I call for another repair man."

"Okay," said Greg, looking confused. "Maybe we could see each other socially and see where this goes?"

"I'm married," said Wynette flatly, ushering him toward the door.

"Hmm, does your husband allow…"

"No, does Rent-A-Hubby allow you to sleep with your customers?"

"Oh, no, I guess we'd better keep this just between the two of us."

"I think that would be a really good idea," she said and shut the door behind him. She went straight to the phone, feeling the stickiness between her legs and wanting to take a shower.

"Hello, Angela, the guy you sent was good, but I just didn't feel a connection between us where work was concerned. Oh, no, it was nothing he did. Could you send someone…say…a bit shorter…?"

***

The sun baked through the window at Haldeman Insurance while Steven did paperwork. He was bored and wished that he could finish up quickly then maybe he could cut out early. Nothing interesting ever happens around here, he thought. Getting up, he went to stand in his office door and stretch his legs.

Gloomily he looked out over the sea of Haldeman employees. Worker bees, he thought, drones printing, stapling, faxing and filing paperwork of one kind or another all day, ever day…

Suddenly the entrance door swung open and the most gorgeous young woman he'd ever seen in his life entered the outer office.

At first he didn't recognize her. She had grown up so much in the two years since he'd last seen her, it was Joe Haldeman's daughter, Kendra. While he was traveling as marketing rep for the company, little Kendra had blossomed into a beautiful young woman. *Damn! She could be a model,* Steven thought, as he enjoyed looking at the lovely young creature. Kendra had grown into a slender, tall, young woman with developing breasts. She had lovely blue-green eyes and long, flowing brown hair with gorgeous highlights. Steven could imagine her doing lingerie ads in a low-cut, lacey, white bra and panties and thigh-length white hose in spiked heels while a light, refreshing mist sprayed down on her making her beautifully smooth, lightly tanned skin moist… In a more risqué scenario, her young taut nipples stood erect through the strategically placed openings in her skimpy, lacey bra and her clean shaven pussy was surrounded by her crotchless panties. He started to drool and lowered his eyes to his own crotch with a worried glance as he tried to push the erotic thoughts from his mind.

"Mr. Harris, are you okay?" Kendra asked.

"Yeah, yeah," he said, snapping back to reality. "I just had a wonderful idea I'd like to run pass your father." He considered what would happen to him if her father ever learned of his recent thoughts. The outcome was obvious even in his befuddled condition.

Steven pulled out the chair to his desk and motioned for Kendra to have a seat, excused himself and tapped on his boss's door.

"Mr. Haldeman, your daughter is here to see you," Steven said, sticking his head in upon hearing his boss call to come in.

"Well hell, boy, send her in! I never get to see enough of her."

Apparently neither do I, thought Steven. "I'll get her in a minute, sir. I wanted to run something past you first, though."

"Yes?"

"Well, it is a family business, and I was thinking it would be a good idea to turn her on, I mean to get her involved with the business. Surely she can type and file? Why don't you hire her to work part time around here? I always need help filing and she couldn't possibly screw up the record keeping anymore than that ditz, Katrina."

"Well now, that's a fine idea, a fine idea indeed. She's old enough to start learning the family business, good idea Harris. Send her in and I'll talk to her about it."

Steven was pleased. He went back out to the main room and asked Kendra to follow him into her dad's office. She stood beside her dad while he explained that it was time for her to begin learning the family business and that the idea had been Steven's. Kendra looked less than thrilled until he mentioned Steven and then she smiled at Steven.

"Will I have to work long hours?" she asked her father.

"Oh, no, pumpkin, we work nine to five around here."

"But, maybe there will be some late night work toward the end of the summer," she said, continuing to smile at Steven. "Besides, I know you take business trips."

"Well, Kendra, I'm not traveling as much these days." Steven began to get a weird feeling. She kept looking over at him and smiling. Then she licked her lips right in front of him! He decided immediately that he wouldn't mention news about the company's new hire to Wynette and certainly not that she was making eyes at him.

"I would never send you on a boring business trip, pumpkin, that's Steven's job," Mr. Haldeman told his daughter.

"Okay, Daddy." Her lower lip jutted out in a pout that Steven found undeniably sexy.

"Then, it's settled," Mr. Haldeman turned back to his paperwork. Kendra followed Steven out of the office.

"Mr. Harris, can I do anything for you right now?" Kendra tilted her head and licked her lips again. She moved her eyes over his body.

"Um, no, but I'll see you first thing tomorrow, I guess," said Steven nervously.

Kendra smiled and picked up her coat.

"Well, I guess it won't be quite as boring here from now on," she whispered at him as she left.

No, I guess not, Steven thought as he watched her go.

***

The neighborhood decided to have an ice cream party at the cabana. The kids scampered about, eating ice cream cones, dripping them on each other and all over the place while the adults relaxed in the lounge chairs and checked each other out. Giji, Ariella, and SueAnn stood together, gossiping among themselves.

"Oh, SueAnn, I guess we can look forward to seeing more of you," Giji teased. "What'll it be? Are you going to drip ice cream all over yourself and suddenly discover that your clothing has dissolved?"

"Careful, Giji," SueAnn warned, with a knowing smile as she walked towards Nick. "I know what's been in your trunk!"

"What's been in your trunk?" Ariella asked Giji as SueAnn walked over to Nick.

"Oh, never mind," Giji said.

Suddenly the gate flew open with a bang.

"I'm here!" Mrs. Hoover announced. "Let the party begin!"

Everyone turned around to see the elderly, heavy-set Mrs. Hoover in a plaid Doris Day bikini. Shock turned to frowns and most people tried to look away and avoid looking directly at her again. The old bat looked absolutely hideous!

"How can she not know how she looks?" Giji whispered to Ariella.

"I guess at her age she just doesn't care!" Ariella replied.

"I wonder what SueAnn will do to show off her assets today," Giji wondered out loud. "She's a subconscious exhibitionist, you know."

"What's that mean?" Ariella wanted to know.

"Subconsciously she wants to get attention by showing off her body," Giji explained. "Ever notice how she has these little 'accidents' that leave her overexposed?"

"So," Ariella observed, "she's like you only slightly more introverted."

"Hey," Giji said loudly and grabbed her firm, round breasts through her thin top. "I don't need happy accidents to put these puppies on a leash!" She glanced around to see if anyone had noticed, but everyone seemed lost in their own little world.

Beside the pool, the men sat uncomfortably and tried to enjoy their ice cream. Steven suggested they make a game of the situation, since none of them especially wanted to be here, watching children and their wives, and least of all Mrs. Hoover. Surely, she had taken more than a few nips from her bottle before venturing out.

"Watch how they eat their cones," he said to Lex.

"Why the hell would I want to do that?"

"You can tell how a woman gives head by the way she eats ice cream," Steven said, "Didn't you go to college?"

"You did that in college?" Marco leaned over. "We did that in high school."

***

Connie chose vanilla ice cream and ate with prim and proper, with tiny licks, her tongue was barely visible. Carefully and meticulously she ate her ice cream cone, avoiding messy drips. Lex nudged Marco, "That's my girl, very proper."

Wynette licked her peach ice cream like a true Southern Belle, dainty but with enough aggression to show intent. She seemed to be eating slow, neat and tidy, but she was on her second cone before the other ladies had finished their first!

"Oh, yeah," Steven said under his breath to the other guys, "That's exactly what she's like, taking it all for herself instead of finding out if anyone else wants some." At this they all giggled like a sewing circle, and Mrs. Hoover looked up, scowling.

Ariella chose chocolate; the mocha Latina princess ate her ice cream cone with a fiery passion, licking the ice cream with long, slow licks around the edges, across the top. Marco wished she would display that kind of enthusiasm in their sex life like she did before they were married. Since the other guys didn't know that, he set back in his lounge chair and smirked knowingly at the other men. Eventually, his mouth got the better of him and he leaned over to his wife.

"Why don't you lick me like that?" Marco whispered. "You know how much I enjoy oral!"

Ariella sighed, ignored him and continued eating. The guys weren't the only ones who began to make observations. Giji chose cherry. She would, SueAnn thought, Giji ate her ice cream cone quickly with a sassy attitude as if she would really like to be licking something else!

"Oh, Nick," Giji called. "I could use some help here. Why don't you lick one side, I'll lick the other, and we'll meet in the middle and see where we go from there!"

"Sorry, Giji," Nick called. "I promised I'd help SueAnn. Besides, I can only have a little lick or two. I'm lactose intolerant." SueAnn couldn't suppress a desire that he would become Giji intolerant.

"Well, she could use some help," Giji said under her breath and pouted. "Your loss," she called out, "I lick as well as I do other things!" Giji headed toward the cute ice cream guy, who was handing out cones and looking like he wanted to be somewhere else. Mrs. Hoover had just stepped up to order a double.

"I'll bet you do," Nick said, watching SueAnn, who chose strawberry and ate hers clumsily, and sloppy, licking quickly and still not avoiding the drips. At one point she almost dropped the ice cream cone down the top of her blouse, which gave Nick an idea. He sided up to her, just in time to avoid an ass grabbing by Mrs. Hoover, who was working through her double with her teeth.

"We should save some ice cream for later," he told her and winked. "We can have our own little ice cream party, if you get my drip... I mean drift."

SueAnn smiled. "I do." She looked at him and licked her ice cream cone, "I would enjoy it as much as you!"

"Oh, I know I'd enjoy it," he assured her, grinning.

"I'll bet you would," SueAnn grinned, still licking her ice cream cone while the other men looked on.

"Then it's a date, you and me and a half pint of chocolate cherry, I'll see you later!" Nick teased and the look which passed between them wasn't lost on Giji, who pouted even harder.

Mrs. Hoover walked to an open lounge chair, and worked her girth into the chair so that she was comfortably sitting in it. She continued to gobble at her Neapolitan cone with such fervor that Marco squirmed, remembering their encounter. He was still squirming when she ceremoniously finished licking and suddenly bit the head off!

Ariella leaned close to her husband. "Are you okay? You look a little green..."

***

Giji stomped home, still pouting about Nick's rejection at the ice cream party. She didn't think it was fair that clumsy SueAnn had caught his eye. He was so cute! She would take a hot bath and relax, maybe get ready for bed, she thought as she entered her bedroom.

The house phone rang just as she finished undressing for bed. She had the blinds open, since the handsome plumber's house was next door and she wanted to make sure he saw what he was missing!

It never occurred to her that someone else might be getting an eyeful, too. Not even when that someone started calling, every other night....

She answered her cell phone to the sound of the usual heavy breathing, this guy had been calling several times a week for the last two weeks, usually just as she was getting read for bed or to soak in a warm bath, and Giji wondered if it was someone who could actually see her getting undressed. The thought was a bit scary - and also a bit of a turn on. Still, she had to admit it did seem weird that the calls came when she was about to undress for the night. That could just be a coincidence, she decided, unwilling to believe the caller could actually be watching her, able see her every move....

"Oh, if I knew where you are," Giji said playfully. "I would do something you'd never forget!"

The person on the phone breathed deeper. She did a little heavy breathing of her own, moaning.

"Hmmm," she added. "I bet you're wondering what I'd do, right? Well, speak up! If you really want to know, all this breathing is keeping you alive, but it won't get you laid!" The heavy breathing continued. She thought she heard a quiet chuckling in the background. She held the phone to her ear as she ran her bath, pouring in bubbles and taking off her blouse with one hand.

"Okay, I deserve more than just a lot of heavy breathing! If you've ever seen me, you know I'm not named Giji Brickhouse for nothing! Listen, you freak, work with me here! We can make this obscene call mutually gratifying. I can call a sex chat line if I want to hear this bull."

The line went dead.

Giji looked at the phone in her hand for a second, and then pressed End Call. Your loss, loser, she thought and sank into her warm bath. After her bath, Giji went down to see if Mrs. Hoover wanted to watch some television before turning in for the night.

From the kitchen door, Giji could see Mrs. Hoover outside the back stoop pacing and smoking. She hadn't realized Mrs. Hoover was a smoker–then opened the door just a bit, took several deep breaths and detected the distinct, arid aroma of marijuana!

***

Gladys paused for a moment outside her walkway and she strained to see through Mrs. Hoover's curtains. She had known Martha for years, and it wasn't like her to not be out watering her front flowers by that time. She thought that she saw movement through the curtains and stepped over to get a closer look. She tried to pull her glasses to her face, they hung on a silver chain around her neck most of the time, but today she wasn't wearing them.

Crossing the small pathway between the two yards, Gladys crept up to the window and patted her pocket, then she felt them. She started to put them on when a movement caught her eye.

Her dear friend Martha was being raped by that awful Marco who lived down the block! It looked like he was forcing the poor woman to perform fellatio on him! She tried to call out but her voice wouldn't work. She had to do something. She had to get help! Her heart pounded in her chest

Gladys ran for the first time since before her husband Jack died. She made her way through her friend's backyard, through the path she and Martha had worn between the hedges over the years and into her own yard. She paused briefly to try to catch her breath, but it was no use, her heart still raced, her breath was short, weakly she stumbled to her back stoop and entered her house.

Her heart pounding in her chest, Gladys dialed 911, but as she was about to speak, she dropped the phone and slumped to the floor.

"Until next month," Mrs. Hoover said as she shut the door behind Marco.

Marco was glad to get out of the crazy old bitch's house; he hurried back to his own home, hoping that no one saw him leaving Martha's.

Martha Hoover felt like gelatin. He had a big cock and she

giggled at the thought that her throat was dry. *I'll make some nice gelatin and catch the rest of my soap,* she thought to herself.

Rummaging through the kitchen only reminded her that she virtually lived alone. If she hadn't taken in Giji, she wouldn't have anyone to cook for. She decided to visit Gladys next door, and see if maybe she might have an extra packet of gelatin lying around.

She hummed to herself as she found her sweater. Marco was a great distraction from her lonely life, even if it was just once a month. She crossed the path and found Gladys's door ajar, which seemed very unusual indeed.

"Gladys! Gladys, I was wondering if you might have an extra packet of the Jell-O, you know the kind we stocked up on sale at the Sure Save?" Martha called out as she came in. What she saw made her stop in her tracks, but what she heard in the distance made her blood run cold. In Gladys's hand was the telephone, and the sound growing louder–was an ambulance. Gladys must've been trying to call for one as she had a heart attack! *Oh poor Gladys!* Martha knelt by her friend as the paramedics rushed in.

***

After the funeral service, Giji sat on the couch with Martha. The last of the mourners had gone home and Martha was left alone. Giji curled up on the couch next to her and patted her hand. Martha could not believe her best friend was gone. She remembered how they'd both moved into the neighborhood as young wives. They were just naive girls, away from their families for the first time. They gravitated toward each other, found comfort, solace, and kinship in each other. These newlywed wives believed that somehow their lives would be perfect because they believed they'd beat the odds and would live happily ever after.

However, that wasn't meant to be. The two young wives found they had other things in common, like the inability to conceive.

Each woman accepted they would never give birth, never be mothers even as they watched younger wives in the neighborhood carry their babies to term and give birth, others starting families while they could not. In the prime of their lives, they'd been widowed. First Martha's husband Earl had become ill and died suddenly, then Gladys's husband Jack had been killed in an automobile accident while he was away on business. They were totally alone except for each other.

"I can't imagine why Gladys would have gotten so upset that she had a heart attack," Mrs. Hoover said.

Giji patted Mrs. Hoover's hand softly. "It probably came on suddenly," Giji said quietly, "It was just her time to go."

Martha nodded, her eyes watering. "I guess you're right," she admitted, "but I'm going to miss Glad."

"I know you will," Giji said, surprised that she could feel such compassion for Mrs. Hoover, but she could see that the older woman was genuinely touched by the loss of her friend. "Glad was quite a feisty little woman."

Suddenly Martha smiled. "Yes, she was," she admitted, her eyes seeming to lighten up now, "Glad was always a fighter, had to be to survive."

"I'm sorry for your loss," Giji told her.

Suddenly Martha's expression changed, her eyes grew cold again. She could not stand the thought of anyone feeling sorry for her. "Well, in all honesty," she began, now sounding like her old self again, "I haven't lost much. Gladys wasn't the best friend a person ever had. The woman wasn't capable of telling the truth. You couldn't believe a word she said!" Then Martha Hoover completely broke down.

"Poor Gladys," Martha sobbed. "I didn't even know she had a weak heart, I guess she didn't want to burden me with that." She sniffed. "I always thought she'd die of a prescription drug overdose or food poisoning. God knows she wasn't much of a cook."

Giji handed Mrs. Hoover a tissue from the box on the coffee

table. "Really?" Giji asked, trying to recall if she'd ever eaten any food Gladys had made. Oh yes, she remembered now. "Gladys made some wonderful deviled eggs for Mary Lynn's wake."

"You ate some of her eggs?" Martha asked, surprised. Giji nodded. "Well, you're lucky to be alive," Martha told her. "A few years ago, I had a really bad chest cold and Gladys made me a pot of chicken soup. I almost died!" She rolled her eyes. "Yes, I'll miss Glad, but I won't miss her cooking!"

Her cooking couldn't be any more deadly than yours, Giji thought. "Glad was a wonderful friend to you," Giji said, trying to sound comforting.

Mrs. Hoover nodded. "She was," she said. "I guess the trees will miss her, too."

"Huh?" Giji wasn't sure she'd heard correctly.

"Well, when Glad started knitting, she made tea cozies and bunny covers for rolls of toilet paper," Mrs. Hoover explained. "Lately, she was measuring the trees around her property. She was planning to knit sweaters for them!"

"No!" Giji gasped.

"Yes, Glad said when the trees lost their leaves during the winter, she didn't want them to be cold!"

"Th - that's interesting!" Giji stammered, trying not to say what she was thinking.

"Who are you kidding!" Mrs. Hoover rolled her eyes. "That's just nuts. I tell you, Glad was one step away from the loony bin!"

Giji shrugged, surprised at what she was hearing. Standing, she asked, "Are you going to be okay?"

Silent now, Martha nodded.

"I'm going to go up and get changed," Giji told her and started up the stairs.

"Giji?"

Giji paused halfway up the stairs. "Yes?"

"Thank you."

Giji smiled. "That's what friends are for," she said and went on up the stairs.

Martha had found Gladys' glasses outside her back door stoop. Her friend never went anywhere without her glasses… She wondered if her friend could have… No, it was unlikely Gladys had seen anything, she decided. Glad had probably felt the tightness in her chest, panicked, and dropped her glasses as she hurried home to call 911. *Yes, Martha was sure that was probably what happened.*

8

The Boss's Daughter

Steven did his best to welcome Kendra to her first day on the job, although he alternated between thinking about her and trying not to make eye contact. He noticed that she was always licking her lips around him, especially when she stood behind her father while Mr. Haldeman was talking to Steven. She pranced around the office, just outside his door, twitching her tight ass in a little skirt as she flitted about. He thought she was filing, but on closer observance he saw that she was merely moving papers from one pile to the next and looking very busy as she did it.

She looked over and caught his eye, and began to make a swirling motion around one of her breasts with her finger. Steven smiled self consciously at her and shut his door. At his desk he reclined back in his chair and soon drifted off, dreaming of Kendra on his desk nude, lying on her back, her long, gorgeous legs up in the air. She's smiling, licking her lips, playing with her tits and fingering her pussy–all at once!

He was so excited he felt his cock begin to spasm again and again wildly. Feeling wetness around his hard cock and something touching his mouth, Steven awakened with a start to find Kendra in his office and standing over him. She licked his lips with her tongue and let the tip of her tongue dart into his mouth every now and then.

He sat up in his chair, trying to hide his hard cock in the folds of his slacks. "Wha... what are you doing?" he asked uneasily.

"Oh, I dunno," Kendra said lightly, "I came in to see if you needed me to file something for you. I decided it'd be fun to lick your lips and see if you'd wake up. And guess what? You did!"

"Ah, yes," Steven said, still confused, "I did."

"You know something?" Kendra began. "You were snoring! Does my father know you sleep on the job?"

Steven held his breath, eyes wide, mouth parted slightly, his face revealing the shock he could not hide.

Kendra grinned. "I won't tell if you don't!"

Steven took a deep breath, sighed with relief, and tried to smile. "Than... thanks," he stammered. "I appreciate that."

"Not a problem," Kendra assured him, then turning to leave she paused briefly. "By the way, nice hard-on." She winked as she turned.

Steven was speechless.

Kendra started toward the door, then paused and bent over to wipe a smudge from the toe of her shoe. "Sure I can't do anything for you?" she asked in a sultry voice.

Her short skirt slid up revealing pink and lavender flowered panties. Little girl panties, Steven found himself thinking.

"No, thanks," he said weakly.

After Kendra left Steven leaned back in his chair and breathed heavily...but not because he was turned on. His hard-on was long gone and he couldn't help thinking that something wasn't right about all this. He was very turned on when he was fantasizing about making the moves, but once Kendra made the first move, somehow it wasn't as appealing. *Maybe it wasn't such a good idea,* he thought as he started drifted off again, realizing what had just happened, and snapped fully awake.

***

Giji Brickhouse wasn't a spiteful woman and she had her share of both good and bad luck throughout her life, like most people. But, when Nick asked her to house sit for him overnight without telling SueAnn, her mischievous streak showed itself the next morning.

Nick called her late the previous night and asked her to house sit the rest of the afternoon and the next day while he went on an emergency service call out of town. He was supposed to get new satellite TV and didn't want to miss the installation.

"Why didn't you ask SueAnn?" Giji had asked.

"She has a book club meeting at the nursing home the next afternoon and I might not be home by then," Nick had said.

"I'd love to," Giji's eyes twinkled. SueAnn nearly fell over as she reached down and picked up her Saturday paper from her front lawn. There was Giji on Nick's lawn, getting Nick's paper... dressed in Nick's shirt! And from the looks of it, nothing else!

"Hi, SueAnn," Giji said with a gloating grin as she bent down to pick up the paper. "I hope you slept well last night. As for me...I didn't get any sleep at all!"

Giji headed back inside Nick's house with the paper just as Nick pulled up in his SUV.

SueAnn went right over and slapped him across the face. "You... you pig!" she screamed.

What she didn't see was that the window blinds on at least three houses moved behind her.

"I can explain," Nick said, putting a hand to his stinging cheek.

"Ah, Evander, I think you loosened a tooth!"

"I hope so!"

"It's not what you think," Nick told her, still holding his cheek.

"Oh, please, I know what I saw!"

"You didn't see what you think!"

"What?"

"I mean it's not what you think," he said, sighing deeply. "I was out of town overnight. Giji needed a break from Mrs. Hoover and I have the satellite guy coming today, so I asked her to her stay at my place last night."

"Oh." Susan suddenly felt the fight drain from her. "I see."

"If you would just listen," Nick said, "and not jump to conclusions..."

Susan kissed his reddened cheek. "I'm sorry, Nick," but then she drew back. "Why didn't you just ask me?"

"I knew you had your book club this afternoon with ladies at the nursing home, besides, it's not like Giji has anything right now, not even a place to live and I was willing to bet that she didn't belong to your book club, if you know what I mean."

"Oh, you where thinking of me!"

He pulled away from her and started across his lawn. "Trust, SueAnn, trust," he called over his shoulder.

Deflated, SueAnn took her paper and went inside. There she lay on her sofa and sulked. *How was I to know?* she thought, wishing it were a better excuse, at least I apologized. He even remembered my book club today, what guy who I just started dating would remember that?

Nick came into the living room where Giji was opening the newspaper to her favorite section, fashion.

"Did you say anything to SueAnn or did she just come up with that conclusion by her self?"

"What conclusion?" Giji looked at him over the paper. "What did she say?"

"Don't play coy with me, Giji. You said something, didn't you?"

"I did no such thing. But I'll tell you what, she's clingy. You'd better watch out. Imagine, her thinking two good friends like us fooling around behind her back!"

"Are you sure you didn't say anything?"

"I told her I didn't sleep a wink; if she took it wrong, then you might want to look at how much she trusts you." Giji turned a page nonchalantly.

"Or, how much she trusts you!"

"I know how much she trusts me," Giji put her thumb and finger together, "about that much! I've always known where I stand with your Miss SueAnn. The question is, do you?"

"Then it was a test?" Nick couldn't believe it. Why was it any of Giji's business how his relationship with SueAnn was going? Could she really be that lonely or jealous?

"Maybe."

"For her or for me?"

"Whomever it helps the most, Nick, whomever it helps the most."

"Well. Thanks for watching the place, I can take it from here." Nick looked at her coldly. Jeez, he thought, you try to be nice...

Giji got off the couch with a huff tossing the paper aside. "Let me get dressed!" She went into the other room while Nick stood looking out the window toward SueAnn's and rubbing his cheek.

SueAnn was feeling worse than ever. Having mentally gone through a list of all of her past relationships, SueAnn realized that she was jealous and mistrusting. She sat down with pen in hand and began to write.

***

Wynette dialed the phone. When the receptionist for Rent-A-Hubby answered, Wynette thought about disguising her voice for a minute. She had called so much lately and it was embarrassing to tell the receptionist that she "just wasn't connecting" with the other men that were sent.

"I have some plumbing problems in the kitchen, could you send someone over right away?"

"Of course, Mrs. Harris, any preferences?"

"Uh, no thank you, just someone who can help me with my pipes," Wynette chuckled to herself as she hung up, and then went to change into a broomstick skirt.

When he arrived, Wynette noticed he was tanned and wore tight jeans, just the way she liked them. He smiled and asked her to show him the kitchen. When he crouched down to examine the pipes under the sink, Wynette had to catch herself from moaning out loud. He had an incredibly tight ass in those jeans, and he seemed like the quiet type.

Wynette swished the broomstick skirt around her knees and watched. He was very handsome, but not too young. She found she liked them a little older since they didn't talk as much as the younger men, and she didn't really need a conversation. She leaned and rubbed her ass against the counter as she continued to watch him. Her mind began to wander and she lowered her hand in front to rub herself through the thin fabric of her skirt. The fabric became damp and she was caught up in the moment.

She didn't realize he had lifted his head from under the sink to ask her a question and he caught her touching herself. Her eyes snapped open when she heard him chuckle. A bright red blush covered her cheeks and she smelled her scent on her fingers as she tried to cover the blush.

With a knowing smirk, he leaned back on his elbows and asked, "Like what you see?"

"Umm hmm," Wynette moaned as she tried to decide what to do with her hands. She was very pleased and even more aroused when she noticed that he was beginning to get a righteous hard-on. The form fitting jeans showed his cock straining against the heavy denim fabric and there were gaps between the buttons on the pants.

"It looks like you are coming out of those pants," she purred and giggled as she thought of the double meaning of her words. She knelt beside him. "Can I help you with your... tool?"

He glanced at his toolbox and raised an eyebrow.

She shook her head, "Not that tool." Wynette traced her finger along his leg and grabbed his crotch. "This is the tool I want."

He laid back and closed his eyes as she massaged his cock through his jeans. She unfastened the buttons and he sprang free of the confines of the jeans. Wynette reached an experienced hand around his shaft and began to stroke him. Lowering her mouth, she licked the pre-cum from the head of his huge cock and he bucked up and down underneath the sink and he bashed his head against the pipe.

"Oh, my god, are you alright?" Wynette asked.

"Yeah, it's just a little bump," he replied as the spot on his forehead started to swell. Wynette admired his stamina. If most other men bashed their head like that, they certainly would have lost their erection immediately. But, he was still rock hard and huge – just the way Wynette liked her men.

"Let's move to one of the kitchen chairs. It should be safer," she said coyly. She knew her feet would touch the floor as she straddled him on the kitchen chairs. There were reasons why she chose the kitchen chairs with that design and with no arms. She smiled when she remembered the strange looks from the saleswoman when she bought the set. Imagine the fun if she had had a salesman that day.

Wynette helped the repairman move to one of the chairs and pulled his jeans down around his ankles. He was injured, she should help him. It wouldn't be right for him to get lightheaded bending over, well not yet anyway. She was pretty sure this guy had never had a house call like this one before. He was hot and ready during the few minutes it took for her to lift her broomstick skirt and climb onto his lap.

Even Wynette had rules about fucking strangers. She didn't like to kiss them on the mouth, so she straddled his legs facing away from him. This gave him a great ass to look at and hold as she rocked furiously, holding onto the edge of the table for balance. He ran his hands around her ass and under the fabric of her skirt until he was holding her waist, and pressed up against her as hard as he could while she moaned and pumped.

They exploded together and Wynette wiggled for a few extra minutes; it would make her cum twice if he could stand it and she did, quivering and moaning. They were both wet with the heat of the minute, and Wynette threw him a paper towel as she straightened her skirt.

He wiped himself off and stood up, straightening his jeans and buttoning his fly.

"Do you need a handy man around here often?" he asked as he slide back under the sink again.

"Umm hmm," Wynette answered, "Several times a week, in fact."

"I'll give you my personal cell phone number before I leave," he said. "If you need any work done you can call me directly."

Wynette accepted the slip of paper before he left and was trying to decide if she wanted the same guy to come back or if she wanted try a new one when she saw a UPS truck pull up across the street. It occurred to her she might want to order some things online soon.

***

At Ariella's house, the doorbell rang. Ariella was on the couch and yelled for Sun Li to get the door. When the little Asian maid didn't appear, Ariella sighed heavily and got up to answer it herself. It was Giji, she was visibly upset.

"I need to talk," she said, pushing past Ariella and into the living room. Ariella shut the door and followed Giji to the couch. She hoped this didn't take long, there was a new evening soap starting tonight and she had wanted to watch it.   "I don't know where to start," Giji pouted as she flopped on the couch, "I guess I could start with the obscene phone calls I've been getting."

"Yeah?" Ariella curled her legs underneath her and muted the TV. She wouldn't be able to hear, but she might pick up on the details of the episode while Giji was talking.

"I get them about three times a week and they always seem to be around the same time at night. I'm always alone and I'm always undressing or already undressed!"

"What does this person say?"

"Nothing… just breathing. I try to get them to talk, you know, tell 'em it could work out well for both of us, but they pussy out and hang up. At first I thought it might be Nick."

"Nick?" Ariella laughed, "Sweetie, that's wishful thinking. You saw how he took off after SueAnn at the barbecue. He was like a puppy dog."

"More like a dog in heat," Giji corrected.

"See, you do understand," Ariella said.

"It didn't seem all that unrealistic to think it was Nick. He could've been watching me."

"Uh huh," murmured Ariella. She caught a glimpse of the show; it looked like it would be a good one.

"Yeah, I get it," Giji admitted reluctantly. "But, I love getting under SueAnn's skin. I pranked her good earlier."

"Really?" Ariella sounded doubtful. "How'd you do that?"

Giji explained about how she stayed overnight at Nick's place while he was away and how she came out wearing his shirt to get the paper.

"She must have wanted to scratch your eyes out!" Ariella laughed.

"I'll say," Giji agreed and laughed, too. "She probably wanted to kill me! But she slapped poor Nick instead."

"Trouble in paradise?" Ariella wondered.

Giji shook her head. "I thought so at first, but SueAnn apologized." She said with a pout. "He's already forgiven her, I'm sure."

Ariella nodded, and then got an idea. "Did you apologize?" she asked.

"Apologize?" Giji repeated, "Why should I apologize?"

"Because you're the reason Nick got booty slapped by

SueAnn!" Ariella reminded her.

Giji was quiet for a moment. "Oh, I see what you mean," she admitted. "Hmmm. I guess I'll have to take care of that a little later, maybe after dark."

"Uh-hum," Ariella agreed, "Maybe you can console him if he's still on the outs with SueAnn."

"I'll sure give it my best try," Giji agreed and grinned.

"So, what else is bothering you?"

"I'm okay. I just...just came into the close proximity of several pairs of Mrs. Hoover's granny panties in the laundry! I thought I'd help her by putting the laundry away, and there they were. I thought it was a load of towels. Ughhh, I touched them!"

"You poor thing," Ariella said, comforting. "You've been traumatized!"

"I have! I have!" Giji agreed, giving the Ariella her saddest puppy dog face. "Just hold me!"

Reluctantly, Ariella put her arm around Giji, who nestled her head on Ariella's shoulder. "There, there, you poor baby," Ariella said soothingly and then she felt something weird. Looking down she saw Giji sucking on her tit, one of her tits had slipped out of her robe and Giji had seized the opportunity and the nipple.

Ariella started to push her away, and then hesitated... it actually felt really good. She got an idea. She quickly removed her robe and let Giji really nibble and suck her tits. Giji made a little moaning sound and Ariella held her closer. Ariella had to admit that it felt really good, better or at least different from Marco's pawing and poking. She had played for the other team in college a few times, but as the girl on "Coyote Ugly" said, she'd never go out for the majors.

Giji was gentle and Ariella found herself getting very wet. She wasn't wearing anything but her bathrobe. Giji was dressed in her usual easy-off whoring clothes, a T-shirt that read *Ice Princess* and a hot pink mini skirt. Ariella leaned back and let her robe fall open. As if she had read her mind, Giji was on her knees in front of Ariella, tickling her clit with her tongue and the experience that only women have with clits. Ariella shuddered and came so many times that she wondered if she'd been batting for the wrong team all these years. Giji sure knew how to give good head. She flicked and sucked like a pro.

Ariella reached to massage Giji's breasts. This was the only encouragement Giji needed and she climbed onto the couch beside Ariella. She moved Giji's leg to straddle her mouth and they both buried their heads in each other's pussy. Neither of the women noticed when Sun Li came into the room, but Ariella looked up when the basket of cleaning supplies hit the floor. She couldn't help laughing at the look on the Asian woman's face.

"Won't she tell Marco?" Giji wiped her mouth.

"No," Ariella said, forgetting about the soap, "keep going."

When Giji bent back down Ariella realized she could order this woman around in sex just like she could with Marco. She glanced at Sun Li who was now on her knees retrieving the items she dropped.

"Sun Li, one word to Marco and you're out of here. Got it?"

Standing, the Asian woman nodded and quickly left the room.

Ariella settled back on the sofa, moaning, "Ummm," she cooed, "That feels so incredibly good."

9

Peek-A-Boo!

"Clothing?" Ariella asked absent mindedly as she flipped through a fashion magazine, "Do you mean on his collar?"

The maid shrugged. She had found the stain while doing the laundry and couldn't wait to show it to her overbearing, condescending employer.

"Well, I guess you could say it's on his collar," she hedged. "It's on an opening anyway!"

"Okay, what do you want me to do?" Ariella asked, "I don't do the laundry!"

"Maybe you should take a look. See if it's your shade," the maid looked her directly in the eye, relishing the moment. She held up Marco's boxers. There was a smear of lipstick on the flap that covered the fly of the boxers. It was a smear of deep pink lipstick, not the shade of red that Ariella almost always wore.

"No. No, it's not my shade," Ariella almost yelled, "This is so 1950s. Maybe Mrs. Cleaver or Mrs. Brady cares, but I could care less about laundry. It was probably just a client, you know how people hug and stuff."

"You did see that it is on the fly of his shorts?" Sun Li asked, making sure the point was driven home.

"I did, Sun Li, okay?" Ariella told her, rattled. "I don't care! How's that?"

The maid smiled knowingly and left the room, taking the incriminating shorts with her.

***

Giji pulled up in front of the strip mall and parked. After a quick check of her hair and makeup in the rearview mirror, she got out and started walking toward the small shop, catching the scent of something that smelled uncannily like Mrs. Hoover's codfish casserole. Glancing down the row of rundown shops, she noticed Thai Fish Market. She decided that must be it as she pushed open the door to the psychic shop, the bell clanging over the door.

She had gotten the idea to see the Sexual Psychic from the sign in the front window, and had driven by several times before finally deciding that it couldn't hurt. It would cost her forty or fifty bucks to possibly find the prank caller that had been calling her consistently. She sat in the little waiting room, trying to listen to the murmurings of the session behind the curtain. It sounded like they were in a pretty heated discussion and Giji thought maybe she better come back another day, but then the talking suddenly stopped.

Presently a young woman and a much older man emerged from the back room and glanced nervously at Giji as they left. The small Asian woman came out and motioned her to enter. She was petite, old and very beautiful. Giji hoped she would look that good when she was that old.

"I'm not as old as you think I am," said Kimiko as she motioned Giji to sit across from her.

"I beg your pardon?"

"You thinking I am an old woman," said the Asian tarot reader, "but I'm not."

"How did you know…"

"You never mind. Get to the point. Shuffle these cards, cut them three times, left to right, and set them down in front of you."

Giji did as she was told, totally convinced this woman was for real.

Kimiko placed the cards in a row; face up, one card at a time. She moved slowly and deliberately and she tugged on the arm of her dress as she did it. She held one card to her forehead, and then smiled at Giji as she lay it in front of her.

"Oh, cards show you be plaything for weird couple," she narrowed her eyes. "You kinda like blowup doll, but you big girl in small clothes, whatever that mean."

"That's not important," Giji assured her, uneasily. "That weird couple is out of my life completely."

"Good for you," Kimiko seemed genuinely impressed. "First time I see you, in red latex mini and go-go boots, I think you are trashy plastic bimbo. You surprise Kimiko, a little! Now, these people not right in the head, and you smart enough to see that. I wonder why you are not smart enough to see what goes on right in front of your eyes."

"Good, I'm glad you don't think I'm a bimbo, what do you mean by right in front of my eyes?" Giji asked. "I came here for a reason."

Kimiko raised her eyes. "Oh, Kimiko relieved," she said sarcastically. "I tell myself you just driving through neighborhood and stop for tea!" She patted Giji's hand and drew another card.

"Someone call you?" Kimiko rolled her eyes. "Obviously a very sick person that you know, but they can't be trusted. They want you to think you are their friend, but they only make fun of you behind your back, and you can not see that."

"Really?" Giji asked. Her disappointment was apparent. "That could be any number of people. About the caller, I was hoping it was someone hot, sexy and really sexually liberated. To be perfectly truthful I have been hoping it's my handsome neighbor."

"No, no," Kimiko told her, "it not him, he a good guy. You should not give up on him." She drew yet another card, "Ah, but he not what he seem, two faces, this one. Good guy, though, confused."

"Really?" Giji was puzzled. "Why would he have two faces? Is it like a double life? Could he be a plumber by day and a spy by night?"

"You live in strange dream world," Kimiko told her. "He just may not be completely honest about who he is and where he's been. He's with another woman right now, I'm sorry."

"Oh, he's with SueAnn," said Giji, disappointed. "He was never with me; he's liked her from the beginning."

"Sweet and wholesome, this one is?" asked Kimiko.

"Well, compared to me," Giji had to admit. "Yeah, I guess." She shrugged. She never pretended to be anyone other than who she was…except in sexual role playing games…and she wouldn't apologize to anyone for her lifestyle, especially not this tarot card reader.

"Things are not always what they seem," said Kimiko mysteriously.

"So you have no idea who's prank calling me?" Giji asked.

"I can tell you two things," said Kimiko as she held out her hand for Giji's money. Giji paid her and stood. As she turned toward the door the little Asian woman said, "For one, he not a stranger. He definitely someone you know."

Giji turned back around, surprised "And the other?"

"Everyone thinks I'm older than I really am," she said and sighed deeply. "It was a lucky guess you would, too!"

Feeling more confused than she had before she met the psychic, Giji frowned and turned to leave.

***

"I guess Mrs. Hoover's not at home," Giji said aloud as she entered the house and walked through the kitchen. She paused, thinking she heard noises, maybe it was heavy breathing? She paused in front of the pantry. Loud panting!

Mrs. Hoover sighed with obvious relief, believing Giji had passed through the kitchen and headed upstairs. She was certain Giji had a late afternoon appointment. If she'd known her houseguest would be home so soon, she would have insisted they meet at Paul's house. Oh, she should have known when she asked Giji to move in that the busy little bitch would cramp her style!

Suddenly the pantry door swung open and Giji stood there in her game lame halter top, leather mini and stiletto heels.

"Oops! Looks like I found you. Peek-a-boo, you two!" she exclaimed loudly, a grin on her shiny red lips and a mischievous gleam in her bright eyes. She could see in the dimly lit pantry that Mrs. Hoover was in her bra and panties while Paul's shirt was unbuttoned and his slacks were around his ankles. "Looks like you've been caught bare-assed and blushing!" she added, noticing their undeniable state of undress.

"It's not what it looks like," Mrs. Hoover said, thinking Giji was dumb as a rabid squirrel.

"Looks like you're naked," Giji observed. "Now, what am I missing here?"

"An opportunity?" Paul Young asked hopefully. He'd always wanted a piece of her hot little pussy, ever since he and Mary Lynn moved into the neighborhood. A threesome with Giji and Mrs. Hoover wouldn't be so bad, he decided, especially since he was already banging the old blackmailing bitch! Having Giji in his grasp, he decided, would make it infinitely more enjoyable!

Giji shook her blonde tresses. "No, I never miss an opportunity," she assured him. "What I might be missing though is that you two are in what we in the real estate biz refer to a compromising position!"

"Compromising?" Mrs. Hoover repeated, confused.

"Yeah," Giji said and laughed, "an uncomfortable position!"

"Well, it is kind of cramped in here," Paul said, uncertain where this was leading, "Maybe I should get dressed and be on my way."

"That would probably be a good idea," Mrs. Hoover agreed.

"I expected more of you, Paul," Giji said as if she were disappointed, "Were all the hookers downtown on vacation?"

Mrs. Hoover shot Paul an uneasy glance.

"I just needed a diversion," he said quietly.

"Looks like you found it," Giji told him. "A diversion right here in Martha's pantry!"

Giji turned away while Paul Young pulled up his slacks and tidied himself.

After Paul Young left, Mrs. Hoover put on her skirt and blouse. "Zip me," she said, turning her back to Giji.

Giji obeyed. "I really didn't expect this of you, Martha," she lied; she had suspected that Mrs. Hoover was slipping around with someone.

Mrs. Hoover closed her eyes. "I know," she said apologetically. "It's just one of those things." She turned to face Giji. "It just happened."

Giji nodded, certain this wasn't the first time. She wondered if it was going on before Mary Lynn killed herself.

"Suppose we just forget what we saw here," Mrs. Hoover suggested, "and I'll forget half of next month's rent?"

"Umm," Giji said and pretended to be considering Mrs. Hoover's offer. "Let's say you forget all of next month's rent and we have a deal!"

Mrs. Hoover rolled her eyes. "Okay, it's a deal," she reluctantly agreed, thinking she'd find a way to get all of the rent back and more, "now, how about some of my meatloaf casserole for dinner?"

Giji got an idea. "Umm, that sounds delicious," she lied, feeling her stomach churn, "but I have an even better idea!"

Mrs. Hoover raised her eyes suspiciously. "More delicious than my meatloaf casserole?"

"Maybe not more delicious," Giji said, thinking quickly, "but I was thinking we could go out for a bite. My treat! We'll use the money I'm saving on next month's rent."

"Well," the older woman hesitated, "I did make that meatloaf casserole especially for you."

"It'll keep," Giji told her. Forever, probably, she thought to herself, "Come on. What do you say? We deserve a night out!"

Mrs. Hoover grinned, thinking: *You clever little bitch! You figured a way to get me to go out to dinner, invite yourself along, and have me pick up the check by using the rent money you're bilking me out of! Clever, clever. Enjoy your meal because it'll just mean more casserole – maybe I'll make a good ole liver and cod casserole for later!*

***

Marco slipped off his shoes and tipped toed up the stairs. When he opened the bedroom door, he realized Ariella wasn't asleep. She aimed a vase directly at his head, and even in the dark her aim was dead-on. If he hadn't ducked, she would have shattered a large ceramic vase against his head.

"What the hell are you doing, Ariella?" Marco demanded, "You almost hit me with that vase!"

"Too bad!" Ariella screamed, sitting up in bed. "My intention was to hit you! Next time I won't miss."

Ariella raised her hand with yet another vase ready to throw, and Marco dove for the bed to wrestle the vase away from her. Once he had the vase and set it on the nightstand, he turned back to his wife, who was turned away from him.

"What is this about?" he demanded. "Have you lost your mind?"

"One of us has," Ariella spat, turning to him now.

"Baby," Marco said in a sweet, soothing voice, "This isn't like you. Tell me what has you so upset, sweetheart. I'm sure we can work this out."

Ariella turned on the bedside lamp, and then she pulled a pair of Marco's boxers from beneath the covers.

"Maybe you can explain this," Ariella told him in a tight voice, holding up his underwear. "I'd love to hear it! You want your cake and eat it too, you... you two-timing cake eater! The maid took great pleasure in showing me a stain on your boxers she couldn't get out!" Ariella's eyes flashed with anger, but Marco couldn't imagine what kind of stain would get her so worked up.

"What?" he asked, "Maybe I got turned on by something you did and I dripped –"

"Oh, I'm sure you got turned on," Ariella said. "I'm sure you did!"

"Accidents happen," Marco sounded almost pleading. He knew his woman was an absolute nut case when it came to any imperfections in the household, even stains on clothing. She could be really weird about it.

"Well, your cock-sucking whore obviously had an accident," Ariella went on, "She got lipstick on the fly of your boxers!"

For a moment, Marco was struck speechless. This was not at all what he had expected. Damn Tia! She had been careless with her sloppy oral sex! He had warmed her to be extremely careful or something like this could happen, and now it had. There was only one thing he could do, Marco decided. Lie! Lie! Lie! After all, he surmised, he was a used car salesman, lying was like a second language to him!

"It must have been you, baby. It could have only been you. Remember on the couch the other day?"

Ariella was caught off guard. It did sound like a plausible explanation. The color of the lipstick was very similar to the tube she wore the most often, and she had been fooling around with the young gardener lately, maybe infidelity wasn't such a good subject to bring up...

Marco drew in his breath sharply after finishing his explanation. Man, he thought, who knew I could come up with something that good on such a short notice! Even Ariella seemed unsure what to believe now, after all, it was possible and maybe even plausible. Marco sounded like he was being truthful; she could usually tell when he was lying because his face would twitch slightly. *No twitching*, she thought. Besides…

"I hope you're not lying to me," Ariella began.

"You know I would never do that," Marco lied with his more sincere face. "I love you too much to ever do anything that might jeopardize what we have and what we share. Our love means everything to me."

Ariella threw back the covers and went to stand in front of the dresser, looking at her reflection in the mirror. She saw him lying on the bed, looking down at the covers, unsure of where things were going.

"I still have the humiliation, Sun Li seeing that stain and making sure I saw it," she said, but her voice sounded less angry.

He looked up at her. "I'll speak with Sun Li in the morning," he assured her, and then he stood. In the mirror, she could see him coming up behind her.

Marco knew the quickest way to get to his wife's heart, other than money, was good sex! He came up behind Ariella and wrapped her in his arms. He kissed her neck slowly, softly, breaking down her resistance, soothing away her anger. He pinched her erect nipple through the sheer fabric of her teddy.

"I still don't fully believe you, you know," Ariella said, looking at Marco's reflection in the mirror. But he did feel good, kissing her neck like that.

"I know, baby, I know, but these things happen. It was just a silly misunderstanding."

She continued to watch him in the mirror as he lifted up the red teddy she was wearing. She hadn't put on any panties and felt her own juices run down her leg as he leaned her forward before putting his huge, Latin cock inside her. She thought to herself that this was why she had married him, besides the money, and knew that no matter what happened between them, that she wouldn't be able to give up this kind of satisfaction.

Marco reached around her waist and began massaging her clit

as he moved in and out of her; she watched him in the mirror and rotated her hips to the movement. His other hand was on one of her breasts, alternating pinching and rubbing. He felt so good, she wondered what it was that that fascinated her about other men, other than the need to get off constantly. She threw her head back as Marco came, and they both collapsed onto the bed.

10

Truth Or Dare?

SueAnn looked through the peephole and saw her neighbor, Mrs. Hoover. She wanted to just ignore her, but she'd seen Mrs. Hoover outside earlier and waved to her, so Mrs. Hoover knew she was at home.

Opening the door, she put on her best forced smile and said, "Oh, Mrs. Hoover, what brings you over?"

"Well, dear, I was looking through my latest Martha Stewart Living and there was a super recipe for a potato casserole. The recipe called for a 9 by 9 baking dish, and I remembered that I loaned my dish to you!"

"Oh yes, let me get that for you," she said, purposely not inviting her neighbor in. She started toward the kitchen and realized Mrs. Hoover was hot on her heels. She could almost smell the old bitch's hot, putrid breath on the back of her neck.

Fumbling through the dishes in the cabinet, SueAnn finally found the dish beneath a set of nesting bowls. "Here it is," she announced, taking it down and handing it to Mrs. Hoover.

"Oh, SueAnn, I see you're having your little monthly get

together," Mrs. Hoover said, looking into the dining room. "I see you have wine and cheese. Do you...?"

"Well," SueAnn shrugged helplessly as the others shook their heads behind Mrs. Hoover.

Mrs. Hoover was on the wine and cheese as if it were a religious experience.

"We were just discussing current events," Wynette said, hoping the topic would send their unwanted guest packing.

"Yes," Ariella said, thinking fast, "like Britney Spears' latest marriage and the Celebrity Death Match between Tom Cruise and Brooke Shields and individual rights."

Nibbling on a hunk of cheese like a giant rat, Mrs. Hoover swallowed hard several times before speaking.

"On personal rights or whatever, I'm in agreement with that sexy George Bush," Mrs. Hoover said with a proud smile.

"Sexy?" SueAnn choked.

"Oh yes," Mrs. Hoover rolled her eyes like a love struck schoolgirl experiencing her first crush. "He's in favor of only true Americans having rights, not queers and people who read smut and stuff. Perverts! Gay people weren't here when the country was founded and now they want rights! You can't trust people who are in the closet!"

Giji looked thoughtful. "Mrs. Hoover, didn't I catch you in the closet the other..."

"Well," Mrs. Hoover said quickly and stood to leave, "That casserole isn't going to cook itself. I'd better run along. Martha Stewart doesn't make house calls, you know!"

***

"The game is truth or dare poker, ladies," said Giji as she dealt the cards. All the wives gathered at SueAnn's for an evening of poker while the guys watched the game at Connie's house. The conversation was heated and the women were in a fine mood, helped along by the wine that Ariella supplied.

"I dated an ass-chest once," Giji admitted.

"An ass...?" Connie started to repeat the word, and then stopped herself.

"What's the hell is that?" Ariella wanted to know.

"I'll take this one," Wynette offered. "An ass-chest is a guy who has no mid-section."

"No corn belt?" SueAnn asked, puzzled.

"No, no," Wynette told her. "You know... no real waist."

Ariella still looked confused.

"His chest appears to be sitting on top of his ass," Giji said bluntly. "It's like those nerdy guys who pull their slacks way up."

"Oh," Ariella nodded. "Like Steven Urkel?"

"Yes," Wynette chimed in.

"Except since an ass-chest has no waist," Wynette explained further, "it's like his belly button is in the center of his chest! If his navel is an outie, it's like he has three nipples!" Ariella laughed loudly and poured more wine.

Connie turned a bright shade of crimson, a few shades lighter than her flaming red hair. "Oh my!" she gasped.

Ariella continued to giggle. "Wow, I'll have to watch out for those!"

"I dated a guy once who was almost as wide as he was tall," SueAnn said out of the blue. "He was only five-foot-six. It was like dating Sponge Bob Squarepants!"

"There you go trying to steal my momentum!" Giji complained and rolled her eyes. "You just can't stand it when I'm the life of the party!"

"Well, I just... felt left out," SueAnn said softly in an almost childlike voice.

"Hey, you guys," Wynette refereed, "we all get equal time here. Besides, I once dated a guy who had defective genitalia!"

Connie suppressed a giggle behind her napkin.

"Do tell!" Giji prodded, interested.

"Okay," Wynette began. "He had one big ball and one small ball and a cock that was bent weirdly in the shape of a 'z'!"

"No!" Connie gasped, shocked by what she'd heard. "That's unreal."

"I'll say," Wynette continued. "He had one of those cocks that bend back toward the guy's stomach or to the left or right on its own. It kind of looked like those long balloons clowns use to make wiener dogs."

"Really?" Ariella sounded skeptical.

"Only his looked like someone tried to tie it in a knot!" Wynette said, and then grinned. She got up to get some more chips, and they could hear her from the kitchen. "I'll say one thing about him though; sex with him was a real pussy-pleasing experience! That weirdly shaped cock was all over the place while we did it–and he hit my G-spot every time!"

Everyone laughed.

"You really shouldn't tease us like that," Giji said and winked at Ariella. "Some of the present company will actually believe it!"

"I dated a guy once who had a third leg, literally," Ariella said, laughing. "All the girls called him 'Tripod'!" She paused thoughtfully. "I wonder whatever happened to ole Tri?"

More laughter.

"Once, before I married Lex, I dated a guy once who thought he was being stalked by celebrities," Connie announced spontaneously. "While we were making out in his room, he would say, 'Be ready, Kathie Lee may leap from my closet at any minute'!"

"Kathie Lee," Wynette repeated and shook her head.

"Okay," SueAnn said, looking down at the deck of cards. "Where were we?"

"Gee," SueAnn said. "I thought I had that one!"

"Truth or dare?" Wynette asked.

"Truth," SueAnn said.

"When I started writing, I tried writing adult fiction, you know, erotica," SueAnn admitted reluctantly. "My editor said my characters were…"

"Wooden?" Connie interrupted.

"Squeaky clean?" Giji ventured and snickered.

Ariella laughed, too.

"Now, ladies, let her finish," Wynette pleaded.

"No," SueAnn answered in a quiet voice. "He said my characters were touching each other inappropriately."

"Is that all?" Giji wanted to know.

"Oh, he had plenty to say," SueAnn continued. "He said some of the bizarre positions my characters were engaging in might lead to their being decapitated! He also said he couldn't tell if my characters were having sex or if they were unconscious!"

"Do you have any of these stories in your basement?" Giji wanted to know, and then she and Ariella looked at each other and burst into rollicking laughter. Wynette and Connie laughed softly.

"So," Connie said uneasily, "That's how you came to write children's books?"

SueAnn nodded. "Pretty much. That, ten years in a miserable marriage, a child, and a need to be able to eat three square meals a day! I certainly couldn't depend on my undependable ex…"

"Okay," Wynette said quickly. "Enough 'Truth or Dare'!"

"Okay, looks like I lose again," SueAnn said.

"Truth or dare?" Ariella asked, laughing.

"Truth," SueAnn said with a deep sigh.

Giji rolled her eyes. "Now that's original. I don't think you've ever chosen 'dare'! This better be good. Let's have it!"

"I slept with a little person," SueAnn announced, determined not to be out done by Giji.

"You slept with a midget?" Giji asked, clearly shocked.

"They prefer to be called little people," SueAnn told her. "And yes, I did."

"Are they little all over?" Ariella wanted to know.

"Ariella!" Connie spoke now, shocked.

Ariella shrugged. "Well, I've always wondered."

SueAnn shook her head. "No, they're actually pretty large in the place that counts!"

The room came alive with knowing giggles.

"Would you look at that," Giji said in a playful voice. "Lady Luck has pimped me out!" She licked her lips. "Dare!" she said suddenly, determined to be different than SueAnn who always chose 'truth'.

"I dare you to go outside topless!" Ariella said quickly.

Giji grinned. "Well, I certainly can't do that again!" she exclaimed, squeezing her breasts together with her hands and giving them a little lift and bounce. "Truth, please!"

"Wow," Wynette observed. "Those things have a life of their own! Are they real?"

Giji feigned mock surprise and batted her violet-blue eyes. "Why, a lady never tells!" she said in her best Scarlet O"Hara impression.

"Since when are you a lady?" Ariella sniffed.

"Careful," Giji warned. "I take offense at that." Then she smiled, lightening the mood. "Since I don't pretend to be prim and proper, I'll just say they're real now."

"Fair enough," Ariella said, pleased. "Now, can we touch them?"

Giji leaned back proudly and pushed out her massive chest. "Be my invited guest," she agreed. "Here they are, ladies. Have at 'em!"

Giji enjoyed her moment while each of the ladies took turns feeling Giji's 36 double D's, except SueAnn who stood and watched. Giji almost moaned it felt so good, especially when Ariella gripped her nipples in her tight, fiery Latina grip! Feeling her pussy juices soaking her panties, Giji closed her eyes and breathed deeply, savoring the sensation. She almost never wore panties, but she did wear them to the monthly poker parties with the girls... just in case they played strip poker, which she had often suggested.

"My god, Giji, what are you doing? Having a freaking orgasm right here in my dining room?" SueAnn stared at Giji's enormous boobs. "You always have to be the center of attention, don't you?" she asked sarcastically. "I hope you have on undies!"

"Okay, okay, SueAnn, don't get your panties drenched," Giji said. "I admit I'm an attention whore." She winked at her arch-nemesis. "Last chance to cop a feel, SuSu," she chided. "I wouldn't want you to miss out on the floor show!"

SueAnn rolled her eyes. "I'll pass," she said, grinning, "after all, I can always touch the real thing!" She pushed out her much smaller chest. "See!"

Giji nodded. Ariella frowned. And no one else said a thing.

"Of course, you can!" Giji said finally and stood up, "and while you're busy molesting yourself, I'll just be running along!"

"Oh, Giji, I almost forgot," SueAnn said as Giji headed for the door. "I just heard there's a peeping tom watching teenage girls in the neighborhood."

Giji paused and turned around, grinning. "Ooh," she said. "I'll have to remember to leave my window open–I mean–closed."

SueAnn smiled, then said matter-of-factly, "Giji, I don't think it matters."

"Why?"

"Well...I did say he was watching teenage girls."

Giji pushed up her firm boobs. "I know." She grinned. "But you never know when he'll decide he needs a real woman!"

"Giji, you're incorrigible!" SueAnn said sarcastically and the other wives laughed.

Giji gave her best smile. "I know," she agreed, "Great, isn't it? And I'm not about to change!"

***

Giji and Ariella sat on Ariella's couch, watching music videos on MTV2 and playing footsie under the throw that Ariella had found. They each lay against opposite ends of the couch. Sun Li flitted in and out of the room, dusting and carrying laundry, but both women knew she was spying on them in case their footsie turned more... erotic. Sun Li had been shocked when she found the two women playing with each other a few weeks ago, but now she seemed as voyeuristic as the person who called Giji every night when she would ready for her bath.

"Mrs. Hoover's smoking pot again," Giji piped up. "She says her doctor prescribed it for her asthma!"

"I've never heard of using pot for asthma before." Ariella seemed surprised. "Really?"

"Yeah!" Giji laughed. "And Paris Hilton is still a virgin!"

"Did she let you have a toke?"

"She offered, but, hmmm...I was afraid she was trying to get me high..."

"So she could molest you again?"

"Exactly!" Giji said. "It smelled like primo stuff, but I couldn't chance it. She might get all handsy! Ugh! The old bitch is hands on enough when she's not high!"

Ariella got an idea. "I know what we can do," she announced enthusiastically.

"Marco has a stash he thinks is a secret, but Sun Li found it. She claimed she was cleaning, but snooping is more like it! Anyway, I know where it is and we can roll ourselves a joint!"

"I'm in," Giji agreed, pleased.

The two went upstairs slowly and quietly as if it were a top secret mission, but the main reason to be quiet was so Sun Li wouldn't get suspicious about what they were doing. Sometimes Ariella felt like there was a spy in the house, watching her every move and listening to every sound and Sun Li would run to Marco and spill everything. If Ariella wasn't trying to make sure that Sun Li wouldn't say a word, she would make sure Sun Li didn't work in the Fluentes household anymore. But, she liked the control.

In the master bedroom, Giji followed Ariella to Marco's closet and stood behind her as she rummaged around before coming up with a wooden box off the top shelf.

"Only top shelf weed for my Marco," Ariella joked as she pulled the box down.

The two women curled up on the bed with the box that contained everything they needed and Ariella tried to roll a joint.

"Geez, let me do that, where did you learn how to roll?" Giji laughed half way through. Ariella sighed and handed over the box. Within minutes Giji had a nice fatty rolled and they were toking.

Giji took a long toke and slowly exhaled. "Mrs. Hoover claims she has the most primo stuff," she said, "but this isn't bad."

"I'll say it's not," Ariella agreed. "This is from Marco's private stash. He only smokes the best."

Giji and Ariella kissed and blew smoke from the joint into each other's mouths. They giggled and listened for the sound of Sun Li's footsteps on the stairs. When they didn't hear anything, they continued smoking and giggling.

"So, what are you going to do about Nick?"

Ariella leaned back on her elbow and wiggled her toes in Giji's crotch.

"I don't know, I went to that psychic the other day. You know, the one out by the strip mall? She said not to give up on him, but that maybe he couldn't be trusted."

"Trusted?"

"Yeah, she said that sometimes things aren't as they seem."

"I'll say." Ariella fingered Giji's wet pussy. Giji sighed and leaned back on the bed. Ariella climbed on top of her and began massaging her breasts through her top.

"Nick's fine," said Ariella as she bent over and nibbled on Giji's breast.

"Yes, he sure is," Giji agreed, closing her eyes. "Hmmm, that feels so good."

"I sure wouldn't say no to a piece of his action," Ariella giggled.

"Ariella Fluentes, are you saying you'd step out on that Latino hunk of yours?"

Giji rolled another joint. They both took turns passing and inhaling deeply.

"Oh, I already have," said Ariella mysteriously.

"No! With who?"

"Whom," said Ariella. "What do you think we're doing right now?"

"Ah, it doesn't count. A little harmless fooling around between friends," said Giji.

"Between friends," repeated Ariella.

They both jumped as Sun Li, entered the bedroom with a full laundry basket.

"Sun Li," Ariella said.

The Asian woman rolled her eyes. "I know, no tell Mr. Marco," she said.

***

"Don't worry, I'll get it," Kendra got on her knees and crawled under Steven's desk to retrieve the pen she dropped. Steven continued to move papers on his desk. All of a sudden his fly was being unzipped! For a minute, he didn't know whether to let Kendra continue or grab her hands. He started to grab her hands when he felt the most wonderfully warm and wet tongue on his cock! Completely out of his slacks now, Kendra had his cock in her mouth, swirling her tongue around the shaft, deep throating him and taking it farther than any woman he had known! He shuddered and leaned back in his chair, one eye on the door and one hand on the back of her head.

Both horrified and excited at the naughtiness of it all, the possibility of getting caught and the shudders of orgasm as they welled up inside him, Steven had never felt so alive...or so uneasy. Kendra continued to gently squeeze his balls with one hand and massage his cock with the other, all the while taking it all the way to her throat. He couldn't help lunging forward as he came. She handled his cock like a pro, he realized it wasn't her first time giving head.

"How was I?" she asks afterward, taking his handkerchief

from his jacket and wiping her lips.

"Unexpected," was all he could think of to say.

"When I want something, I just go for it!" Kendra said proudly. She started to leave the office, and then paused just inside the door. With her hand on the knob, she looked over her shoulder at him.

"Next time, it's my turn," she smiled at him.

Steven leaned back, torn between the enjoyment of the unexpected and the fear of a young girl who was either very free-spirited or spoiled to the point of being out of control. He couldn't shake that 'ole uneasy feeling.

Kendra is unpredictable, he thought, and the last thing he needed was her spilling anything to her father and his boss, or even worse, Wynette!

He watched her flit back and forth outside his office, bending over a little too far to put paperwork away, glancing back at him and smiling through the half cracked office door. He wondered what other plans she had for him and was caught between the feelings that seemed to overpower him.

Little did he know that less than halfway across town, Marco was putting his secretary into a car and sending her away.

***

"Well, I guess this is goodbye, then," said Tia as she started to get into her car.

"Tia, it really is the only way. Ariella would never give me a divorce and think of the scandal around the office. You need to go home to your mom's so she can help you after the baby is born. I'll send money when I can, I promise."

"You promised you'd find a way for us to be together," pouted Tia.

"I know, baby, but what am I supposed to do now? We could have gotten together as much as we wanted, except that you got pregnant."

"It's not like I got pregnant all by myself," Tia reminded him.

"I know, I didn't mean it that way, really I didn't." Marco reached into his jacket pocket and brought out a wad of cash. "Here, this should help get you set up."

"Is this how you handle all of your problems? You just throw money at them? I thought you really liked me."

"I do really like you," Marco said, ignoring the bit about the cash. "But, what did you think was going to come of this, realistically?"

"I thought we would be together," Tia said, wiping away a tear.

"Now, don't cry. You be strong and we'll make it right somehow."

"How?"

Marco was getting irritated. He hadn't ever made plans to leave Ariella, even though she was good for a raging case of blue balls at least twice a week. She had money, her family had money and she was an excellent trophy wife. She knew how to behave at business parties and what to wear. Marco knew that part of why he was doing so well was Ariella's way with men at the social functions they attended. She knew what to say and how to flirt just enough to seem coy but professional. She should since she was raised by the right people, attended the right schools, and was quite the debutante. A good business wife and Marco wasn't about to jeopardize anything just because he'd had a fling with a hot little thing who ended up pregnant. He didn't think that he was a bad guy, he just needed this problem to go away, and when Tia refused to have an abortion, he didn't have much of a choice but to send her away and look the other way for awhile.

"I don't know the answer to that yet, sweetie. We'll stay in touch and who knows what the future will bring?"

You could be sued for child support and then lose your where little wife, Tia thought. She trusted Marco and thought he needed her. He never turned down sex in all the times she offered herself to him, since that first day in his office. It seemed a long time ago, although it was only a few weeks.

After that first day they had stolen many lunch hours at the motels out by the highway and Marco couldn't say no to her. She had perky breasts, the kind of body Marco wanted and was willing to do it in any position Marco fancied, from dressing up as a French maid to letting him take her from behind. She did anything for him. He had the biggest cock she had ever taken into her mouth, but she thought he loved her, maybe just a little bit. She hadn't planned on getting pregnant, at least that's what she wanted Marco to believe. The truth was she'd stopped taking the pill the very first time they'd slept together in his office. She'd thought if she became pregnant with his child, Marco would find a way for them to be together. Now he was simply pushing her aside without a thought, but with a handful of cash. She put on her seat belt and looked up at him once more. He looked like he was in a hurry to get out of there as soon as he could.

"Well, how will I keep in touch with you?" she asked.

"Write a letter addressed to the office and tell me where you are," Marco said quickly, looking around.

"Okay, I guess I'll be going now." She seemed hesitant. "I love you, Marco."

"Take care," was all Marco said as he shut the door to the car.

He watched her pull out of the parking lot and turn onto the interstate ramp.

***

Giji loved the way the sun hit her pink Cadillac, especially when she was driving it fast on the freeway. She had fallen in love with the large pink Cadillac the second her father had given to her just before her high school graduation. She had been standing on the front stoop with her mother, expecting a tiny little compact, when her father pulled into their driveway in a huge car that literally took her breath away. The car glistened like a true gem in the afternoon sunshine, sleek and gorgeous, and Giji could not take her eyes off of it. Quickly she developed an enduring relationship with her graduation gift, and she realized she was always in a good mood when she drove her pink Cadillac.

As she drove along, bopping to the radio while singing and humming along with Diet Dr. Creeper's 'Shorty Loves to Party,' " Giji didn't have a care in the world. "Are y'all ready to party," she sang. "Everybody where you at? Where you at party people? Where ya at? There's shorty right there. Oh. Hey, party people you're in the place to be, the place to be, the place to beeeeeeeee!"

Just as she was rounding the slight curve near the off ramp, she noticed a patrol car on the shoulder, checking for speeders. She sighed and slowed down, only to see him pull out into traffic and begin to follow her, sirens blaring.

Oh, great, I hope he's cute, she thought as she looked for the best place to pull over. There wasn't one, so she took the next off ramp and pulled into a dirt road, leaving the end of the car sticking out from the trees so the cop would know that she had tried to pull over.

He was cute: he had dark hair, a muscular build and piercing green eyes. Giji loved those tight pants patrolmen wore. He got out of his patrol car and came up to her side of the window. She rolled the window down and shook her blonde curls at him.

"I was speeding, wasn't I, Officer?" she smiled up at him.

"Yes, you were way beyond the speed limit back there." He leaned in the window and looked in her back seat.

"Have you been drinking?"

"It's not even one in the afternoon!" Giji sounded insulted .

"I could give you a sobriety test," the cop smiled at her.

"We could pull farther down this dirt road so we wouldn't be disturbed," smiled Giji back at him. He was very young, probably new to the force, and Giji couldn't help herself. He didn't look like he wanted to take her (to the station) especially with the bulge that was building in his pants.

Giji motioned for him to follow her and pulled the pink

Cadillac further down the dirt road. When they were both parked she got out and got into the passenger side of the cop's car.

"Put your seat all the way back," said Giji. The young cop did as he was told and Giji unzipped his fly. Taking out an enormous cock; Giji couldn't help but moan as she took him in her mouth to get him ready. It didn't take long.

"Now lean back," she told him. She remembered the biker in the trunk of the other car, having to call SueAnn to rescue her and she began to giggle.

"What's up?" asked the cop

"I was just thinking of something funny," Giji said quickly. "Wouldn't it be funny if I got my foot got stuck in the horn?"

"Not really," said the cop, but he started to relax. Giji was good at getting guys to relax and she climbed onto his lap and began to rock back and forth in the cramped space.

But, that's exactly what happened. Giji's spiked heels got caught in the steering wheel and the horn blared at least three times during sex. The young cop was mortified, and turned red every time, but Giji just laughed and untangled herself.

"Maybe we should move to the back seat," he said once.

"No, I'll be done in a minute," Giji breathed back. She twisted and wriggled on top of his lap, and just as they both were about to cum the second time, Giji's spiked heels got her into trouble again, this time by hitting the siren button!

"Officer down!" Giji screamed playfully. "Going down on an officer!"

"Oh, my god," said the cop, leaning frantically forward to shut off the siren. Giji couldn't tell whether he was exclaiming about the siren or the sex and she got up and wriggled again, this time back out of the car.

Giji turned the dials on the police. "Come in, headquarters," she said loudly in a playful voice. "This is Officer Hot Bod! I've apprehended a naughty, naughty boy!"

"You're going to get us both in trouble!"

"I'm just pranking you!" Giji told him, laughing.

"You had me going," he admitted.

While Giji straightened her clothing, the young cop leaned against the door, lighting a cigarette.

"Can I hit that?" Giji asked as she took it from his lips. She took a puff and let it out, beginning to cough since she didn't really smoke. They both laughed and Giji headed for her pink caddy.

"Will I see you again?" asked the cop.

"Just keep an eye out for a pink Cadillac!" Giji winked as she sped off.

Giji hit the on ramp and turned out to the freeway. She looked in the rear view mirror but the cop wasn't behind her. She doubted she would run into him again, after all, she hadn't run into the biker or any of her other freeway conquests. She shook her head and slid a CD into the player, turning up the volume and throwing her head back into the sunshine. She hummed along with Sex On the Beach's "Burning for You." For the moment everything was right with the world, and Giji was in control again.

11

Girl Crush

Ariella's living room was littered with potato chip bags and bottles, some were pop and some were beer. This week's get together was in full swing, and the subject was crushes.

"My first crush was David Cassidy," Connie revealed. "I had his pictures up all over my bedroom. Hmmm, I had fantasies about him, that funny tour bus, and his tight ass in those even tighter jeans!"

"Yeah, I remember him and then his little brother upstaged him as a Hardy Boy," said SueAnn, licking her fingers and reaching back into the potato chip bag.

"Oh, gross, wipe your hands first," said Ariella, grabbing the bag and laughing. She tossed the bag back and popped open another can of soda. "What was his name?"

"Who?" said Connie

"David Cassidy's little brother."

"Shaun," Wynette spoke up.

"Oh, yeah, what was the other Hardy Boy's name?"

"Colin Grey."

"No, that was the 1995 series," Wynette spoke up again. "You're talking about Parker Stevenson."

"Well, someone was a fan!" giggled Giji.

"I once had a dream about Angelina Jolie," Ariella said proudly. "In my dream she accosted me in the ladies' room. One thing leads to another and we ended up kissing in one of the stalls!"

Silence.

"What?" Ariella asked as if insulted. "Like none of you have ever dreamed about a hot woman. Those lips just kill me!"

"Ariella, I never would've guessed you played for both teams!" Wynette said.

Giji and Ariella glanced at each other, but none of the other wives saw them.

"Well, I did have a crush on Miss Jane from 'The Beverly Hillbillies,'" Wynette admitted, trying to lighten the moment.

"Who?" the wives asked in unison.

"'The Beverly Hillbillies,' you know..." Wynette trailed off as she realized they didn't.

"Sounds like our little Wynette watched a lot of TV as a child!" Giji giggled again. "What's with the name Wynette?"

Wynette winced. "My mom was a big Tammy Wynette fan," she answered.

"Oh," Giji said, then a thought occurred to her. "Good thing she wasn't into Boy George!"

Wynette gave a self-conscious laugh. "I know!" she said loudly. "I'm thankful for that every day of my life!"

"Anyway, I never watched those hillbilly shows or whatever," Giji said. "My parents didn't approve of television, so I didn't watch a lot of TV as a child."

"You were actually out whor..." SueAnn started, but Ariella cut her off,

"As a matter of fact, I did have two lesbian experiences, one in high school and one in college." Ariella looked down and smoothed her skirt.

"Well, are you going to tell us about them?" asked Wynette.

"Not much to tell, in high school, we were in the locker room after a game and changing our clothes. The rest of the team had gone already…"

"What did you play?" interjected Wynette.

"Who cares?" said Giji.

"Volleyball, and as a matter of fact we went to state that year," Ariella said. "We were in the locker room and I had just come out of the shower. The girl asked if she could dry my back and I said yes. One thing led to another and she kissed me and started fondling me. It felt better at the time than anything the boys had done."

"Okay," Giji announced. "None of us will ever get laid like this!" She stood to leave. "See you guys after my next conquest!"

"Giji, I guess you've never really had any crushes," SueAnn said sarcastically.

"What's that supposed to mean, SuSu?" Giji said in a mocking voice. "Huh? That I'm such a slut; I just sleep with any guy who happens to walk by at any given time!"

"I'm sure, Su…I mean SueAnn didn't mean it like that," Wynette said.

"Maybe I did!" SueAnn said quickly.

"Well, SueAnn, for your information," Giji started, "I have had crushes, many crushes. I once had a crush on Marilyn Manson. There, in your face, top that!"

"Easily," SueAnn said confidently, "I once had a crush on Julia Child."

After a moment of silence, Giji said loudly, "That's just sick!"

"That is kind of sick," Wynette agreed, "but I admitted I had a crush on that cute Miss Jane from 'The Beverly Hillbillies.' "

Silence.

"I dated a guy with clown feet once," Connie spoke suddenly.

Everyone seemed surprised, more by the fact that Connie had spoken on the topic than by her revelation.

"You mean he had really big feet?" SueAnn asked.

"No, silly," Connie said smiling. "He was with the circus!"

A few laughs went around the table.

"I have a cousin like that," Ariella admitted. "She has big feet, I mean. She's so big and manly. She drives a tractor, wears guy clothes and carries a tool belt for a purse!"

"No!" Connie gasped.

"Unfortunately, yes," Ariella said and rolled her eyes. "She's feminine dysfunctional or hormonally deficient or something!"

"Or, maybe she's a lesbian," Connie ventured.

"That could be," Ariella agreed, ignoring the implications, "I never really thought of that, mainly because she's so butch other lesbians are afraid of her! I've never seen her kiss a girl… or a guy… but she does hum along with Melissa Etheridge!"

"There you go!" Giji said, "That's the litmus test for lesbians!"

"Is not," Wynette said, laughing lightly. "There is no litmus test. Either you're a lesbian or you're not."

"Okay," Giji announced. "None of us will ever get laid like this!" She stood to leave, and then grinned. "See you guys after my next conquest!"

"You said that already," smirked Ariella, looking right at her.

"Well, here I go!" Giji went out of the room, and the wives heard the screen door slam.

***

Giji watched the last of the bath water drain away as she wrapped herself in a towel. Just as she squeezed the toothpaste, her phone rang. It had been like this all week, every night after her bath the phone would ring, almost as if someone knew when she finished her bath. She sighed and answered the phone, maybe this time it would be different.

"Hello?"

Same as always, the only sound she heard on the other end was heavy breathing.

"Like I told you before," Giji spoke to the breather, "you have to work with me. We can make this mutually pleasurable but only if you're willing to participate, and I don't have all night...unless you want me too," she added playfully.

Still nothing; the loud breathing sounded labored, as if the caller was having a hard time keeping quiet, except for the sound of their breath.

"Say something," Giji chided. "Hey, I have an idea. Talk dirty to me, okay? Say something really naughty or tell me to do something sexy, and I'll do it while you, ah, listen."

Loud breathing.

"Okay, okay," Giji said playfully, "work with me here. I have on my see-through pink teddy! I'm ready for bed but not necessarily sleeping."

More loud breathing.

"I'm touching myself!" Giji told the caller. "Go ahead. Ask me what I'm touching. Better yet, guess! Betcha'll never guess!"

Louder breathing, the noise faded for a second, as if the caller was holding the phone away from their ear for a moment. It occurred to Giji that they might be laughing at her.

"This isn't Mrs. Hoover pranking me, is it?" Giji asked, and then it occurred to her that maybe SueAnn was getting even with her for all the not so nice things she'd said and done to her. Nah, she finally decided, SueAnn doesn't have it in her! She'd never come up with something this clever, Giji decided, almost wishing it was SueAnn because not knowing who was on the other end of the line was the most unnerving part...

Before she could tempt the caller further, the line went dead. Giji held the phone for a moment, and then started to press End Call– then she remembered that she could press star 69 and find out where the call originated. But, almost as soon as her finger pressed the button, her cell phone began to ring again. Her heart raced, with a combination of excitement and fear. She was sure it was the caller calling back.

"Hello?" she answered quietly.

"Giji?" It was a woman's voice, a familiar voice that Giji recognized as her receptionist at the office.

"Charmaine?"

"Yes, I just called to remind you that you have an early appointment tomorrow."

"Thanks, Charmaine," Giji said, picturing the bookish young woman. Charmaine wore her hair in the tight roll like so many corporate ladder climbers did, and she was sure that she'd move up, one day. She was cute, too, Giji thought, in a bookish sort of way. Thin and blonde, with actual horned rimmed glasses like you'd see in a hair color commercial where the strict teacher lets loose on Friday nights. Giji had more than one impure thought about Charmaine and she giggled about it.

But back to business, she answered the phone, so now star 69 would only show the office as the last call. Giji, hung the phone back on its stand and vowed to get the mouth breather next time.

***

Since the evening she confronted Lex about his indiscretion, he had been keeping doctor's hours. No more nighttime consultations!

For the most part, things had gone back to normal, whatever that was! Their perfect little family seemed unblemished, at least on the surface. The kids, especially Danielle, had been uneasy for a few days, sulking more than usual, looking afraid as if waiting for the next bomb to fall.

But, there had been none. Connie had made sure of that.

She fantasized about following Lex and confronting his lover (whoever she was) and letting her know she would never be more than a mistress. She would never act on it, although running over Lex with the family Volvo again and again did have a certain macabre appeal. Connie found more strength and control in making sure the affair went absolutely nowhere. How she would love to see the look on Lex's slut's face when she realized this was it. There would be sex but nothing more, ever.

Connie would never let go and Lex knew that. He also knew

better than anyone that she would not allow any disruption that would threaten their family, so arguing was pointless. She and Lex were essentially unchanged by the revelation of his affair

They shared a bed, but they hadn't really been intimate. The last time they were intimate was such a long time ago that Connie had forgotten when it had been. How many weeks? Months? She didn't know, but she had stopped pretending to be interested in sex with her husband once she realized he was no longer interested. It had almost been a relief, she recalled. But then there had been the revelation that he was not going unfulfilled… She pushed the thoughts from her mind.

Connie lay on the bed, trying to be interested in her book, but listening for movement from downstairs. Presently, she heard the sounds she expected, Lex coming home and climbing the stairs to the master bedroom.

Lex entered their bedroom, closing the door behind him. She glanced up quickly, then back at her book.

"We need to talk," Lex announced.

"Then let's talk," she said and closed her book, letting it remain on her lap. Taking off her reading glasses, she placed them on the book and looked up at him.

"I'm all ears. What's so important?"

"You want things to be like they were when we were younger," Lex began quietly, "close I mean. We need to work on that."

"What do you suggest?" Connie wanted to know.

Lex shrugged. "I don't know," he lied. "I was thinking…I saw an ad on the bulletin board at the hospital for a sex therapist."

"Really?" Connie sounded surprised, "A sex therapist?"

"Yes." Lex sat on the edge of the bed beside Connie and turned to face her. "She's called the Sexual Psychic."

"What kind of sex therapist has a name like that?" Connie demanded. "That doesn't sound like a legitimate sex therapist to me."

"She may be a little unconventional," Lex admitted. "But, I'm sure she's a qualified professional…"

"Well, I'm not sure," Connie said. "I'm not going to see someone who works out of a rundown strip mall or smutty porn shop to discuss the most intimate details of my life. If you want to see this Sexual Psychic, then you'll have to go alone."

Lex stood, shoulders slumped. "I was hoping you'd be a little more open minded," he said, disappointed. "I was under the impression that our marriage is worth saving."

"I'm not the one having the affair," Connie threw at him, her tone of voice flat and controlled. "I thought I made it perfectly clear the other night that our marriage is in no danger, only your love life!"

Lex threw up his hands. "Okay, fine," he said, defeated. "I give up."

"If you want to see this sexual pervert or whatever," Connie called after Lex as he stormed out of the room, "be my guest!"

Connie lay back against her pillow and closed her eyes. Initially, after finding out that her husband was seeing someone else, Connie wanted to change, to be more spontaneous, more like the woman Lex said he had always wanted. That was just a knee jerk reaction when she realized she had lost any control she had.

It was true that she wanted to be more spontaneous, to enjoy life a little more than she had during most of the years she'd been married, but she wanted it for her sake. She wanted to let go, throw caution to the wind and not worry about the outcome, but she had learned that when you feel comfortable and let your guard down, things slip out of your hands and you learned things about people that you never wanted to know. Control was all she had…

12

The Fruit Salad

"See you later, Giji," Mrs. Hoover called. "Be sure to be home for dinner, I'm making another scrumptious casserole!" Mrs. Hoover didn't wait for an answer, just let the door swing closed after her. Giji watched from the window as she got in her old car and fired it up. As soon as she saw the old woman veer off down the street, she grabbed her towel and tugged on the bottoms of her new, sheer, lime green bikini and went out into the back yard.

I'll have to make alternate plans for dinner, she thought to herself as she laid the towel over the lawn chair. She lay back and closed her eyes, thinking about the handsome cop she had spent a few minutes with in the back of his patrol car the other day, and felt herself begin to get wet. She squirmed and changed position, lying on her side, and then her back again, facing up so that the sun could hit her just right.

She was half asleep when she felt someone kissing her neck. Well, actually, licking her neck, and in her half asleep state she was sure it was Nick, who lived just across the yard. She was still half asleep when the licking went lower and lower, stopping at her stomach, and then made its way down to her pussy, big, soggy laps through the sheer fabric of her new, lime green bikini.

She decided not to move, if this was the way he wanted it, so be it. She had held still for worse pleasures. But when she felt him nose into her, she bolted upright, wide awake. No guy had a nose that big and wet.

"Stop it, Bismarck!" she yelled. "Stop it!"

Oh, gross! It wasn't Nick after all, but his huge golden retriever, Bismarck!

She heard the bushes move, and pulled away from the huge dogs tongue just as Nick crashed through. He got the dog by the collar and pulled him back. Giji saw that he was trying, unsuccessfully, to keep from laughing.

"I'm glad you find this so humorous," she said, standing and grabbing her towel. In an unprecedented move Giji covered herself with it.

"I'm sorry, Giji," Nick apologized, "It appears he's really taken with you. I've never seen him this enthusiastic."

"Yeah, wow," Giji said sarcastically, "he's a regular Rudolph Valentino!"

"You must just… smell nice," Nick said and looked away, determined not to laugh again.

"Hmmph!" Giji said, disgusted.

"What can I do to make it up to you?" Nick asked.

Giji thought for a moment.

"You know, Mrs. Hoover is such a lonely old bird, why don't you come have dinner with her tonight?"

***

Pulling into the parking area in front of the rundown strip mall, Lex recalled Connie's comment the night before about being "located in a rundown strip mall or porn shop." Here was the Sexual Psychic nestled among a single row of tiny shops, many had gone out of business. He parked and sat for a minute, looking at the front of the shop. He wondered how things had gotten so out of control between them and then he went inside.

The shop was exactly as he had imagined. Dark but clean, he sat in the same chair Mrs. Hoover frequented, without his knowledge, and was about to pour himself a cup of tea from the ever present pot when a small Asian woman came from behind curtain that lead to an adjoining room. She greeted him with a polite, if somewhat gummy smile, then introduced herself and asked his name.

Presently he found himself sitting across from Kimiko, shuffling her cards and cutting them three times to the left. The little Asian woman dealt them out.

"What the trouble with you?" she asked.

"I'm not …getting what I need at home anymore," said Lex self consciously.

"I see that, you having affair." The small Asian woman looked up from the cards. "I ask again, what the matter with you?"

Lex looked surprised.

"I'm a psychic that what the sign says," Kimiko reminded him. "You want advice? You going to have to be straight with me."

"My wife doesn't understand me and seems to have lost interest in sex," said Lex, "I didn't know what to do, this was my last resort."

"Last resort?" Kimiko frowned. "You try marriage counseling? You try being nice to her? I don't think this your last resort at all, that's what I think."

She studied the cards and her voice softened.

"You be sad all the time. You not getting what you need at home, your wife is punishing you, but you deserve it."

"Yes, I guess I do," said Lex, standing up to leave, "how much do I owe you?"

"You sit back down, Kimiko not finished with you," she gestured to the chair.

Lex sighed again and sat back down. He realized he sighed a lot, lately.

"It not her fault," said Kimiko as she turned another card.

"Yes, we already established that this is my fault," said Lex.

"No, no that not what I mean. She had...how you say it? Trauma in childhood. Doesn't trust anyone. Never has, never will. Need for perfection, need to have everyone see she is always ok. Very controlling that one."

"That's amazing!" Lex said, his voice rising excitedly. "You can see all that?"

"Of course, I see." Kimiko gave him a mysterious look. "I can help you this once, too."

"How, what do I have to do?"

"Kimiko teach you sacred, ancient sex ways to make her feel good. You try on her, you have one happy wife."

"What is it, a book?" said Lex, thinking she was going to try to sell him a copy of the **Kama Sutra**.

"No, no book, you will need hands on experience, I think," said Kimiko. She stood in front of him and in one movement dropped her kimono. She was older and small, but very shapely and strong looking. Her Asian skin was dark and smooth. She pulled a pin out of the bun in her hair and it fell across her shoulders in a wave. Lex could feel himself begin to get aroused, even though he fought it. It didn't seem right.

"I know it not seem right," said Kimiko said. Apparently she can read minds, Lex thought. "But it the only way."

She led him to an old ratty couch and undid his belt. She then gently undid his jeans and pulled them down. Pushing him onto the couch, she climbed on top of him and put his now hard cock inside her. She was tight, much tighter than Lex had expected. He moaned and she smiled.

"Ancient oriental exercises," she explained, "I practice all the time, keep tight for your pleasure. You can teach your wife to do them, too, but for now just listen to me."

Lex took both of her hips in his hands and began to push against her.

"No, no touching," she said, "you just lay there, it is called

Tantric, and neither of us move until it over."

"But why?" pleaded Lex, who was going crazy. She felt so good.

"Trust," Kimiko told him. "Your wife need to trust you again. If you don't move, just lie there and look at her, she will learn that you are thinking of her, not other woman."

She continued to sit on him and look deep into his eyes. Neither one of them moved.

Soon Lex felt something growing inside him. It built up and came in a rush, all of a sudden. He climaxed so violently that they almost fell off the couch.

When he was done, Kimiko got off of him and went into another room, Lex figured she must be cleaning up, as he hadn't cum that hard in as long as he could remember, not with the women he had affairs with and certainly not Connie.

"You go home now and remember that," said the psychic as she came back into the room. She pulled her kimono around her and in a flash had it tied her hair back up in a bun.

Lex tried to stammer something but she gently pushed him toward the door, stopping only to get the money for the reading. As Lex sat in his car in the parking lot he tried to figure out what had just happened and then shrugging his shoulders, headed home.

***

SueAnn glanced once more at the clock. There was just over an hour before Nick would be home from work; it was time to get busy on the little surprise she had in store for him when he walked through his door. She smiled when she thought of the look her new neighbor would have on his face when he walked through his bedroom door.

Peering into her refrigerator, SueAnn gathered a basket full of food items that were an essential part of her plan. She filled the basket with some cherries and sliced bananas, which she had prepared earlier that day. For Nick's delicious fruit salad surprise, she would need whipped cream.

How tantalizingly sweet this fruit salad would be for her, when her new neighbor sampled the fruit as he made his way to her more forbidden fruits. SueAnn shivered with excitement, anticipating her delight when Nick finally began to taste her forbidden fruit.

Once she had gathered all the necessary ingredients for her surprise salad, SueAnn made her way next door to Nick's house. Letting herself in the front door, she headed straight for his bedroom.

After removing all her clothes, SueAnn climbed onto Nick's bed with her basket. Slowly, she sprayed the whipped cream until her whole body was covered with cool, white puffs. She then took the sliced bananas and put a line from the cleavage between her breasts all the way to the mound between her legs. SueAnn then filled her bellybutton with a large cherry and topped off her special salad with a cherry on each nipple. The cool whipped cream against her hot skin added to her excitement.

SueAnn kept an almost continuous watch on the time, with the help of a small alarm clock that sat on the nightstand next to Nick's bed. While she lay there, time crept by painfully slow. The time when Nick should have been home came and went, and as the minutes continued to tick by, SueAnn became increasingly nervous.

Nick was never late coming home from work. In fact, he was so predictable you could set an alarm by him. Why did he have to pick the one day that she wanted to surprise him to be late?

SueAnn knew she was melting; sticky sweet fruit juices were spreading all over her body. She could feel the juice seeping down her breasts and her thighs. The sticky liquid was making its way onto her hairy mound and down between her pussy lips. She was overwhelmed with the sudden urge to wipe away the sticky juice, but instead she continued to lie there, not moving. The last thing she wanted to do was ruin the effect.

She began to wonder if maybe she shouldn't have planned this surprise without giving Nick some hint to make sure he was home on time. SueAnn was just about ready to get off the bed and clean herself up when she heard the front door open. Listening closely, she realized that there was more than one set of footsteps. She should do something, but she was shocked and found it nearly impossible to move.

SueAnn had no idea who could be with Nick, but she desperately hoped that they remained downstairs.

With her heart racing she listened as footsteps made their way up the stairs. She desperately hoped they were Nick's footsteps. With hindsight, she should have closed the bedroom door before climbing onto the bed and making herself into a fruit salad.

SueAnn kept her eyes on the doorway; knowing that she would be fully exposed to whomever it was coming up the stairs, but she also realized there was no time to cleanup before the person reached the bedroom door.

Her breath caught in her throat when the stranger stepped through the open door. The older looking man came to an abrupt halt when his eyes caught sight of her lying on the bed.

A few seconds later, realization dawned in the man's eyes and a look of amusement spread across his face.

"Hello, I almost didn't see you laying there."

"Hi," SueAnn had to force the greeting from her lips.

"You must be Nick's new girlfriend. I'm Nick's dad, Mac. I'll be visiting for a few days."

"Nice to meet you," she said as she was making an attempt to be polite even though at that moment she just wanted to completely cover herself in the wilting fruit.

Nick's dad was smiling mischievously. "It's nice to meet you, too. Nick has told me a lot about you, but apparently there are a few things he left out."

The older man paused as he studied SueAnn with a thoughtful gaze.

"What are you suppose to be, some kind of fruitcake?"

So embarrassed she could only nod, SueAnn tried to cover her most intimate parts with her hands, but it was no use. She couldn't cover everything!

SueAnn heard more footsteps and looked toward the door. "Oh," Nick said stood in the doorway. He looked at SueAnn then at his dad, who seemed amused and maybe slightly aroused by the scene before him. "I see you two have met."

SueAnn nodded and tried to smile. "It was supposed to be a surprise," she said weakly as she looked at Nick's handsome face and then down at the fruit and whipped cream that covered part of her body. "I guess the surprise is on me!"

Nick cleared his throat. "Listen, Dad, let's clear out so the pretty lady can have some privacy," he suggested, placing a hand on his dad's shoulder.

Nick gave her a helpless look as he and his dad started out of the room.

SueAnn slipped out of bed the moment she heard their footsteps on the stairs. In the adjoining bathroom, she quickly wiped herself on a towel, but the whipped cream had dried and would not wipe off completely. Unwilling to take the time to shower given what had occurred and wanting desperately to be in her own home with her head under the covers, hiding like she did when she was a little girl after being embarrassed by her dad falling down drunk in front of her friends. SueAnn took Nick's thick, oversized bathrobe from the hook on the back of the bathroom door and slipped it on.

SueAnn crept slowly down the stairs, hoping she would not bump into Nick or his father which was the last thing she wanted. At the bottom of the stairs, he heard Nick and his father talking in the living room. She couldn't make out what they were saying, but occasionally they punctuated their words with loud laughter. Imagining they were laughing at the stupidity of her fruit salad idea and the scene they'd walked in on, she hurried through the kitchen and out the back door. Almost running, she headed straight for her own back door and hoped that no one saw her!

13

Doin' It... In the Dirt!

SueAnn practically ran across Mrs. Hoover's lawn, then into her own yard and in her backdoor. When she stepped inside the door, she slammed it closed behind her and leaned against it, relieved to be home and away from everyone's prying eyes. She felt like she would die of embarrassment.

She could only imagine what Nick's father thought and she hoped Nick wasn't too upset with her. It was humiliating as she closed her eyes and thought about it. Looking back it occurred to her that the entire mess probably looked like something Giji would do. Then it occurred to her that even Giji might not do something that humiliating.

It would be nice to just block out the entire incident, then she realized it would be better to go back and erase it. She didn't want anyone to know what she had done. Thankfully, Nick's dad lived out of town. He wouldn't be able to tell anyone and she hoped Nick wouldn't either. If anyone in the neighborhood found out, she would not be able to face her neighbors again–not even the ones who were her friends!

She wasn't sure how long she leaned against the door, but after a while she heard a knock and it was followed by another knock. She peeped through the hole. Nick was carrying a bag which contained her neatly folded clothes, so no one could see them.

"Thank you," she said softly, opening the door but she couldn't look him in the eye. She took the stack of clothes and placed them on the small table beside the door. "I appreciate that," she added, relieved that she didn't need to retrieve them from Nick's house.

"You're welcome," Nick said.

She was relieved he didn't sound angry. She glanced down at Nick's soiled robe.

"I'll wash your robe," she said, "and get it back to you."

"Thanks," he put his hand under her chin and lifted her face to his.

"SueAnn, I know what just happened was... embarrassing for you, but it's really not a big deal."

"Then why do I feel so awful?" she asked, unconvinced.

"Because it was uncomfortable and embarrassing," he told her, "but it's not that big of a deal. My dad was pleasantly surprised, not shocked."

"He must think I'm the worse kind of person," she guessed.

"No," he said sincerely. "He thinks you're a great girl, really attractive and definitely not boring!"

She laughed softly. "Well, I guess that's not too bad." She looked him in the eye. "What else did he think?"

He took her in his arms.

"Oh, if he was young, he'd give me some competition for you!"

"Ooh, I like your father," SueAnn said, smiling.

"Wanna meet him?"

"Again?" SueAnn asked incredulously. "Now?"

Nick nodded. "Uh-huh. Right now."

"Well," SueAnn tried to decide how to phrase her explanation. "I'm kind of still... getting over the embarrassment of our first meeting."

"I see." He seemed disappointed.

"But, I'd love to see him again, the next time he visits." SueAnn said quickly.

"Okay," Nick agreed, then gave her a quick kiss. "I gotta run."

"So soon?" said SueAnn, "Can't you stay a little longer?"

"I wish I could." He sighed heavily. "But my dad is here and I do have to visit with him."

"Of course," SueAnn agreed. "Tell him it was nice...well..."

"I'll just tell him you appreciated the compliments," Nick said.

"Yes," SueAnn sounded relieved. "That would be great."

He kissed her again, this time a little longer.

"Are you really sure...?" she asked quietly.

He nodded and let go of her. "I'm sure, but we'll pick up where we left off soon," he promised.

"I would like that," she said as he turned to leave. "Promise you won't tell anyone what I did?" She thought of the teasing she'd get if Giji found out.

"Cross my heart, he said, "it'll be our little secret, just the three of us."

She smiled and shut the door behind him. As much as she liked Nick, she couldn't help but feel there was still something he was keeping from her.... At that very moment, though, it didn't seem that important.

***

For the first time in a long time, Lex didn't roll over and turn his back to Connie as soon as they were in bed. Connie wondered why as she closed her book, removed her reading glasses, and placed them on her nightstand. Lex glanced over at her as if he wanted to say something, but he didn't speak.

"I guess we should get some sleep," Connie said quietly and turned out the light.

"Uh-huh," Lex agreed, but he didn't turn over.

She could feel his warm breath on her bare shoulder. The warmth made her long for his touch, but she was determined not to reach out for him. Instead she lay on her back in the dark and didn't turn away from him, either. Connie closed her eyes and placed her head against his bare chest, feeling his strong arms around her. It had been so long. It felt so good, but she was curious about why Lex wanted to be close to her.

"What happened, Lex, why are you doing this...now?" she finally said, pulling away from him just a little bit.

"What?" Lex asked incredulously. "Can't I spend time with my wife and be close without being interrogated?" He wanted to try the Tantric position that Kimiko had shown him, but didn't know how to approach the subject. Instead, he immediately reverted back to being defensive.

Connie sighed. "Yes, Lex," she said. "I'm sorry. It's just not like you lately. It's been so long. I've forgotten..."

"I haven't," he told her. "I miss this. I miss you, Connie."

She looked up at him in the dark, seeing the flash of his eyes and wanting desperately to believe him, but there was a part of her that just couldn't fully believe in him or trust him again, no matter how much she wanted it.

"I miss us," he said softly.

Connie said nothing.

While Lex kissed her neck and worked his way down, Connie thought about dinner tomorrow night. Feeling she had no control over the situation, she laid still as he tried to get her to get on top of him, eventually giving up and making love to her as best as he could.

Connie wondered why Lex had made love to her for the first time in months. She wanted to believe that he'd done it because he wanted her. But, she couldn't help being suspicious that he felt guilty for something that she did not know about or his lover rejected him and he had nowhere else to turn.

Unable to find the answers she sought, Connie finally turned away from Lex and made herself think of other things. Shortly, she found herself thinking of preparing meals, specifically about what she would make for dinner the next evening. Of course, she could borrow a casserole recipe from Mrs. Hoover, but the last time she did that, they threw the casserole out and ordered pizza. Wishing she could come up with a wonderful unique dinner for her family, Connie drifted off to sleep....

***

Even though Connie spent the time she should have enjoyed making love with her husband thinking about food, she still couldn't figure out what to make for dinner. Out of ideas and feeling a little disjointed, she decided to take a cooking class at the local community college. She remembered seeing the ad for a new class, and how attractive the instructor was... Chef Real Charbonneau. What a wonderful name! So masculine, so sexy, she decided. Dark skin seemed even darker against his crisp white chef's attire, with strong features and piercing eyes that seemed as though they could see into her soul! Yes, she decided, a cooking class was exactly what she needed. In the back of her mind, she began to wonder what food had to do with sex, and control...

She found the Sunday newspaper's Home & Food section and circled the ad. There was a black and white newsprint picture of the locally famous chef. He was even more handsome than she remembered.

But she quickly snapped back to reality. "I should be interested in taking a cooking class, not in how gorgeous the instructor is!" she remonstrated herself.

Connie dialed the number and when a young lady answered, she said "Yes, hello, I saw your ad in the Sunday paper for a cooking class...?"

"Chef Real's class?" the girl asked.

"Yes, yes, that's the one," Connie told her. "He will be the instructor for the class... I mean... he'll be actually teaching the class himself, right? Not one of his assistants... or protégés?"

"Oh, yes, Mr. Charbonneau, Chef Real, will be the instructor."

"Great," Connie said, pleased. "Then sign me up!"

***

Ariella followed John out to the side of the house and looked at the area between the porch and the hedges. She pulled her bath robe closer and glanced around the neighborhood. Nope, no one could see into the side yard. She watched her young gardener move around through the shrubbery and couldn't wait to feel him inside her. She asked him about some extra curricular activity yesterday when he had come to start the hedges, but he had had to put her off until today.

"You said you wanted to do it in the dirt," John reminded her.

"I know," Ariella admitted, "but that was just said in the heat of the moment. I'm not even sure this is sanitary!"

"I have an old tarp," John told her and held up a dingy, stained piece of canvas.

Ariella frowned, wondering which would be cleaner–the bare soil or the filthy old tarp. But she felt her nipples beginning to get hard against the thin material of her robe, and knew that she would do this. The wetness between her legs confirmed it.

"Okay, okay." She reached a quick decision. "Spread it out."

John, who had been doing lawn projects for Ariella and Marco since they had moved in, noticed Ariella looking at him and licking her lips all summer. She was great looking, and he didn't have a moral problem with the fact that she was married. He had taken his share of bored housewives over the season and considered it one of the perks of the job. They never wanted to become attached, didn't call him late at night, and there was never any pressure for something more. He winked at her and spread out the old tarp, motioning Ariella to lay down on it.

She wondered for a second what on earth she was doing this for and then threw her head back as John started to tweak and pinch her nipples lightly. He stripped off his shirt and she could see a rippling chest – he could probably have any girl he wanted. But, he was on his knees in her side yard between the hedges and the house, mouthing her and fondling her in a way she hadn't been touched in a month, unless you counted the cable guy the other day…

He pulled his jeans down to just below his tight ass, and paused long enough for her to get a good look at what she was getting. He was young and hard, and he smiled down at her while he put his hand between her legs. After what seemed like an eternity of fingering her and looking her in the eyes, he playfully placed the head of his cock against her clit and held it there. Ariella thought she would explode with that, but he winked and pushed himself inside, moving in and out of her like a pro. She sighed and licked his neck, which made him pump her that much harder. She arched her back and began to grind against him, stopping only to change position slightly when a rock found its way into the small of her back. She would cum this time for sure and she hadn't even been aroused by the cable guy, but this one was hot. As she reached the peak of climax she tightened her legs around John's waist…

"Ariella, I'm home!" Marco called from inside the house.

"Get off of me quick!" Ariella said loudly into John's ear as he worked his expert tongue over one of her nipples. *Damn,* she thought, *missed it again!*

John rolled off, still in the throes of ecstasy, his cock having just shot its load in the final frenzied moments of increased excitement by Marco's sudden presence, stood erect. He quickly stuffed it back into his tight jeans and zipped up while Ariella got to her feet and pulled her robe tightly around herself. Ariella gave the young gardener a cautioning look, then she turned and walked around the side of the house onto the patio.

"What were you doing?" Marco asked, standing just outside the French doors that led from the patio into the house.

"Oh, John was just showing me the new plantings," Ariella lied easily. John appeared at the side of the house, rolling up the tarp and looking around, seemingly for his shovel.

"New plantings?" Marco repeated, confused. "There aren't supposed to be any new plantings."

"Did I say new plantings?" Ariella saved quickly. "I meant newly trimmed hedges."

"In your bathrobe?"

"That's my fault," John said as he came toward them. Ariella froze. "I have to leave right away, but I needed your missus to tell me if the hedges were straight."

"We have some other trimming to do tomorrow, John, if you could come back then," Ariella said, pushing a damp strand of black hair from her face.

"Sure thing, ma'am," John said.

Ariella kissed Marco quickly on the lips as she walked passed him, just in time to wink back at John, who was shaking Marco's hand and carrying the rolled up tarp under his arm.

14

Those 1970s Pants!

Mrs. Hoover had already turned in for the night when it occurred to her that she should make sure her little red book was in its proper hiding place. After all, if Giji got up during the night or beat her up in the morning, she didn't want her nosy houseguest finding her diary and her secrets! Anything of value is worth protecting, she told herself as she climbed out of bed, stuck her feet in her slippers, quietly left her room and headed downstairs.

Not wanting to risk breaking her neck, Mrs. Hoover made her way slowly and cautiously down the stairs and entered the den. There, she clicked on the desk lamp and set about opening her secret drawer. Her late husband designed the spot to hide a little money or small valuables like jewelry or old coins. First, she removed the contents and the drawer appeared empty. The old papers, some legal stuff and bills that needed to be paid, a couple of pictures, nothing anyone riffling through it would find interesting, sat on the top of the rosewood desk.

When the drawer was empty, she reached underneath and flicked a spring, making the bottom of the drawer pop up. This was where all the secrets of the neighborhood were kept, all the juicy tidbits that would finance her retirement and make it possible for her to travel. She was almost giddy every time she opened it.

Except this time… it was empty!

Martha Hoover couldn't believe her eyes. She ran her hand around inside the false bottom, but if she couldn't see it when she opened the drawer, it just wasn't there. The drawer wasn't big enough for the precious little book to have slipped behind something, but she dug out the bottom and looked underneath, anyway.

She felt herself starting to panic. Who would have come in here and known where to look? Who possibly could have taken it?

Giji, that's who, that's the only person who might have seen her one evening putting the book away. Giji must have stood outside the door and seen her putting the book into the false bottom drawer. Mrs. Hoover glanced toward the open doorway. Yes, Giji could have stood there without her knowing it. What if Giji read it already? She couldn't take that chance. Giji was sleeping upstairs and Mrs. Hoover would have to go into her room and search tonight.

She crept slowly up the stairs; her heart was beating so fast! She opened the door to Giji's room and took a couple of tentative steps inside, only to trip over one of the slut's stiletto heels! She landed on Giji with a loud "hrrumph!" Giji let out a scream and pushed the old woman off of her. Martha landed on the floor with another "hurrumph."

"Who-ooo is…?" Giji said, suddenly awake and hoping her groper was at least someone who she wanted feeling her up.

"It-it's me," Mrs. Hoover said slowly.

"What are you doing on top of me?" Giji wanted to know.

"I - I was well," Mrs. Hoover stammered and she did not want to tip Giji off that her little red book was missing. Suppose Giji offered to help her look for it? The last thing she wanted was her nosy houseguest getting her busy little hands on the diary before she did. "I was just looking for the cat. I thought I heard her in here."

"What?" Giji said in a loud voice. "Mrs. Hoover, you don't have a cat, remember?" Giji couldn't believe it. First this old bat had gotten her all liquored up and molested her, and now she was taking it further by coming into her room at night! Right in the middle of one of her Harrison Ford dreams!

"Hmmm, you're right," Mrs. Hoover agreed. "I guess I was dreaming and walked in here in my sleep. That's it, I was sleepwalking."

"Since when do you sleepwalk?" Giji asked suspiciously.

"Sorry, Giji," Mrs. Hoover said, slowly climbing to her feet and ignoring Giji's question. "Go back to sleep, dear."

"Whatever," Giji said as she rolled over. It was late and she didn't want to get into it. Besides, if she went back to sleep right now, she may be able to find Harrison where she'd left him.

Mrs. Hoover stumbled through the darkened room, making her way slowly and cautiously back to the door. She closed the door behind her and sighed. *Damn! Where could her diary be?* She was almost sure that Giji had found it, but didn't want to risk going into her room again. After Giji left for work in the morning, Mrs. Hoover would snoop around her room. She went into her own room and decided to read for awhile before turning out the light.

She flipped on the light and there was her little red book, right where she'd left it, on her bedside table. Then she remembered that she was making notes before she fell asleep last night. A little embarrassed, but more relieved that her secrets hadn't been found, she grabbed the book and shoved it as far back into her headboard shelf as she could. She would return it to its proper place in the morning and she would have to be more careful! She climbed into bed and thought about what would happen if the book ever fell into the wrong hands. Her thoughts also wandered to the fact that Giji slept in the nude.

***

"Look what I found in the attic!" Mrs. Hoover held up a pair of multi-colored psychedelic short-shorts. She had been rummaging in the attic and when she found them, all she could think about was landing on a naked Giji the night before. She had grabbed them up and practically ran down the stairs.

"Ah!" Giji's eye lit up. "Are those what I think they are?"

"Hot pants!" Mrs. Hoover chimed.

Giji threw her magazine aside and stood up. "Wow, I haven't seen those since… I was a little girl!"

Mrs. Hoover's eyes twinkled. "Want to try them on?" she asked quickly. "You have a slim body, like I did. I bet they'll fit."

Giji pushed her tight shorts down and kicked them playfully off her toes while Mrs. Hoover watched. Standing there in her tiny black thong, she felt a bit self-conscious, especially with Mrs. Hoover's eyes glued to her. Quickly she took the short-shorts from Mrs. Hoover and with a little effort poured herself into them.

Wow! Mrs. Hoover thought, licking her lips. I can see everything. Tight hot hips and sweet, pouty pussy lips! Now if I could just get SueAnn in a pair…"You look sensational!" she gushed as Giji spun around, showing off her obvious assets.

"You mean sex-sational!" Giji chimed, and then she noticed something she had somehow missed.

"Whee! Whee! Look at me!" Mrs. Hoover said cheerfully, dancing around, shaking her enormous bubble butt. "Don't I look sexy?"

Giji couldn't believe Mrs. Hoover had found a pair of stretch hot pants covered with pink and yellow daisies and had somehow squeezed herself into them. It was a hideous sight–especially the way Mrs. Hoover's ass seemed to giggle as she danced. Like watching gelatin fight for its life, Giji decided, repulsed.

Obscene!

"Yeah," Giji finally said, trying to hide her shock. "Look at you!"

"Look at us," Mrs. Hoover corrected and started bumping her lower body against Giji's much smaller hips. When the older woman started backing her lower posterior toward her, Giji suddenly froze. All she could see was two huge mounds of ass flesh jiggling and wiggling as if trying to break free of the tight confines of Mrs. Hoover's hot pants.

"Hey, look," Giji said suddenly, pointing out the living room window. "There's SueAnn getting her mail. I should show these off to her. Show her what a real woman should look like. Maybe she'll finally trade in those god-awful sweats she wears!"

"Yeah," Mrs. Hoover agreed, still shaking her enormous rump. "Ask if she'd like to try on a pair." She licked her lips, already visualizing SueAnn's sweet pussy and firm ass being held tightly in a pair of faux leather hot pants. "I have more where these came from!"

"I'll bet you do." said Giji, leaving so quickly the screen door banged shut behind her. She practically skipped to the street to where SueAnn stood at her mailbox.

"Hey, SuSu," Giji greeted SueAnn. "What's shaking?"

"They caught the peeping tom," SueAnn announced, not looking up from her mail. "And don't call me SuSu."

"Really?" Giji was surprised. Here was some information she might be able to use.

"Yeah, it was a chubby teenager a couple of streets over. His lawyers are blaming it on his receding hairline and erectile dysfunction or something."

"Ooh," Giji said and shivered, thinking of her obscene phone caller. She wondered if he could have been the caller. It went completely over her head to ask what a teenager was doing with ED and a receding hairline. "So he had Ed?"

SueAnn giggle at the way Giji said it. "No, silly, E.D. its short for erectile dysfunction, it's not pronounced Ed like a person!"

"Silly me!" Giji laughed. *Arrogant know-it-all bitch,* she thought. Before she could ask when they had caught him, SueAnn continued.

"I went out with Nick night before last," SueAnn said, gloating.

"Oh." Giji sounded disappointed. "Hope you two had a lovely time."

"Uh-huh." SueAnn pretended that it was just conversation–that she didn't mean to get under Giji's skin about Nick, even though she was having a hard time sounding casual about it. She looked up from her mail and was stunned to see Giji in short-shorts.

"What's wrong?" Giji asked, confused by SueAnn's expression. "You've never seen a woman in hot pants?"

"Not since the 1970s," SueAnn lied, taking advantage of every opportunity to get under Giji's skin, while trying to sound casual.

She just couldn't help it. Giji made an ass of herself around Nick ever since he had moved into the neighborhood. Nick was nice enough to give her his key and ask her to watch his place when he was out of town. But, Giji couldn't get it through her head that he was being nice and giving Giji a break from Mrs. Hoover when he was on a business trip. It made SueAnn alternately feel sad for her and angry at her that Giji couldn't see Nick's kindness for what it was, and instead she assumed it was a come on.

"Well, for your information," Giji snapped, "guys love them!" She paused, but when she didn't get a reaction from SueAnn, she added; "Besides I hear they're making a comeback!"

SueAnn looked right at her and laughed out loud, "Yeah? Right behind eight-tracks and Coppertone appliances!"

"Mrs. Hoover has extras in her attic," Giji said, realizing she wasn't getting anywhere with this conversation. "Want to try on a pair?"

"Mrs. Hoover has extra hot pants in her attic." SueAnn repeated and gave a long pause continuing to look Giji in the eye. "Hmmm, I'll try on a pair of Mrs. Hoover's hot pants say about the time hell freezes over!" SueAnn stuck her mail in her sweatshirt pocket and turned away.

"Well," Giji said with a knowing grin, "Sounds like you're going to need a heavy coat. Mrs. Hoover has a couple of those, too!"

***

"I am Chef Real," Real had said while introducing himself to the class. "Real Charbonneau. I am French-Canadian." He looked out at the class, a proud look in his warm eyes, with a pleasant smile on his face. "I will be your instructor."

Connie couldn't help thinking, *Ooh La La!* He had the effect of bringing her out of herself and she wanted to resist the freedom it provided, but she enjoyed feeling unrestrained. She'd been lonely and bored during the problems with Lex. For the first time in what seemed like an eternity, she was actually excited about something, about something that did not include her husband, her family, or housecleaning. She was excited about the community college cooking class and she could hardly sleep the night before class started. Just like a school girl, she chided herself before going to bed. She took an extra hot shower that morning and was dressed a little too nice for a college cooking class Connie got to class early and picked out a spot near the front. When he finally came into the room and the class started, she could hardly believe her eyes. Chef Real was such a handsome man! He was much better looking in person than in the photo with the newspaper insert with the advertisement for the school.

Right before they began to work on the Béarnaise sauce she went up to introduce herself to him.

"Hello, Chef Real," Connie had said shyly, "I'm Connie, and I've been looking for a good all purpose sauce for my chicken." *You idiot!* she thought. *How lame is that?*

"No, Real. Ree-AL. I'm French-Canadian."

"Ree-al."

"Yes. You say it much better than I do." They looked into each other's eyes, and suddenly it was as if the room receded into nothingness and everyone else ceased to exist, it was just Connie and Chef Real for eternity. After the short break, the Béarnaise sauces were simmering and he walked about, checking on each student's progress. When he reached Connie's area, he paused and looking over her shoulder, which made Connie a bit nervous and more than a little excited.

"Béarnaise," said Connie, "it sounds so exotic!"

"Actually, béarnaise sauce is just a fancy way of saying hollandaise; it's made with tarragon and white wine, that's really the only difference." Chef Real said as he looked deep into her eyes for longer than either of them realized. The rest of the class noticed and a few giggled like the schoolgirls that Connie had warned herself against earlier that day. Chef Real leaned over Connie's simmering pot and tasted the sauce off the end of a big, wooden flat spoon.

"Warm?" she asked as he licked his lips. He seemed to be mulling over the spice content, then he winced a little and looked as if he might spit. He set the spoon aside and took one of her hands in his. Guiding her hand over to the spoon, he held it over the edge of the pot.

"You need to stir it slowly," he said.

"Oh," said Connie.

"You must be gentle with béarnaise, it is delicate and will break down if not handled properly…much like a beautiful woman."

"Hmmm," Connie said, not realizing that two of her classmates were making gagging noises behind them.

"Hot!" said Chef Real.

"Ohh, yes." Connie set the spoon down beside the pot and took some more tarragon in her palm. Chef real took a pinch out of her cupped palm and threw it into the pot. The other women in the class looked more than a little annoyed.   "Hmmm, Sweet?"

He looked right into her eyes. *"Very."*

"Oh." Connie seemed surprised. "Naughty... I mean tangy?"

"Tasty!" said the chef.

"Does it taste...good?"

"Delicious," he purred and took her hand in his and kissed it gently but with an air of sensuality.

He seemed to snap out of it and hurriedly went back to the front of the class. The rest of the instruction went on without incident, even though it was obvious to everyone in the room that Connie wasn't exactly protégé material for a master cook. The rest of the class began to roll their eyes behind her, but Connie never noticed, or cared. All she could think of was when the next class would be.

***

Giji was anxious to tell Ariella about her crazy night. She still couldn't get over Mrs. Hoover sneaking into her room in the middle of the night.

"Hey, Ariella, you wouldn't believe what that sex crazy, Mrs. Hoover did last night. She snuck into my room calling for her cat. The bitch doesn't even have a cat. I know she was only pretending to be sleepwalking or whatever."

"She might have been hunting for a little pussy... I mean a little cat." Ariella burst out laughing. "Seriously, maybe she's really loosing her marbles. I mean old people get like that when they're senile."

Giji sneered, "Senile my foot. You're right about what kitty she was looking for and my pussy doesn't come when called. At least, not when called by old ladies stumbling around in the dark."

"Does it meow?" Ariella chirped in mischievously.

Giji pushed Ariella playfully. "I wouldn't go so far as to say that. Under the right conditions my pussy can meow mighty loud as well you know. Want a reminder?" They looked at each other and burst out laughing.

Giji settled down and told Ariella the entire story. "She landed on top of me and tried groping a feel and you know I don't sleep in my clothes. I could have killed her; Harrison Ford and I were getting into some serious loving-making when she interrupted my dream. Try as I might, I couldn't pick up where we left off."

Ariella, ever willing to try anything new to spice up her sex life, decided to tell Giji about watching one of Marco's porn videos. "Forget about Mrs. Hoover. I saw the coolest thing on one of Marco's lesbian porno videos."

Curious, Giji asked, "What was so great and different about this lesbo film?"

"Maybe I shouldn't tell you," Ariella teased.

"Come on, girl, tell me already. What was it?"

"Well, these two lesbians had a two-headed dildo and one inserted it in her pee-pee-"

"OK, we're not three year olds here; it sounds very nasty when you have to call a pussy a pee-pee. Since when did you become such a prude?" Giji threw herself onto the beige sofa in Ariella's living room. Ariella wrinkled her nose and stuck her tongue out at Giji.

"OK, one of them inserted one end of the dildo into her pussy and the other came over her, hunched down a little and pushed herself onto the other end. It was something to see. They were having real fun banging each other. Matter of fact, it was so hot I came in my pants. Uh huh, I can see you want to try it?" Ariella was getting turned on as she watched Giji squeezing her legs together.

"Do you have one?" Giji asked. "It sounds like fun. That way both of us can get fucked at the same time."

"Nope, not yet. Let's go to the dildo store and but one or two. Maybe we can even look around for some handcuffs and stuff. It's been a while since we've done anything really wild." Ariella, sat across from Giji and began rubbing her nipples through her T-shirt. She could feel the hot juices running down her legs.

Giji, hands between her legs, hissed through her teeth. "Ok, we'll go to the adult toy and book store, but that's later. I'm in need of some serious loving right now. Come here, girl." She beckoned Ariella over with her fingers.

"I thought you'd never ask," Ariella teased.

Ariella wasted no time kneeling before Giji's open legs and realized that she wasn't wearing any underwear. The sight of her smooth shaven pussy was too much for Ariella. Licking her lips, she inserted one finger inside her before licking it suggestively. Giji quickly took her pink tank top off. Without any need for words, Ariella reached up and began twirling first one nipple and then the other between her fingers.

"Mmmmm...you know just what I need," Giji murmured as Ariella pinched her left nipple. The sensitive bud tightened at the sensation. Liking Giji's reaction, Ariella lifted her head and took the other nipple in her mouth, flicking her tongue across the tip. She bit back a satisfied smile as Giji trembled at her ministrations.

"Ouch! Ariella, what do you have in this chair? It's bruising my butt," Giji exclaimed.

"Ok, let's go into the bedroom. I promise there are no hard objects on my bed to damage your beautiful body," Ariella replied, a bit sarcastically.

They hurriedly stood, wrapped their arms around each other and they took the few steps into the bedroom. Without missing a beat, Giji threw Ariella onto the bed and knelt above her. "How should I punish you, my fair lady? You were so naughty watching that video without me." Bending her head, Giji gently bit Ariella's love swollen lips. "You are sweet...yep, nectar of the gods." Ariella reached up to touch her, but Giji shook her head to stop her. "Not yet. Lie back and enjoy," she commanded.

Ariella closed her eyes and allowed Giji to have her way with her body. She could hardly breathe as Giji quickly changed positions so that she could lick her cunt. Ariella jerked at the sensation of Giji's tongue against her swollen clit.

***

After bolstering his strength, Marco decided to visit his new son and his mother, Tia. He knew Tia's mom wouldn't welcome him with open arms. She wasn't very happy when she found out that Tia was pregnant. Being a strict Catholic she wasn't very happy that her unmarried daughter was pregnant by a man who couldn't marry her. Nonetheless, he had to see them.

Ringing the doorbell, Marco waited anxiously for Tia to open the door. He was looking forward to seeing his week old son. He knew Tia understood that he couldn't come before but he still felt badly. Clutching the bouquet of yellow roses in his hand, he wondered what his son looked like.

Tia opened the door, a bundle in yellow in her arms. He found it strange that he bought her yellow roses and his son was wrapped so securely in yellow as well. Although not superstitious by nature he wondered if it was a sign.

"Come in," Tia said, seeming pleased to see him. "Put the flowers on the table," she instructed.

"Hi, Tia," he smiled tentatively as he moved to sit beside her on the sofa. He adjusted his butt as a piece of spring from the torn furniture jabbed him in the rear.

Marco looked at Tia, and kissed her quickly on the cheek. "So what's up? Are you doing OK?" Marco was truly concerned. He felt like a heel for getting her in the situation. "How's your mom treating you?"

"She's OK. She adores our son," Tia replied. She smiled down at the bundle in her arms. "He's her first grandson. You know she wished he was born under different circumstances, but it's all good." She looked at him. Marco didn't miss the sadness in her big brown eyes.

"I'm sorry, baby. I wish things were different. If I could marry you I would in a heartbeat." Taking Tia's free left hand in his, he tenderly kissed her fingers.

Tia said nothing.

"What's his name?" Marco questioned.

"I named him Ricky after Ricky Martin," she replied quietly.

"Ricky," he repeated. "It's a good name. I like it."

"I wanted to call him Marco after his daddy, but with you being married and all…" Tia looked at him as she trailed off. "Mama discouraged me, said I've brought enough shame on her family." She paused, then added, "Plus she said you didn't deserve to have him named after you."

Releasing her hand, Marco stood and walked to the window. He looked out at the early morning traffic on the street below. He stood with his back toward Tia, once again overcome with grief for his blunder.

"Marco, do you want to hold your son?" Tia called softly from the sofa.

Marco turned and looked at her. He did love her but there just wasn't a place in his life for her right now. "I sure do, but I'm afraid that I might squeeze him too tightly. I don't want to break anything." Marco had never held a newborn before and was scared.

"Don't be silly. You won't break him," Tia said lightly. "He's not that fragile. Once you support his head he'll be just fine." He held the small bundle out to him. "Come on, hold him."

Marco came to sit beside her again. Tia handed the baby to him. Marco gingerly held his son for the first time. As he looked at his son, tears welled in Marco's eyes. There was no missing the proud look on his face. As the baby opened his eyes to look at him, Marco softly whispered, "I'm your daddy." He looked across at Tia and silently mouthed, "Thank you." Looking back at his son, his heart filled with love for the tiny creature he had helped to create, Marco traced a finger across his son's cheek. "He's so tiny. It's hard to believe that he's real." He smiled at Tia. "He has your smile, Tia," he commented glancing at her.

Tia smiled at his statement. "Mama says the same thing, but he has your kind eyes and strong chin," she said. "I find it hard to look at him and not see you."

"Yes, that pointy chin is definitely his daddy's," Marco beamed. "What a handsome little guy," he added, pride evident in his voice.

"Just like his father," Tia looked lovingly at Marco.

Marco noticed the look in her eyes and was overcome with guilt again. Had he given her false hope that they would have a future? Did she think they would have a life together where they could raise their son and have a family? Thinking of his wife, he felt a stab of sadness. He always thought that he and Arielle would be sharing this moment together after she had just given birth to their first child. Sadly, his wife had never shown any interest whatsoever in starting a family or becoming a mother.

"I probably should go," Marco said, handing the baby back to Tia.

"You just got here," Tia protested, taking their son. "Are you sure you can't stay longer?"

He shook his head. "I have an early flight in the morning," he replied. "I really wish I could stay longer, but I can't. Thank you for letting me see him."

"Okay," she said quietly. He heard the disappointment in her voice. "I'm glad you got to see your son."

"Me, too," he said.

"Tia, I'm back from the store," a woman's voice called from the kitchen.

"Who is that?" Marco asked, startled.

"Oh, no, Mama is back. She helped me find this apartment." He saw the fear in her eyes. "I forgot to tell you she's staying with me to help with Ricky."

Marco looked at her, concerned. "Oh, I see," he stated in a tight voice. "That's good."

"You should leave now, Marco," Tia said. "My mama, she is very…"

As Marco stood the door opened and a heavy-set woman with a murderous look in her eyes stared at him. The hard expression on her face said all there was to say, she thought he was scum. He nervously eyed the broom in her hand.

"You!" she bellowed. "What are you doing here?"

Marco looked to Tia for help. The angry women in front of him looked capable of murder. "Missus, ahh…" Marco stammered. "I… I came by to see your daughter and the baby."

"It's okay, Mama," Tia said in a pleading voice. The baby stirred, waking from his sleep by the noise. Tia gently rocked him back to sleep.

"If you need anything, call my cell," Marco told Tia.

"We'll be fine," Tia assured him.

"I'll take care of my daughter and my grandson," Tia's mother said.

Marco walked over to Tia, kissed his son and told Tia goodbye. He turned his back when Tia's mom delivered the first slap with the broom in her hand.

"Mama, no!" Tia called to her mother.

Ignoring Tia's pleas, her mother whacked Marco again. He ducked his head in a futile attempt to avoid the full force of the descending broom. "You're a married man and you do this to my daughter. She's a good girl and you bring shame on my family, my daughter." Each word was accompanied by another whack of the broom. Dust swirled in the tiny room.

"Ouch!" Marco protested. "Are you crazy?"

"I'll hurt you worst yet," Tia's mother shrieked. "You hurt my baby, now I hurt you." Another blow struck Marco's upraised hands. "I haven't drawn your blood yet." Her demonic look wasn't lost on a whimpering Tia.

The baby was awakened by the ruckus and began to cry at the top of his lungs. The sound jolted everyone in the room. "No, Mama. No!" Tia pleaded. "Not around Ricky. Look how scared he is, plus all this dust isn't good for him."

Her mother put the broom down, pointing a finger at Marco. "See what you cause, you dog. Get out!" she admonished.

Marco quickly left with a reminder to Tia to call if she needed anything.

"You're a fool," her mother told her. "You should let me beat him. He's brought you shame."

"I love him," she said helplessly.

"I wish you didn't. He has hurt you and he will always hurt you," her mother said matter-of-factly. "I know his type. No good."

Tia remained silent as she nursed her son.

"He'll never be with you like the father of a child should be," her mother noted before returning to the kitchen, broom in hand.

15

Two Heads are More Fun!

Together Ariella and Giji went to the adult toy store in search of a dildo. They found a battery powered double-headed dildo. Giggling they made their purchase and hurried home to experiment. Once they got home, Giji had second thoughts, sort of. Gigi looked at Ariella, a faux frown on her face. "You do realize that this is kind of lesbian, don't you?" Her pretense at disapproval wasn't evident to a horny Ariella.

"Yeah, you're a regular tri-sexual. I know, I've heard it all before, you'll try anything once," Ariella snickered.

Giji enjoying the moment, quickly added, "Well, if you'd rather find someone …"

"No, you'll have to do," Ariella interrupted her. "Now how do we do this?"

"What are you asking me for? What do I look like, a porn star?"

Ariella gave her a knowing look. "Well, it didn't exactly come with instructions now did it!" She examined the box she had taken the two headed dildo from. "Made in China, no wonder there aren't any instructions."

"Are you sure you haven't done this before?" Ariella asked Giji.

Giji gave her a blank stare. "Yeah, sure," she said sarcastically, holding the dildo and trying to figure out how they would insert one end into each of their pussies. "I did it with that tall red-haired girl from 'That 70's Show'! She was kind of butch, but really soft!" She gave a short burst of laughter. "Come on, if I'd ever done this before do you think I'd be doing it again. By the way, you're the one who saw the lesbian porno! So, how'd they do it?"

"It didn't look that hard when they were doing it. Anyway, I was too turned on to pay attention to the technical details. They inserted it into the big girl's pussy and then the smaller girl leaned over her and slowly inserted it into her own pussy. You know, like when you're riding a cock. It really seemed easy. Once it was in both pussies they pumped together until the heads of the dildo was making good contact with their pussies. I can still see it."

"Okay, lie on your back. Yes, like that, now spread those legs wide so that I can insert this cock inside your warm cunt," Gigi ordered. "We'll figure it out if we practice." Giji licked her lips and felt herself grow wet. "Now that's a nice sight." Her eyes drooped as she looked at Ariella's exposed clit.

As Giji positioned one end of the dildo between Ariella's pussy lips, while the Latin beauty used her fingers to spread her lips wide. Gently, Giji pushed the rounded head of the dildo deep inside Ariella. As she pushed and pulled the device in and out of her pussy, Ariella arched her hips and groaned.

"You like being fucked, don't you?" Giji asked, pushing the dildo in Ariella's pussy, moving rapidly.

"Yes, yes," Ariella groaned.

Ariella reached down and started rubbing Giji's pussy, smiling as Giji jerked against her fingers.

"Okay, hold on," Giji said. "Use you hand to hold this in place and help me get in position." Placing the other exposed head of the dildo between her pussy lips, Giji slowly lowered herself onto it. She wiggled her ass a little and her tight hole grabbed hold of the fake cock pulling it inside her. With a satisfied smirk, she grinned at Ariella.

Giji tried to pull the dildo from her pussy with no success. "Uh oh," she said.

"What?" Ariella asked. "Get off me, you're not exactly featherweight."

"I can't," Giji replied.

"What do you mean, you can't?" Ariella sounded alarmed.

"I believe we are stuck. It's stuck in my pussy. Thanks to your wonderful idea we're joined at the pussy," Giji muttered. "Maybe if we urinate..."

Ariella gave her a sobering look. "Hell, no!" she spat. "That's disgusting. There has to be another way."

"We could run some warm water in the bathtub and get in together," Giji suggested. "Maybe the water will loosen the dildo and allow it to slip out of our cunts."

Ariella nodded. "That sounds like a good idea," she agreed, "Some bath oils may help."

"Let's move together," Giji instructed. Ariella shifted to the edge of the bed. After some difficulty they stood in unison and slide across the smooth tile floor towards the bathroom.

Hearing footsteps outside the bathroom door, Ariella and Giji exchanged worried looks. For a split second, they both had the same thought: Marco! Had he come home earlier than expected from his business trip?

They both released pent-up breaths when the door opened and Sun Li entered, with a load of freshly-washed towels in her hands. "Ooh, what do we have here?" she asked, her eyes twinkled with amusement.

"Nothing of interest to you," Ariella assured her in a stern voice. "Now, put the towels down and leave, please!"

"Oh, funny girls take bath together!" Sun Li chuckled.

"Just keep your wide trap shut and get out of here," Ariella told her, hoping she'd leave before she spotted the dildo and realized their predicament.

Sun Li placed the towels in the cupboard, snickered and left.

"Bitch!" Ariella said angrily under her breath.

"Forget about her," Giji suggested. placing her hand on the center of the dildo, she gave a little tug. "Does your end feel any looser?"

Ariella frowned. "Not really."

"Maybe if we wiggle it," Giji said, twisting the dildo from the center, "it'll loosen up some."

Ariella closed her eyes and leaned back against the edge of the tub. "That feels gooooood," she said.

"Well, it's not suppose to feel good," Giji admonished her, then admitted "but it does." Giji twisted the dildo so that it moved a little inside both their pussies.

"Oh!" Ariella gasped. "Don't stop! I'm going to…I-I'm cumming big time!"

"Me, too," Giji told her, still twisting and wiggling the dildo. "Here I-I goooo!"

Ariella and Giji slid down into the now lukewarm water, enjoying the euphoric afterglow.

"Wow!" Ariella said. Still weak with pleasure she slurred the words. "That was freaking incredible!"

"It sure was!" Giji agreed, raising her hand from the warm water she displayed the dripping wet dildo."

"Never underestimate the power of a pussy!" Ariella said, laughing.

"Or two satisfied pussies." Giji laughed as well.

***

Marco was pacing in his hotel room, his thoughts on his situation. He missed his son already, but there was nothing he could do. He was already packed for his early morning flight back to his life, back to Ariella. A knock at the door jolted him from his thoughts.

Peeking through the keyhole he was surprised to see Tia's face. He hurriedly opened the door, anxious to see his son again before he left. He quickly recovered and hid his disappointment when he saw she was alone.

"How did you…?"

"I called around." Tia smiled timidly. "I wanted to see you before you left." She sounded apologetic. "We had so little time during your visit."

"It's not your fault," Marco reassured her. Stepping aside he beckoned for her to enter the room. The sight of her full breast straining against her T-shirt caused a stirring in his loins.

"I'm sorry for my mother's behavior," Tia apologized. "She just …"

"I know," he interrupted her. "She loves you."

Tia nodded, pleased that he understood. "Yes." She looked up at him now. "Yes, she does, and she wants the best for me and my son. She's from the old school and disapproves of sex before marriage and all of that."

"Our son," Marco corrected. "I'll be there for you both, you know that. I plan to play a part in his life."

Tia turned adoring eyes on him. "Yes, our son." She smiled, and then the first tear trickled down, followed by another until she was in full crying mode.

In an effort to comfort her, he took her in his arms. He held her, brushing her brown curls from her forehead. Before Marco knew what was happening they were kissing. Despite telling himself briefly that they shouldn't, he lowered her onto the bed. He slowly removed her T-shirt. As he unhooked her lacy black bra, he was surprised at how much larger her breasts had become.

"Courtesy of your son," Tia said, noticing his fascination.

"Mmm," he responded, flicking his tongue across first one nipple and then the next.

Tia arched her hips so that he could tug off her shorts. She was hot and wet, ready for him as usual. She was young but Marco made her feel like a woman. He did things to her no nineteen year old could. No, she didn't want a boy her age.

Marco didn't know when he lost his clothes, but he couldn't stop himself. Tia stroked his already erect cock, using her thumb to circle the tip. He was already lost and couldn't stop. He needed her warmth and innocence. "Oh, Tia, baby I don't deserve you. I never have," Marco whispered against her neck.

Tia's only response was to take his cock and direct it into her throbbing pussy. She needed to remind him of how good they were together. "Marco, I love... how you make me feel," remembering how he reacted the last time she told him that she loved him.

"I love fucking you, too, baby. You are just the best," Marco told her. "You make me feel so alive and loved."

Stretching lazily, Tia turned to Marco. Smiling coyly, she caressed his cheek.

"I should go," Tia said, wishing she didn't have to go, she would prefer to snuggle close in his strong arms all night. "My mother will start to worry if I'm not home soon." In her heart, Tia hoped that Marco would tell her that he would divorce his wife when he got home and return for her and Ricky.

"I know." He kissed her and rose from the bed.

Tia rose and dressed slowly, dreading leaving without knowing when or if she'd see him again.

Taking her hand in his, Marco told her to call him if she or the baby needed anything. "Remember, call me on my cell phone, okay."

"I will. I miss you already, Marco." Her eyes welled with tears.

"Come now, little one. No more tears. Promise." Marco kissed her passion swollen lips.

Tia nodded, afraid to trust her voice. She gave Marco a quick kiss and walked through the door. As it clicked closed behind her, she pressed the elevator button, praying she wouldn't cry.

Long after Tia had left, Marco lay awake with his thoughts to keep him company. He wished that he hadn't given in to the temptation to make love to Tia. He felt bad about using her. She is such a sweet and naïve girl, and I really made things bad for her, he mused. He was thankful her mother was there for her and his son, for that he was truly happy. He didn't want to think of her all alone. He hated to admit it, but her mother was right, she did deserve better. For a fleeting moment he entertained the thought of taking his son and raising him with Ariella.

He had images of them as a happy family playing in the park. He could actually see himself and Ariella lying on a blanket watching as Ricky ran around playing with the dog. Could he get her to forgive him about getting someone else pregnant and agree to be a mother to his child? Would she be willing to take Ricky as her very own and treat him as such? With thoughts of Ariella laughing and playing with Ricky in his head, he fell into a dreamless sleep.

***

Lingering after class, Connie hoped that Chef Real would talk to her. Fumbling with her bag, she slowly packed her stuff. Her ploy worked as Real approached her.

"Hi again, Connie," Real drawled. The way he said her name sent tingles down her spine. There was no mistaking the smoldering lust in his eyes.

"Chef Real, the class was excellent as usual," Connie said. She tried to still the rapid beating of her heart. She laughed a bit self-consciously. "I think you'll make a first-rate cook out of me yet!"

"Call me, Real," he said, pleased by her compliments. "And don't worry, Connie, you're doing excellent."

Connie smiled, she loved the way her name rolled off his tongue with a fluidity that could only come from his French background. "Thank you, Real," she said pleased. "I'm giving it my all."

"And doing very well," he reiterated. "I have been noticing how graceful you are and how well you follow direction. Very commendable."

Connie nodded but did not speak, she was wondering where Chef Real was headed with the conversation. He seemed to be leading up to something, but she wasn't sure what. Whatever it was, she had a feeling she was going to like it.

"How'd you like to be my assistant on a cooking show?" he asked

"Me?" Connie asked, looking behind her just in case he was speaking to someone else. This was the last thing she expected; she didn't feel her efforts were outstanding. In her opinion, there were certainly more capable students in the class. Maybe Chef Real saw something in her that she did not. The thought was somehow exciting.

"Yes, you," Real answered. "I've been offered my very own cooking series on a local access television station and I want you to be my assistant. What do you say?"

"But... but I'm not a great cook," Connie said, surprised by the offer. "I mean, I'm learning to be a better cook, but... I don't know what to say." Connie knew she wasn't making any sense but couldn't help herself. "I am overwhelmed that you would think of me. I just don't feel qualified."

"Well, what better way to learn than with the master? Come on you'll have fun and I'll teach you how to really cook," Real said, smiling. "Listen, I've thought about this for a while and you're the best choice. You have great sense of style and class. Plus, I like the gusto and enthusiasm you show in class. You'd make a wonderful assistant. Also, I don't want someone who'll steal the show, if you know what I mean. Think Vanna White and Pat Sajak." He winked at Connie, knowing that she wouldn't say no despite her protests.

"Okay, I'll do it," Connie said excitedly, but even as she said the words, she could hardly believe they were coming out of her mouth. *After all,* she thought, *how could I possibly pass up spending more time around such an exciting man?*

"I am so pleased," Real said, taking her hand in his, Turning it over, he kissed the palm of her hand, before taking her little finger into his mouth. Connie shuddered, feeling her pussy quiver at the touch of his warm, wet mouth on her skin.

"You taste like honey, sweet Connie," Real whispered.

Connie felt shaky, her legs like gelatin. She had heard the French were a passionate people, but she'd never dreamed she'd experience it firsthand. "Thank you, Real," Connie said, almost moaning. "I-I am so excited by-by your offer!"

***

SueAnn was a bundle of nerves; finally she would get the chance to spend some quality time with Nick. She was still feeling a little weird about their last encounter but looked forward to seeing him again. She jumped when she heard the knock at the door.

"Wow, you're looking hot," Nick complimented her. SueAnn blushed, but couldn't hide the satisfied grin that spread across her face. At least her efforts to look beautiful for him had paid off.

"Thank you," SueAnn responded. "You aren't looking bad yourself." She took in his tan colored slacks and well-fitted silky white dress shirt. Beneath the thin material, his muscles were evident as he moved. She bet he spent a lot of time at the gym keeping that body in shape.

"Let's get out of here before I undo all your great work," Nick suggested and he held the door open for her. His attentiveness and gentlemanly behavior wasn't lost on her. Arriving at the elegant restaurant he had selected for their first date, SueAnn was afraid she was under-dressed, in her simple pale blue blouse and matching skirt. Nick however put her at ease, telling her that she was perfect.

After ordering, SueAnn broke the silence that enveloped them with small talk about her work. They were rescued from an uncomfortable silence by the serving of the appetizer.

"SueAnn, you must taste the grapefruit bowl, it's delicious. Pink grapefruit is my favorite fruit," Nick said. He offered her a taste from his spoon.

"Really, I like it, too," SueAnn exclaimed, although she couldn't help thinking of Giji Brickhouse every time she saw anything pink. "I first had pink grapefruit when I visited Jamaica a few years ago." SueAnn took the offered delicacy between her lips.

Taking the opportunity to get to know him better, SueAnn said, "Giji didn't tell me a lot about you, Nick. I believe you said you grew up in New Jersey?"

"Yes, I grew up in a city called Rockaway," Nick answered. "I had a great childhood there, lots of fond memories. It's a great place to live."

SueAnn looked up at him, curiosity in her eyes. "You ever think about moving back?" she wondered.

He shook his head. "I used to," he admitted, "but not anymore. I do go back every few years to visit family and friends, though." He suddenly smiled. "I have been seduced by the sunshine state."

"Me too," SueAnn admitted, enjoying the warmth of his smile.

"How about you?" he asked, curious. "Are you from around these parts?"

"Oh, no. I grew up on the East Coast, Pennsylvania," SueAnn told him. "I moved to California when my husband, now ex-husband, got a great job in Silicon Valley."

"Sorry things didn't work out," he said.

SueAnn shrugged. "Well, it was a while ago."

"What happened if you don't mind my asking?" His smile was her undoing. He had the kind of smile that made it impossible to deny him anything.

"It's okay, all water under the bridge now," SueAnn assured Nick.

"Not only did he get a new job in Silicon Valley, he also got a cute young assistant as part of the package. Once I found out I gave the rat his walking papers." SueAnn took a sip of wine before continuing. "Anyway, that's a whole other story. Enough about me," she said. "I'd like to hear more about you."

Nick reached across and took her hand in his. "Good for you and lucky for me," Nick replied and smiled.

"Lucky for you?" SueAnn asked, wondering if Nick were intentionally trying to steer the conversation away from his past. Nick released her hand and waited for the waiter to clear their partially eaten appetizer away to make way for the main course. As soon as the waiter was out of ear shot he dazzled her with another mega-watt smile before responding. "I know this may sound selfish, but it's the truth. It's his lost and my gain. Your husband, ahh, ex-husband was a fool to cheat on a treasure like you. So, do you still have family on the East Coat?" Nick asked.

"Yes, I sure do," SueAnn replied, then quickly asked, "What about you? You said you have family in New Jersey. Do you have any family members close by?"

"Sure, don't you remember meeting my dad...a while ago?" The twinkle in his eyes made her blush. Remembering her wanton behavior when she planned a little surprise for him, she wished she could erase the entire episode.

With her blush deepening, SueAnn lied, "Yes, I vaguely remember meeting him. I had forgotten about that." She took another sip of wine before taking a bite of her stuffed fish. "What about your mother? Doesn't she live here as well?"

For a fleeting second Nick's features changed. It was almost as if a cloud had passed over. "My mom passed away a few years ago," he said quietly. "It was sudden, unexpected, she had a stroke. After her death, my dad moved out here to be closer to me."

SueAnn reached across and gently touched his hand. "I'm sorry. It's not easy to lose a parent. Were the two of you close?" she asked, her curiosity peaked by his expression. "If it's okay to ask..." her voice trailed off, she didn't want him to continue if it was too painful to discuss.

"We were close." He nodded. His voice became almost a whisper. "She was a wonderful lady, a great mother. We were very close, she was my best friend."

"That's great Nick. Not very many people can say that about their parent," SueAnn comforted.

"Thanks," he said and managed a smile.

The rest of the meal passed pleasantly. Nick and SueAnn shared stories of childhood pranks. SueAnn was a little disappointed when Nick paid the bill and pushed his chair back. She hated for the evening to end.

Standing, he came around beside her chair and helped her. "Thank you for a wonderful evening, SueAnn. I had fun," Nick took her hand under his arm as they walked outside.

On the drive back to her home, Nick and SueAnn found that they shared similar taste in music and movies as well. They both gushed over little known actors who they thought were overlooked in Hollywood. Too soon they were driving into her driveway.

"Want to come in for some coffee," SueAnn offered. "The evening is still young, unless you have something else to do of course," she added.

"Coffee would be great. Thanks," Nick following her inside her living room.

"Make yourself comfortable while I go put on the coffee," SueAnn told him

"No problem."

They sat sipping their coffee, enjoying the quiet after their evening out, SueAnn nestled in close to Nick, leaning her head against his strong shoulder. "It really has been a great evening," she said quietly and turned and kissed his cheek lightly. As her lips brushed his cheek, Nick turned and kissed her full on the lips.

Before she knew what happened they were locked in a passionate embrace. SueAnn shivered as Nick trailed his tongue down her neck. His hands were everywhere putting her on fire. When he pushed her dress off her shoulder and took her nipple in his mouth through the lacy bra she was wearing SueAnn moaned aloud. Suddenly she realized what was happening and why she felt it wasn't such a good idea.

"Nick, please stop," she asked. Her body was aching for release but she was determined not to give him. She wanted him, but she also wanted this to be more than just about sex.

"What?" Nick raised himself on his elbows, looking down at her perplexed. "What's wrong, SueAnn. Did I hurt you?" He sounded genuinely concerned.

"No, I just can't do this right now. I'm sorry." Seeing his hurt look SueAnn hastened to add, "It's not you, Nick."

Reluctantly, Nick got to a standing position. He had to shift his pants to accommodate the massive hard-on pushing against his pant front. He helped her up, still holding onto her hands he asked her what was wrong.

"Nothing is wrong. I swear, Nick. I just want some time to think about this, okay?" SueAnn looked at him pleadingly, hoping he'd understand. "I just need to sort out how I feel."

"I probably should go," Nick said, still unsure if he'd done something wrong, "if I don't I may not be able to."

"Okay," SueAnn agreed, wishing she had been a little less abrupt in her response to his interests. "I had a truly great night with you and hope we can get to know each other better over time…" her voice trailed off, she hoped that Nick didn't miss the note of expectancy in it.

Pulling her into his arms, gently, he gave her a gentle kiss. "I want that too," he reassured her. "Goodnight, sleep well," he called as the door closed behind.

SueAnn closed the door, leaning against it to support her suddenly weak knees. Her first real date with Nick was more than she expected, so much more. She could only hope she hadn't blown her chance of taking it to the next level by refusing to sleep with him again. But she knew that her budding relationship with Nick had the promise of being so much more than just about sex….

16

Timber!

Ariella arrived home and noticed that Marco was back. His car was parked in the garage which surprised her since he's never home this early, not even when he's just returned from one of his many trips.

Going inside she saw him lying on the sofa watching TV. Something else Marco rarely did. Suspicious she wondered what was happening. Hearing her enter, Marco sat up and smiled, then got to his feet to greet her.

"Hi, babe," Marco said, pulling her close. He gave Ariella a long, lingering kiss that was passionate but with a tenderness that Marco usually didn't show. After the kiss, he said, "Hope you were okay in my absence?" His words sounded awkward, his voice nervous, another thing that wasn't like Marco.

"Sure, everything was okay?" Ariella wondered. "I hope your trip was successful."

Marco nodded. "It was," he assured her and not too convincingly added, "Everything went fine. Just fine."

"Are you hungry?" Ariella asked. "I could fix you something

quickly since I gave Sun Li the day off."

"Don't go to that much trouble," he urged. "Would you like to visit the restaurant of your choice, sweetheart? It's been so long since we had a real date," he continued, "just the two of us going out like we did when we were dating..." his voice trailed off.

Taken by surprise, Ariella stared at Marco, unable to respond for a couple of minutes. Looking at him closely she wondered again what was up with him.

"Sure, that sounds really great, babe," she replied, still not sure why Marco was in such a nostalgic mood. "How about *Chez Paradise*?" she asked.

"Anything you want, babe," he agreed.

Ariella smiled, she liked the sound of that, even though she was still a bit puzzled by his behavior. "Let me go have a quick bath."

Marco took the opportunity to call and make a reservation at *Chez Paradise*. They had eaten there once since the restaurant opened, and he knew Ariella enjoyed the ambiance. She had been dropping hints enough ever since the place opened six months ago. He felt a little guilty about lying to her about his trip; he just hoped his wife wouldn't catch on to what was behind his sudden attention.

Somehow, he was sure she would never guess.

He spent most of the trip back home thinking about the future. There was no doubt in his mind that he wanted his wife to raise his son. Tia would try to be a good mother, but she didn't have the financial means to make it alone. He also wanted to make it easier for her to go back to school and start her life over without a child holding her back.

After they returned from dinner, Marco was in the bedroom getting undressed when Ariella came out of the bathroom. For the first time in months he actually felt real lust for his wife. "Wow, when did you get that full body tan? You are gorgeous," Marco complimented Ariella. "I love it!"

"Thank you," Ariella responded hesitantly. "I went to the

salon while you were away."

Her surprise was complete when Marco took the lotion from her.

"Let me do the honors," he said. Leading her to the bed, he told her to lie on her stomach. Squeezing some into the palm of his right hand he rubbed both palms together warming the lotion. Starting at her shoulders he began a sensuous massage.

Ariella relaxed, enjoying his touch as he stroked her naked flesh. She almost arched her body off the bed when he lowered his head and ran his tongue down her spine.

"I love every inch of you," Marco whispered against Ariella's neck. Turning her over, Marco stared deeply into her eyes.

In the heat of the moment she removed his shirt, buttons flew across the room. They kissed passionately, a reminder of their early days.

Ariella was about to return the kiss when she saw the nasty purple bruise on his forearm. "My God, what happened to you?" She pointed to the nasty looking bruise.

"Oh, that. It's nothing; it happened at hotel last night. I walked into some bushes," he explained. "Trust me, it looks worst that it really is. Now, let's get back to the business at hand," he said bending his head to take a nipple in his mouth.

"What kind of bush could do that much damage?" Ariella asked, not convinced.

Marco, anxious to turn attention away from his arm responded nonchalantly. "As I said it was dark, it could have been some shrubs or bushes. You know how it is when you're in a strange place at night."

"No, I don't. Anyway, I think you should let me take a look at it," Ariella persisted "Looks like something that can become infected if not cleaned properly."

Realizing that she wasn't about to give up, Marco sat up and allowed her to get the stuff needed to clean the area. Returning from the bathroom with the necessary first aide items Ariella got to work. On closer inspection she suspected he wasn't telling the truth. While the bruise and a few minor cuts could not have been caused by bumping into bushes as Marco claimed, she knew her husband, he wasn't accident prone. He was the most careful person she knew.

Ariella suspected that he was beaten up by a jealous boyfriend or husband. She was always having doubts about his frequent business trips. "Serves you right," she mumbled under her breath when he winced as she cleaned the area.

"What?" Marco asked. He was nervous that Ariella would realize that he was lying.

"Nothing, love," Ariella answered sweetly. "I know this must sting, but I have to make sure it's clean."

"Thank you, sweetheart. You're truly the best wife a man could ask for," Marco said, looking at her. "I know things haven't been great between us lately, but I want to change that. I want to save my marriage," he finished.

"Save our marriage?" Ariella lifted one eyebrow. "What's wrong with our marriage?" she asked, concerned.

"I haven't been as attentive as I should be," Marco admitted. "I spent far too much time at the office. I want to change that."

Ariella was taken aback at the sincerity she heard in his voice. She was shocked at his words. It was like the time when they first started dating, Marco held the door open for her, pulled her chair out and was charming.

"Thank you for a wonderful night, Marco," Ariella told her husband. "I had a wonderful time, sweetheart."

"The pleasure was all mine," Marco responded. "I do plan on wooing you all over again," he said. "I'm going for a late night swim in the pool. Come with me," he urged.

"Sure, but you go ahead. I'll be down to join your shortly."

Ariella went into the bathroom to remove her makeup and to hunt for a bathing suit. As soon as she heard Marco hit the water she looked at the clock. She knew at 10:00 Giji was probably in bed, especially under Mrs. Hoover's bedtime regime, but she felt like she needed someone to talk to. She quickly dialed Giji's cell and waited.

After the fifth ring, a grumpy sounding Giji picked up the telephone. "This had better be good," she said, yawning.

"Giji, hi," Ariella whispered. "I just want to call and let you know Marco's home."

"That's it?" Giji asked, sounding irritated.

"Well, no," Ariella replied. "He came back from his trip in a weird mood. I don't know what's going on with him. He took me to *Chez Paradise* for dinner tonight and he's being so loving and attentive –"

"And you're complaining?" Giji asked incredulously.

"I'm not complaining exactly," Ariella told her. "I'm just not sure what he's thinking. Something's going on. I'm not sure what."

"Maybe he just missed you," Giji ventured.

"Maybe." Ariella did not sound convinced. She decided not to mention the bruise on his forearm or his excuse.

"Enjoy it while it lasts," Giji urged. "You know how guys are, tomorrow he may be back to taking you for granted!"

"You're probably right," Ariella said. "I guess I'd better make the most of it while it lasts. So, I've got to run, he's waiting for me by the pool."

Ariella put down the phone, glancing out the window she saw Marco lounging on the side of the pool, dangling his feet in the water, obviously waiting for her. Deciding against a bathing suit she walked out onto the patio in glorious nudity.

***

Connie and Lex had a late lunch in the kitchen. "How come you've haven't commented on my cooking?" she asked him. "I learned to make a French omelet in my cooking class," she continued.

Looking up from his plate, Lex grinned at Connie. "I noticed, hon, but I wanted to finish eating before saying anything."

"Really, you noticed?" She seemed genuinely surprised–and pleased.

"Hon, this is great. Of course I noticed. It's really good," Lex complimented her. Putting the last spoonful in his mouth, he licked his lips in an exaggerated gesture.

Connie beamed. "The class is really going great and I'm enjoying myself tremendously. Chef Real, the teacher asked me to be his assistant on a new cooking show he'll be hosting." She glanced up at Lex.

"You? An assistant on a cooking show?" There was an edge to Lex's voice.

Connie smiled, it seemed he was jealous. "Lex, aren't you happy for me?" she asked. "This is a great opportunity for me to earn some money, plus improve my cooking even more," she explained. Connie was glad that her cooking class was having a benefit she hadn't anticipated.

"Of course I'm happy for you. Let me show you just how happy," he suggested with a leer on his handsome face. Pushing his empty plate aside he came to her side of the table. He pulled her to her feet and held her around the waist. Looking deeply into her eyes, Lex lowered his head and kissed her lightly on the lips. "Let's spend the rest of the day in bed to celebrate," he suggested, grinding his semi-erect cock against her pussy.

"It's afternoon and we've just finished lunch," Connie stated, pulling away to look into his face.

"So what?" Lex asked. "There's no set time for love and lovemaking," he cajoled. "Come on! Don't you remember when we were dating, our hot and heavy time on the freeway in rush hour traffic?" he whispered.

Connie laughed, joining in reliving some of their wild times. "Do you remember that time we got caught by the zookeeper going at it in on the wall by the animal enclosure," she asked. "I'll never forget the look on her face. You'd think she'd never been fucked in her life." She laughed self-consciously at what she had just said. Fucked! She forgot that she once spoke that way when they were alone. It seemed like such a long time ago.

"Maybe she was and still is a virgin. Poor thing!" Lex reminisced. "Hey, at least , the monkeys were enjoying the show!"

"It's Saturday and most of our neighbors are home. What will they think?" Connie asked coyly. To take away the sting, she came into his arms, smiling up at him, snuggling close. "I'll make it up to you tonight. Honey, I promise…."

"Speaking of honey," Lex pulled her to him, "I want to taste some of yours right now," he said and put his hand under her short shirt and rubbed her pussy through her panty.

Connie groaned and pressed into his fingers. She opened her legs slightly allowing him to pull the leg of her panty aside. She jumped as he slid a finger inside her, his thumb caressing her sensitive clit.

Weak with desire, Connie leaned into him.

Lex, easily lifted her and walked to the bedroom. Depositing her onto the bed, Lex easily stepped out of his shorts. His cock stood proud, pre-cum already coating the purple-pink tip.

"Seriously, the neighbors may hear us," she protested.

"We're not inviting the neighbors into our bedroom," Lex said frustrated. "It's just a little alone time for the two of us," he stated obviously put out. "Anyway, fuck the neighbors, we are adults and can do whatever we want. Since when have you been concerned about the neighbors?" Lex asked. Grabbing her hands and holding them above her head, Lex used his head to push her shirt up exposing her belly button. He placed teasing flicks of his tongue just below it. Connie jumped. She was extremely sensitive just above the pubic area. Effortless, he released her hand and ripped the shirt from her body. "I'll buy you another, two if you wish," Lex said, before tugging her shorts off.

Throwing the shorts aside, he buried his head between Connie's legs. Pushing the leg of her panty aside, Lex licked the exposed clit. "Yes, most definitely honey," he said coming up for breath.

With great effort, Connie pulled away. "Seriously, Lex, I can't do this now. I have to go get some more books for my next class."

"You've got to be kidding me," Lex said in frustration. "What's this about?"

Springing from the bed, Connie dodged Lex's efforts to catch her. She actually found it erotic to have him chasing her, his erection standing out from his body proudly. Looking over her shoulder at him as she dashed down the stairs and into the living room, Connie laughed aloud as Lex tripped over the edge of the large Oriental rug.

Lex's responding laugh was cut short. Connie turned to the window he was staring through. Her eyes met Mrs. Witherly's, their elderly neighbor. Hastily, Connie used one hand to cover her bare breast.

At the look on Mrs. Witherley's face, Lex burst out laughing, seeing the humor in the situation. He unabashedly walked towards the open window, his semi-hard cock swaying gentle with every step. Mrs. Witherley stood transfixed her eyes glued to Lex's package; Connie all but forgotten. Startled as if coming out of a trance, Mrs. Witherley covered Pixie's eyes. The cat meowed and jumped out of her arms.

A red faced Mrs. Witherley, pulled down her window shade.

Still laughing, Lex pulled the drape. He collapsed onto the carpet. Looking at Connie, he beckoned her to join him. She did so, with slow measured steps. "I guess it's not too late to finish what we started," she said. "One neighbor has already seen the goodies."

She bent over him taking his cock in her mouth. Instantly, it stiffened as her tongue expertly rimmed the edge, licking away at the moisture gathering there. Lex groaned as she worked on, coming close to the brink, he pushed her away. "Hot stuff, babe," he said before switching position.

Without another word, Lex drove into her. Connie cried out in surprise. Lex covered her mouth with his, stilling her cry. "Congratulations at being a success at your cooking class," he said before slamming into her again. "I'm so proud of you."

"Shut up and fuck me," Connie ordered. Rising her ass off the rug, she met his next thrust. Feeling her climax nearing, Connie buried her nails into Lex's shoulder and closed her eyes. Imagining Real fucking her, Connie put her all into it, wanting to please her new lover.

"Yes, baby, fuck me hard," she encouraged him, riding the wave of pleasure. "You know I'm a bad girl. Fuck me, Real. Yes, Yes, just like that," she persisted. As she reached her peak, Connie cried out, "Oh, Real, it's so good!"

Lex grew still above her. "What did you just call me?" he asked as his erection disappeared. Connie opened her eyes to see him staring at her, obviously mad.

"Sorry. I guess because we were talking about him I got carried away," she tried explaining. "Honestly, Lex, there's nothing going on between Real and me."

"Yeah, fucking right!" Lex exploded.

Connie went into the master bath to clean up and get dressed, slamming the door behind her.

***

A small shower of something hitting her window caused Giji to go peek in an effort to see what it was. Her first thought was about her obscene caller. Scared, she turned out the light and crept to the window. She was surprised to see Connie and Lex's son, Andrew looking at her from the top branch of the tree beside her window.

"Andrew, what are you doing up there?" Giji asked opening the window.

Grinning self-consciously, Andrew answered her. "I've a little problem," he said uneasily.

"What kind of problem," Giji asked concerned.

"Well, some of my friends were daring each other to…," Andrew licked his suddenly dry lips before continuing, "I… I…"

Before he could complete his thought, the branch broke and he was on his way down. Giji watched helplessly as the boy plummeted to the ground.

"Hey, are you okay?" she called.

"I think so," Andrew responded. He stood, brushed himself off and climbed back up the tree. Reaching her window level, Andrew grinned foolishly.

"Are you sure you're okay?" Giji asked in concern. "That was a nasty fall."

"Yeah, I'm fine. Luckily I didn't land on the one thing that could have broken my fall," Andrew assured her. Seeing her confusion, Andrew laughed.

"What are you talking about anyway?" Giji asked still confused by his comment.

"It's kind of embarrassing," Andrew said.

"I've heard just about everything," Giji assured him. "Fire away, I bet you can't embarrass me!"

"Okay, here goes, but don't say I didn't warn you. If you want me to stop, just say so," Andrew said. "On a dare my friends and I ordered some pills being advertised on TV. You know, the ones for erectile dysfunction," he explained.

"Oh," Giji said, shocked and more than a little uncomfortable. "Andrew, please don't tell me you took any," she exclaimed. "Anyway, why order them, kids don't normally have that kind of problem. Which pills did you get?" she asked out of curiosity.

"You know, the one that offers bigger and harder…erections," he replied. "It's hard to miss the ads." He paused, giving her a long, pleading look. "Can I come in, Giji? The next time I fall I may not be so lucky."

"Sure." Stepping aside she helped him through the window. "Come into the kitchen and I'll make you some cocoa while we talk. You know, I don't watch a lot of TV," Giji said quickly, noticing the bulge in his jeans. Trying not to stare, she couldn't avoid stealing a look every now and then as she prepared the cocoa. "So you took these pills on a dare," Giji concluded with a sigh, "and this is how you ended up." She looked pointedly at his protruding erection.

He nodded.

"Andrew, this could be serious," Giji worried. "I saw on TV that you could go blind from taking these kinds of pills."

"If I don't get some relief soon," he told her, urgency evident in his voice, "I'm going to go blind!"

For a while, Giji was quiet, not sure what to say or do.

"You gotta help me, please," he begged. "I can't go home looking like this, my mom would freak out."

"I could call 911 or something," Giji suggested.

"No, my parents would really kill me," the teenager protested. "I don't want them to know that's why I came to you for help." He smiled sheepishly at her. "Please, don't call them or anything like that." His voice went up as he protested.

"Okay, okay, keep quiet," Giji warned. "The old cow snores loudly, but sometimes I think she can hear a pin drop!"

She turned her attention back to the fully aroused teenager. "So, what do you want me to do? I'm not a nurse or anything, you know," Giji said. "You're not suggesting that..."

Andrew nodded in the affirmative. Giji looked at him, she was sure that banging him would be unwise. Her eye traveled to the impressive bulge in his pants and made her decision. "How old are you anyway?" she asked. "I don't want to get my ass thrown into jail for having sex with a minor or anything!"

"I'm seventeen," Andrew lied, thankful that he looked older than his sixteen years. "That's the age of consent, right?"

"I guess so," Giji responded with a shrug."

"Just don't be lying to me and don't you dare tell anyone if I do this." She glared at him, but knew she was game; her pussy was already jumping in anticipation.

Andrew looked down at her breasts pressing firmly against her sheer see-through gown. "So, are you gonna help me?" He pressed in a helpless, little boy voice.

Giji nodded reluctantly. She was sure that it would be over

pretty quickly, especially since he took medication to get in the state he was in. Again, she glanced at his cock poking through his pants.

"Okay, get undressed. Be quiet about it," she instructed. "Come with me," she told Andrew and headed back to the living room, the cocoa forgotten on the counter.

Putting a finger to her lips to caution him to be quiet, Giji lead Andrew quietly back upstairs. There, she glanced toward Mrs. Hoover's door to make sure the old woman was still sleeping soundly. She listened for a few seconds until she heard Mrs. Hoover's loud snoring, then she took hold of Andrew's hand and pulled him quickly into her bedroom.

Giji quietly closed the door, slowly so that it would not creak and risk awakening Mrs. Hoover. When she turned back around, Andrew was undressed, standing there, waiting. His young body was tight and firm. *His erection would put many a grown man to shame,* she thought briefly. It stood almost in line with his flat six-pack.

Giji drew in her breath and tried to quell her conscious with a reminder that she was just helping the kid with a medical problem. With a silent admonition not to enjoy the look of his firm youthful cock and the promise it held. Nonetheless as she closed the short distant between them and he took her in his arms, she knew he was more man than kid. His touch sent quivers down her spine. His touch was electric; the excitement caused goose bumps on her shoulders. Her pussy quivered at what was to come.

Andrew pulled her down on the bed and helped her remove the red night gown. His eyes grew huge as her breast spilled out. He took one nipple in his mouth, moving his tongue across the tip like an expert. After a hot session on the bed, they moved to the floor, realizing the bed was making too much noise. Giji's grandmother's rug with the pink roses protected them from the cold floor, not that either of them would have noticed. Giji had lost count of her orgasms, giving up after five. She was surprised at Andrew's stamina. She thought it was all over after he came on the bed… wrong. She wondered what pills he'd taken?

"Let's try another position," he said, inclining his head towards the old chair in the corner. It belonged to Mrs. Hoover. Giji was tired but still game. Joined at the hips they sidled to the chair. Andrew slowly sat, taking Giji down with him. Riding him, Giji was able to take as much of his cock inside her juicy pussy as she wanted.

"Giji, I really appreciate this," Andrew groaned. Holding her hips firmly, he rose to meet each thrust with a thrust of his own. Sweat dripping from their bodies, it rapidly cooled, keeping them from getting too hot. "It feels so good."

"You fuck good for a little boy," Giji teased, moaning.

"Little boy," Andrew replied. "Can a little boy do this to you?" With that he rammed everything in her. Giji almost shrieked out loud as another spasm racked her body. Soon they moved to the small bathroom in the hall as Andrew asked to take a leak. No sooner was he done, than he bent her over the sink and was ready again.

"How many of these tablets did you take?" Giji asked.

"Twelve," he responded proudly.

"No wonder," Giji answered. She couldn't believe that she was getting the best fuck of her life from her young neighbor.

"Giji, are you okay in there?" Mrs. Hoover called from her room.

"Yes, Martha," Giji answered uneasily. "My tummy is a little… queasy. I guess the codfish and cabbage casserole upset my stomach a bit. I'll be okay." She pressed her finger against Andrew's lips.

"You're as bad as my late husband," Martha Hoover said. "Poor man, he had the runs for nearly thirty years. He spent more time on the toilet than he did on me!"

Giji had to clamp her hand over Andrew's mouth to stifle his laughter. Yes, I have no doubt what gave him the runs, Giji thought.

"Sssh!" she hissed at Andrew while he fucked her hard against the cold porcelain toilet. The excitement of nearly getting caught was heady. "Slow and deep, slow and deep," she instructed the youngster.

"Is this your first time?" Giji asked. She wanted to know because he wasn't acting like a first-timer.

"Yep," Andrew admitted, before proudly adding, "I'm no longer a virgin."

Feeling a mix between honored to be his first and worried about being found out, she looked at him hard. "That's right," she agreed. "You're definitely no longer a virgin, but we might want to keep this quiet. If your mother finds out she'll make us both wish we were still virgins."

"Yep, I guess we'd better keep this between us," Andrew responded.

"Yes, let's do that," Giji added. She kissed him lightly on the lips.

He licked his lips, obviously having enjoyed the kiss. Suddenly a thought occurred to Andrew and he looked worried. "Does that mean we can't have sex on a regular basis?" he asked.

"Not even on an irregular basis," she told him.

Shortly before daybreak Andrew's hard-on relaxed and Giji ushered him quietly down to the kitchen and out the door before Mrs. Hoover woke. Climbing into her bed, she was exhausted, but thoroughly fucked and satisfied.

17

Bikini Snafu

Taking a seat on her sofa, SueAnn looked directly at Nick. "I called you to come over for a reason," she began, "we need to talk."

Nick shifted in his chair, nervous. He didn't like where this was going. Those words, he knew, were almost never followed by anything good. "Are you sure?" he asked, almost sure of where this was going. SueAnn was going to break off their relationship, he was almost certain of it.

SueAnn nodded. "I've given it a lot of thought," she told him. "I'm sure."

Nick swallowed hard and waited, bracing for what he was sure was to come.

"Recently I've been pulling away from you," she said evenly. "I'm not sure if you've noticed." She paused and he nodded. "I have noticed that sometimes when we're together, you seem like a diffcrent person."

For a few moments, Nick could not speak. This was the last thing he'd expected to hear. He had noticed SueAnn's distancing herself from him, but he never guessed it was because she sensed that he was not being totally honest with her. He thought she was scared off by how fast their relationship was developing and had taken a step back to allow things to develop more slowly while they got to know each other. Now he knew that wasn't it at all. As hard as he found it to believe, SueAnn had tuned in to his being dishonest with her – and she was right.

"I'm not sure what's going on," SueAnn admitted. "Sometimes when we get together it's like I'm talking to someone I don't know, the Nick I thought I knew seems to fade away and he's replaced with a stranger." She paused as if she were watching his reaction. "Even when we kiss, it's like I'm kissing a total stranger!"

Nick opened his mouth, and SueAnn thought he was about to speak. Her heart leapt that he might finally explain why his behavior seemed so inconsistent. At the same time she couldn't shake the sinking feeling that the truth might drive them further apart.

Nick shrugged, relieved the conversation had not gone as he expected, but still stunned at what SueAnn had just revealed. "I-I guess I try too hard sometimes," he stammered, unsure of what he should say. One thing he now realized was that he had been holding back, not letting SueAnn get too close, because of the deception. "I'm sorry, SueAnn. All I can do is promise to try to make it up to you if you'll give me a chance."

SueAnn nodded. That was what she wanted to hear. "I was afraid you were losing interest in me," she admitted and smiled, relieved. "I had this crazy notion in my head that you were entranced by Giji! At least, I hope it was crazy…" her voice trailed off expectantly.

"Giji's fun to be with," Nick told her, looking her in the eye, "but I care about you. I have since the first day we met and that hasn't changed."

"I feel the same way," SueAnn told him and stood. "Come on, give me a hug."

Nick stood and took her gently into his arms, pulling her close to his chest and his racing heart. He was tempted to tell her the truth right there, but he was afraid it would only make matters worse. If she knew the truth, she might never trust him again.

"I feel so much better," SueAnn said against Nick's chest.

"I'm glad," Nick said quietly, wishing he could say the same as he gave her a light kiss on the lips and turned to leave.

"Sure you have to rush off?" SueAnn asked as she followed him to the door.

He put his hand on the knob and paused, but he did not turn to face her. "Yes, I need to go."

"I'm really glad we had this little talk," SueAnn said.

"Me too," Nick said, opening the door. "Listen, I'll see you later."

You sure will! SueAnn thought. "Thanks," she said quietly, feeling better for the first time in weeks about her and Nick. Maybe they could move on from the distance that had grown between them, she hoped, watching Nick walk away....

Nick glanced back at SueAnn standing in the doorway. Despite SueAnn's reassurances, he could not shake the feeling that all was not right. She had picked up on his deceiving her even though he had tried to hide it as well as he could, and, when she learned the truth, he couldn't help feeling she would never forgive him.

***

Deciding to surprise Nick, SueAnn turned up at his door with a bottle of expensive wine and two wine glasses. She thought it would give them a chance to know each other better.

When he opened the door, Nick was pleasantly surprised to see SueAnn standing there. "Hi there, beautiful," he greeted her. "What are we celebrating?"

"I just wanted to spend some time with you, get to know you better," SueAnn explained. "Maybe this is a bad idea," she said, turning away.

"No, it's a brilliant idea. I'm sorry I didn't think of it. Come on in," Nick said. Seeing SueAnn looking down at the towel around his waist, Nick smiled. "I was in the hot tub out back when I heard the door bell," he explained. "Why don't you join me," he suggested.

"I don't have a bathing suit," SueAnn said. "I'll just sit and watch you."

"No problem. I'm sure I can find a suit to fit you," Nick offered. Seeing the look of disdain on SueAnn's face, Nick hastened to clear the air. "I have a few suits my sister left at my old place and she's about your size."

"Oh, sorry for jumping to conclusions." SueAnn felt stupid. "Anyway, I had no reason to react that way," she apologized. "It's not like we have an exclusive relationship."

"Forget it," Nick encouraged her. "Let's go find you a bathing suit." He led her down the passage to a room at the end. Opening the closet he told her to look through a drawer full of various bath suits. "I'll be back shortly," Nick told her. SueAnn settled on a blue bikini with a floral pattern. It seemed the most decent, she decided, since all the others were mere wisps of cloth in strategic places. She was trying to stand firm in her resolve to slow things down between them. A "barely there" bikini wouldn't help that plan.

True to his word, Nick returned minutes later. They went out onto the deck where he directed her to a changing room at the end of the deck. "You can change in there. Don't be too long." He winked at her.

"I won't be," SueAnn replied.

SueAnn put on the bathing suit, a turquoise blue color with white hibiscus flower pattern, a bit dated looking, she decided, but the cut was rather stylish, with thin straps. It was a bit more revealing than SueAnn had expected, but she thought it looked good on her. She was certain Nick would like it.

"Come in and join me," Nick invited. He was sitting in the tub sipping some wine. He held her hand and helped her get comfortable in the swirling waters. "Comfy," he asked, the perfect host.

"Yes, thank you," SueAnn answered.

Without another word he handed her the other glass of wine. "Cheers to a beautiful woman and to a long and beautiful friendship," he said, he winked playfully, "and maybe more."

"Here, here," SueAnn clinked her glass against Nick's, giggling like a school girl when some spilled over. "It's a beautiful night isn't it?" she stated, looking up at the starry sky.

"Yes, it is," Nick agreed. "I love it out here at night. It's one of the things I love best about living out here in the suburbs, the beautiful and unobstructed view of the night sky."

"Good," SueAnn observed, "because you don't seem like the city type."

Nick chuckled, pleased. "I'm not," he assured her. "I'm just a country boy at heart."

"I like that," SueAnn said, wishing that meant he was a bit less complicated. But always in the back of her mind, no matter how well things seemed to be going, was the feeling that something was just not right.

"I'm glad," Nick said quietly, looking at her as he shifted and moved a bit closer.

SueAnn relaxed, enjoying the soothing beat of the water against her skin. *This is almost as good as an orgasm!* she thought. The water from the jets stimulated her pussy, getting her slightly aroused.

The water churned around them, soothing her to a state of near sleepiness especially when combined with the wine. The water level reached below her chin and some splashed into her face and mouth. She hated the unpleasant taste of the chlorine. In an effort to avoid getting the water in her face SueAnn attempted to raise herself up. As she rose to adjust herself she realized that her bikini top was missing. Using her hands, SueAnn searched around hoping to find the missing garment without arousing Nick's attention. Unfortunately, the hot tub took that moment to automatically turnoff. As the water calmed, Nick looked down at her and grinned.

"You're a naughty, naughty girl," he observed, his eyes glued to her chest. "I like that, I like that a lot!"

Before she could react, Nick was beside her. She raised herself from the water, feeling the evening breeze cool against her skin. She was trying to wrap her arms around her breasts when he took one of her nipples in his mouth. The warmth of his mouth against her cool flesh caused her nipple to pucker and harden. SueAnn leaned into Nick, enjoying for a brief moment the pleasant sensation, but she couldn't dispel her concerns. She really hadn't come there to have sex with him. She battled between giving in to her desires and doing what she thought was right became harder as Nick's hands and tongue continued to work their magic on her. All she wanted was to close her eyes and let Nick to have his way with her.

"Okay, this is all wrong," SueAnn protested, pushing him away. Hugging her arms across her breast she tried to stand. Losing her balance she almost fell. Catching herself against the edge of the tub, she rushed from the porch.

"I thought this was what you wanted," Nick sounded offended. "Didn't you take your top off? What'd you expect me to...? Wasn't it all part of the plan?"

"I did not plan this," she assured him. "It fell off," she cried.

"You mean your top just fell off like that?" Nick asked in disbelief.

"Yes, that's exactly what I'm saying. Now let go of me," SueAnn cried.

Grabbing a towel off the closest chair, SueAnn dried herself off quickly and entered the house. She quickly dressed, unaware Nick had followed her, dripping wet.

"Please let me at least apologize?" Nick asked from the open doorway. SueAnn was surprised at the pleading tone of his voice. "Please, sit down for a moment. I promise I won't touch you,"

Nick said. He waited until she was seated before taking the chair beside her. "Listen, I'm sorry I didn't believe you about the top. I should have known better. I know some women like to play games but I should have given you the benefit of the doubt," he continued.

"Thank you, Nick. I accept your apology," SueAnn whispered. "Anyway, I think it's best if I leave now." Rising she smiled at him tentatively. "I guess I can see how you could have gotten the wrong idea," she confessed, blushing. "I know things started off pretty heated between us..." she closed her eyes as she spoke, "but I-I...I wanted to believe we could have something more...."

That left him speechless.

***

"More coffee, anyone?" Wynette asked, glancing through the French doors at her sons playing in the backyard. "I can make more."

Ariella shook her head. "I'm good. I had a latte at the Java Hut earlier."

"I'm good, too," SueAnn said, looking absently down at her empty cup.

"Are you sure, SueAnn?" Wynette asked, coming closer. "Are you okay?"

SueAnn glanced at Ariella as if reassuring her then looked up at Wynette. "Yes, I'm fine. It's just...well... I saw Nick again last night?"

"And?" Wynette asked, pulling up a chair. "How'd it go?"

"Don't hold out," Ariella chimed in. "Give us details!"

SueAnn shrugged. "Well, there's not all that much to tell." Should she skip the bikini snafu altogether? she wondered. "We had wine at his place under the stars in the hot tub, and it was —"

"Come on," Ariella urged.

"Awkward."

"Awkward?" Wynette repeated, seeming disappointed and

confused.

"Yes, it was awkward," SueAnn said. "Nick's like a chameleon sometimes."

"In bed, you mean," Ariella assumed, more interested now, giving the conversation her full attention.

"In bed, out of bed," SueAnn said. "He changes so much from the time I see him till the next, it's like dating more than one guy. And yes even making love with him is different. Sometime it's like I'm in bed with a stranger. He's just so different, his touch, his kiss."

Ariella smiled. "At least you never have to worry about getting bored in bed!"

SueAnn gave a little smile. "I agree, but the changes in his behavior bother me." She paused, remembering her childhood. "I guess it goes back to my childhood. My dad was an alcoholic and he was like a total stranger when he drank. He would get mean and angry over the smallest things. I just don't want to ever go through that again."

"You don't think he's an addict, do you?" Wynette wondered, concerned.

SueAnn shook her head. "No, no, I don't believe Nick's mood swings are from an addiction," she assured her friends. "I just don't know why he behaves this way and it concerns me."

"It's totally understandable that you would feel that way," Ariella agreed.

Wynette nodded. "His behavior is odd," she observed. "Have you tried talking to him? Maybe there's a reason for his mood changes. He could be intimidated by you for some reason."

"If he's not intimidated by Giji," SueAnn told her quickly, "I don't think I have to worry about that!"

"You've got a point," Ariella agreed.

"Well," Wynette shrugged, "it was just a thought."

SueAnn looked at her. "I know." She sounded apologetic. "And, I appreciate it. I have tried talking to Nick, and afterwards it seems like things are better, but it doesn't seem to last. Before I know it he's creeping me out again, like he did in the hot tub."

"Maybe you're not right for each other," Ariella suggested.

"Nick's changes in behavior make me wonder sometimes," SueAnn admitted, but she wasn't ready to give up on Nick or their potential relationship.

Wynette got a playful look in her eyes. "His mood swings are unusual," she said lightly. "Maybe he has male menopause. I've heard some men get that."

"From the sounds of this," Ariella said and laughed, "he may have female menopause!"

"Manopause," Wynette interjected. "The change."

"Even if that were true, isn't he a little young for the change?" SueAnn wondered.

"He's fortyish," Wynette said, "I've heard of women going through menopause in their twenties, sometimes younger."

"Okay, that's it," Ariella said, standing up. "You two are creeping me out with all this talk about menopause! I'm going to go home and try to banish this conversation from my thoughts... forever!"

After Ariella left, SueAnn stood up and was about to leave when she noticed a flyer on Wynette's buffet.

"I was about to throw that out," Wynette said.

SueAnn picked up the thin, bright yellow sheet of paper and began reading. "The Sexual Psychic," she said aloud.

Wynette nodded, an embarrassed look on her face. "That's what it says." She laughed self-consciously. "I picked it up at the grocery...or...someplace."

"Oh," SueAnn said flatly as she put the flyer back on the buffet. "I wonder if she could tell me about Nick's behavior."

Wynette shrugged, unconvinced. "I guess it could be, if you believe in that sort of thing."

"I guess it couldn't hurt."

"Hey, okay, but think about it." She laughed. "After your caffeine buzz wears off, it may not seem such a good idea."

SueAnn nodded, turning to leave. She paused at the window in

Wynette's dining room and stared out the window. Giji was washing her car in Mrs. Hoover's side yard, her clothes wet and clinging to her voluptuous body. "There's that sneak...I mean, snake now," SueAnn said.

"Who?" Wynette wanted to know and came to stand beside SueAnn.

"Look at her," SueAnn said as she looked out Wynette's dining room window. "A woman her age in low rise jeans and a tank top so tight it looks like both of her breasts will explode!"

"Yeah," Wynette sighed. "It's too bad that we can't all wear those teeny tiny little outfits and get away with it!"

SueAnn turned to face her friend. "Whose side are you on?" she asked a bit defensively.

Wynette shrugged. "Yours, hers, the clothing manufacturer's, I don't know. Sometimes I just wish I could turn back the clock and be nineteen again and wear those little clothes and chew gum and smile!" She paused. "Maybe even jiggle... I meant giggle!"

They both burst into laughter.

18

Sex & Soccer

After spending a lot of time looking for the Sexual Psychic, SueAnn finally found her shop. Just as she imagined, the shop was tucked into a small, rundown strip mall on the outskirts of town. She pulled into the parking lot in front of the shop and got out. Walking towards the small, dimly lit shop, she worried if she was making a mistake. I need to know, she reminded herself. She didn't really believe in psychics or the ability to foretell the future or anything else for that matter, but she needed some insight into the reason behind Nick's ever-changing behavior. Still, she had a sinking feeling that the psychic wouldn't be able to help her. Once she had watched Montel Williams' talk show and saw a psychic named Sylvia who seemed to be real and who appeared to give people helpful advice, but she still wasn't convinced, not completely.

Hopefully the Sexual Psychic would be in. She couldn't imagine the psychic would be closed on a sunny weekday afternoon. Besides, if this person really had psychic abilities, she mused, wouldn't he or she know a customer was coming at precisely 3:15 this afternoon? Even a skeptic like herself had to admit that might be expecting too much.

Frowning at the very distinct smell of rotting fish which, she decided must be coming from the Thai Fish Market next door, SueAnn entered the shop and paused briefly just inside the door and waited for her eyes to adjust to the dim lighting. Once she could see clearly, she glanced quickly around the shop, which appeared even smaller than she imagined. It wasn't much larger than a walk-in closet, she thought, and the dark, dated red and gold wallpaper made it feel even smaller. There were a few nondescript posters on the walls, mostly pleasant scenes of deserted white-sand beaches, serene lakes surrounded by greenery, and mountains rising into ethereal clouds. The pictures might have been more appropriate in a travel agency, she decided. Then she finally noticed the small Asian woman peering at her from a doorway that apparently led to an adjoining room.

Still apprehensive, SueAnn approached the woman.

"Yes, I help you?" the woman asked, trying to give her a gummy smile, with thin lips and very small teeth.

SueAnn nodded, fighting the impulse to turn and run. "I... I need a reading," she stammered, noticing the bar stool in front of the counter, but she did not sit.

"Good, good, you come to right place." She held back the faded silk curtain that had once been a deep, blood-red but now was only a dull rose color and gestured for SueAnn to enter.

SueAnn entered the slightly larger adjoining room and took the seat the small woman offered at a table in the center of the room. Once they were seated facing each other, the woman introduced herself, "I Kimiko. And you?"

"Oh, I'm SueAnn Day."

"SueAnn," the Asian woman repeated but it sounded more like "Su-enn" when she said it. "Good meet you, yes," she added, handing SueAnn a card and a pen. "Fill in."

SueAnn hesitated.

"In case I start website or something," Kimiko explained.

"Oh," SueAnn reluctantly filled in the card with her name and phone number.

Kimiko took the card and pen and placed them to the side. "Now how I help you?" the Sexual Psychic said, beginning to shuffle the cards that lay on the counter in front of her. "What you want to know?" she asked, still shuffling. "Or, you want random reading?"

"I have a concern about my boyfriend," SueAnn admitted.

Kimiko looked up. "A pretty girl like you," she observed and shook her head.

"Thank you," SueAnn said, although it occurred to her that the statement was more an observation than a compliment. "I'm not sure what's going on with him..."

"I see," Kimiko placed the freshly shuffled deck in front of SueAnn. "Cut deck," she instructed and made a small gesture with her hand.

After SueAnn cut the deck, Kimiko dealt a series of cards, placing them in a straight line on the counter between her and SueAnn. The psychic began to study the cards, one by one, and occasionally she went back to earlier cards and studied them again in sequence with the others. SueAnn watched, still skeptical and concerned that she should have asked the psychic's rates before the reading began.

"Oh!" the small woman said as if she had experienced an epiphany.

"What do you see?" SueAnn asked anxiously.

Kimiko rolled her eyes. "He good-looking man being chased by tramp in hot pink and heels!"

"That would be Giji," SueAnn rolled her eyes at the thought of Giji.

"Hmmm, she big competition."

"I guess so," SueAnn admitted.

"Man have two faces," Kimiko told her.

"What does that mean?" SueAnn asked, confused.

"He has secret," Kimiko nodded her head.

"What kind of secret?"

Kimiko shrugged. "Cards not say, not clear." She paused, studied the cards again and added, "He not who he says or who he seems to be."

"He's not being honest with me?" SueAnn panicked.

"No, he someone else."

"That doesn't make sense," SueAnn felt even more confused. "What does it mean?"

"It mean he lie to you," the small Asian woman said matter-of-factly. "He not be honest. He not who he say he be. You be duped."

"Is that all?" SueAnn wanted to know. "Can you tell me more?"

Kimiko studied the cards again. "Hmmm," she said, "and you not who you say. You used to be man before sex change!"

"I did not!" SueAnn said outraged. "I have always been female. I have a child for chrissakes!"

Kimiko looked up from the cards, pursed her lips and said, "You adopt?"

"No!"

"Those real?" Kimiko pointed at SueAnn's breasts.

"Yes they are!" SueAnn said, feeling her anger boil.

"Nice. I touch them?"

"No, I would rather you didn't," she spoke quickly but not quickly enough. The small woman reached over the table and placed her equally small hand on one of SueAnn's boobs, squeezing it as if she were shopping for produce at the supermarket. SueAnn backed away and crossed her arms, suddenly feeling underdressed.

"I give you deep pussy discount!" Kimiko offered. "Half price."

"If I let you... cop a feel?"

The little Asian woman nodded. "That pretty much right. What you say?"

"I say no way!"

"Then I no pleasure you today," Kimiko said and smiled, "and you pay me."

"How much do I owe you?" SueAnn wanted to know even though she felt any price was too high for the vague reading she received.

"That be fifty bucks," Kimiko told her.

SueAnn took a fifty from her purse and handed it to her without another word.

Kimiko thanked her then added, "Next time, maybe you get freaky deaky discount!" She winked as she ran the counterfeit pen over the bill. "You get freaky deaky discount, you see you like!"

SueAnn said nothing as she turned and left the shop.

The small Asian woman tossed her head back. "Hee hee, sometimes even psychics get bored with boring people, like to give shocker, hee hee," Kimiko said out loud when the shop was empty.

***

Wynette was busy trimming the hedges along her walkway when SueAnn returned from the Sexual Psychic. SueAnn parked in her driveway and walked over to speak to her.

Wynette stopped clipping as she approached and turned around, smiling. "Hey, you're back. How'd it go?"

SueAnn gave a small shrug. "Okay, I suppose."

"The Sexual Psychic stinks, huh?" Wynette asked, wiping perspiration from her forehead on one of her gardening gloves.

"Pretty much," SueAnn said, then she went on to explain exactly what the psychic had told her. "She told me that Nick cannot be trusted," she concluded. "Fifty dollars for a vague reading."

"Well, I wouldn't take anything she says too seriously," Wynette cautioned. "She's probably just a quack out to make a buck."

"I know, I know," SueAnn said quietly.

"But something she said rattled you?" her friend pressed.

SueAnn nodded. "A little," she admitted. "I didn't tell her anything about me and Nick except my misgivings about him and she zeroed in on what I was feeling about Nick. She seemed to know what I meant about his behavior without me saying it."

"Nan-no, nan-no," Wynette teased, mimicking the Twilight Zone theme. "Spooky!"

SueAnn had to laugh at that. "Kind of."

"The Sexual Psychic said Nick has two faces?" Wynette said after their laughter had subsided. "I've heard that Native Americans believe that gay people have two souls and, thus, are very wise, but…"

"So you think Nick is gay?" SueAnn interrupted.

"You slept with him," Wynette reminded her. "Did he seem gay?"

SueAnn shrugged. "Well," she thought, "no. He didn't even seem mildly bi-sexual!"

They laughed.

"Well, I'm glad Nick is such a hottie in bed," Wynette observed and winked, "but it still sounds like you just blew fifty bucks!"

SueAnn nodded. "I guess so. At least she confirmed my feelings, though."

"You're not saying you believe in that kind of thing, I mean psychics?" Wynette chided.

"Not entirely," SueAnn assured her, "but she was right about Giji."

"Probably a lucky guess."

"Yeah, probably." SueAnn laughed, looking at the clippers her friend held as if she were noticing them for the first time. "So, how's the repair guy doing?"

Wynette sighed. "Not so great," she admitted, frowning. "I tried Rent-A-Hubby, but that isn't work out, so far, unfortunately."

"Too bad," SueAnn said, thinking it seemed odd that Wynette hadn't found anyone who could do the odd jobs around her house, especially since the agency had sent over a dozen or so repairmen!

"I'll probably have to try again," Wynette said, "Since Steven never seems to have time to do anything around the house. Maybe I'll try a different agency next!" Her mind reeled with the possibilities of all those new men. "If Rent-A-Hubby doesn't… you know…work out."

SueAnn turned to leave, then paused. "How about a glass of tea while you rest?" she asked. "Who has time to rest!" Wynette said, taking a deep breath. "I have to meet my sons' soccer coach at 5!"

"I hope it's something good."

Wynette frowned. "Ah, I doubt that," she said flatly. "I have absolutely no idea what they have done this time." She sighed. "Anyway, I've got to finish this up, then shower and be on my way!"

"Good luck," SueAnn called over her shoulder as she turned and started across the lawn to her home.

"Thanks," Wynette called, thinking I'll probably need all the luck I can get.

***

Wynette took the handwritten note her twin son's brought home from the soccer coach. As usual, it seemed her sons were misbehaving and not listening to the coach.

The coach was drenched in man sweat after a close, intense game. Wynette could smell him across his massive desk, intoxicating and oddly appealing. He seemed to sense that Wynette wasn't getting what he was saying, that it just wasn't sinking in, because he stood and came around his desk, standing in front of her.

She couldn't concentrate on his words, although he was saying something about kicking her sons off the team. She found herself drawn to the movement of his wet mouth as he formed words. Her eyes drifted down to his broad, wet chest, his damp T-shirt that clung... Hmmm, she licked her lips and hoped he wouldn't notice.

He was standing so close. She knew she shouldn't... she shouldn't, but she did. She touched the front of his T-shirt, feeling the dampness of him against her fingers. Beneath his wet shirt she felt his hard, muscular chest, her fingers glided across his nipples. Several previous Rent-A-Hubby's passed in front of her eyes and she felt a flicker, like a drug addict in the first few weeks of sobriety, and knew she would do this.

"You must work out," she said with an uneasy smile as she looked up into his dark, puzzled eyes. Later she would think it sounded like a cheesy come-on line, but the important thing was that it worked.

"Yea-yeah," he stammered, surprised and a bit shocked by the contact. He had fantasized about some of the soccer mom's before, even about two of the hotter moms ambushing him in his office after a winning game and having their way with him. It was unlikely that would happen, but this was happening. He could hardly believe it and he found it arousing, even stimulating.

Wynette couldn't remember the coach being such a handsome man, with his thinning black hair, thick porn star mustache and square jaw.

"You like?" He smiled with that dirty wet mouth she wanted clamped to her juicy hot pussy.

"I... I was just thinking you might catch cold," Wynette lied and dropped her keys, which fell between his dirty white sneakers.

When she reached to pick up her keys, she found her face very close to his bulging, damp crotch. She inhaled deeply, smelling his sweaty manly-smelling crotch. And suddenly all that mattered was that she wanted... desired... no, needed him. She pressed her face into his sweaty crotch, feeling the dampness of his regulation, reinforced coaching shorts against her face. So cool, so hot, so inviting!

He didn't resist! Instead, he leaned back against his desk so her face would make even closer contact with his crotch. He started to get hard and she made a request. The coach nodded and eased down the shorts so that his cock was right in her face; hard, red, almost angry. Wynette smiled up at him before she took him in her mouth. She was continually amazed at the effect sex had on men; an aggressive woman could get them to do anything. Giji had always known that, but it was no time to think about Giji.

She swallowed him, taking his cock slowly into her throat, licking the underside as a boyfriend from long ago had shown her, and felt him push up against her as far as he dared. They both were tense listening for any sound that might mean that they would get caught and that excitement along with the coach's fantasies about other soccer moms caused him to shoot off a little sooner than he normally would. Wynette didn't mind since she always found giving head a tiresome way to get her needs – other than sexual–met.

Suddenly there were several bangs and what sounded like kicks to the office door.

"Sounds like my kids have arrived," Wynette told him, getting to her feet. "I guess I should…"

The coach gave a sort of half nod and he may have grunted, Wynette wasn't sure given the racket her kids were making, but he didn't speak. Wynette took her purse from the chair, turned and left the office without a word.

"What were you doing in there?" Petey asked.

"Yeah, what took you so long?" Pauly chimed in. "We were getting worried."

"Oh, there's nothing to worry about," Wynette assured her twin sons with a satisfied smile, carefully pulling the door closed behind her. "I was just making sure the coach keeps his two best players on the team where they belong."

"Us?" they said in unison as if they couldn't believe what they were hearing.

"Yes, you, silly guys," Wynette told them. "Now let's go home. I don't know about you two, but I'm exhausted."

19

A New Way to Cook

When Connie arrived on the set, it was dark with just enough light to see your way around the counters and stools. She dropped her bag on one of the stools in front of the island and stood behind the island as if she were doing the show herself. That was when she thought of Real. She really couldn't imagine the show without him since he was the force that made it special and made her want to be a part of the TV series.

Connie wandered through the dark kitchen, wondering what the first episode would be like. She was pleased Chef Real had asked her to be a part of it and she spent many hours thinking about what it would be like to do something like that with him. Well, that and other things… Connie started to dance slowly, seductively, unaware that someone was watching. She placed the spatula between her legs and rubbed it against her pussy, enjoying the friction of the spatula against the fabric of her skirt over her labia. The sensation was pleasant, even pleasurable, she decided and increased the movement until she felt she could reach orgasm with a little more encouragement. *Ohhhhh!* She almost moaned out loud as she closed her eyes and thought of Real, imagining he was here with her, pleasuring her....

While she fantasized, she used the whisk to lightly touch her breasts through her blouse, letting the rounded part of the whisk center on her erect nipples. Making small circles around the area of her blouse where her right nipple was, Connie began to feel the arousing sensation the wire whisk made as it stimulated the sensitive skin beneath the thin cotton fabric of her blouse. *Ah! That felt wonderful,* she thought, wondering why Lex didn't pay more attention to her breasts. She'd always felt it was because her breasts weren't as full as he'd like, judging from the issue of Juggs she'd found in the back of his closet, she decided it was an accurate assumption. She never encouraged him to play with her breasts, kiss them or lick them, or suck her nipples while they were having sex. If she asked and he didn't show any interest or refused, she would have been crushed and having sex with him would have been less pleasurable, maybe even unbearable.... She rubbed her nipples through her blouse and threw her head back, leaning against the side of a stainless steel counter for balance.

"Wow," Real said from the shadows, "I've never seen cooking utensils used in this manner, but I would love to try the dish sometime."

Embarrassed, Connie suddenly stopped and dropped the utensils on the counter in front of her. "I was just...ah...just fooling around a little."

"That was very creative," Real said in a lively voice. "I am very impressed."

Suddenly he was much closer. *Very close,* Connie thought, smelling his manly, appealing aroma, kind of like a combination of nutmeg and *Aqua Velva.*

It should not have been such a heady situation. Connie could have easily pulled back a little and started another conversation without letting him see that she knew he was interested and it might have all ended there but she suddenly felt a sense of abandon. For a split second, she thought about her life and why she took the class in the first place. She thought of all the things she had never done because they weren't acceptable socially, and in that moment she made a decision.

Her pussy was still feeling the effects of the spatula, her pussy quivering excitedly, even more so when she was caught in the act by her teacher.

It was like being caught masturbating, she thought.

She leaned into Chef Real and smiled. He pushed aside the thin lace of her panties with one hand as he held her face with the other.

"Is this what you want?" he whispered in her ear. Connie didn't say anything; she just pressed her finger to his lips and pressed her pussy against the curve in his hand, which now cupped her completely.

That was all they did, that time. He moved his hand around her like he was folding sweet spices in one of his cooking bowls, leaning her head and neck as she moaned and moved against him.

It felt so good, Connie thought. This must be what it feels like to really be in lust. Certainly, she had felt that way with her husband at one time, but she pushed that thought away as she leaned against the counter. She could feel him pressing hard against her leg and wondered for a minute whether or not she should take this encounter a step further.

She felt a sense of abandon, of a sexual power she had never felt before. It was overwhelming and incredibly liberating. The fear that held her back for so long was gone. She drew closer to Real and gave him a soft, promising kiss on the lips. A kiss that promised more to come....

He seemed surprised. She could see it in his eyes. "What was that about?" he asked, but he knew. How could he not feel the same longings she felt?

She smiled, licking her lips, tasting him on her tongue. "Just something I felt like doing," she told him matter-of-factly.

He laughed, that wonderful deep and manly laughter that sent shivers down her spine. "Well, since we're being honest, there's something I've been wanting to do since the first time we met," Real said, coming even closer, his handsome face just inches from hers, "Since that day when you came into my class."

Connie could hardly believe he was speaking the words she wanted to hear. "What's stopping you?" she taunted.

With that, Real took her into his strong, muscular arms and held her close, tight, his lips pressing hard to hers in the deepest, most passionate kiss she had ever experienced. She held on to him as if her very life depended on it. "Take me," she whispered breathlessly. "Take me now!"

Suddenly Real began to change, to fade away.... She screamed "No!" so loudly that it rang in her ears, it was so loud and so real that when she woke, she wasn't sure if she'd screamed out loud. What if Lex heard her? She rolled over toward her sleeping husband. He was lying on his back, snoring like a runaway locomotive. She took a deep breath, relieved Lex hadn't heard her and she turned away from him. He stirred slightly, then rolled over on his side away from her, ending the snoring.

Thank God it was just a dream, she thought. *Masturbating with cooking utensils?*

Shivering more from realization than chill, she reached down to pull up the covers and felt a dampness between her legs....

***

"What do you mean you've run out of Rent-A-Hubbies for me?" Wynette demanded, like an addict talking to her dealer. "I have work that needs to be done. What should I do?"

"Well, since you asked," the woman said firmly, "I suggest you call an escort service!"

"What?" Wynette asked outraged. "How dare you... Hello... Hello?"

The doorbell rang and Wynette quickly put down the phone and went to answer the door. She looked through the peephole. Good! It was SueAnn. Maybe she'd have a suggestion. After all, she was the one who gave her the idea to hire a hubby!

***

The wives met at SueAnn's before they headed next door to Wynette's house for an intervention, similar to the intervention their friend Mary Lynn staged when Wynette was addicted to daytime soap operas. This intervention, made that one seem tame by comparison because it now seemed their friend and neighbor Wynette was addicted to sex. SueAnn went over first to pave the way.

"I don't see the big deal," Giji told them on the walk over to Wynette's house, "after all, Wynette is just having sex. It's not like she's a crack whore or a meth addict."

"Any addiction can be harmful to your life," Connie told her, "and one addiction can lead to another."

"So, Wynette could become a crack whore turning tricks for sex?" Ariella asked.

"Something like that," Connie said. "Besides, even if it were only sex, it can't be good for her family or her marriage."

"What do you think Mary Lynn would do?" Ariella asked softly.

Giji shrugged. "What we're doing, trying to help a friend in need."

"She'd stage an intervention," Connie answered matter-of-factly. "Like the one she did when Wynette was addicted to soaps."

"Okay," Ariella said as they walked up the walkway to Wynette's front door. "Let's just hope she's between lovers!"

Once they reached the door, Giji took the lead and rang the bell. The wives exchanged nervous glances as they waited for the door to open.

***

Dozens of catalogs were strewn haphazardly on the coffee table. SueAnn briefly peeked at some of the titles: Pottery House, Park Avenue, Chic Image, and many more.

"Wow, Wynette," SueAnn said, looking up, "I see you've been catalog shopping."

A look of panic crossed Wynette's thin face. Worriedly she ran a hand through her unkempt blonde hair. "I'm not addicted!" she said quickly. "I only buy what I need."

"I know," SueAnn said quietly and seated herself on the sofa. "I know
you're not addicted to shopping and that's not why I'm here."

Wynette sighed, relieved. "All right. You just want to talk?"

"Well, not exactly," SueAnn admitted. "The other girls are on the way over."

"Really?" Wynette seemed curious. "If I had known I could have made drinks with those funny little umbrellas for everyone."

The doorbell rang.

"Here they are now," SueAnn announced and hurried to the door.

"What's going on guys?" Wynette asked when they were all in her living room facing her. "I feel a little out numbered." She laughed, pretty sure she knew what as coming. "Really, what is this about?"

Ariella sighed. "It's another intervention," she admitted.

SueAnn nodded. "Yes, it is, Wynette."

Wynette said calmly. "Who's turn is it?"

"Unfortunately," Giji said firmly, "it's your turn again!"

"You have a problem," SueAnn told her. "You may not even be aware that it's a problem, but it seems to be getting worse and worse."

Wynette shrugged. "So, I have a glass of wine after dinner," she said, playing stupid. "It's not like I'm an alcoholic. I just like a glass of wine or two after dinner to relax before bedtime."

"We're not referring to wine," Connie said uneasily.

"No, we're not," SueAnn agreed. "The kids are away at camp,

and you have a lot of time on your hands. It's not unusual that you would try to find something to fill the void, but sex with strangers is not the answer."

"We count on you to be the sensible one," Ariella said, "The level headed one when the rest of us spiral out of control. If you keep spiraling out of control this way, it'll throw off the balance of nature."

"How can we count on you when you're shagging every guy who

sports a large tool..." Giji paused before adding "belt!"

"Giji!" SueAnn gasped.

Wynette spoke. "I don't have a problem. It's just..." her voice trailed off.

"An insatiable appetite?" Ariella ventured.

"You're all hypocrites!" Wynette shouted and in a quieter tone she added, "Except maybe Connie."

Connie frowned and lowered her eyes as if she was embarrassed by being excluded. But, she valued her privacy and if you can't have privacy, discretion is the next best thing!

Wynette put her hands up for a moment as if the topic were off limits. "I'm not comfortable discussing my sex life with my friends or anyone for that matter," she started. "I don't think my husband would appreciate that very much."

SueAnn took a deep breath. "Hon, it's not your sex life with Steven that we're talking about. You're having sex with other people, and it's happening more and more. It's beginning to affect your daily routine. Steven and the kids need you to be there for them completely."

Wynette sank into the sofa, buried her face in her hands and started to weep. "How do I beat this?" she asked between sobs.

SueAnn sat beside Wynette and rubbed her back. "You can start by getting help," she said quietly. "See a professional, a therapist who can help you beat this addiction before it consumes you."

Wynette looked up, drying her eyes on her sleeve. "Okay, I'll call a therapist," she said. "I'll do it now."

While her friends watched, Wynette reached for the cordless phone on the end table. Looking down, Wynette paused before dialing. She could just see the edge of the flyer from the Sexual Psychic. Fortunately, it was the edge with the phone number - 1-800-Sex-Psyc. Thank goodness the number was in plain view, she felt clever as she dialed the number.

"Hello, Kimiko, Sexual Psychic."

"Hello," she said calmly. "I'd like to make an appointment. The earlier you can see me the better."

"Oh, you be impatient. Tomorrow good for you too?"

"Oh, yes." Wynette smiled. "Tomorrow will be great."

Satisfied that Wynette was making the effort to get the help she needed, her friends said a few words of encouragement and milled out one by one. SueAnn lingered behind. "I'm so proud of you," she told Wynette.

Wynette smiled. "Thank you," she said simply, wondering if the Sexual Psychic could offer her an alternative to her current sexual exploits, after all, good men were getting harder and harder to find!

***

Feeling a tiny twinge of guilt, Wynette kept her appointment with the Sexual Psychic. She promised SueAnn and the other wives that she would seek the help of a therapist and that's what she was doing. Of course, they probably expected her to see a legitimate sex therapist. The Sexual psychic is a sex therapist, she decided, trying to make herself feel better. The words "Sex Therapist" were right there on the sign, right between "Sex Dream Interpretation" and "Celebrity Gossip"! Besides, how much trouble could she get into with a woman? Men were her weakness.

It wasn't long before she was called back into the small room with the table and the red drapes. She took a seat in front of the most demure Asian woman she had ever seen.

"My friends feel I should get some help," Wynette admitted. "They think I have a problem."

Kimiko looked closely at the tall blonde before her. "What problem?"

"They think I'm addicted to sex," she told the small Asian woman and lowered her voice as if someone might hear even though they were the only ones in the shop. "I saw on your sign that you're a sex therapist. Can you help me... with my problem?"

"I sex addict once, too," Kimiko admitted. "I kick the habit."

"How'd you do that?" Wynette really wanted to know.

"Oh, I keep busy," the small Asian woman answered. "Kimiko raise family of eleven. Run full-time business as Sexual Psychic. Read two books a week, sometimes only one. Watch lots of TV. Watch "American Idol!" That Simon Cowell slay me! He big giant homophobe, but in good way."

Surprised by what she'd just heard, Wynette raised her eye brows.

"Is there a good way?"

"Sure, sure," Kimiko replied. "If Oprah say so, it okay. Simon make goo-goo eye at Oprah. She all like laughy and bubble over!"

"Okay, I'm trying to follow you here," Wynette told the small Asian woman, "but I don't think Oprah has swung that far to the right."

"Not yet," Kimiko spat, a note rising in her shrill voice. "I Sexual Psychic. I see future. I say she break bread with George Bush on White House lawn before next election!"

Wynette shrugged and gave a little laugh. "I say your psychic connection has shorted out!"

Kimiko looked at her directly, her small eyes now dark and cold. "Listen, girlfriend, you don't want to get on my bad side," she spoke quickly, perfect English, with almost no accent. "Keep your predictions to yourself. Let's not forget who the psychic is here!"

"You speak perfectly good English!" Wynette said accusingly.

"You keep my secret, I keep your secret," Kimiko told her, her voice suddenly calm again. "How you say, what happen in Sexual Psychic shop stay in Sexual Psychic shop!"

"Ummm," Wynette said, suddenly feeling better. "I like that. Kinda like that Vegas slogan that was used so many times in so many different places and now it sounds ridiculous!"

Kimiko laughed even though she wasn't sure exactly what Wynette was getting at. "You make funny," she said, "like ha ha!"

"So... you think you can help me?" Wynette asked.

Kimiko shrugged. "I think I have just the thing."

"Really?" Wynette sounded doubtful.

The small Asian woman nodded. "Oh yes," she said, enthused. "Best part is it make you feel," she paused thinking, "how you say marvelous!"

"I can hardly wait," Wynette said, still not convinced.

Wynette watched as Kimiko moved under the table and felt a soft hand on her thigh. She jumped at the initial touch, but then stayed still as the woman's hand slid toward her pussy. Surely, she wasn't going to... A moment later those hands grabbed her hips and pulled her forward on the chair.

The little woman lifted her head and pushed the table cloth out of her way. She reached inside the elastic of her panties and pulled them from Wynette's body. Wynette was too stunned to say anything and too curious to stop her. She leaned back on the chair and slid her hips and her wet pussy toward the edge of the chair. Kimiko looked at her and gave her a wicked grin. The Asian woman buried her face in Wynette's wet pussy.

Wynette lifted her hips toward the woman's moist mouth and skillful tongue. As the small woman ate her pussy, Wynette could not suppress a moan. It seemed like years since she'd had oral sex. She had forgotten it could be so stimulating—or maybe it was Kimiko. It was like Kimiko's small mouth fit perfectly to her vagina and that small, pointed tongue was perfect for licking pussy! Her small, thin tongue, was perfect for going in deep and licking around Wynette's clit, occasionally licking her clit.

Wynette had never had anyone work her clit like that–it was as if the small tongue was everywhere at once! She could feel her orgasm stirring, building and an incredibly satisfying climax hit her at once. Wynette shuddered as her excitement continued to build to almost unbearable heights of ecstasy.

The pleasure was so intense that Wynette wondered why more men weren't into giving oral–they were certainly into receiving! Whatever the reason, she made a mental note to insist that her next Hire-A-Hubby, salesman, coach or whomever must be orally inclined and experienced.

As Wynette reached the most incredible orgasm she'd experienced in her life, she realized she truly had found a cure for her problem…or at least a solution. For now…

"I see you same time next week?" Kimiko asked, taking the fifty from Wynette and marking it quickly with the counterfeit detecting pen.

"You sure will!" Wynette said without any hesitation and humming softly to herself.

Any doubts she'd had about the Sexual Psychic were gone now!

20

A Bump in the Dark

Connie stood just off the set as Real thanked viewers for tuning into the first episode and invited them to tune in every week. As the credits rolled the lights went down and Real joined her. She had half-hoped he would not see her standing there, so she could sneak off.

"Great first show, eh?" he asked, grinning proudly.

Connie nodded. "Yes, yes," she stammered. "I'm exhausted, though."

He chuckled. "Me, too," he admitted, but she could see from the twinkle in his eyes that he'd enjoyed every minute of it.

"I wish things had gone smoother," she said quietly, apologetically, recalling that she'd overheated the sauce, spilled the spices and somehow managed to lose the main entree. "I am such a klutz. It wasn't intentional, I promise. I'm usually less accident prone. Just first show nerves, I guess." She paused, taking a deep breath. "I'll get better, I promise."

"You were fine," he said and seemed sincere. "I didn't expect the first episode to go off perfectly. From what I hear, they rarely do. Things happen. That's the beauty of live TV!" He paused as if unsure he was convincing her. "We'll both get better," he added and took her hand in his, caressing it.

She smiled, fully aware of his touch, feeling the tingle of electricity between them. "We will," she said simply, then pulled her hand from his. She glanced at her watch but did not see the time. "I have no idea what time it is," she worried. "I... I should get home."

He frowned. "I was hoping we could go out for a drink," he admitted, "To celebrate the success of our first episode. A few of the crew are going to a local bar for a round of drinks. I agreed to join in the celebration. I thought you might want to come along."

Reluctantly, Connie shook her head and looked away. "I wish I could," she begged off, "but I have a million things to do. I have to pick up something for dinner on the way home." She paused, took a deep breath, then added, "I'll have to take a rain check."

"Okay." He sounded disappointed. "Maybe some other time, then."

"Definitely," Connie assured him. "Yes, of course. Some other time."

Real said good night and walked back across the set where the crew members were talking, laughing and slapping each other on the back. Looks like the celebration has already started, Connie thought, watching as Real joined them, his strong voice and laughter ringing above the others. She watched as they filed out, wishing she had accepted Real's invitation but knowing all too well why she hadn't. Lately there were so many uncertainties in her life, she decided, and if she had gone with Real and his friends, she wasn't sure where it would lead....

***

Giji's stiletto heels clicked on the worn asphalt as she walked toward the Sexual Psychic's small, dark shop. Giji opened the door to the Sexual Psychic's little shop and waited patiently until a young couple was escorted to the door, giggling, by Kimiko. "You remember what I said, you will be happy," said Kimoko as she shut the door behind them. She smiled, thin lips, thick gums and small teeth, then she saw Giji and frowned. "Oh, it you."

She turned to Giji, recognizing her from the other day.

Giji ignored the slight as she approached the small woman. "Hi," she forced a smile. "I told you I'd be back."

"Yes," Kimiko said flatly.

"But you probably knew that," Giji said with a slight laugh, "after all, you are a psychic!"

"Yes, that be true," the older woman agreed, still frowning. "Can't put one over on you. How I help you?"

"Oh, I dunno," Giji answered, not wanting to be too obvious. "I thought we could start with a reading."

"You follow me," Kimiko told her, pushing aside the faded silk curtain.

Once they were seated at the table in the larger room, Giji noticed a stack of business cards on a small plastic tray. Picking up one of the cards, she gave it a quick once over, noticing the obvious. *Cheap,* she thought, sloppy design, poor printing on thin cardstock. It didn't scream class, she thought, then recalling her surroundings and decided it was somehow appropriate. But, it gave her an idea.

"I see you're new in business," Giji said, gesturing with her eyes toward the card she held.

Shuffling the deck of Tarot cards, Kimiko shook her head. "No, no," she corrected, "I be here since…ah…1999. These for Grand Re-Opening. I try get new business." She looked up. "I just get those," she added proudly. "Late from printer, so I get free upgrade from Economy to Premier package. Better quality paper."

Giji tried to smile, wondering what the Economy cards would have been like. "Oh, yes, very nice," she lied.

"You like design?" Kimiko continued, still shuffling. "I do it myself on home PC."

"Really nice," Giji said, working up to her plan. "So, you're trying to drum up business?"

Kimiko finished shuffling the cards and placed the deck on the table in front of Giji to be cut. "Yes," she answered. "TV ads too expensive. I want to do ad like Miss Cleo, but she phony. Her accent not real." She sighed. "She get readings from Harry Potter book or something. I dunno. I call in, she say I psychic. Before that I sandwich artist at KFC!"

Giji hurriedly cut the cards. "Hmmm," she said, "I can probably send you some business. My whole neighborhood is sexually dysfunctional!"

"That be great," Kimiko said, her soft voice a mixture of skepticism and hope.

Giji smiled, pleased by the response. "I won't ask for much in return."

"Oh?" Kimiko's thin eyes widened. "What that be?"

"Have you heard the expression "you wash my back, I'll wash yours?"

Kimiko seemed shocked. "You want me to bathe you?"

"No, that's not really what I had in mind," Giji assured her, "although a tongue bath might be nice every now and then."

Kimiko frowned.

"Listen, I the Sexual Psychic," she said firmly, "not the Bi-Sexual Psychic!"

"Who are we kidding?" Giji said disbelievingly. "When dropped a little cash, you licked my cunt like a cat licking cream! You didn't seem to have a problem going down for a twenty!"

The small woman shrugged. "I gave you introductory discount, price usually fifty. But you bring me interesting clients, I give you lick on the house."

"Well, I will settle for free sessions to start," Giji agreed without any hesitation, "Later I'd like a small portion of the profits I bring in. How's that?"

"What make you sure you deliver?"

"I know where there is a little red book filled with pertinent information about everyone in my neighborhood," said Giji.

"What kind of information?" asked Kimiko.

"Secret information," Giji said and winked.

"Can you do this?" Kimiko wanted to know.

"Of course," Giji assured her, confident she can get her hands on the coveted book. "She'll leave it lying around, and I'll bring it to your hands!"

"Good, that make Kimiko very happy," the small Asian woman said and smiled.

The names in Mrs. Hoover's little red book alone should be able to create a thriving business! That tramp should be able to bring her lots of business if she's not sleeping with them all first! She smiled
broader and passed the tarot cards over to Giji, who shuffled and cut.

"What do you see in my future?" Giji asked.

Kimiko spread out her tarot cards, and studied them.

"Hmmm," she said, still looking down at the cards. "Future look bright. Much pleasure come your way soon." Then she added in an excited voice, "Kimiko predict you have an orgasm real soon!"

"Mmm," Giji said, pleased. "I can hardly wait."

Kimiko gathered her cards and put them aside. Then she closed the blinds, flipped the "We're Open" sign on the door to "Sorry, We're Closed," turned the lock and dimmed the lights.

"You are so tense," Kimiko told her. "You pussy like jaws of life or something!"

Giji sighed. "I know I'm tense," she admitted, closing her eyes. "Living with Mrs. Hoover will do that to a person."

"Oh." Kimiko understood. "That woman have mean spirit. But little red book good idea for us. We make lots of money."

"Yes," Giji said in a less tense voice, "lots of money. Mmm. Feels so relaxing, so good. Ooh. You were so right. I'm going to orgasmmmmmmm! Oh! You should call this place the G-Spot Cafe!" Giji gasped as the Sexual Psychic went down on her pussy for a second time.

The small woman raised her head. "Then Kimiko get busted. Kimiko go to jail. Big girl make Kimiko love slave. No. I not change name!"

"What about Mrs. Hoover's casseroles?" Giji wanted to know. "Am I endangering my health? My life?"

"If you keep eating like that, you going to look like Buddy Hackett!" the small Asian woman told her.

Kimiko finished licking Giji's pussy clean, then she tidied up and followed Giji into the outer room of the shop.

Giji smoothed her skirt, then began fumbling through her purse for her cash.

Kimiko looked out the window and saw a young police officer walking around Giji's car. He stopped near the front of the car, took out his notebook and started writing. "You meet a nice young man in uniform soon."

"Really!" Giji sounded excited. "Is he hot?"

Kimiko squinted. "Tall. Nice butt, yes, but he not too bright. Attic dusty. No, no, swept clean." She raised her arms to demonstrate incoming tidal wave, "as if he had been hit by tsunami."

Giji smiled partly at Kimiko's sense of the dramatic and partly because she kind of liked her guys dumbed down. They were a lot more fun when they weren't so serious or complicated, not really thinking of anything but having sex and having a good time. But mostly having sex!

"How soon till I meet this hot hunky guy?" Giji wondered.

Kimiko smiled, almost a grin as she held out her hand. "Put fifty on my palm and hurry, you probably catch him before he finish writing ticket!"

***

Giji tossed her keys on the bedside table and sat on the edge of the bed. It had been a hard day and she was looking forward to her nightly bath. She slipped out of her clothes and into her hot pink satin robe. She started the bath, adding the new bath beads she picked up at the drugstore on her way home. *Vanilla Twist*, she wondered what the twist would be, and poured a liberal handful into the running water. Once the steam from the water began to fill the small bathroom, she realized the twist was an added lemony freshness. Hmmm, she thought, not bad. Kind of soothing.

While her bath ran, Giji crossed the hall and went into her bedroom, leaving her door open so she could hear the water. She stretched out across her bed and leafed through the latest *Frederick's of Hollywood* catalog, trying to recover from the latest casserole dinner she had shared with Mrs. Hoover. Tonight it was Mrs. H's infamous hamburger and goat cheese casserole, the combination left her stomach a little queasy.

Giji was studying a shiny faux leather jumpsuit with optional handcuffs when her cell rang. She took the phone off the night table and looked down at the screen. She did not recognize the number; it could be a client calling about a property. Hesitating, it occurred to her that it might be him, the caller, but she didn't want to miss a call from a client. So she pressed a key and put the phone to her ear. "Hello?"

Heavy breathing was the only reply.

"Hey, breather," Giji said in an almost playful voice. "Stop wasting my time and do something besides breathing loudly into the phone." She giggled. "It was a bit of a turn on at first, but now it's tired. We need a new game. What do you say?"

Loud breathing.

"Could you just cough or clear your throat or something?"

Loud breathing. Giji sighed, frustrated.

"Well, at least I know you're still alive!"

A little cough.

"There!" Giji beamed triumphantly. "Now if you will speak, this can get exciting."

Loud breathing.

Giji got an idea. "Hey I know a game we can play," she announced breathlessly. "I'll say word and you say the first word that comes to mind. Let's see." She paused, thinking. "Sex!"

"Whore!" he finally spoke. A male voice, deep, slightly nasal.

Giji paused, thinking, but she could not put a face to the voice. There was something familiar about the voice. Where had she hard the voice before? She wondered. But she could not recall exactly.... maybe she could keep him talking until she figured it out.

"Cock!"

"Whore!"

"Cunt!"

"Whore!"

This was getting boring quick, and Giji was beginning to get nervous, maybe this wasn't such a fun game after all. "I don't like your tone, Mister!" Giji said indignantly. "That's no way to talk to a lady!"

"Screw you, bitch!"

"Okay," Giji said, thinking, "I have something that you'll enjoy. I'll describe myself for you. You'll like this a lot." She decided to give it one more try; after all, he was on the other end of the phone...

Loud breathing. "I'm wearing a tight Catholic schoolgirl uniform," she told him in her sexiest voice. "I have on fishnet stock –"

"You're a lying bitch!" he snapped. "Don't fuck with me. I don't like games. Got it?"

The line went dead.

Giji looked at the phone. "If you keep that up," she said aloud, "I'll stop taking your calls!"

Suddenly, Giji realized if her caller knew she was lying he must be able to see her. She tore open the curtains and looked up and down the street. Nothing, no cars parked out in front of her house, and no vagrants wandering the street. Okay, he might have been bluffing, he might have been guessing that I was lying, but if that's the case, how did he know when to call? He always called around the same time, always in the evening, usually while she was undressing or about to undress and have her evening bath. Maybe she should change her routine, she thought. In the meantime, her bath was ready, but this time she locked the bathroom door behind her.

***

"Whew, that taping was brutal!" Chef Real said as they wrapped the scene and began to head out of the building.

"Yes, it was," Connie agreed, "I could use a cup of coffee to clear my head."

"Would you like to go get one?" Real asked.

Right into my trap, thought Connie. She said "You know the best kept secret in town is that the best coffee is in the hospital cafeteria."

"Really?" Chef Real looked doubtful. Hospital coffee was notoriously bad.

"Really," Connie lied. "Come on, I'll drive over in my car, and you can follow me."

Connie got into her car and waited for Chef Real to pull up behind her, and then drove to the hospital, where she knew that Lex would be taking his dinner break soon. He often ate a late dinner while working, it was easier than packing a snack at home, and that was fine with Connie; less cooking for her. She didn't really know why she was doing this, except that the thought of Lex's reaction to seeing her having coffee with such a handsome man might make him realize what he was missing at home. Mostly she just wanted some excitement in her life and maybe the fantasy that two men would fight over her. Chef Real held the door open for her and they ordered at the counter. Holding the scalding thin Styrofoam cups, they chose a small table in the back near the wall and sat down. Connie was careful to take the seat that looked out over the entire cafeteria, which she thought was a great vantage point to see who came in.

"What do you think of the lighting?" Chef Real asked after they had made themselves comfortable.

"Well, it's bad for the complexion, but I guess people don't linger here much," said Connie, looking around and up at the florescent lights.

"No," he laughed, "I meant on the set."

"Oh, on the set. I guess its okay, I don't know much about those kinds of things." Did I just bat my eyes at him?

"I think you have more of an opinion than you let on," winked Real as he sipped at the boiling swill. She doesn't know much about coffee, though, he smiled between sips. Still, she was a fascinating woman in his opinion, multilayered, he decided, and intriguing. There was so much more to Connie, he believed, than she was willing to allow others to see. He felt she could really let herself go, if she'd only loosen up a little around him.

Connie started to answer, but the words caught in her throat. There was Lex, carrying his tray to the table, predictable as ever, but someone was with him. What would he be doing with Deanna at this hour? She was the hospital administrator, and usually went home around 5 p.m., with the rest of the office people. It was nearly 11 p.m.! Connie watched Lex laugh, balancing his tray in one hand and pulling out her chair with the other. He even pushed it in without spilling anything from his tray! When was the last time he pulled a chair out for her?

"… and that's how it all started." Chef Real looked like he was waiting for her to say something.

"What? I'm sorry, I thought that I saw someone I knew," said Connie.

"I was telling you how the show came to be," said Real.

"I'm sorry, I forgot to do something at home and I really need to be going. Thanks for the coffee, Real. I'll see you at the next shoot." Connie excused herself and left. Chef Real caught up with her in the parking lot.

"Connie, wait up," he called out behind her. She stopped and turned around, allowing him to catch up.

"Did I say something?" he worried. "Did I do something wrong?"

"No, not at all, I just saw my husband with another woman."

"What would he be doing in a hospital cafeteria?"

"He works here, he's a doctor," whispered Connie. Chef Real was silent for a minute, and Connie could only guess what he was thinking. He must have guessed why she had wanted to come here for coffee. She waited for him to say it served her right for bringing him here since she knew her husband would be in the lunch room, but he didn't. He simply leaned against her car and thought for a second. It seemed like an eternity.

"Well, don't jump to conclusions," he finally said, "After all, you were here with another man. What's a cup of coffee between coworkers?"

"I guess you're right," she admitted. They said good night and she drove home, but Connie had every intention of finding out.

***

It was well after two in the morning when Connie finally heard Lex's car pull into the driveway. She thought about pretending to be asleep when he came in, but changed her mind and snapped the light on next to the bed, picking up her book from the side table and opening it. She would be reading and waiting up for him, she decided, and she managed a look of distain when he opened the bedroom door.

"You look tired," she greeted him.

"I am," said Lex, sitting across from the bed and taking off his shoes.

"I'll just bet you are!" Connie blew.

"What's that supposed to mean?"

"I saw you with the hospital administrator tonight, I saw you having coffee with her. What did the two of you do after that?"

"When was this? You came into the cafeteria and didn't even

say 'Hi' to me? Where were you?"

Connie realized that if she went any further with this that she would have to explain herself. There was an awkward silence, then she said, "I was coming to have a late dinner with you, but when I saw the two of you together I figured three's a crowd and left." Nice save, she thought.

"Nothing's going on with me and Deanna, she met me to discuss the candidates for another administrator. She's accepted a position with another hospital, out of state. She's leaving."

"Oh," said Connie in a small voice. Lex shrugged and went in to take a shower. Connie felt foolish but at the same time realized just how much she loved her husband. Like a school girl, she thought of Chef Real; how charming and understanding he was, he was so spontaneous and made her feel special. Alternating between feeling sick and excited, Connie snapped off the light and waited for her man to come to bed.

***

It was around three o'clock in the morning when the sounds woke Giji from a quiet sleep. First a crash, and then she heard a moan. She started to get out of bed, but something pushed her down. Giji wasn't a weak woman, she swung as hard as she could and the assailant fell with a thud.

"Ah ha, caught you, you asshole, knocked the hell out of you, didn't I?" The adrenaline was flowing and Giji was mad as hell. She snapped on the bedside lamp only to find Mrs. Hoover scrambling for the closet door.

"It's me, it's me!" Mrs. Hoover held her hand to her head.

"What the hell?" Giji was still angry and more than a little frightened. After the increasingly threatening obscene phone calls she had been getting, anything but sound asleep made her edgy at night.

"I heard noises downstairs and came to get you, or see if it was you But, I tripped and woke you up, and you hit me!" Mrs.

Hoover said accusingly.

"You deserved to be hit! You scared the hell out of me!"

The two women were calming down.

"Let's go downstairs and see if anything's missing," Mrs. Hoover said finally.

"Let's call Nick to come over first," said Giji.

"No, I don't want anyone else involved in this, let's just go downstairs." Mrs. Hoover got to her feet and with Giji's help made it to the kitchen. The door was wide open.

Apparently, the intruder jimmied the door to break in. Giji started a pot of coffee and took a bottle of brandy from Mrs. Hoover's cupboard. She wondered to herself if the obscene caller, who obviously watched the house, had snuck in. She dismissed the thought and was glad she hadn't said anything, it would have sent the old bat into hysterics. If there was one thing Giji couldn't stand–next to a silent obscene phone caller–it was hysterics.

"I won't be able to sleep another wink tonight," Mrs. Hoover said and sipped her coffee.

"Neither will I," Giji admitted. "I just keep thinking he might come…"

"No, no," Mrs. Hoover said comfortingly. "Intruders never come back unless they lost something or forgot something."

A thought occurred to Giji. "What do you think the intruder was after?"

Mrs. Hoover shrugged. "I don't know," she lied. "It could have been anything. I don't know what the intruder wanted. He could be a drug fiend looking for money to get his next fix. I just don't know."

Mrs. Hoover closed her eyes, remembering how she woke in the dark with someone moving around her bed in the dark. At first she thought it was Giji snooping around, trying to get her hands on her little red book. But, she saw the light from a small flashlight and she knew it was an intruder. She wanted to scream but no sound would come out of her mouth. She watched as the dark figure take her beloved little book and flee. After taking a few deep breaths, she got out of bed and followed the intruder to the kitchen but by then he was long gone… and so was her little red book. Unfortunately, she had continued to leave her diary on her bedside table, even after the night she'd mistaken thought Giji had swiped it. If only, she thought, but that's not going to help now, she decided.

"Maybe we should call someone. Like the pol-," Giji interrupted her thoughts.

"No!" Mrs. Hoover snapped. "We can't involve the police. We don't want them poking their noses around in…things. I mean, we both have things we'd rather keep quiet."

"The intruder may be watching the house; he'll know we didn't call the police and he may come back!" Giji told her, and then she said it again, "Maybe I should call Nick and have him come over to protect us."

Mrs. Hoover shook her head adamantly. "I don't think that's a very good idea, either. We don't want to involve anyone else."

"I just thought we'd feel safer if we had a big strong man to protect us…"

"No," Mrs. Hoover interrupted. "It's not a good idea. The fewer people who know about this, the better."

"So you plan to do nothing?" Giji asked incredulously. "I mean there was a break in and something could have been stolen."

"I know what you're saying, Giji," Mrs. Hoover said, "but nothing good can come of involving others. It'll just complicate things." She took a deep breath. "There are things I just don't want being made public. I'm not proud of some things I've done." She put a hand on her chest as if she were having difficulty breathing.

"Are you okay, Martha?" Giji asked, concerned. "Should I call an ambulance?"

Mrs. Hoover waved a hand, dismissing the idea. "No, no, I'm fine," she told her houseguest. "It's upsetting is all… scary."

Giji nodded. "Yes, it was." She patted the older woman's hand.

"I'm glad I wasn't alone." Mrs. Hoover appreciated Giji's presence for the first time. "It would have been even scarier. Having you here and not having to go through this alone was a real comfort."

"I'm just glad we're both okay," Giji told her. "Are you sure nothing was taken?"

Mrs. Hoover nodded and lied. "I don't know what this person could have been after...."

Giji and Mrs. Hoover were certain they couldn't sleep a wink after the break-in They were left frightened and nervous that the intruder might return, but sometime in the wee hours, they felt calmer and more at ease and tried to get some sleep before daybreak.

Giji was surprised to hear Mrs. Hoover's snoring loudly a few minutes after they turned in. The old bat must have fallen asleep when her head touched the pillow, Giji thought when she got up and closed her door to block out the sound. She clicked the lock on the door, feeling safer, just in case....

The next morning Giji slept late. When she woke, Mrs. Hoover was still asleep. Giji knew Mrs. Hoover was asleep as soon as she opened her bedroom door and heard the older woman snoring loudly.

Pulling on her robe, she crept quietly crept downstairs. What a night! Thankfully, she didn't have any appointments for showings this morning. Wearily she sank onto the sofa. She planned to make breakfast, maybe surprise Mrs. Hoover with breakfast in bed. But she felt so tired, she wasn't sure she could summon the strength. She would try to make breakfast a bit later and she laid her head back against the comfortable cushion-backed sofa.

She had just dozed off in a peaceful slumber when the doorbell rang. Wondering who it could be, she got to her feet and shuffled to the door. "Yes?" she said after she opened the door.

An older man stood there, tall, gray haired with horn-rimmed glasses and a wrinkled gray suit that almost matched his hair. He smiled pleasantly. "Good morning," he said in greeting.

"Can I help you?" Giji asked, certain her appearance was frightful and not feeling up to socializing.

"Yes," the man said, smiling warmly. "I'm here to see Martha."

Giji suppressed a yawn. "I'm sorry, she's not up yet."

"I see," he said, and after they introduced themselves, he took an envelope from the inside pocket of his jacket. "Maybe you can give this to her for me?"

Giji nodded, taking the envelope from him. "Of course." She turned and put the envelope on the console table in the entrance. Although the thin envelope was sealed, she saw it contained cash, a lot of cash. When she turned back she saw Reverend Daley had followed her. "Oh," Giji said uneasily, "would you like… to… sit for a while? I'd offer you coffee, but –"

The Reverend waved a hand in the air dismissively. "No, no thank you," he followed her into the living room where they sat on the sofa. "I already had my two cups."

"If you're thirsty," Giji began, not sure what to say to the Reverend, "I can get you –"

The Reverend watched her closely, as if he were studying her physique.

Giji felt more self-conscious than she had before and as if he were undressing her with his eyes. Pulling her robe tighter around her breasts, she noticed his eyes followed each movement and she could have sworn he was drooling like a dog in heat!

"So," Giji began, trying to think of something to say to distract him, "how long have you known Mrs. Hoover?"

"We go back a long, long way," the Reverend admitted with a heavy sigh. He explained that he'd known Martha Hoover since he came to First Methodist Church. He was young, naïve, newly married and it was his first appointment. Dealing with the likes of Mrs. Hoover proved very stressful to say the least and through the years it only got worse. "God's way of testing me, I suppose," he added and laughed good-naturedly.

"I guess so," Giji agreed.

"Yes, yes." The Reverend was looking at her chest again.

"So, Mrs. Hoover is a good Christian lady?" Giji spoke to get his attention and at the same time she wanted information from him about Martha Hoover, since he'd known her longer than almost anyone.

He swallowed hard. "Well, she's in church every Sunday," he told Giji and tried to smile.

Remembering the cash the Reverend brought in the envelope for Mrs. Hoover, Giji thought of Mrs. Hoover's little red book, full of secrets. Before she caught herself she blurted out, "Is Mrs. Hoover blackmailing you?"

For a few seconds the Reverend seemed shocked by her question, but once he regained his composure, he cleared his throat, "I would exactly call it blackmail."

"What would you call it?" Giji asked, sure her hunch was correct.

He shrugged and gave a small, sad smile. "Payback," he said.

"Payback for...?"

"Miss Brickhouse, I want to save your soul," Reverend Daley interrupted, changing the subject, then paused and licked his thick lips as he stood, "and touch your spirit."

Giji grinned, realizing she would get no further with the Reverend on the subject of blackmail or Martha Hoover. "You sure that's not all you want to touch?" she chided, standing up.

"Well, first things first," the Reverend smiled. He gave her a hug, holding her tightly to his body. Giji thought she felt a little poke, but it could have been a pen or his belt buckle. Then one of his hands brushed one of her tits while the other lightly cupped one of her buttocks.

Giji pulled away and winked at the frisky old man. "Reverend, you'd better go before you get us both in trouble!"

He grinned. "Oh, no, I wouldn't want that!"

"Mrs. Hoover will be down here any minute," she told him, deciding to keep quiet about the break-in, "and she hasn't had much sleep."

"Then by all means, let me be on my way!" He headed for the door.

Giji walked with him. "Here," she said and handed him the envelope. "I have a feeling Mrs. Hoover won't need this."

He smiled appreciatively as he took the envelope from her. "Thank you."

After he left, Giji searched downstairs for Martha Hoover's little red book, but she didn't find it. She wondered briefly if that was what the intruder wanted. Exhausted she sank back onto the sofa just as she heard Mrs. Hoover stirring upstairs....

21

The Psychic's Warning

When Mrs. Hoover came down, Giji had breakfast almost finished, eggs, grits, toast, juice and coffee. She encouraged the older woman to have a seat and allow her to wait on her. After bringing Mrs. Hoover coffee and juice, she prepared a plate for her.

"This is really nice of you, Giji," Martha Hoover said as if she weren't used to having anyone do anything nice for her.

"I thought you could use a little pampering after last night," Giji said quietly as she put a plate of food in front of Mrs. Hoover. "I hope it's okay. I haven't prepared a meal…ever."

"It smells delicious," Mrs. Hoover said, smiling as she took a bite of eggs. She closed her eyes, but she could not hide the frown brought on by the taste of the food. "Heavenly!"

Giji smiled, relieved. "Great," she sat across the table from Mrs. Hoover.

The older woman looked up from her food. "Aren't you having any?"

Giji shook her head. "Nope," she answered. "I never eat

breakfast."

Martha Hoover sighed loudly. "Oh, I forget," she said, taking a sip of her coffee.

"Martha, the Reverend Daley came by while you were asleep," Giji told her.

Mrs. Hoover gave her a quick, uneasy glance and looked down at the plate of grits Giji had just placed in front of her. "He did," she said finally.

"Yes," Giji said.

"He told me you've been blackmailing him for years," Giji lied and watched Mrs. Hoover's reaction to what she had just said.

Mrs. Hoover started to take a bit of her food and frowned again, but this time Giji figured it wasn't because of the taste. Mrs. Hoover put her fork down. "I might as well come clean," she said. "The Reverend and I had a fling after my husband died; he was married at the time. I cared for him…" her voice broke off.

"You loved him," Giji finished.

Mrs. Hoover nodded. "Yes, I did," she admitted. "But, he wouldn't leave his wife even though he said he loved me too. He felt it would be too much of a scandal to divorce his wife for another woman. He thought his wife might be angry and vindictive and create a backlash in the church." She looked at Giji and took a deep breath. "So he ended our relationship."

Giji listened.

"I was devastated for a long time, but later I was just angry. So I came up with the idea of blackmailing him, kind of a way to get even."

"That wasn't the best thing to do," Giji said, but she found herself feeling a bit of sympathy for the older woman.

Martha Hoover nodded. "I know," she said quietly. "I'm not proud of it."

"I am glad to hear that," Giji said, trying not to be too hard on Mrs. Hoover especially after their ordeal the night before. "I did drag most of the information out of Reverend Daley. He was willing to talk a little, but he was more interested in staring at my bust—and copping a quick feel!"

Suddenly Mrs. Hoover put a hand to her forehead, her expression harder now. "I should have known that dirty old pervert would spill everything the first chance he got!"

"Play nice, Martha," Giji warned, but from Mrs. Hoover's reaction, Giji realized how deep the woman's feelings ran for Reverend Daley. "Remember, you're the one in the hot seat here."

"I'm sorry," Mrs. Hoover apologized. "I'm still angry about the past." She paused briefly. "Funny, I thought I was over that."

Giji nodded, knowing how hard it was to get over losing someone you love. Looking at Mrs. Hoover's fountain pen lying on the table, an idea occurred to her. "Martha, where is that infamous little red book of yours?"

"It was stolen last night during the break in," Mrs. Hoover explained, looking down at her food. "Apparently that was what the intruder was after. Once he had that, he fled. I knew it was gone immediately," she added, looking at Giji now, "I wasn't sure there was a reason you had to know until now."

"Are you being honest with me?" Giji had doubts. Martha Hoover wasn't known for her honesty.

Mrs. Hoover exhaled loudly out of frustration. "Yes, Giji, I am," she answered, "I usually keep it locked in my safe, but I had been writing some things down." Her voice seemed to catch on the word things. "I left it on my bedside table... again... unfortunately."

Giji could usually tell when Martha Hoover was lying, and this time the older woman was telling the truth. *There goes my deal with the Sexual Psychic,* she thought, then an idea occurred to her: Could the Sexual Psychic have stolen the book – or did someone steal it?

Mrs. Hoover sighed quietly. "I guess I'll never see it again," she realized, "but at least we're okay."

Wondering, Giji glanced at the older woman. "Martha, exactly what was in your little book?"

Mrs. Hoover took a minute to respond, as if thinking over

what to say. "I wrote down things...little things I learned about people who live in this neighborhood," she stammered, closing her eyes as if she were ashamed. Her voice dropped to a whisper, "Secrets..."

Giji hoped her face didn't show her uneasiness. "Secrets?" she repeated. "What kind of secrets?"

Mrs. Hoover shrugged. "All kinds," she said as she let out a deep breath, almost as if letting out a sigh of relief. "All kinds."

"Mostly bad?" Giji wanted to know.

Mrs. Hoover nodded.

"How bad?"

"My little book has the sexual exploits of everyone on Erotica Lane and the surrounding neighborhood." Mrs. Hoover fell silent.

"Sexual exploits?" Giji gasped, thinking. "Do you have anything in there about me?"

"Yes..."

"Why would you do this?" Giji asked, suspicious. "I suspected your little book might contain secrets about people around the neighborhood, but sexual secrets?"

"People are willing to pay me money to keep their secrets quiet," Mrs. Hoover admitted, "especially the more sordid... sexual... ones."

"I'm not paying you a dime!" Giji snapped, finding it hard to believe she felt sympathy for this vile woman just moments earlier. She knew Mrs. Hoover was writing things about the neighbors in her diary, but she had no idea she was using her so-called secrets, to blackmail her neighbors.

"Well, my dear," said Mrs. Hoover knowingly, "yours aren't exactly secrets, if you know what I mean. So, I can't go after you, can I?"

Giji thought for a minute. "So, the Reverend Daley wasn't the only person you were blackmailing," Giji assumed. "You're probably making pretty good money, aren't you?"

Mrs. Hoover nodded, thinking. "Sometimes I didn't get money."

"What did you get?" Giji realized she might regret asking.

Mrs. Hoover gave a slight shrug. "You know...sexual...favors..." she answer slowly, embarrassed.

Giji cringed visibly. "Let's...just not go there," she begged.

"I was just trying to be honest –"

"You have no idea who took your little book?" Giji interrupted, anxious to change the way the direction of the conversation.

"It could have been... anyone." She paused, thinking. "Whoever it was, I have a feeling this thief got exactly what he came for."

Thinking of Mrs. Hoover's little red book, being in the hands of an intruder, possibly a stranger who might use the sordid secrets to his own end, sent a shiver down Giji's spine.

***

"I wanted to call Nick and have him come over and protect us," Giji said, looking directly at SueAnn. "He could have slept in my bed...with me, of course."

"Of course," Wynette said sarcastically.

Giji called a meeting to spill the beans on Martha Hoover and her little red book. If everyone knew she had it, she could no longer use it to blackmail the residents of Erotica Lane. The afternoon conversation with the lecherous pastor made up her mind, even though she had to admit the thought of some of these women being blackmailed didn't bother her in the slightest, but Giji Brickhouse had some integrity.

"Well, Martha wouldn't hear of it," Giji continued. "She wouldn't even let me call the cops. She didn't want anyone to know..."

"Know what?" Ariella asked.

"She kept a diary of sordid little secrets about the people on Erotica Lane," Giji said, relishing the stunned looks on her friend's faces.

"What kind of secrets?" Connie spoke for the first time.

Giji shrugged. "All kinds of things, I guess. Mostly sex secrets, I imagine. Things people do in private and don't want anyone else– even their neighbors and sometimes even their spouses–to know about."

"Most of us have nothing to worry about, right?" SueAnn said. "Giji, you didn't get a peek?"

"I didn't even get a fleeting glimpse," Giji admitted. "Mrs. Hoover guarded her diary as if her last breath depended on it!"

"Come on, Giji," Wynette prodded, "you sure you didn't swipe it?"

Giji shook her blonde tresses. "Unfortunately, no." she paused, a thought having occurred to her. "I know someone who may have taken it," she admitted, thinking of the Sexual Psychic. "If she didn't steal it, it could have been anyone."

"Well, who?" Wynette pressed.

Giji took a few seconds to look around the table at the other women. "I'm not in a position to say," she said evasively, "but it's someone who knows Mrs. Hoover."

"Great, that means a stranger could be privy to all our–I mean– the secrets in Mrs. Hoover's diary," Connie observed uneasily. "I wish we knew what was in there."

"At least your little indiscretion went public immediately," Giji said. "God only knows what that vile old bitty has on everyone else in that nasty little book of hers."

"Yeah," Ariella said absent-mindedly, trying to think if there was a chance Mrs. Hoover could know about her numerous affairs.

Connie rolled her eyes and stood up.

"Where are you going?" Wynette asked.

"Home," Connie answered. "There's no use sitting around here worrying. We can't change what has happened. Besides, the diary may disappear forever."

"Oh, it could resurface," Giji said confidently.

"How can you be so sure?" Wynette wanted to know.

"Because," Giji answered, "if someone wanted it bad enough to steal it, he or she is going to use it." She paused for dramatic effect. "I wouldn't be surprised to see it published on the Internet!"

Everyone gasped. Suddenly their worst fears were even worse than they had imagined. For a while no one spoke, it was so quiet, it seemed hard to believe anyone was actually breathing.

"I'm sure we have nothing to worry about," Wynette said finally, sounding worried.

"That's probably what Mary Lynn thought before she learned whatever caused her to blow her brains out," Giji said.

"Gee, Giji, thanks," SueAnn said sarcastically. "Way to go! You certainly know how to make everyone feel better."

Giji grinned. "What can I say, it's a gift!"

"Too bad you can't return it," Ariella said crossly as she stood to leave. "Listen, I have to get home. I have to make dinner for Marco."

As soon as the door closed, Giji sighed. "Who is she fooling? She never cooked a meal in her life!"

***

SueAnn took her bag and her keys from the console sofa table and was about to head to the grocery when the phone rang. Reluctantly she picked it up. "Hello?"

"Su-enn?" a thin female voice said on the other end.

"Yes."

"This Kimiko. I call to warn you. Be careful. Your life in danger!"

"What?" SueAnn asked as if she had misunderstood.

"Be safe," Kimiko answered. "Get here for reading soon. I close six on dot."

"Okay," SueAnn told her. "I'm on my way."

SueAnn opened the door and pulled it closed behind her just as Wynette started up her front steps.

"I was just coming over to see how you are," Wynette told her. "Where are you headed in such a hurry?"

"I'm not sure you'd believe me if I told you," SueAnn admitted, "but I just got a call from the Sexual Psychic and I'm going to see her."

"What did she say?" Wynette leaned against the porch rail.

SueAnn quickly explained about the psychic's warning that her life could be in danger, that she should be very careful and come in for a reading as soon as possible.

Wynette laughed. "Oh, I see where this is going," she said. "This psychic, and I do use the term loosely, just wanted another customer today and an extra 50 bucks. She just wanted to scare you. She knew that would get you scrambling to her for a reading, and apparently it worked."

SueAnn shrugged. "You really think she's just lying to get the money for a reading?"

Wynette nodded. "Yes, that's exactly what I think."

SueAnn looked at her keys. "Well, you may be right," she conceded reluctantly, "but I need to know if this is about Nick or something else." She took a deep, nervous breath. "I just need to know." She walked pass Wynette, down the steps and then paused. "Besides, I was headed to the grocery anyway. Can I pick you up anything?"

Wynette shook her head. "I'm good," she answered. "Just be careful."

Wynette watched SueAnn get into her small silver sedan and leave. Afterwards, she looked up and down the street. She checked her watch. *Where is that damned salesman?* she wondered, starting back toward her own house. *Oh well, guess he took a different route today.*

22

Cunts & Robbers

On her way to see Kimiko, SueAnn realized she was low on cash and needed to make a withdrawal from the ATM. She wheeled her car into the entrance at the bank and there were several cars at the drive-thru and she walked up to the ATM by the bank entrance. Later she would realize that if she had gone through the drive-thru, the day might have ended differently. Instead she parked and walked to the machine, fumbling for her card as she went.

At the ATM, SueAnn waited for her cash to drop into the slot when she saw two men dressed in dark clothes passed the ATM and headed toward the bank entrance. One looked back at her, and she thought about people who were robbed at ATM's each year. He only glanced at her and went inside with his buddy. Letting out a deep sigh of relief, she wondered what was taking the ATM so long. The enclosure was hot and dirty.

As SueAnn came out of the ATM enclosure, someone screamed, "Oh my god! The bank is being robbed!"

People scurried about. SueAnn was about to make a run for it when she saw the two men she saw earlier coming quickly from the bank entrance. They were the same men, but they were wearing ski masks over their faces and carrying weapons.

No, this can't be happening! SueAnn thought as two of the robbers, one on either side practically carried her from the ATM. Why the hell do they need me? I'll be late for my appointment! SueAnn fought against the men in black, biting down hard on one of their arms. Her mind raced between survival and her appointment with Kimiko. Later she would wonder why people think such strange thoughts during a crisis. The guy she bit swore and slapped her, hard enough to scare her.

"Quit fighting and I won't hurt you, I promise," he whispered in her ear, his voice thick.

They whisked her around a corner toward a waiting car with a driver inside at the ready. As they neared the car, SueAnn caught a flash of bright pink heading for them! Not Giji, she prayed. She started to breath deeper. Oh, no, she worried; Giji will get us both killed!

The pink skirt came around the side of the ATM enclosure and it was Giji. Police cars pulled up on the other side of the building, responding to the silent alarm.

"Hey…Hey!" yelled Giji at the men who had SueAnn. She was pushed into the backseat of a small coupe and before she knew it, Giji was sitting beside her.

"What the fuck!" Giji started to kick the back of the seat in front of her, getting a hard smack across the face from the guy in the passenger seat.

"Shut up!"

"Do you know who you're messing with?" Giji put a hand to her stinging cheek and continued kicking the seat, paying no attention to SueAnn.

"We should just throw this one out," the driver said as they screeched around a corner and down the block. Police cars were everywhere, and the street in front of them was blocked off when they approached the intersection. The car broke through the blockade and kept going, turning onto a nearby freeway entrance.

"Why didn't you tell me to run or something?" Giji turned to SueAnn.

"Jesus, Giji, I tried to! Why did you have to start kicking and screaming?"

"Well what the hell? Did you expect me to just sit quietly and get kidnapped?"

"'Well why didn't you turn the hell around and run?" snapped SueAnn.

"So they could shoot me in the back?" Giji asked incredulously. "Do you really think…"

One of the robbers turned from the front seat and said, "I swear if you two bitches don't shut up, I'll shoot the two of you–and then turn the gun on myself!"

SueAnn and Giji were stunned silent by his outburst–and frightened by his threat.

"You wouldn't do that would you, boss?" one of the guys asked.

"Shoot myself after I off these two? Hell, no!"

"I meant…"

"Everyone just shut the hell up!"

The car continued on the freeway for what seemed like miles. Eventually the driver slowed down and although he stayed in the fast lane, it looked as though they might get away. Giji reached across the seat and squeezed SueAnn's hand. They looked at each other but no one dared say another word, not even the other bank robber.

***

Eventually the bank robbers turned off the freeway and headed down a main street. They were getting out in the county now, and SueAnn was nervous. She assumed that Giji was nervous as well, but she sure couldn't tell by looking at her. Lips pursed and eyes like daggers, Giji was burning a hole in the back of the driver's neck with her eyes. SueAnn was glad that if she had to go through this ordeal, then at least she was with Giji. Even though she could have gotten them killed with her mouth, she was tough enough to be a comfort.

The car took a sudden turn onto a gravel driveway, for what seemed like an eternity, they bounced along and hit every pothole before they stopped at an abandoned farmhouse. The three robbers took them inside. They shoved the girls into a corner and talked among themselves for a few minutes, looked over at the women occasionally and snickered.

Neither one was tied up and they didn't have any gags on their mouths, but they didn't dare move or speak. The robber who had told them to shut up took a beer out of the refrigerator and motioned them both over to a rickety table.

"We'd like to see a little show. You can go girl on girl or choose one of the guys, but you're going to do it. We have to hang out here for a few days, and if you're good..." he paused here and winked, "we'll let you go."

"Couldn't you just shoot us?" Giji retorted.

"Another remark like that and I will. The boys want to see a little kissing, a little fondling," the leader took a big gulp of beer, wiping the drool from his chin.

"I'm not kissing, licking or touching anything below the border," SueAnn said, "I know where she's been!"

"Yeah, right," Giji said, "like you're so pure you came over with the Puritans on the Mayflower!"

Their lips barely touched...

"Well, you know what you have?" Giji asked.

"Perfectly normal lips!" SueAnn said confidently.

"For a moose maybe!" Giji taunted.

"What!" SueAnn gasped. "You heard me!" Giji snapped. "You, my dear, have moose lips!"

"I do not!" SueAnn protested. "I don't even think mooses... or is it meeses...have lips."

"Sure they do," Giji said knowingly. "They look just like

yours!"

"Now who's being childish?"

"You dish it out, then you have to take it!"

"Oh, okay, fish lips!"

"You have big 'ole Bullwinkle lips that scare small children!"

"I do not! Children love me."

"Or maybe they just think you're a lovable cartoon character like Bullwinkle!"

There lips barely touched again.

"Ooh," Giji said and frowned like the would-be kiss left a bad taste in her mouth. "It's like kissing a dead fish."

"Well, kissing you was no pleasure either," SueAnn assured her while wiping her lips with her hands. "Kissing you is like kissing a dead fish's butt."

Giji rolled her eyes. "Oh, brilliant!" she exclaimed. "That's totally juvenile. Like dead fish have butts!"

"Sure, they do," SueAnn said, pleased she'd rattled Giji. "The butt is right where your lips are!"

The two women clumsily touched each other's breasts, playfully squeezing and fondling them and lightly pinching their nipples, which were erect more from fear than the temperature in the old house, which was a bit stifling.

"You bit my boob, you mouthy twit!"

"I'm new at this." SueAnn reminded her. Giji slugged her.

"You bit me!" SueAnn yelled, "I now have one and a half nipples."

"You'll get no sympathy from me!"

"You two are pretty boring," one of the guys interjected.

Giji started to speak, but the lead thug beat her to it. "Okay, knock it off! One more word and you will be swimming with the fishes!"

"Well, we're not exactly lesbians," Giji said.

"Tie 'em up, boys," the leader said.

"Do you have to?" Giji asked, suddenly aware that if they didn't play along, that they could both be killed, and if they did play along, there might be a chance to escape. She gave SueAnn a long, hard look, and SueAnn seemed to get it; she nodded slightly.

"We promise to get along," SueAnn said.

Giji and SueAnn exchanged uneasy looks, but neither of them felt brave enough to speak no matter how badly they wanted to.

SueAnn lightly pinched Giji's enormous erect nipples through the thin, silky material of her blouse.

"Nice, huh?" Giji teased as she pinched SueAnn's much smaller nipples.

"Not bad for silicone," SueAnn said, "They're like two big bouncy balls!"

"Bouncy balls!" Giji repeated, and then she lifted her huge breasts, one in each hand, and let them drop. Her breasts jiggled and bounced while Giji laughed and giggled playfully. "Bouncy boobs are more like it!"

The guys snickered.

"At least you didn't have to do a strip search to find mine!" Giji smirked, "I'm not sure if I'm pinching your nipple or your entire breast!"

The guys laughed

"Just for that you can touch your own nipples!" SueAnn spat indignantly. "Let's see your suck your own nipples!"

"Okay, I will," Giji told her, and then she removed her blouse.

The guys cheered her on.

Giji took one of her large, fleshy firm breasts in her hands and slowly raised the tip to her mouth while the three guys watched, almost drooling. The room was so quiet a person could hear their own breathing as Giji took one of her huge, erect nipples into her warm, wet mouth and startled to suck slowly at first and then harder and harder until she was almost moaning!

"You want me to off these two, boss?" the quieter of the bank robbers asked.

Manny sighed. "Ummm, it's damned tempting," he admitted, staring at the two chatterboxes until he saw the glint of fear in their eyes. "But, we may need them. Besides, the show is just starting to get good." The thug nodded and went back to looking through an outdated edition of the local news rag he'd found thrown in a corner of the shabby, dirty living room. Visibly shaken the two women almost sighed with relief.

"You've sufficiently lost your mind," SueAnn spat.

"You can't sufficiently lose your mind," Giji disagreed. "You've either lost your mind or you haven't."

"Well, you have," SueAnn assured her. "You've lost your mind and very sufficiently."

Giji started to speak, but she thought better of it when she noticed Manny listening closely and watching their every move!

***

Wynette watched her afternoon soaps, just to catch up on what was going on with Victor and Nikki and the other characters on "The Young & the Restless" when the program was interrupted by a news bulletin: Two local women had been taken hostage by bank robbers as the armed men fled Federal Savings & Trust with an undisclosed amount of money taken from the tellers in the holdup. When Wynette heard the identities of the two women taken hostage, she immediately called the other housewives and told them to come over to her house right away. Before she hung up the phone on the last of the calls, her door was already opening.

"I can't believe it," Ariella said as she, Connie and Wynette sat in Wynette's living room in front of the television. "It's like a Lifetime movie of the week."

"Or a crime story on Court TV," Connie said flatly.

"Yes," Wynette agreed. "I just keep thinking this is a bad dream, and we'll wake up and none of this will be happening." She sighed. "Poor SueAnn! Imagine being held hostage with Giji Brickhouse of all people!"

Ariella rolled her eyes. "Pulleeze!" she said suddenly.

"SueAnn is a pill. After a while, with her whining and constant nagging, you want to strangle her."

"Ariella's right," Connie agreed. "SueAnn can get on your last nerve, but then so can Giji. The two together are…"

"Lethal," Ariella finished for her. "We have to face it. We may never see our friends alive again."

"Oh, come now," Wynette refused to listen to such talk. "SueAnn and Giji are survivors! They'll be fine. Just wait and see. They'll get out of this unharmed and just fine."

"I hope you're right," Ariella worried.

"Of course, I am." Wynette assured her friends.

Connie shifted her weight and turned her attention back to the newscast. The remaining wives watched the news coverage of the hostage situation.

"I can't believe it," Connie said, "first Mary Lynn and now this."

"Who would have ever thought SueAnn would be taken hostage," Wynette said.

"And with Giji," Ariella said, "I guess truth really is stranger than fiction."

"Mrs. Hoover called earlier," Wynette told the other wives. "She pretended to be upset, sobbing. She went on and on about how Giji and SueAnn were goners for sure, and she wanted to know if she could donate Giji's things to Goodwill!"

"What'd you tell her?" Ariella wanted to know.

Wynette sighed. "I told her not to give up hope just yet," she replied, "and that seemed to upset her even more!"

"How typical of her," Connie said dryly, her eyes glued to the television and the continuing news coverage on the local access channel.

"I can't believe our friends are being held hostage by armed and dangerous bank robbers," Ariella said, her voice having an edge of excitement. "If it weren't so scary, it'd be cool! But, knowing what we know about our friends, it's scary."

"Yeah," Wynette agreed. "I just hope the genuine dislike and ongoing battle for Nick doesn't cause SueAnn and Giji to do anything stupid."

"They've been captured by armed bank robbers," Ariella reminded her. "I'm not sure they can do anything any more stupid than that!"

"I know," Wynette said, "but with those two, you never know. They're like kids, always into something, usually bad, and…"

"Just say it," Connie encouraged her, "you think they could drive the bank robbers crazy enough to shoot them to shut them up."

Wynette nodded. "Pretty much," then she smiled, "Hey, I'm sure it won't come to that. I'm sure SueAnn and Giji will be on their best behavior."

Even as the words were leaving her mouth, Wynette could not believe what she was saying….

23

The Great Escape

The leader and another guy went to check about a private plane to fly out of the country, but the other robber wanted more girl on girl action. He agreed to join them and untie them if they promised to be good girls and not try to escape.

"You've been a bad boy, you deserve to be spanked but not before me!" Giji said, teasing him and trying to get him hot enough to forget that he was supposed to be watching them...not watching them.

The girls managed to get in a tangle of bodies. Amid the moaning-mostly from him–Giji and SueAnn maneuvered his hands and feet long enough to bind him with the duct tape the robbers left after binding them.

"Grab his cell phone and call the police!" Giji hissed at SueAnn as she worked the duct tape across the robber's bare, hairy back. SueAnn fumbled with the cell phone.

"Shit!"

"I don't know about you, but I'm going to get the hell out of here, make my way through the woods to the main road and wait on the cops!"

"Stupid, stupid, stupid!" SueAnn said, "he just heard the plan!'

"How do you know that?" Giji started working on the robber's hairy legs. He twisted to try to get out, but that just made the duct tape bind tighter. He was starting to look uncomfortable and more than a little worried. His hard-on was long gone now, and he was making deep grunting noises as he fought to break free.

"Because I accidentally hit redial! They heard everything! They're probably on their way back right now! Giji, do you hear me? Giji, we're supposed to be making our escape. We didn't tie up this guy so you could tongue him!"

"I wasn't tonguing him," Giji protested. "I was making sure he was securely taped up!"

"DO YOU HEAR WHAT I'M SAYING TO YOU?"

"Another good use for duct tape!" Giji announced, after tearing another piece and placing it over his mouth. "Did I tell you what I did with duct tape once?"

SueAnn sighed. "I'm not sure I want to know."

"Well, it was for a bikini contest," Giji said proudly. "I made a bikini out of duct tape!"

"Gee, that sounds pretty original." SueAnn knew it was fruitless to yell. Giji was in *Giji Land*, and they could be discussing her duct tape exploits when the robbers crashed through the door and shot them both. SueAnn sighed again.

"It was," Giji said. "I believe I was the first to attempt this feat and I would have won first place. But things went horribly wrong during the talent portion of the competition."

"Really? What'd you do?" SueAnn could care less. "Spring a leak?"

Giji rolled her eyes. "Not exactly," she replied. My top came loose during the talent portion of the competition. I was yodeling Celine Dion's 'My Heart Will Go On' while twirling my —"

"Okay, enough!"

"Baton!" Giji finished as she took the cell phone from SueAnn and dialed 911.

"... an old farm house somewhere off Canyon Road. Yes, Canyon," Giji repeated. "I have a weak battery. I'm losing the signal. Are you still there? Hello?"

Giji flipped the cell phone closed and turned to SueAnn. "I hope the 911 operator heard me," she worried. "She wasn't sure about the street name. I just hope she heard it before the signal went out!"

SueAnn nodded, still distraught over accidentally hitting redial and tipping off the other robbers.

"We have to get going," Giji told SueAnn. "The other robbers could come back at any time and we need to be long gone before they get here." The girls opened the old screen door and went down the rickety steps, Giji paused to throw a kiss to the duct taped, naked robber. He's going to have some explaining to do to his buddies and the cops, whoever finds him first," she commented and she giggled on the way down the gravel driveway.

"Are you sure that's the way to the main road?" SueAnn worried.

"No, but if it doesn't get us to the main road," Giji called over her shoulder and kept walking, "maybe it'll get us to a house where we can get some help. Are you coming?"

Reluctantly SueAnn hurried to catch up with Giji. "I'm not sure about this farmland," she told Giji breathlessly. "Maybe we should walk in the pasture along the road coming in."

"If we do that," Giji quickly pointed out, "and the killers –"

"Bank robbers!" SueAnn corrected.

Giji gave her a blank stare. "If they catch us escaping, it won't take much for them to go from bank robbers to murderers," she assured SueAnn. "I don't know about you but I'd like to go on living for a long, long, time."

"But the land along the road looked smoother, less hilly," SueAnn pointed out.

"I'm sure it is," Giji agreed. "Unfortunately, that makes it easier for those madmen to spot us if they drive along the road coming in."

"Okay," SueAnn relented, "good point."

Giji got an idea. "Jeez, I wish a certain plumber were here!" she said, knowing her comment would get to SueAnn. "He could carry me out!"

"Speaking of Nick," SueAnn said, ignoring Giji's jab. "How much do you really know about him?"

"I enjoy his company," Giji answered and shrugged. "What else is there to know?"

"Lots," SueAnn assured her. "Did you think he could be... dangerous?"

"Dangerous?" Giji repeated, surprised by SueAnn's question. "I like to think all men are dangerous, especially the good-looking ones!"

"So you don't know anything about him either?" SueAnn assumed from Giji's response.

"The man is a plumber, not a secret agent or a bank robber," Giji said. "I don't think he's dangerous in the same way Manny is, for instance."

SueAnn smiled, trying to feel relieved. "You might as well know, I asked the Sexual Psychic about Nick, and she said he is not being honest about who he is."

Giji looked at her, clearly surprised at what she'd just heard. "Well," she said finally, "I'm sure it's nothing major. After all, no one is one hundred percent honest."

In the silence that followed, SueAnn had to admit, unfortunately, Giji was right.

"You sure fall apart in a crisis," Giji observed. "You get all clumsy and klutzy and you say the damnedest things! I keep thinking I'm going to have to slap you!"

"If you do," SueAnn pointed down the sloped terrain that lay ahead of them, "you won't have to worry getting down to the main road in those heels!"

"Really!" Giji said disbelievingly. "You only resort to threats because you know I'm right. You fall apart like cheap panties when things get tense."

"I do not," SueAnn protested.

Giji rolled her eyes. "Sure you do," she remained firm. "Just like you got all clumsy and pressed redial on the robber's cell phone. Now thanks to you we have to walk through the old farm pastures which are overgrown with brush and briars," Giji said loudly, "and it's hell walking in these stiletto heels!"

"I guess that's an argument for sensible shoes," SueAnn glanced down at her comfortable Keds. "Where'd you buy those things, the Adult Whore Superstore?"

"Gee, what a nice thing to say," Giji snapped, wobbling slightly and almost losing her balance. "For your information I only shop at Frederick's of Hollywood!"

"It shows," SueAnn said under her breath, then added, "What kind of person wears stiletto heels on her job?"

Giji stopped and looked at SueAnn. "Excuse me for trying to look nice," she replied sarcastically. "I wear what I like and feel will look good on me, okay? Besides, it wasn't like I was expecting to be kidnapped by three bank robbers on the run with a flaky brunette!"

"Flaky!"

"Like a Betty Crocker pie crust!" Giji quipped as they came up to a fenced pasture with a herd of cows grazing just a short distance away. "Now can we just walk and not talk?"

SueAnn shrugged and suddenly stopped dead in her tracks.

"What's wrong now?" Giji asked. "You don't like the way my ass looks in my spandex mini-skirt?"

"I'm afraid of livestock," SueAnn said apprehensively.

"Well, I guess you'll have to decide if you're more afraid of a herd of docile cows," Giji told her as she climbed through the wire fence, "or Madman Manny and his two sidekicks!"

"Okay, okay," SueAnn relented, climbed through the fence and ran to catch up to Giji. "Since you put it like that!"

"Don't hold on to me like that," Giji complained. "I'm walking in heels, you'll make me fall."

The cows raised their heads and mooed a few times as the women passed the herd. Unsettled by the attention of the large animals, SueAnn held Giji's sleeve like a small child seeking protection, but Giji pulled away.

When SueAnn and Giji reached the lower road, they didn't see anyone at first, and then they saw a vehicle coming down the road towards them. Fearing it might be their captors, they clung to each other, not sure if they should run or remain frozen in place.

As the car got closer, they could see the lights on top and nearly collapsed with relief. Giji recognized the young police cop, Officer Mark Hayes, as soon as he stepped from his patrol car, and despite her somewhat unkempt appearance, she could tell he recognized her as well.

***

Within seconds it seemed, police cars, ambulances and news reporters swarmed the scene waiting for the bank robbers to return. While the paramedics made sure they were fine, the police officers questioned SueAnn and Giji about what led to their kidnapping and what happened while they were in captivity. After they were finished, the two women were hounded by reporters from local newspapers and news crews from radio and television stations.

"When the paramedics were checking my vitals, I volunteered to ride with them next Saturday," Giji told SueAnn proudly as they waited to be released and taken home.

"But you don't have any training," SueAnn reminded her. "Do you know CPR?"

Giji shrugged. "Well, I've kissed a lot of guys," she said proudly. "That should count for something!"

"Shoving your tongue down someone's throat isn't likely to save a life," SueAnn said sarcastically.

Giji winked, enjoying SueAnn's distress over her announcement. "That may be true," she agreed, then added, "but it can certainly make a guy feel more alive!" She pretended to pout. "You aren't jealous, are you?"

"I'm just concerned for the patients," SueAnn said.

"You're just jealous, SuSu," Giji taunted. "Get over it already!"

SueAnn burst into uncontrollable laughter.

"We've just been kidnapped and here you are laughing like a deranged hyena!"

"Laughter is the best revenge!" SueAnn told her.

Giji rolled her eyes. "Really, you must be suffering from that delayed post-response syndrome or whatever it is that people have after a traumatic experience."

"Maybe I'm just tired from being held captive for 24 hours." SueAnn paused for dramatic effect. "With you! Or…maybe…I just find the picture of you as a paramedic hilarious!"

"Ha! Ha!" Giji said sarcastically. Giji got an idea. "I was just thinking."

"Gee, I'm impressed," SueAnn said sarcastically, wishing she were with anyone but Giji Brickhouse. Well, almost anyone.

"This affects both of us," Giji told her. "What do you say we agree not to tell anyone about our…girl-on-girl action?"

"Like I would want to brag?" SueAnn said incredulously, her eyes wide. "It wasn't that great, you know."

"I was there," Giji reminded her impatiently. "What's it gonna be? Deal or no deal?"

SueAnn stuck out her pinkie. "Deal," she said.

After their pinkie swear to seal the deal, Giji sighed. "I don't know about you, but I feel a helleuva lot better!"

"I felt better the minute we were rescued," SueAnn told her, thinking the less time she had to spend with Giji, the better.

"I guess since the reporters seem mostly interested in you, god knows why," Giji began, "I'll concentrate my efforts on the cops. I saw several really hot ones! Maybe I can help them solve a few cases and work off some of their pent up adrenaline!"

SueAnn rolled her eyes. "You really do live in your own little world!" She sighed. "I thought you were interested in that cute young reporter?"

"Well, I was and he was really cute," Giji said, "but he was only interested in an interview!"

"The nerve of that guy!" SueAnn said sarcastically. "What was he thinking?"

"I know!" Giji pretended to be oblivious. "I asked if he had a hard one and he pulled out his microphone!"

"You poor thing," SueAnn teased. "What are you going to do?"

"You get the reporters," Giji said, "and I get the cops. Mine trump yours. Mine can put yours behind bars and they carry loaded weapons and…" Giji winked… "their own handcuffs!"

"I don't want to know what you're taking about, really I don't," SueAnn said, smiling as she stared at the gathering crowd. "Is that Matt Lauer? Matt? Oh, Matt!"

"He looks so much taller on TV," Giji said and headed off towards the uniformed cops nearby....

***

"How about a lift home?" Officer Mark Hayes asked Giji as the crowd began to disperse.

Giji nodded appreciatively. "Thanks, Mark," she said as he put an arm around her and walked with her to his patrol car. He opened the front passenger side door for her and she got in.

"What a day, huh?" the young officer asked getting into the driver's seat and started the engine.

Giji nodded and sank back in the seat. "Weird," she said, giving a little laugh. "Definitely not my typical day!"

Mark glanced at her, nodding as he navigated through the maze of people scurrying about and onto the road. "I'll bet," he said, making small talk. "I'll bet you're exhausted."

"A little." Giji glanced over at his strong profile, wondering if he had something in mind. If so, she would be a willing participant. Although she was a bit tired, she could summon the energy. As she recalled the last time they were together, the young cop was a good fuck!

"Are you up for a little... diversion?" he wanted to know.

Giji put a hand on his bulging forearm, letting her fingers glide across his skin. "Hmmm," she began slowly, teasingly, "I could be persuaded."

He grinned. "Really?" he seemed surprised but pleased.

"Uh-huh," Giji told him, "what'd you have in mind?"

"A motel room," he told her. "You, me and my friend, fooling around a little and seeing where it goes."

"Sounds like fun," Giji said, her curiosity and excitement growing. "Count me in!"

"Okay, if you're sure?" the young cop asked again, then went on to explain that someone wanted to meet her.

Giji grinned, curious to know who wanted to meet her. "Hey, I feel my second wind coming on," she told him. "Besides, there'll be lots of time to rest later. Right now it just feels good to be alive and doing something." *Or someone*, she thought, still curious about the person who wanted to meet her. She imagined it was another young officer he had bragged to. That wouldn't be so bad, she decided, hoping she was right. She would really enjoy two young hot cops having their way with her after what she'd just been through.

Mark pulled into a small motel on the outskirts of town. Giji had driven pass the motel once or twice before. It was an old brick structure, somewhat rundown, with over grown flower beds, giving an over all effect that reminded her of the infamous Bates Motel!

After parking, Mark led Giji to Room 12 and knocked. "Do I look okay?" Giji asked, smoothing her pink blouse and her matching mini skirt. "That farm house was dirty and dusty."

"You look great," the young officer assured her, smiling.

"You couldn't look bad if you tried." Giji grinned at him pleased. "Thanks," she said, pushing her chest out to make her best first impression as the door opened.

An older man, dressed in tan slacks and a blue dress shirt, grinned at them, then turned his attention to Giji and looked her up and down. "My, my, my!" He whistled. "What have we here!"

"Chief, meet the girl I told you about," the young officer said proudly, "she's the fast one, I told you about."

"Giji, this is Police Chief Harold Burke."

Giji hoped she hid her initial disappointment as she smiled at the leering man.

The police chief was a big man, rugged, over 6 feet tall, somewhat muscular with an extra tire around his waist, salt and pepper cropped short and thinning on top, he had dark eyebrows and lively eyes, especially when he looked at a beautiful woman. He took Giji's delicate hand in his big, rough hand and kissed it softly. "You look good enough to eat, hot stuff!"

Maybe you'll get your chance, Giji thought, smiling. "Good to meet you, Chief Burke."

"Ah, shucks," he said in a boyish voice, "call me Harold." He winked. "We're all friends here."

"I told you she was hot," the younger officer said excitedly.

The police chief looked Giji up and down, his eyes glued to her body. "You did say she was hot," the chief agreed, "but hell, man, she's smokin'!"

The younger officer had a nervous, pleased laugh.

"You put the hot in burn!" the chief said excitedly.

Giji tried to smile even though she found the comment somewhat corny although a bit flattering, too, especially coming from the chief of police. "You're not so bad yourself!" She grinned.

Giji wasn't sure what to make of this situation. Hoping she wasn't being setup for something that could come back to haunt her, Giji entered the room when Mark placed his hand in the small of her back.

Inside, the motel room was pretty much what Giji had expected, dark and dated, with paneled walls and worn dark olive carpet, worn furniture that was probably original to the decade in which the motel had been built, Giji guessed the 1950s, and a musty smell like an old house that had been closed up for years.

The police chief turned to young Officer Hayes as soon as the door closed. "Hey, how'd everything go after I left the scene?" he asked.

"Fine," Mark assured him. "As you know, the bank robbers were all apprehended and it looks like with Giji and her friend's testimony, they'll be looking at a nice long life behind bars."

"Okay then," the police chief said, his voice alive with excitement. "Let's get this party started!"

After they undressed, Giji spun around for the officers' admiring eyes.

"Damn!" The police chief whistled. "If you were any hotter, that would be a crime!"

"Thanks, Harold," Giji said, grinning.

"I told you wouldn't be disappointed," Mark interjected.

"You did," the police chief agreed, his eyes still on Giji. "And for once, kid, you were right!"

From their previous encounter, Giji knew the younger officer had a well-built, well-toned body and a cock built for pleasure. However, Giji was surprised the older cop's body wasn't half bad, much more toned than he had appeared dressed and he had a large package that was already erect and ready for action.

"I hope you have a permit for that concealed weapon!" Giji teased the chief, looking at his erect cock. Giggling, she turned and ran into the bathroom. The police chief followed, trying to catch her, with the younger officer close behind.

Giji leaned against the far wall of the bathroom, feeling the cool tile against her warm skin. The two officers caught up to her, and what followed was a series of hands all over her body amidst their laughter and her giggles. "No fair," she protested, "that tickles!"

"We're just funning you," the police chief drawled playfully.

Noticing the shower, Giji got an idea. "Hey, let's get wet!" she suggested.

"Okay," the police chief agreed, thinking a naked, slippery wet Giji would be even more fun. "Wet it is!"

The three of them crowded their naked bodies into the shower, which was barely large enough to accommodate two people, and began to enjoy each other beneath the steady, pulsing downpour of the water.

Giji could feel the chief's hairy chest against her back, the hair prickly feeling against her skin as he put his arms around her, pressing his huge, erect cock between her buttocks and up into her wet pussy. He started to ride her slowly, kissing the back of her neck, her shoulder, and occasionally pinching her nipples between his big, strong fingers.

"That feel good?" he whispered as the water pelted them.

"Uh-mmm," Giji moaned.

While the police chief fucked her from behind, the younger officer was beneath Giji, his head between her legs, licking her wet pussy, licking around the chief's cock, she noticed, wondering if the younger officer had homoerotic interest in his commanding officer. She wondered if that explained why he was so eager to for a threesome and why he was so anxious around the chief? If this were true, Giji found being used this way, a bit insulting, but at the same time she found it oddly exciting.

"It's not a flotation device!" Giji teased the younger cop.

"I don't know," the chief said in her ear, "I've known 'em to save a life or two!"

Giji laughed at the chief's comment as he continued grinding his cock into her pussy while Mark kept licking and sucking around her pussy as if he were trying to get the chief's cock out of her cunt and into his eager mouth!

Turning off the shower suddenly, the police chief pulled his cock from Giji's pussy before he came and suggested they move their party to the bed. Still dripping wet, Giji ran from the bathroom and dove into the center of the bed, then got to her knees and pushed the covers down. The two naked cops followed and the chief nudged the younger officer playfully. "Watch this!" he said excitedly and leapt on the bed rolling onto his back and pushing his head under Giji, his mouth on her pussy.

Giji could feel the chief's warm mouth on her pussy, his wet tongue pushing her pussy lips apart, slowly and deliberately as his tongue slid into her, deeper and deeper. He started licking around her clit with the tip of his tongue, making small circles, then suddenly he began tongue-fucking her wet pussy with vigorous thrusts. His bristly mustache tickled her pussy lips and his nose rubbed against her clit with each thrust. Giji found the sensation intoxicating!

Moaning loudly now with each movement of the chief's tongue, Giji started to ride the chief's face, pressing her pussy closer and tighter to his mouth, wanting his tongue deeper and deeper inside her. Giji noticed the younger officer seemed transfixed as he watched his commanding officer's erect cock bobble up and down with each movement.

Finally the younger officer moved to the bed and knelt beside her, he took one of her breasts in his hand and the other in his mouth, sucking on her nipple while gently pinching the other between his thumb and forefinger.

It added another element to her excitement, Giji had to admit, but nothing could compare to the pleasure the older man was giving her with his incredible tongue!

The louder Giji moaned the faster the chief's tongue moved inside her pussy and the more he licked her clit with the tip of his tongue. The closer she came to orgasm, the more Giji clenched her pussy muscles around the chief's tongue. Giji settled into a steady rhythm, her movements against the chief's face matching the movements of his tongue.

Suddenly Giji felt her excitement peak as her pussy convulsed, grinding against the chief's face as her pussy juices flowed onto his eager, sucking mouth.

While she was still reeling from the most powerful orgasm she'd had since her last visit to the Sexual Psychic, Giji got an idea that seemed like it would be fun when it occurred to her. She noticed the young officer's handcuff on the bedside table and she reached over and picked them up. Giggling, she pulled the cuffs apart and placed one of the bracelets around the younger officer's wrist and snapped it closed. He looked up at her, surprised, but he didn't say anything. He just watched while she took the other bracelet and locked it around the chief's wrist.

Giggling playfully Giji slid off the chief and got to her feet, waiting for the police chief to realize he was handcuffed to his young officer.

"What the hell!" the police chief erupted, noticing the handcuffs for first time and that he was cuffed to the younger officer. "Get these damned things off me!"

"Mark, where do you keep the key?" Giji asked, laughing at the chief's reaction.

"In my car," Mark told her, laying beside the chief. "Over the visor."

"Okay," Giji said, putting on her clothes. "It'll take me a minute."

"Just get these damned cuffs off of me," the chief bellowed.

"Okay, okay," Giji said, pulling her blouse over her head. Smoothing her blouse, she slipped her feet into her heels and started for the door. She paused, an idea occurring to her. "Your car isn't locked?" she asked Mark.

Mark nodded. "Yeah, it is," he answered and pointed with his free hand toward his uniform thrown across a chair.

Giji went to the chair and took his keys from the pocket of his slacks. "Now we're good to go!" she said, trying to sound upbeat despite the fact that her playful idea had backfired on her. "I'll be right back.

Giji unlocked Mark's patrol car and quickly found the key above the visor.

"I have the key," she announced, entering the room and closing the door.

"The sooner you get these things off me the better," the chief said, sounding relieved.

Giji held out the small key as she approached the bed. As she reached the edge of the bed, she stopped and looked down.

"What's wrong?" Mark asked.

"Oops!" Giji looked up at the officers.

"What have you done?' the chief demanded.

"I-I," Giji stammered, unable to believe what had just happened. "I-I dropped the key down…down the air vent!"

"Can you fish it out?" the younger officer asked.

Giji shook her head. "It fell all the way in," she replied. "There's no way I can reach it."

The police chief closed his eyes and put his free hand to his head. "Oh, my god, I cannot believe this is happening," he groaned. "I should have known this would end in disaster."

"You both knew I hadn't had much rest or any sleep after my ordeal, sorry," Giji said apologetically. "I'm still shaky from the whole kidnapping ordeal. I guess a threesome doesn't seem like such a good idea now?"

"Are you kidding?" the police chief asked, a rising note of anger evident in his voice. "Get someone to cut these cuffs off ASAP! And make sure it's someone who doesn't have a big mouth!"

Giji pursed her lips and tried to look thoughtful. "Well, it's in the middle of the night…" her voice trailed off helplessly.

"I don't care what you have to do or what it takes," the chief told her, his voice now erupting in full-blown anger. "Just do it, dimwit!" He paused, the vein his forehead swollen and pulsing. "Or you'll be the one in cuffs!"

Giji frowned. "Now that's just not nice."

"That really wasn't very nice, sir," the deputy agreed.

"Who's side are you on?" the chief asked.

"I'm on your side," the deputy assured him. "I mean we are handcuffed together –"

"We sure are!" the chief blew. "And who's fault is that?"

"Mine and Giji's, sir," the younger man stammered. He sighed nervously and closed his eyes. "Mostly mine."

"You got that right!" Silence. "Hey, you just touched my –"

"I didn't mean to," the deputy apologized. "It's just so...I believe it touched me, sir."

"It certainly did not!" the chief said indignantly. "Keep your hands to yourself or I'll have your badge!"

"Yes, sir. I promise not to –"

While they argued, Giji quickly dressed and slipped out of the room.

"You, sonofabitch, you did it again!" the chief accused. "You stay on your side of the bed and I'll stay on mine, got it?"

"Got it, sir."

Suddenly the room seemed quieter.

"Hey, where the hell did she go?" the chief asked.

Giji went to the motel office and asked the clerk to call her a cab. It took a while for the taxi to arrive and even longer for them to weave through the traffic downtown on the way to the suburbs and to her bed at Mrs. Hoover's.

During the ride, Giji reflected on the unfortunate situation. She wished she could have helped the officers, but she wasn't sure what to do. Maybe she could have helped the officers get dressed from the waist down, but she didn't think of it at the time. Besides, she was afraid of the chief's temper, his yelling just made her more jumpy and uncertain of what she should do, and that's why she had fled.

She sighed as the cab neared Mrs. Hoover's house, hoping the old bat had already turned in for the night. She wasn't up to answering any questions about the hostage situation or anything else.

Too bad such a fun beginning had ended on such a sour note, she thought as the taxi stopped in front of Mrs. Hoover's house. She hoped the officers would be a bit more forgiving when they had a chance to calm down a bit. At any rate, she was pretty sure she wouldn't have to worry about them wanting to have a threesome again. *Then again,* she thought, *you never know!*

***

Giji finally arrived home after her ordeal. Mrs. Hoover seemed more interested in "Wheel of Fortune" than in her houseguest's safe return.

"Well, aren't you glad to see that I survived being kidnapped by three dangerous bank robbers?" Giji asked after Mrs. Hoover's lackluster welcome back.

"I never doubted that you'd be fine," Mrs. Hoover admitted, turning only slightly away from the glow of her television, "I wasn't so sure that dainty SueAnn or the bank robbers would make it back alive, but I never for one moment doubted that you would!"

"Oh, thanks," Giji told her. "I think."

"You look pretty good considering," Mrs. Hoover observed. "Did you have a shower? At the police station? With an officer?" Mrs. Hoover paused, snickering like a teenager. "Or two?"

"No, I'm on my way upstairs to shower and rest now," Giji lied, "I've already had my interrogation for the night, thank you."

Mrs. Hoover laughed at that comment. "Is that what took you so long?" she wanted to know. "SueAnn got home earlier in the day? Did you do the police force?"

Giji rolled her eyes. "I had to repeat my story for the head officers," she lied again. "Unlike dainty SueAnn, they were actually interested in what I had to say."

"Knowing you," Mrs. Hoover said, taking a quick sip of iced tea. "I doubt that."

"What's that supposed to mean?" Giji was starting to get pissed. Her life was no business of this meddling, arrogant old woman.

"Ummm, welcome home, Giji," Mrs. Hoover said, ignoring her houseguest's question, and was about to turn back to her television program when she remembered something from earlier in the evening.

"I just saw the strangest thing on the newsbreak. Two cops handcuffed together naked in a hotel room...queer perverts on the police force! Fleecing America using tax payers' dollars for perversion... It was like 'Reno 911' or the parts they cut out of 'Cops'! I haven't laughed so hard since the cast of 'La Cage Aux Folles' lit themselves on fire!"

"They did not!"

"Then why did all those queers have to draw on their eyebrows with a pencil?"

"You're going to hell, Martha!"

"I'll be there waiting for you!"

"I fully expect you will," Giji started upstairs, "I can see your forked tail and pitch fork now," she called back over her shoulder.

"Yep," Martha Hoover called after her, "I'll keep you a nice toasty spot!"

24

ParameDicks!

When SueAnn answered her door, she was surprised to see Nick standing there, holding a huge bouquet of flowers, a mixture of her favorite daisies, dahlias, bachelor buttons, zinnias, rosebuds, with baby's breath sprinkled among the other flowers.

"Hello," she said quietly and tried to give him a small smile as she looked from the bouquet to his smiling handsome face.

"Hello," he greeted and handed her the flowers. "These are for you."

"Thank you," SueAnn said, accepting the bouquet. She gave the flowers a quick sniff, enjoying their fresh floral fragrance. "That's so nice. These are beautiful and you remembered my favorites."

Nick nodded, pleased that she noticed. "Of course," he said. "I know what you like by what you plant in your garden."

"That's so nice," SueAnn said and meant it despite the recent distance that had been growing between them. "I'll get these in some water."

"Mind if I come in?" he asked.

She was about to turn to go inside, but she paused briefly, smiling. "I can hardly say no to a man bearing flowers now, can I?" she said playfully, then given the tension that seemed to be growing between them recently, she regretted that she didn't say "Sure" or "Come on in."

Nick followed her into the kitchen where she placed the bouquet on the counter. Taking a large vase from the windowsill, she filled it with water.

"Did you get some rest?" he asked, concerned.

SueAnn shrugged. "A little," she said, turning off the faucet and placing the vase on the counter. "It'll be a while before I can sleep soundly, I'm afraid."

He nodded. "That makes perfect sense," he told her, "I'm just glad you're okay physically..." he took a deep breath, "and emotionally you'll be better soon."

"I hope so," she said, wishing it wasn't so awkward, so uncomfortable. She slipped the colorful plastic sleeve off the bouquet and started to arrange the flowers, one by one, in the vase of fresh water. "It was scary and unnerving." She shuddered.

Nick caught her arm and turned her to face him as he pulled her into his arms and gave her a comforting hug. SueAnn closed her eyes and placed her face against his broad chest, enjoying the safety of his strong embrace.

"I wish I could have been there to protect you," he said softly and kissed her forehead. "I felt so helpless when I heard what happened. I was afraid those monsters would hurt you."

Suddenly SueAnn was jolted back to the present by his words, and she pulled free of his embrace. "I-I'm fine," she assured him, then turned and resume arranging the flowers he'd given her. "It'll take a little time to get pass the shock and stress of the ordeal, I guess."

"Of course, it will," he agreed.

"I just need a little time."

Taking that as his cue, Nick put his hands on SueAnn's shoulders, and gave her a little kiss on one cheek. SueAnn closed her eyes and did not attempt to turn to face him. "I'll see you later," he said tightly. "If you need me –"

"I'll be fine," SueAnn interrupted.

"I know you will," he said. "Just take it easy."

SueAnn placed the last of the flowers in the vase, a tightly closed rose, and stepped back to admire her arrangement. Not bad, she thought, then started to rearrange some of the taller flowers, placing them near the back of the vase. "That's better," she said, pleased. "Don't you think –?"

She turned to get Nick's opinion and realized while she concentrated on the flowers, he'd left. She was disappointed, but somewhat relieved because the visit was so awkward. She wondered if she'd been too hard on him. Although she was afraid to let him get close to her again, she was even more afraid that she would push him away…

***

A few days later, after SueAnn got a chance to rest a little after her ordeal, she sat on SueAnn's patio with Wynette and Ariella and caught up with them.

"So, do you feel like talking about it?" Wynette asked.

"What do you want to know?" SueAnn sipped at her drink. She had recently begun drinking a Mandarin Cranberry at all times. She could taste the mandarin vodka mixed with the tart cranberry juice.

"Were the bank robbers sexy?"

Ariella gave SueAnn an uneasy glance.

SueAnn frowned. "I thought you were over your addiction to men?"

"I was just wondering, you know, curious."

SueAnn put her head in her hands.

"Giji says one of the guys was semi-hot, muscular, but a creep. I imagine being in this situation can bring two people who don't have much in common very close." Wynette leaned in, expectantly, "Did it?"

The women looked up as Giji opened the back gate.

"I thought you'd be back here, no answer at the front door. Hey, can I have one of those?" she gestured toward SueAnn's glass.

"In the kitchen," SueAnn answered, then after Giji returned with her drink, she added, "Wynette was just asking if I thought the robbers were cute."

"The leader Manny was sexy in a malevolent sort of way," Giji mused, "rugged, macho –"

"Trigger happy!" SueAnn interjected. "And bug ugly!"

"I believe the term is butt ugly," Ariella corrected.

"Well, nobody's perfect," Giji said to SueAnn.

"He certainly wasn't!" SueAnn assured her. "You're all about how sexy he was now. When he had a gun pointed at you, I didn't see you trying to seduce him."

"You're just jealous because he found me more attractive than you!" Giji quipped.

"Oh, please, he called you dumpster dive Barbie!" SueAnn reminded her.

"Well, he was a little rough around the edges," Giji said quickly.

"Sounds like he was rough around the edges, up the back, down the front, inside, outside and all over!" Wynette joked.

"That sounds about right," SueAnn said, her words sounding just a little slurred.

A thought occurred to Wynette. "You could really get close under such stressful conditions," she pointed out looking from SueAnn to Giji. "It has been known to happen, sometimes even when mortal enemies have been thrown together in a life-altering situation, they emerge friends or at least having a better understanding of each other."

"Oh, please, that would be so made-for-TV!" Giji quipped. "I'd rather French kiss a bullfrog!"

"You probably have," SueAnn observed.

Giji grinned. "Well, I have kissed a few toads!"

"Well, Giji and I are definitely not closer," SueAnn said, ignoring the laughter of the other wives. "We hate each other as much as ever!"

"Maybe more," Giji added.

SueAnn went in the kitchen and came back out with a litre of mandarin vodka and a gallon of cranberry juice. She poured drinks all around, and the women sat quietly for a minute. "So, did they catch the robbers? I mean other than the one you tied up?"

SueAnn nodded and took a sip of her drink. "Yes, they caught them," she said, pausing briefly for dramatic effect, "while trying to get decent service at a fast food restaurant!"

The wives laughed.

"I'm volunteering with paramedics tomorrow," Giji announced proudly. "With any luck, I'll be riding between two hot hunks and before the end of our shift they can take turns giving me mouth-to-mouth!"

Ariella rolled her eyes. "Yeah, right," she said, and then shrugged. "Well, if you can have a nice big helping of Mrs. Hoover's codfish and death casserole before you head out in the morning; you can probably get your wish!"

"I'm not sure it'd be worth it." She pretended to think it over. "I could die. Besides, mouth-to-mouth is no fun when you're really sick!"

"Good point," Ariella agreed. "And they would have to be really dedicated to their jobs and then some to kiss anyone who'd just eaten codfish casserole! So, forget about those hunky paramedics and get out there and save some lives."

Giji grinned. "You're asking an awful lot!" The women laughed and sipped their drinks. For a moment, it was good to be out in the backyard with the fresh air with SueAnn, Giji, Wynette, and Ariella.

"What would you do in a situation like that?" Ariella asked Wynette.

"I would never be in a situation like that; I don't need to go to an ATM for anything."

"Okay, but what if it was a hostage situation, never mind how you got there?"

"I'd kick their asses," said Wynette, her short, blonde hair swept back on her head with an earthy sage green scarf.

"You'd wet yourself," Giji quipped teasingly.

"The truth is, no one knows how they would act in a situation until they are in it," SueAnn spoke up.

"What do you think Connie would do, or Mrs. Hoover?" said Wynette, ignoring Giji.

"Heart attacks, both of them, no question about it," said Ariella.

"Speaking of Mrs. H," said Giji quietly, "she sounded almost dejected that I didn't get killed, when I came home. She was really mean, more so than usual."

"She's a lonely mean old woman," said Ariella. "Don't let her get to you. Your best bet is to get the hell out and get your own place. Your house sold months ago, why don't you try looking for a nice, small house somewhere?"

"I know where there is an abandoned farmhouse that needs some work," SueAnn teased.

"Hey, that's not a half bad idea," Giji said, "I could fix it up, buy it at market loss, I'll bet. It was dilapidated. I could hire a cute plumber to come over and stay for days at a time helping me get things together." She winked at SueAnn, knowing that it would get her goat.

"And you could have parties where you play cops and robbers, and charge admission, oh no, wait, that's kind of like prostitution, isn't it?" SueAnn retorted, her words a bit slurred.

"I think we've all have enough to drink," offered Wynette.

Ariella sighed. "Some things never change!"

***

The Saturday afternoon she was to volunteer with the paramedics, Giji kept her plans a secret from Mrs. Hoover. So, after a quick breakfast, she told Mrs. Hoover she had a couple of house showings and wouldn't be home until the evening.

At the hospital Giji met Ken, one of the paramedics, who checked her and SueAnn after their hostage ordeal. Ken was a good-looking guy, muscular, with close cropped dark hair and a goatee. He introduced her to the other paramedic who would be riding with them, a younger guy named, Jason, who was slim, tall, with light brown hair, a bit longer than Ken's and the dreamiest green eyes Giji had ever seen!

Giji squeezed into an orange jumpsuit

Ken whistled. "You make the suit look good!" he said.

"Thanks," Giji said, pleased, and turned to Jason, hoping he would comment, but he didn't.

***

That evening, after their shift had ended, Giji called Ariella and asked if she wanted the details of her afternoon. Interested, Ariella told her Marco was working late, and to put on a bathing suit and come on over, they could have Sun Li make them strawberry daiquiris to sip while they lounged by the pool.

Giji quickly changed into her tiniest bikini, a hot pink number, with spaghetti straps and a thong-style bottom. Throwing her see through sarong over her bikini, Giji went down the backstairs to avoid Mrs. Hoover's questions and roving eyes, and headed the down the block to Ariella's.

Giji entered the side gate as Ariella had instructed and went around to the pool. Ariella was already there, with two strawberry daiquiris on a small table between the teak lounge chairs. She looked up, giving Giji a welcoming smile. Giji said hello and seated herself, leaning back comfortably against the soft cushion on the chair. "Ah," she moaned, "this feels so good."

"So how'd your volunteer work go?" Ariella asked, curious.

Giji grinned. "Awesome!" she chimed. "I went out on calls with two of the hottest hunky paramedics!"

Ariella took a sip of her daiquiri "Really?"

Giji swooned with her eyes. "Oh, did I ever!" she said. "They were so incredibly gorgeous."

"And?"

"And we had a wild three way," Giji said quietly, seriously. "The most fantastic ménage a trois!"

"Are you serious?" Ariella could hardly believe what she was hearing.

"Cross my heart." Giji made the gesture with her fingers across her breasts.

Ariella smiled, genuinely impressed. "Wow, way to go, Giji," she said. "Now fill me in on everything! I want details, and don't leave anything out!"

"I sat between these two very hot and sexy guys and I couldn't help being aware of how close they were. So close I could feel their body heat warming me! The occasional brush of an elbow and the unexpected shift of a knee added to the heat. Each movement produced more contact and my pussy was more energized! In my mind, I was imaging my favorite fantasy of being with two super sexy guys in uniform! I could only imagine how wonderful it would be, but as it turned out, I didn't have to imagine for long!"

Ariella turned a little on the couch, so she was directly facing Giji. "Is this story going to be about saving lives or having sex?"

Giji shrugged, giggling. "Mostly sex."

"Mmm," Ariella said and giggled too. "That's what I was hoping you'd say!"

"Wait till you hear!" Giji told her excitedly.

"Well, don't keep me in suspense," Ariella prodded.

"Okay," Giji agreed, then explained how her morning had begun at the hospital, meeting the paramedics she would be riding with, getting her uniform, and starting out for a day of volunteer work tightly squeezed in the ambulance between two hunky paramedics.

Ariella nodded. *This should be interesting!* she thought and licked her lips in anticipation.

"At the end of our shift, Ken, that was one of the medic's names, said, 'Let's do something exciting!' "

" 'Like what?' Jason asked.

" 'I dunno,' Ken managed to keep his eyes on the road ahead as he drove, 'any suggestions?'

"At this point Jason shrugged. His body rubbed against mine and it felt good, but I was hoping for more than a shrug. I wanted him to speak up and join in so we could have an exciting meeting of the three of us."

Ariella took a quick sip of her drink, not wanting to miss any of Giji's story.

"I knew what I wanted and trying to make my fantasy come true, I said, 'We could fool around a little, play a game, maybe role play.' I tried not to sound excited! 'One of us could pretend to be a patient and the others could perform CPR. We could see where it goes from there.'

" 'Only if you're the patient,' Ken said to me with a great big grin on his face. He glanced over at me to check the look on my face. I tried to contain my enthusiasm, but I was getting more excited by the minute!" I turned to Ken and asked what he thought?

"He said, 'I say what does Jason say?'

" 'I say let's do it!' Jason spoke quickly, finally a note of excitement I his voice.

" 'Let the games begin!' I said and reached out my hands, which were shaking with excitement, on either side of me. I placed my hands on their crotches, feeling their cocks beneath my fingers. Their cocks were both large; Ken's seemed fatter and Jason's longer but thinner. Both were rock hard, throbbing slightly beneath my fingers and reaching straight up! Ken let out a pleased sigh as my fingers massaged his cock head and Jason's. Ken used one hand to unzip the fly of his uniform and his cock leapt into my hand. The head of his cock was wet, dripping pre-cum already. I massaged his cock head using the pre-cum as a lubricant beneath my fingers. It was warm and silky smooth! Unfortunately, Jason wasn't as bold as Ken, but Jason surprised me by placing his hand over mine and pulling my hand tight against his cock. He was literally humping my hand as we drove!

"Ken turned down a less traveled side road, then onto an old road that was rough and grown up, almost like an old logging road. He drove for a quarter of a mile or so, and then he parked in a wooded area. I wondered if he had been here before, possibly with the female paramedic who usually road with them, but I decided it didn't matter. I was more interested in what was about to happen.

Ariella sat up suddenly as if she could not believe what she was hearing. "Wow!" she exclaimed. "This is hot."

Giji grinned knowingly. "I told you!"

"Go on," Ariella urged.

"I quickly let go of the guys and slipped from the cab into the back of the ambulance. 'Come on, guys,' I said playfully, giggling like a schoolgirl discovering sex for the first time. 'Let's have some mouth-to-mouth!'

"They turned and looked back at me as I unzipped my orange uniform and revealed that beneath the thick material I wasn't wearing anything! They glanced at each other and exchanged pleased smiles as I kicked off my boots and slipped out of my uniform. I stood before them, completely naked except for my white socks! I sat on the edge of the stretcher and removed my socks, and then I lay back on the stretcher just as a patient would, flat on my back with my legs straight, my arms at my side.

"Both of the guys scrambled to join me in the back, each trying to see who would be the first to administer CPR, I guess. Jason got there first, which pleased me as I found myself most attracted to him and his edge of mystery. He started to kiss me without hesitation, a deep, long kiss with a hint of tongue at first and more as the intensity grew. Not to be left out, Ken pushed my legs apart and crawled up between them on the stretcher. He quickly started to administer CPR to my pussy lips!'

Ariella placed a hand between her legs against the dark material of her bikini, lightly touching her pussy as Giji took a quick sip of her drink and continued with her story.

"While Jason was kissing me and exploring my mouth with his tongue, Ken was kissing my pussy and exploring my pussy with his tongue, hot, wet and deeper and deeper! While he was still kissing me, Jason put his hands on my breasts and started to rub and squeeze them and pinched my erect nipples between his strong fingers. It felt incredible having one hot guy kissing me and playing with my boobs while the other hot guy ate my pussy and rubbed my clit with his tongue until I was close to ecstasy overload (if that's even possible! It just felt sooo good!) I pulled my legs up and clamped them firmly around Ken's head as he continued to lick my pussy and my clit. Jason ended the longest kiss I'd ever had in my life and started licking, kissing and sucking my breasts. Then he put his warm, wet mouth on my hard nipples and began to lick with the pointed tip of tongue, first licking around the edge of my nipple, and then licking the center. Finally he sucked my tit into his mouth and sucked me long and hard!

"The reality was so much better than my fantasy! It was almost overwhelming, I felt like I could come at any time. It was a good thing they eased up! Ken opened the rear door of the ambulance and he picked up one end of the stretcher while Jason picked up the other end. They carried me out of the ambulance on the stretcher and placed me just behind the rear door. They positioned the stretcher so that my face was even with their bulging baskets! I was relieved the moon was full and I could enjoy our ménage a trios without being totally in the dark. There was enough moonlight to see everything that I needed to see. Before I knew it, Ken had his huge, thick cock out and in my face. I took his cock in my hands and put it to my lips. I kissed the wet tip, tasting his sweet cum on my tongue. Then I licked with the tip of my tongue around the edge of his cock. I let the tip of my tongue lick the tip of his cock head as I squeezed his shaft to get all of his seeping cum to my eager mouth! While I concentrated o Ken's hard cock, Jason lifted my feet to his mouth, kissing them, licking them. He let his tongue dip down between my toes, flicking in and out. I had never had anyone concentrate on that incredibly sensitive area. It felt so exhilarating! Finally he sucked my toes and I almost lost my concentration on Ken's cock! Mind-blowing!

"Jason was still sucking my toes while Ken was unzipping his uniform. He quickly untied his boots and slipped them off. He stepped out of his uniform and stood there in his boxer briefs. His bare chest was broad and muscular, showing a thick growth of hair in the center of his chest. He pushed his briefs down and off, then he slipped his boots back on, which I found very exciting! Strong muscular guy was never sexier than when he was wearing nothing but his boots! Jason, on the other hand, was just sexy. Period. No matter what he wore–and when he wore nothing!

" 'Rip 'em off me!' Jason demanded in a firm voice that excited me for the first time since we'd met. I reached out my hands and caught his shorts and pulled hard ripping the stretchy material apart. His long, hard cock leapt through the ripped material towards me. I could see in the moonlight that it was a beautiful cock with an enormous head, pre-cum glistening on its tip. I ripped his underwear again, almost shredding them this time. The pieces fell to his ankles and he kicked them off. He stood completely nude above me. I licked the sweet cum drop off Ken's hard, throbbing cock while he moaned. I knew from his breathing and the tightness of his balls he was close!

"I slid my lips up and down his cum-filled shaft. He thrust his hips, fucking my face faster and faster until he exploded, shooting his huge load of warm cum down my throat. I licked his giant cock head clean, and then I licked my lips! Ken lowered the stretcher and sank to his knees on the bottom end of the stretcher. He lifted my legs, placing my feet against his hard chest, I could feel his pecs and with the soles of my feet I could feel his hard nipples beneath my toes.

"He rubbed his wet cum-soaked cock against my pussy lips, teasing my pussy over and over as he let his cock slip just inside my pussy then pulled back out, each time he went in a little deeper until he had sunk his huge, fat cock deep into my wet, quivering pussy and was thrusting his hips. I could feel his cock rubbing against my hard clit. My pussy was on fire!

"I wanted Jason's long, hot cock in my pussy, pounding me for all he was worth! I think I found my G-spot tonight! Ken, Jason and I made a *sex sandwich*! Ken lay on the stretcher. I lay on top of him, letting his big cock slide up in my hot, juicy pussy from behind. Jason climbed on top and slid his long, thick cock in me. They thrust in me, two huge, cum-dripping cocks in my pussy at the same time! Their cocks rubbed my clit and all my hot spots at once! I heard myself doing the deepest moan ever with two hunky guys pounding me at once! The guys continued to thrust in somewhat different rhythms, which seemed to add to the excitement. I felt myself about to come, orgasming wildly and my pussy began to –"

"Seriously, Giji, you're wild, one of the wildest, freer women I have ever met, but don't you think–" Ariella stopped herself. "Hell, what am I saying? Your story is so hot, when Marco gets home, I may have to get my groove on!"

Giji laughed and fanned herself with one free hand and spoke with a ragged voice. "Let me finish, I'm almost done. The guys started to grunt loudly, very primal, especially outdoors in the dark with only the moonlight shining down on us. Suddenly Ken started to thrust wildly as he shot his load deep in my pussy. As if spurred on by Ken's cumming, Jason started to cum, too. His long cock shot his huge load in a series of orgasmic squirts! It felt so good. Having two guys shoot their loads in me while both their cocks were inside my pussy was unbelievable! I would never think of a sandwich the same way again!"

Ariella laughed at Giji's last comment. "That is definitely a close encounter of the hot kind," Ariella told her. "It's pretty damned incredible!" She winked, getting an idea. "I may have to do some volunteer work myself!"

"It was so much fun, hanging out with those hunky guys," Giji said, "and Nick was so hot!"

"You mean Jason?"

Giji giggled. "Yeah, of course, I meant Jason," she said, a bit self-consciously. "Just a little slip of the tongue!"

"Uh hmmm," Ariella said, unconvinced

Laughing, Giji got to her feet. "Well, I just wanted to let you know how things went today."

"Thanks for sharing," Ariella said, wondering if she could ever get Marco to go for a ménage a trois. The *sexual sandwich* Giji had described had left her very interested and *very, very turned on!*

25

Lights! Camera! Action!

Giji pulled back the lacy curtains in the front window of Mrs. Hoover's living room. Nick was out in his yard fiddling with a lawn mower, which was upside down on the grass. As she watched him squat down next to it, his already tight Levis straining against his thigh muscles, she had an idea.

She opened the creaky screen door in such a way to make as much noise as possible and pretended that she was going to check the mail. As she stepped on the last stair, she threw herself onto the brick pathway, crying out and holding her ankle. As she rocked and held her foot, she sneaked a peek across the street. Nick stood up and was running across the road toward her. She smiled to herself and cried out again.

"Hey, are you okay?" Nick knelt down beside her.

"I was just trying to check the mail, how could I be so clumsy?" Giji smiled at him through her alligator tears.

"Here, let me see it," Nick reached for her ankle. She jerked back and held it tighter, trying to make it swell from lack of circulation.

"I'm okay, really," she said.

"I heard what happened, well, everybody did. I'd like to take you to dinner, when your ankle is better, of course," he smiled at her.

"It was a trying time for me and SueAnn, but it was especially awful for me," Giji forced a few more tears, letting him think she was overcome with the memory of her ordeal.

"Well, let me know when you're ready," said Nick. "Can I help you into the house?"

"That would be nice of you, thank you," replied Giji.

She stood up, leaning a little too long on Nick's shoulder, and allowed him to half drag, half carry her back up onto the porch.

"I can take it from here, thanks," she simpered at the doorway.

"Just a minute," said Nick. He turned and sprinted to the mailbox, opened it, shrugged, and called back to her.

"All for nothing, I guess, no mail yet," he called out.

"Silly me. I'm feeling better already, you still want to go to dinner?"

"Sure," he glanced over at the up turned lawnmower, "the lawn can wait."

Just then Giji saw SueAnn come out of her house a little ways down the cul-de-sac. *Even better,* she thought.

"Give me five minutes," she called to Nick.

"Fine, I'm just going to put this bad boy in the garage," Nick called back. He squatted again next to the mower.

Giji limped over to SueAnn, who was busily watering the hanging baskets on her porch.

"I just came over to gloat. Nick asked me out," she said when she got close enough that Nick wouldn't hear her. SueAnn looked up. She watched Giji limp closer.

"What happened to your ankle?"

"I went out to check the mail and silly me, tripped on the stairs. Nick was kind enough to come to my rescue, and now he's taking me to dinner," Giji said proudly. "I have a date with Nick Delfino!"

"Sure you do," SueAnn said disbelievingly, "and I have a date with Simon Cowell!"

"I do," Giji said firmly, "and good luck with Simon. From my personal experiences, I'd say he's rather hands on!"

They both waved at Nick as he righted the mower and started to wheel it toward his garage.

"Well, gotta go get ready," said Giji. She turned away and started skipping back to Mrs. Hoover's house, not a limp in sight.

"You've lived here for years," SueAnn called loudly after her, "you know the mail doesn't come for another two hours!"

***

SueAnn angrily watered the rest of the hanging baskets and stomped back into her own house. *Who gives a damn?* she thought. *I have more important things to do. I've got to get ready for my dinner with my editor.* She jumped in the shower and within half an hour was headed toward one of the nicest restaurants in town, *Chez Paradise*.

"So, Peter, I was thinking about a series of books on morals," SueAnn said to her editor after they had both ordered. She ordered the steak, because after all, this was on Peter's expense account. He ordered the prime rib.

"Great, great, how many books in the series?" Peter asked but he seemed occupied with something under the table. He kept twisting and finally reached down, disappearing from the edge of the table for a second.

"Are you okay?" asked SueAnn.

"Fine, fine, just wanted to adjust my shoe. New, you know. A little tight." Peter often started sentences by repeating the first word. SueAnn originally thought he couldn't hear very well, but found out later all editors do that so they can buy time for something else to say.

At the exact same time that the entrees arrived, SueAnn saw Nick and Giji across the restaurant, and felt something between her legs, the tip wedged against her panties and just inside her pussy. It all happened so fast. The waiter was setting the steak and prime rib before them, she caught Giji's eye across the room, and she felt a shove in her crotch. She continued to hold eye contact with Giji as her chair flipped over. Scrambling to regain both her chair and her composure, she saw Peter's shoe between her legs. Across the restaurant, Giji burst into laughter as Nick looked over. He looked so shocked that the look on his face would have been priceless, if not for the rest of the scene. It appeared he and Giji had heard the thud as her chair tipped over, but they hadn't seen the wingtip protruding from her pussy.

"Ma'am, are you all right?" The young waiter brought there food just as SueAnn fell. He stood there, tray poised on his palm, and seemed unsure what he should do. He just looked from SueAnn to Peter and then back again. "Sir, would you like your shoe back?" The waiter set the food down and was being as professional as possible, given the situation. It was easy to tell that he could barely keep a straight face.

SueAnn pulled the wingtip from between her legs and threw it at Peter, landing a hit to his chest. Already looking injured, he didn't bother to say "Ouch!" He just picked the shoe up from where it landed on the table and slipped it back on his foot.

Fuming SueAnn righted her chair and clumsily got back into it. She couldn't bear to look over at Giji and Nick again. The evening was turning into a nightmare. She waved away the smirking waiter and turned on Peter.

"Next time Peter," SueAnn said, keeping her voice a loud whisper so the other patrons wouldn't hear, "make sure it's about editing and not playing footsy."

"I'm sorry. I thought you were going to take off my shoe," Peter said innocently.

"Why the hell would I do that?" SueAnn demanded.

"I thought you were taking it off so I pushed trying to hold my foot steady..."

This was the last straw. First Giji and Nick, who she felt had betrayed her, being held hostage, the incredible embarrassment, and this jerk thinking he could do whatever he wanted just so she could get her books published, enough was enough. SueAnn was tired in general and with men specifically.

"No, I wasn't. You had your wingtip wedged in my pussy, you ass. Does your wife know you do this kind of thing?"

He looked down.

"Well, actually she left me when she caught me...with her best friend."

"Serves you right," SueAnn hissed, "What were you thinking? I write children's books, for chrissake!"

"I find that kind of sexy, a turn on," he admitted in a quiet voice.

"Oh, if I weren't such a bleeding heart liberal, I'd - I'd-"

"I'm a Republican."

"Don't tempt me, Peter!"

"I'm sorry. I apologize for –" Peter looked around nervously. The restaurant settled down when SueAnn regained her chair and her composure, but several patrons watched the show they were inadvertently putting on.

SueAnn put up her hands. "Save your apology," she told him. "You've already humiliated yourself... and me... enough!"

"But I-I –"

"I'll be working with a new editor," she told him, getting up to leave. She picked up her glass of wine and took a quick sip, then she tossed the rest on Peter. "Bon appetit!" she said and, smiling, she turned and left the restaurant.

***

I can't do this, Connie thought, feeling herself resist, pulling away. Real held her close, tight. He began to kiss her, slowly at first then more passionately; his lips were soft and warm but manly. Connie started to say no, but she remembered Lex and that Sexual Psychic person, and changed her mind. "No... Don't stop!"

she exclaimed.

"You are a most delectable dessert!" he whispered in her ear. "I want to lick you from head to toe, and then eat you like a hot tamale!"

Connie felt herself being caught up in the moment. "Talk sexy naughty food talk to me!" She was surprised the words had come from her own mouth!

Chef Real reached for Connie's shirt and unbuttoned it was ease. He slid it off her shoulders and pulled it loose from her tailored pants. He ran a fingertip along the lacy trim of her skimpy bra. Her nipples hardened and pushed against the flimsy material. She glanced down and saw a definite bulge in Real's pants which was becoming more pronounced as he stripped the clothes from her body. He slid the pants over her hips and revealed the strings of her matching bikini panties.

Connie reached to Chef Real and unsnapped his shirt. She pushed the shirt from his shoulders and couldn't stop herself as she reached for the waistband of his pants. The button slipped free and Connie cautiously slid her hands into his pants and moved them over his trim hips. She stopped short of removing his underwear, but his attraction and erection were obvious.

Real leaned to Connie and flicked his tongue over her breasts and unhooked the bra with nimble fingers. The material floated to the ground when he lowered the straps. Connie felt her body tingle from his touch and didn't notice when he slid her panties onto the floor. He removed his underwear and his hard, thick shaft sprang free from the closure.

Connie took in every inch of his body with hungry eyes and reached for him, but he touched her hand. He lifted his chef's hat onto his head and nodded toward her apron. "Put it back on, but only the apron," he said.

Connie put the apron strap over her head, and maneuvered to tie the strings behind her back, unaware that she had backed into camera one, hitting the auto start button. As they wiggled back to the other side of the room, the little red light came on. They didn't realize they were being aired live during an info-mercial. They spun around like two hot pastries, alone in the studio kitchen. No set people were around to see; they had all gone off to lunch while Chef Real and Connie were supposed to be setting up for the next scene, Broche soup.

Entwined together on the vinyl-covered floor, they brushed against the island that Real used to prepare food during his cooking segments. Chef Real backed her against the cutting board, kneading her breasts with his expert fingers as he tongued her open mouth. A bowl of flour spilled from the island on them, covering their faces and bodies in a white powder just before a pitcher of milk spilled off the counter onto them. They twisted and churned together until their naked bodies were covered in a creamy white batter. As they rolled around, the little red light continued to blink, recording everything. The auto set to rewind and project their images as soon as the commercial break ended. The last images before the show returned live was Connie's face thrown back in the heat of passion while Chef Real thrust everything he had into her. She came in a shuddering climax just as the tape began to rewind.

***

Martha Hoover continued to keep her eyes on the television as Giji lugged the last of her bright pink luggage down the stairs and set them in front of the door. She had finally closed the deal on her new place and was excited to get on with her life. It had been an interesting summer, that was for sure and she would miss the cul-de-sac with all of its characters–but it was time to move on.

She balanced the last small carry on next to the rest of the luggage and sat down next to Martha on the couch. Martha lowered the volume and turned slightly toward Giji.

"What did she think she was on, one of those hot Latin TV novellas?" Mrs. Hoover said and laughed. According to a phone call Mrs. Hoover had gotten from a neighbor two streets over, most of the neighborhood had witnessed Connie's indiscretions on the air.

Giji laughed, "You watch those too?"

Mrs. Hoover shrugged. "I've been known to take a look every once in a while when I'm looking for my cooking shows…or the home shopping channel, sometimes game shows or Jerry Falwell, of course!"

"Of course," Giji said with a smirk. "They are hot."

"So was Connie and her hot French chef," Mrs. Hoover assured her. "They were smoking! I kid you not, they set the kitchen ablaze. Damn, I wish I'd recorded it!"

"Mmm," Giji said, grinning, "that does sound interesting."

"It was," Mrs. Hoover assured her, an excited glint in her eye as she spoke. "The two of them were on fire. I would have expected it from…some people, but not Connie." her voice broke off as she stared at Giji. "She's always so quiet, so refined…"

"If you ask me, it's just an act," Giji said. "I'll bet she's not so prim and proper when she's getting her groove on!"

"Well, we already know that." Mrs. Hoover pursed her lips. "After all, she's been caught in the act and on live TV, no less!"

Giji nodded. "True." Expecting Mrs. Hoover would notice, she glanced down at her suitcase. "I'm glad Connie's not as square as she seems." She smiled. "I admire that she's got booty and knows how to use it!"

"I bet she cusses like a sailor," Mrs. Hoover said and winked. "You know what they say, it's the quiet ones you have to watch, they'll surprise you every time!"

"Oh," Giji said peeping through the blinds. "There's our hot TV star." She turned back to Mrs. Hoover. "I guess I'll be on my way."

Mrs. Hoover nodded. She looked like she wanted to say something but couldn't find the words.

"Well, it's been nice." Giji caught herself mid-sentence. "Hell, who are we kidding? Staying with you has been hell, Martha."

Mrs. Hoover stood up and gave Giji her best faux smile, just the tiniest of curls at the corners of her mouth.

"I love you, too, Giji." Mrs. Hoover spoke now in a sarcastic tone.

"I know you do," Giji said. *And that's more than a little scary*, she thought as she picked up her suitcases. "I'll be by to pick up the last of my things in a day or two."

"Just make sure that's all you pick up," Mrs. Hoover warned. "Your things, I mean."

Giji gave Mrs. Hoover that saccharine smile she'd come to loathe with every fiber of her being. "Of course," Giji said as she started out the door.

Mrs. Hoover stood watching her former houseguest carry the last of her tacky pink luggage to her matching pink caddy and place the bags in the back.

At that exact moment, someone else was watching Giji Brickhouse, someone keeping track of her every move....

26

Christening Giji's Crib

Maybe no one would recognize her, Connie hoped as she pulled into her driveway. After all, she had had flour all over her face and other places! She could still feel the flour between her legs.

She glanced in her rearview mirror before getting out of her car. Here she was in her own driveway donning a disguise. She had covered her head with a floral print scarf and put on her darkest shades.

"Nice pastries!" Giji called across the street as she closed the trunk of her caddy. "Chef Real's buns look pretty tasty, too! Mmm! I'll take a slice of that beefcake! When you take cooking classes you really heat things up. Talk about being too hot in the kitchen!" Giji fanned herself with her hand.

"Just stop it!"

"Well, you don't take a compliment very well, do you?" Giji teased. "I was just saying you and Chef Emeril turned public access into porno access! I'm impressed. I didn't know you had it in you!"

"Go to hell, Giji!" Connie snapped.

"Oh, I'm wounded." Giji laughed. "No need to get your pot roast in a stew!"

Connie slammed the door behind her. For a moment Giji was sorry she had used her saying goodbye time with Connie to taunt her, she wanted to say something more important, but then she shrugged, got into pink caddy, and drove off. She would run into everyone again when she came to get the last of her stuff from Mrs. Hoover's.

***

Feeling an empowering sense of independence that she hadn't felt in a long time, Giji put the key in the lock and opened the door of her new condo. She dropped her suitcase just inside the door and entered the living room, taking a deep satisfying breath, she looked around the room. "I am home!" she said out loud and hugged herself. "Home, sweet, home, at last!"

"It's all yours," a female voice said behind her. "Welcome to the building and your new place, Giji. Hi neighbor."

Giji turned, realizing she had left her door open. "Hi, Charmaine," she returned the greeting quickly, trying to hide her embarrassment. "Thanks."

Giji stood in the living room of her furnished condominium with her friend and new neighbor. The furnishings were clean, with straight lines and neutral earth tones with just a splash of bright color in accessories–like the hot pink sofa pillows and vases Giji had added. She liked putting her own stamp on things; it made it feel more like home to her. Still, even though most of the furnishings were left from the previous tenant, it was definitely her, Giji decided.

Not like that granny chic furniture at Mrs. Hoover's, Giji thought thankfully. I'll definitely not miss living with Mrs. Hoover and her dusty antiques and assorted knickknacks!

"It's perfect," she told Charmaine. "I'm so glad you told me about it the minute it became available. Otherwise, it would have been snapped up for sure!"

"I'm just so glad you love it," Charmaine enthused, "and that we're going to be neighbors!"

"Me, too," Giji agreed. "It's going to be so much fun."

Charmaine nodded, pushing a strand of long blond hair from her face. "Sure is," she said as the doorbell buzzed.

"I wonder who that is?" Giji said starting toward the door. "I wasn't expecting anyone."

When she opened the door, she was pleasantly surprised to see Nick standing there, a warm smile on his face and a bottle of champagne in one hand and a bouquet of pink roses in the other.

"Hello," Nick greeted. "Is it a bad time?" he added, looking past Giji to Charmaine. "Can I come in?"

"I'm sorry," Giji apologized and stepped aside for him to enter. "I was surprised to see you."

"A good surprise, I hope." He handed Giji the roses and champagne.

"The best! Wow, my favorite, a dozen pink roses and no thorns," Giji gushed, then she introduced Nick to Charmaine. "I owe Charmaine a lot," she finished, "she helped me find this great condo."

Nick glanced around the living room. "It's very nice," he agreed.

Charmaine beamed proudly. "Well, I'll be on my way," she announced. "I have an appointment. Good to meet you, Nick."

"You, too, Charmaine," Nick said. "Sure you won't stay and join us for a toast?" He gestured toward the champagne on the cocktail table.

"No one ever accused me of being a third wheel!" Charmaine responded and winked at Giji. "Thanks anyway. Giji, I'll see you later!" she said, flashing her eyes.

"Thanks, neighbor," Giji followed Charmaine to the door. "Maybe we can have dinner later?"

Charmaine shrugged. "Maybe," she said softly, almost a whisper, "if you don't have other plans! If so, all I can say is bon appetit!"

Giji glanced over her shoulder at Nick and whispered to Charmaine, "What do you think?"

"Hmmm," Charmaine swooned. "Yum-myyyyyy!"

"Uh-huh!" Giji licked her lips and they shared a quiet giggle then Charmaine left.

"I was truly surprised to see you," Giji said turning back to face Nick. "I didn't expect you'd come by so soon, but I'm glad you did."

"I wanted to congratulate you on your new place," he grinned, "in person."

Giji came into his arms easily. "I hope that's not all you wanted," she teased. "Ummm?"

Nick grinned playfully, looking into her eyes. "Hey, I'm only human," he played along. "I can be tempted!"

"Now that's what I want to hear," Giji said as their lips met in a long, lasting kiss that promised more to come. "So, you really like my place?"

He nodded. "Yeah, it's great," told her, looking into her eyes as he held her.

"Then you have to help me christen the place," she told him and began to unbutton his shirt, revealing his broad, muscular chest.

"I can handle that," he agreed, smiling at her eagerness.

"I know you can!" Giji exclaimed excitedly. "The only thing sexier than having clean sheets is having someone to help dirty them up!"

"You know something," he teased, "You have a way with words!"

"That's not all I have a way with," Giji flirted.

"You don't have to tell me!" he assured her, slipping his shoes off and tossing them aside. Giji also removed hers, playfully throwing them at him, he caught them, pretended he could put the small heels on then playfully threw them onto the sofa.

Laughing at his antics, Giji started to unfasten his slacks, but he stopped her, taking her hands in his. "Hold up," he urged, chuckling. "I have an idea, something you might like."

He sank to the shag carpet by the cocktail table and took a corkscrew from his pocket. "I thought ahead," he explained, "I figured you wouldn't be able to find yours right away, since you are moving and everything is still packed…" his voice trailed off as he uncorked the champagne, it bubbled out of the bottle and he tried to catch the spill in his mouth.

Giji rolled her eyes as she sank to the floor beside him. "I see," she said, not letting on that she was glad he'd brought a corkscrew because she didn't own one!

Nick opened the champagne and handed her the bottle. "Drink," he said.

Giji hesitated. "Are you sure? I don't think this is proper."

"Go ahead," he urged. "Since when have you been concerned about what's proper?"

Giji laughed. "True," she said, took a sip and handed the bottle to Nick.

"Here's to your new place," Nick said and took a long drink.

Giji took the champagne and took another sip, looking him straight in the eye. "Here's to christening my new place!" she said in a seductive voice.

Nick took the bottle from her hands and placed it in the table. "Here! Here!" he said in a playful voice as he pulled her on top of him. As they rolled together on the soft carpeting, their lips met in a hard, hot kiss, tasting the champagne on each other's lips, exploring each other's mouth in a heated promise of what was to come.

Nick broke the kiss and looked at Giji. "Let's screw our way to the bedroom," he suggested, "and we'll lose one piece of clothing with each fuck!"

Grinning, Giji said, "As long as you take off my clothes and I take off yours!"

"Agreed!" he said quickly, unbuttoning her blouse.

Giji pushed Nick's shirt off his broad shoulders, and he

removed her blouse, leaving her wearing only her pink satin bra. "You know you have me at a slight disadvantage, don't you?" he asked, staring at the under garment.

Giji giggled. "Some men wouldn't see that as a disadvantage!" she snapped, getting up quickly. She picked up the bouquet of roses he had brought her and hit him playfully on the head, pink petals went everywhere. Laughing as Nick was showered with loose the petals, she turned and ran for the kitchen.

Nick was right behind her, and he caught up, pulling her into his strong, and they fell together onto the cool tile floor just inside the kitchen, crushing the remainder of the roses beneath them. They playfully wrestled on the hard floor, the tile cold against their skin.

Scrambling to their feet, Nick held onto Giji, pulling her to his chest, he kissed her hard on the lips, lightly biting her tongue, while he reached around and unhooked her bra, then let go of her. While she slipped the bra off, her breasts bounced freely, Nick got behind her, his hands exploring her breasts and pinching her erect nipples as he held her to his chest and kissed her neck from behind, nibbling lightly on her earlobe.

Giji wiggled in his embrace until she was almost facing him, then she lightly bit one of his nipples until he let go of her. "Ouch!" he said, feigning injury.

Giji giggled at his plight as she unfastened his belt and slacks and pushed them down around his ankles, then she turned and ran from the kitchen, leaving Nick standing there in his boxer briefs, his slacks around his ankles. Stumbling, he kicked his slacks off, running after her.

Squealing like a small child, Giji turned and headed down the hallway to the guest bedroom, with Nick close on her heels, she tried to close the door on him as he got close. He caught the door chased her into the empty room. They fell together on the soft carpet, laughing.

"Got ya!" Nick said, his voice echoing slightly in the vacant room. "What, no furniture in this room?"

Giji shook her head as she pulled away. "No, but I have an idea of how I want to use it," she admitted, thinking of Charmaine's guest room with a computer and pen cam.

"I know how we can use it now," Nick teased, lunging at Giji.

Giji quickly got to her feet and backed away. "Not so fast, we still have a room to go," she said, then unzipped her skirt and slid it off, revealing hot pink panties underneath. Knowing she was expecting him to remove his shorts, he cleverly removed one sock, tossed it up in the air, and then did the same with the other.

"Not fair," Giji protested.

"Fair," Nick disagreed, laughing. "You had one piece of clothing more than I did!"

"Okay, okay," Giji conceded. "I'll let you slide this time!"

"Will you?" he said playfully as he pulled her to him and started to kiss her neck, then slid his mouth down to her breasts, kissing and licking first one and then the other. Giji moaned at the feel of his warm mouth on her cool skin, the sensation sent a quick series of shivers through her that seemed to settle in her quivering pussy.

By the time they reached Giji's bedroom, they were both ready to cum. Wearing only their underwear, they collapsed together on Giji's huge platform bed rolling across her new pink satin sheets, laughing, wrapped in each others arms.

While they shared a deep, wet kiss, their tongues exploring each other, Nick pushed Giji's panties down ever so slowly until they were around her knees, and she pushed them down her slender legs and kicked them off, landing them on the ceiling fan above their heads. Nick looked up. "Nice shot," he said, laughing.

Giji grinned. "I was aiming at your head!" she said playfully.

"You missed!" Nick laughed, as he tried to tickle Giji. Giggling, she started to push his shorts down, his cock sprang out, erect and seeping cum. Giji seized the opportunity and gave the head of cock a quick lick, tasting his salty-sweetness on her tongue.

"Hmmm," she said, looking at Nick.

As good as it felt having Giji's warm, mouth on his throbbing cock, Nick had something else in mind; he wanted to feel her tight wetness around his hard cock! He caught Giji's hand and pulled her close to him, taking her into his arms. Their lips met in a sloppy wet kiss, their tongues exploring each other's mouths. They sucked each other's tongue, tasting each other.

Finally, they broke the kiss leaving them both gasping for air. Nick kissed her bare shoulder, his lips brushing lightly against her smooth skin, making her shiver with excitement. When she let out a soft moan, Nick kissed her neck, then lowered his mouth to kiss and lick her breasts and sucked one of her nipples into his mouth, nibbling gently.

She put a hand under his chin and lifted his face to hers and while they kissed again, this time slowly, lingering, he settled between her legs, pushing his eager cock between her damp pussy lips and deep inside her. He moved deep inside of her slowly, deliberately at first, then in a steady rhythm, thrust after thrust, going deeper and harder.

"Fuck me hard!" Giji whispered in his ear after their kiss broke. She spread her legs wider and pulled them around Nick's naked body, allowing his cock to bury itself even deeper in her warm wet pussy. An excitement stirred inside her, building in intensity with each new thrust. "Don't stop," she begged, moaning softly. "Don't stop!"

As if in response, Nick pounded Giji's pussy harder and deeper, so deep that his cock hit her special place. Each time Nick's cock rubbed against her clit, the feeling of impending pleasure was so intense, that soon Giji began to moan softly, then louder and louder.

As he continued to pump her juicy pussy, harder and harder, Nick started to breathe heavily. Sensing that he was close to cumming, Giji pulsed her pussy around the shaft of cock, faster and faster, tighter and tighter until he began to grunt softly at first and then louder and louder as he shot his warm load, spurt after spurt, deep inside of her. With each shot of cum, Giji felt her pussy respond, her walls throbbing, quivering wildly as she began to orgasm, first in small waves, then in a shuddering climax that left her holding onto Nick as if her life depended on it!

Satisfied to the point of exhaustion, Giji and Nick collapsed in each other's arms, laying together in a tangle of pink sheets. While she lay close to Nick and listened to his steady breathing as he drifted off to sleep, Giji took a deep breath, smiling contentedly to herself. *Yep,* she thought, *it's definitely beginning to feel like home....*

***

"Okay," Connie fumed as she answered the door. "I've had it with the cooking jokes!"

"I just came over to borrow a cup of Chef Real," Ariella gushed, "I mean, a cup of sugar!"

"It's not a good time, Ariella," Connie told her coolly. "Lex and I are having an argument."

"Well, okay, I'll come back later," Ariella told her, and then added, "I wouldn't want to take sides or anything. Still, the whole neighborhood knows you've been sleep…ah… I mean cooking with someone else!"

"I don't think a man who sleeps with a psychic has any room to complain," she said evenly and rolled her eyes.

Connie closed the door before her young neighbor could finish. "Now where were we?" Lex refused to answer her. She sighed and went upstairs, put on her favorite silk gown, and climbed into bed, miserable. She sulked in the bed as Lex opened the door to the room. He didn't give her a chance to say anything, at first.

"All this time," Lex argued, "you've been lecturing me about my sexual behavior, and you're caught on live TV making love with a pastry chef-slash-would-be celebrity!"

"He's going to be huge, the next Emeril!" Connie spat as if it explained everything.

"Well, that makes it all right!" Lex said sarcastically, unable to control his rising anger, "but you're avoiding the real issue!"

"What's that?" Connie asked, enjoying her husband's jealousy even if she wasn't thrilled with the reasons leading to it. "That another man finds me appealing? Why is that an issue when you don't?"

Lex paused, thinking about what his wife had just said. He decided not to pursue it, instead he asked, "Are you in love with this guy?" He took a deep breath. "Or are you just lusting after him." Lex wanted to know, but his words were like a slap in the face.

Connie admitted she had feelings for Real, but she wasn't sure if she was or wasn't in love with him. But, she also knew that she was jealous at the thought of Lex being with another woman. She threw back the bed sheets and sat up in her silk gown.

"When was the last time you even took any interest in this?" she asked, pointing between her legs.

She wasn't sure what happened next, but Lex tore off her nightgown and took her as never before, moaning and devouring her body with his hands and mouth. She enjoyed that her husband wanted her, but wasn't so sure it was because he was attracted to her. She lay there thinking that it could be a reaction to knowing she was with another man. Although she wanted to save her marriage, Connie wasn't as turned on as she had hoped.

Later, lying beside her husband in the dark, hearing the soothing sound of his heart beating, Connie realized she had lost control and surrendered herself to someone else, but this time with no regrets, except when she thought of Real. She felt a little pang of guilt, like she betrayed him…she admitted to herself as she drifted off into fitful sleep that she loved Real but she also loved her husband. The problem was that she wasn't sure which love was stronger.

It also occurred to her that she probably wasn't the first lonely housewife that Chef Real had an affair with. The professional cook didn't seem to mind that she was married. Soon, she needed to decide what to do about her nosy neighbors. She participated in the gossip circles and now the tide would turn on her. She knew the next monthly get together would be interesting and she wasn't sure she would attend.

27

Kendra Gets Busted!

"It's crazy out there on the roads," Giji said, sliding into the booth at the Java Hut opposite Ariella. "I would have been here sooner, but I was almost killed by a soccer mom and a couple of fish people!"

"Fish people?" Ariella repeated.

"Yeah, the ones with the little fish symbol on the rear of their cars!" Giji explained. "They're some of the scariest drivers on the road. The fish people cut me off on the freeway, and then this deranged soccer mom almost ran up my ass!"

"Oh, Jerry Seinfeld did an episode on his show about those fish symbols several years ago," Ariella recalled. "I believe they're supposed to be evangelical Christians." She rolled her eyes. "I call them faux Christians. They're some of the lyingest people you'll ever meet. A couple sold me a fountain once without a pump. Now I ask you how can it be a fountain without a pump? Where's the water gonna come from, huh?"

Giji shrugged. "Same place the fish do, I guess."

"Well, they also have hang-ups about sex."

"Yet they don't seem to have a problem reproducing like wayward little bunnies!" Giji quipped.

"Maybe their symbol should be the bunny!" Ariella laughed.

"Where would we be without sex?" Giji asked.

"Extinct."

"That's right," Giji agreed, "we'd be gone the way of the dinosaur. If dinosaurs spent more time having sex and less time foraging for food, they'd probably still be around!"

"Well, they would probably have lived happier lives, anyway," Ariella said quietly.

"I don't care what two consenting adults do in the privacy of their own home," Giji stated, "as long as they'll let me join in– or, at least, watch!"

Together they laughed.

"I recognize the cross as a religious symbol," Giji told her after their laughter ceased, "but I draw the line at fish!"

"This is a side of you I haven't seen before," Ariella observed, surprised their views on religion were so similar.

"Well, I don't have a problem with religion as a whole," Giji assured her, "just with organized religion trying to force the same lame views on people of other cultures and religions!"

"I feel the same way," Ariella told her, then remembered an incident Giji might find amusing. "Once I saw a crazy driver with a bumper sticker that said 'Jesus is my co-pilot.' After he almost rear ended a bus load of nuns, I said, 'Jesus, when this guy makes a stop, get out!'"

They shared a quick laugh.

"I just saw the weirdest thing on TV this morning," Giji remembered.

"Talk about weird," Ariella complained, "Marco was watching Chelsea Handler last night. That bitch is insane!"

"Well, I can top that," Giji assured her. "Some jackass dressed like an apple was singing you can't overload your underwear right there on TV!"

"No, it's you can't over love your underwear," Ariella told her, frowning.

"Well, that makes even less sense. So, you can't over love your underwear, but you can overload them."

Ariella cringed. "We're not having this conversation." She stared at Giji. "Have you been smoking pot?"

Giji nodded, grinning. "Just a little."

"Oh my God, I could tell. I wondered why you didn't order a latte. Guess you're wired enough!" Ariella told her and leaned closer. "I can smell the weed on your breath!" She laughed. "Besides, it makes you all philosophical, if that's what you want to call it."

"Well, I can't help it, there's so much crazy shit on TV these days," Gigi complained, "and in the newspaper, books..."

Since when do you read, Ariella wondered, but she didn't say it out loud. "I saw a story a while ago where a kid working at a donut shop ejaculated into the glazed donuts!" she said, making a sour face. "Disgusting! I haven't been able to even look at a glazed donut since I read that story."

"Ew," Giji said, "if I'm going to have cum-glazed donuts, I want to choose the guy who does it!"

"Me, too," Ariella agreed, "and I choose George Clooney."

"I don't know," Giji said. "Maybe Brad Pitt or –"

"Or Tom Cruise!" Ariella interrupted, "if he'll promise to stop jumping up and down on Oprah's sofa!"

"You know," Giji said with a smile, "I'm suddenly getting a huge craving for glazed donuts!"

"I agree there is a lot of insane shit on TV," Ariella agreed, "too bad so much if it is true!" She paused, getting an idea. "Maybe we can grab a couple of donuts to go!"

"Okay, but while we're on the subject of TV, I saw Connie after her...indecent exposure on live TV with Chef Hunk-a-licious!" Giji announced. "She was a mess, and I'm not just talking about the leftover food crusted in her hair!"

"I know," Ariella said and gave a slight giggle. "I made the mistake of going over to borrow a cup of sugar."

"Did you really need sugar?" Giji asked and gave her a doubtful look.

Ariella shrugged. Busted! "Well, not really," she admitted reluctantly. "I just wanted to go over and see what was going on."

"Funny," Giji said, mildly amused. "Speaking of finding out what's going on, I have to tell you about the Sexual Psychic!"

"Cute name," Ariella asked. "Is that a new rock band?"

Giji shook her head. "No, remember I mentioned her once before," she said, grinning. "She's a psychic downtown, near the fish market."

"I remember now." Ariella winced. "Ew!" she spat. "Is it that godawful place that smells like rotting carp?"

"Her place is near there," Giji admitted. "Anyway, she's really good, her name is Kimiko, and she's a small Asian woman." She paused, licking her lips and rolling her eyes. "She gives the best oral ever!"

"Better than you?" Ariella wondered.

Giji shrugged. "Well, I don't know," she told her friend. "It's not like I've ever given oral to myself."

Ariella took a sip of her latte and almost choked as she visualized that unlikely feat. "If you ever do," she coughed, snickering. "I'd love to see it! That would be some feat of gymnastics!"

"Or contortion!" Giji chimed in, laughing too. When the laughter had passed, she added,

"You should go see her."

"I have been a little tense lately. You think she could work her magic on me and loosen me up?"

Giji gave her a sarcastic stare. "As if you really need to be any looser!" she teased.

"Watch it," Ariella warned. "Blondes who wear lingerie as business attire should not cast dispersions against other people!"

"Hey, you set yourself up for that one," Giji told her, laughing lightly. "So, what do you think?"

"I think you should lay off the sarcasm if you want to remain friends."

"Okay, okay," Giji agreed. "But, are you going to see Kimiko?"

"Not on an empty stomach, that's for sure," Ariella hedged. "Maybe." She paused, wondering. "How is she?"

"I just told you she's wonderful," Giji said, drawing out the last word. "And I do mean wonderful. She predicted I would have an orgasm, and within the hour, there I was cumming like it was predestined!"

"I'm wary of psychics since that time I called Miss Cleo and she said my lesbian girlfriend was pregnant!"

Giji laughed. "Was she?" she teased.

"Sure!" Ariella played along. "I caught the cunt in bed with my bi-sexual twin brother Enrique!"

"She could tell you what's up with Marco," Giji told her on a more serious note.

"Who says I care?" snapped Ariella.

"I'm not saying you do, but –"

"Okay, if I can't sleep at night over who Marco is bedding," Ariella said sarcastically, "I'll go see this slutty Sexual Psychic!"

"Well, if you do," Giji began, "you might not want to refer to her quite that way."

"Why? I'm a Latina princess with a fiery temper!"

"Just a warning. She'll filet you like sushi!"

"In that case," Ariella frowned, "maybe I'll pass."

"So, you're definitely not going?"

"Probably not," Ariella admitted, "but how is she at making accurate predictions?"

Giji didn't speak. "Really I don't know," she admitted.

Why does that not surprise me? Ariella wondered. "I guess I could find out for myself."

Giji looked at her, her curiosity aroused. "Oh?" she said. "What's going on?"

"Well I have been having a dream –"

"Tell me about it," Giji pressed. "Maybe I can help."

Ariella drew in her breath, not sure she wanted to share certain aspects of her personal life with Giji Brickhouse, no matter how friendly they pretended to be with each other. "It's just a silly dream. I haven't been sleeping well, that's all. You know, one of those crazy dreams where the pieces don't fit and…"

"Recurring?"

"No…kind of."

"Sure you don't wanna share it with me?" Giji prodded.

Ariella shook her head. "Tell me why you wanted to meet here," she remembered, "you said you had some news you just couldn't wait to tell me."

"I do," Giji assured her, grinning. "I've been saving the best news for last."

"You and Nick are getting serious?" Ariella guessed.

"Ummm, kind of," Giji admitted. "Sexually, anyway, but that's not my surprise."

"Okay, I give up," Ariella said, not sure she wanted to hear what Giji was beaming about, but if it didn't involve her, it couldn't be that bad.

"One more guess," Giji pressed.

"You just got laid by every guy on the high school football." Ariella winked. "And the opposing team!"

Giji grinned. "That sounds like fun," she quipped, "but no. Not even close."

"Okay, I give up."

"You sure?"

"Go ahead," Ariella told her, "lay it on me."

"I got my own place!" Giji announced proudly.

Ariella forced a smile. "Great, I guess we'll see less of each other from now on."

"Why?"

"Well, you won't be a few houses down," Ariella explained. "We won't bump into each other unexpectedly. You won't drop by uninvited. Hey, we'll probably never see each other."

"Of course we will," Giji disagreed. "We'll see each other all the time. I'm only fifteen minutes away. You can come see my new digs and tell me what you think of the place."

"Sure," Ariella agreed, trying to be happy for Giji. "You can finally move out of that Hoover-ridden hellhole!"

"She's not so bad," Giji admitted, "at times!"

"Well, at least those horrible casseroles of hers will be a thing of the past."

Giji rolled her eyes. "Ooh, yes, I definitely won't miss those!" she agreed. "My new place really rocks. You'll see. Charmaine –"

"That mousy girl from work?"

"Yeah, she found the apartment for me in her building at Grandview Heights," Giji told her. "She's not mousy at all when she lets her hair down! You should meet her, she's really cool."

"I'll bet." Ariella sounded unconvinced. "Grandview Heights. Swanky digs. Congratulations on your new place."

"Thanks," Giji said. "Very swanky! Anyway, when Charmaine told me about a great apartment available in her building, I was skeptical at first. I imagined an old dated apartment that was stuck in the 1940s, but the apartments at Grandview have been well kept and updated over the years. Mine came furnished. I looked at the place and fell in love with it and it's perfect for me!"

"Great," Ariella was genuinely pleased for her friend. "I'll come see your new place after you get settled in." She paused and smiled. "I'll bring you a house warming gift."

"Just make sure you bring the good stuff." Giji winked. "Marco's primo blend!"

"Only the best," Ariella promised. "You're a bad influence on me, you know!"

"The feeling is mutual," Giji teased. "It hasn't been all bad."

"Ditto."

***

Friday, Steven thought, watching the clock on his desk tick down the minutes, eager to get out of the office before Kendra popped in. Somehow he managed to avoid her all week, mostly by leaving early every day. Today was Friday, and Steven was determined to make it a full week without Kendra. So, he'd decided the one way to guarantee that he would not bump into Kendra today was to leave a bit early. He watched the clock at 4:30, then 4:45, 4:50 and then it was time to make his move.

Quickly he shut down his computer, took his jacket from the coat rack in the corner, draped it over his arm, turned back to his desk and clicked off the light, paused at the door, listening for any sound of movement that might be Kendra. Slowly, he turned the knob and pulled the door open and came face-to-face with Kendra! There she stood, dark, dark hair falling freely about her slender shoulders, dressed in what appeared to be her father's trench coat and a pair of shiny black stiletto heels.

Steven looked at the young woman and licked his lips. He had to admit that Kendra's latest surprise was a bit of a turn on, but he had to admit the thing that worried him the most about her was her unpredictable, impulsive nature! He couldn't help worrying that Kendra's spontaneity would get them both in a whole lot of trouble. Steven glanced around quickly, grateful that most the other employees usually snuck out early on Fridays.

"Where are you going?" she looked down at his jacket. "I was coming to see if you wanted to work some overtime, if you know what I mean?" she added and winked.

Startled, Steven literally could not speak for a few minutes. "I... I know," Steven stammered finally, he knew what she meant. He spoke softly so no one would hear.

"Where have you been?" Kendra demanded with a suspicious twinkle in her eyes. "I haven't seen you all week except for passing you in the hallway a couple of times."

"I-I've been busy all week...at home," Steven lied. "Wynette thought of little projects for me to do around the house after work all week."

Kendra frowned, uninterested. "How domestic."

"I need to-to get home," Steven told her. "Tonight Wynette

wants me to-to change... I mean...clean the rain gutters."

"Really?" Kendra sounded doubtful. "You wouldn't be trying to avoid me, would you?" Kendra asked, looking him directly in the eye.

Steven knew he might be making a huge mistake, unsure what the unpredictable young woman might do, but he decided to seize the opportunity. "Kendra, I'm not sure this is working out," he said as she sank to her knees in front of him. She unzipped his slacks and removed his erection, which was a result of fear instead of sexual excitement. "Us getting together like this, doesn't seem like it's going to work out."

"Of course, it's working out," she assured him. "What's not working?"

Steven tried to resist, but she was getting to him. Worst of all, she knew she was getting to him. "I'm trying to tell you," Steven said, sounding like a young child dealing with an authority figure. "I'm too exhausted to get much work done. You seem to have one thing on your mind most of the time." He thought of his poor cock. Speaking of the weakness of the flesh! he thought. Despite being oversexed for weeks, it was his one weakness where Kendra was concerned. His slacks were bulging out. His cock was hard and pressing eagerly against the fabric of his shorts. It was turned on. It enjoyed Kendra's unrelenting attention. It craved her lips on its tip. It longed to be in her warm, hot mouth and deep in her lovely young throat! He had to get control of it.

Kendra grinned. "I should've been a guy!" she said playfully. "You know how guys reach a certain age and all they can think about is sex...sex...sex!"

Like a deranged sex maniac, Steven thought, realizing she wasn't getting the point, but he was determine to try although he was more and more turned on by Kendra's determination and by her open rebellion. "I know," he assured her in a serious voice. "Well, I'm well past that age. I need some rest. My cock is so sore from your constant attention that I couldn't fuck my wife without taking painkillers!"

Kendra chuckled. "You exaggerate," she told him, sounding adamant. "All your beautiful cock needs is a little TLC, just a little mouth-to-mouth resuscitation."

"No, I'm not exaggerating," he ignored her last comment under the circumstances. "The other night I brushed up against my wife getting into bed and it hurt. It really hurt!"

"You're such a liar!" Kendra laughed.

"I need a break," he told her, "to heal from your nibbling and sucking." Maybe if he played the age card, really concentrated on their age difference, Kendra would see how wrong this was and find someone closer to her own age. "I'm not as young as I used to be. It's not like I'm some young college student who can go at it day and night and be fearless and completely pain-free!"

"If you keep talking that way, I'll think you're too old for me," Kendra told him, her hand brushing the front of his slacks. Her fingertips lingered ever so briefly on his rapidly rising erection.

That's the idea, Steven thought to himself. He couldn't believe he was actually thinking this way. Too old! But Kendra had a way of making him rethink how it would be to have a sweet piece on the side.

Kendra took several steps forward, forcing Steven to retreat back into his office. Once inside, she kicked the door shut behind them. She stood so close their lips were mere inches apart. Feeling intimidated by the closeness, Steven took another step back. As he did, Kendra untied the trench coat. He wanted to look away, but he couldn't pull his eyes from her lovely, smooth hands as she pulled open the coat, revealing that she wasn't wearing anything underneath! There she stood, legs apart, trench coat barely hanging on her slender shoulders, her body toned and tanned. She smiled as he drew in his breath sharply. She took this as a sign she had conquered her prey–and she shifted her shoulders back, pushing her perfectly round, tight young breasts out and dropping the coat off her nude body into a crumpled heap at her feet.

"What happened to your clothes?" Steven asked.

"I managed to lose them," Kendra said proudly. "I started before everyone left for the day. I started with my bra. It's hanging from the ceiling of the ladies' bathroom! My blouse is keeping a dying plant warm in the lounge! My skirt is draped over the water cooler! And my wet panties are on my dad's desk!"

"That's not smart," Steven worried, "you could get caught."

Kendra looked at him through eyes that almost seemed innocent, naïve. "Isn't that half the excitement?" she let her hand brush the front of his slacks. "You look pretty excited to me."

"Well, what are you going to do about it?" Steven asked, admitting he was very excited actually and a little scared. For better or worse, that was part of the excitement, too.

Looking into his eyes she saw a promise of something exciting to come, Kendra took his jacket and tossed it on a nearby chair. "I can think of a million things we haven't tried," she said as she sank to her knees in front of him. She licked her tongue across the front of his slacks, the tip of her tongue finding the head of his cock and massaging it through the fabric. Suddenly she caught the head of his cock between her teeth, chewing his cock lightly through the damp fabric. Steven moaned, it was a mixture of excruciating pleasure and exhilarating pain.

She looked up at him, with playful child-like eyes. "You want me to stop?" she asked, but had no intention of stopping. She quickly unfastened his belt and slacks, his enormously swollen cock almost leapt into her mouth. She took the head of his cock into her warm, wet mouth.

Steven looked down enjoying the sight of her sweet mouth around his hard cock. He tilted his back slightly, closed his eyes for a second. "Oh, noooo!" Steven responded in what was more a moan than actual words.

"Good." Kendra smiled, as she licked out her tongue and ran the tip over his cock. "Is it feeling better?"

"It feels great," he assured her.

"See, I told you it just needed some attention," she said triumphantly.

She held his cock tightly and let the tip touch her breasts, massaging one of her nipples with the head of his cock. Holding his cock between her young pert breasts, she sucked his cockhead between her lips, sucking more of his cock into her warm mouth. She moved it in and out, deeper and deeper until his cock filled her mouth and the entire shaft was down her beautiful, slippery throat. Steven just nodded, so close to cumming he couldn't speak.

They were both absorbed in each other, when Steven's office door opened. He heard a slight creak and saw light from the hallway. Suddenly, realizing Kendra had forgotten to lock the door–or maybe she'd left it unlocked intentionally? She was unpredictable... Steven's eyes jerked open and he stared into the face of Joseph Haldeman III, his boss and Kendra's father! A part of Steven wanted to pull away, but another part, an even stronger part wanted to stay inside Kendra's sweet mouth until he shot his load and achieved the satisfaction they were building towards before the door opened. He knew they should stop, but they'd already been caught, he remembered thinking later. Surely, no explanation was necessary. He didn't want to explain this. Kendra continued to suck his cock with all her energetic youth, seeming oblivious to what was happening. Steven tried to get her attention, looking from her to her father who stood there with a frozen look on his face as if he forgot what he was going to say. It seemed like this was happening to someone else, but Steven reminded himself that it was happening even though it seemed so freaking unreal!

The combination of fear and excitement at of being caught and having his boss watch his daughter give Steven a blow job was overwhelming and Steven's excitement peaked. He was unable to hold back and he started to jerk as he came, again and again, shooting thick spurts of thick cum until his load was spent. Breathing heavily, he pulled his cock from Kendra's grasp and pulled his slacks and shorts from around his ankles, leaned back against his desk for support and waited. He waited for the scene to unfold. Although he was not sure what was to come, he was sure it couldn't be good. He was planning how he would tell Wynette that he'd been fired without telling her why.

Suddenly, Kendra looked up at Steven and he saw from the surprised look in her eyes that she was finally aware that someone else was in the office. Glancing over her shoulder, Kendra remained on the floor, naked, kneeling on her father's coat – frozen in place or bracing for the worse.

As Mr. Haldeman pulled his daughter to her feet, Steven noticed Kendra had a drop of cum in the corner of her mouth, which she licked away with her tongue. "Dad, what are you doing here?" she spoke as if her father were doing something criminally wrong.

"I forgot my coat," her father looked at his trench coat on the floor beneath his daughter's naked body. "Looks like I found it...and a lot more!"

"Daddy, are you upset with me?" Kendra asked in a small voice that sounded like she was reverting back to her childhood.

"Kendra," her father began, his face red, "find your clothes, get dressed and wait in my office. We have a lot to discuss."

"Okay, Daddy," Kendra said, like a child who was caught being naughty.

Kendra scurried away, one arm folded around her breasts and the other between her legs, where she tried to hide her wet pussy. Joseph Haldeman III took a deep breath and looked at Steven with what could only be described as a combination of pity and disgust.

Steven stood there with his slacks around his ankles, a shocked expression on his face, unable to believe it was really happening. It was like a dream... no... a nightmare. Later he remembered thinking it was like a scene from a bad porno movie. But, it was real. He wished it would go away so he could escape.

Without saying a word, Steven pulled up his shorts and slacks, fastened the top button, and sank into a chair, defeated, humiliated and unable to look his boss in the eye. "I'm fire, aren't

I?" he asked weakly.

His boss let out a deep breath. "No, Steven, you're not fired."

"I'm not fired," Steven repeated as if he could not believe what he was hearing, a hopeful note in his voice.

"No, no. Kendra's been a hand full since puberty," the older man admitted. "I thought working here would settle her down a bit. That's why I agreed to let her work here when... you came up with the idea." He cleared his throat. "Get dressed and get out of here."

"Okay, sir, I'm sorry, Mr. Haldeman," Steven apologized, but he still could not look his boss in the eye. He could only look at his boss's trench coat on the floor with noticeable cum stains that had escaped Kendra' mouth. "It'll never happen again."

"You got that right," Joe Haldeman agreed as he turned to leave. He paused in the doorway and added, "Kendra's going to be away for a while... a long while!"

28

She's a Brickhouse!

Giji closed the apartment door behind her and walked down the hall. Near the end of the hall way, she paused and knocked lightly on the door. She heard footsteps inside, then the door swung open. A tall, slender blonde stood there. Giji noticed she was gorgeous and guessed she was a friend of Charmaine's.

"Hi," Giji greeted. "Is Charmaine in?"

"Giji!" a familiar voice exclaimed. "It's me! Charmaine. Didn't you recognize me?"

Giji shook her head. "You look so… so different," she admitted, a little embarrassed by the mistake. She had never seen Charmaine without her glasses and with her hair down. Even when she stopped by to see the apartment, Charmaine wore her hair up. "At work you usually look… so…."

"Mousy?" Charmaine asked, clearly not surprised by the perception. "I don't like to mix my private life with my day job."

"Private life?" Giji repeated, curious.

"Oh, I enjoy an active social life," Charmaine admitted. "It started when I went to clubs with friends in college and later became a dancer at Coyote Ugly."

"Really!" Giji was impressed, recalling Charmaine's appearance at work.

"I was," Charmaine assured her. "I spent almost four years dancing on the bar!"

"Wow, that's cool!" Giji said. "You'll have to show me some moves some time."

"Sure thing." She got an idea. "I may know something else you'd enjoy, but first let me show you around my place."

Giji glanced around Charmaine's living room, which was identical to hers except for the décor. Charmaine had an affection for wild prints, especially animal prints like leopard and tiger, which were on upholstered chairs, a sofa along with accent pillows and rugs. Above the fireplace on the mantel, there were tall, shapely vases that mimicked the shape of a woman; Giji immediately liked these and decided that later she would ask Charmaine where she bought them.

Interesting, Giji never imagined that mousy Charmaine had a wild side!

"Follow me," Charmaine offered, noticing Giji interest.

"Okay, great," Giji said, not sure what to expect next. She was still recovering from seeing Charmaine with her hair down and without her thick glasses! "Lead the way!"

Charmaine stood on the opposite side of the living room, pushing the swinging door open and allowed Giji to peer in. The kitchen was small, galley-style and identical to Giji's, clean white tile and stainless steal appliances.

"I don't use it much," Charmaine admitted. "I mostly do take out."

"Me, too," Giji said.

Charmaine lead Giji down a short hall way to the guest bathroom which was a carbon copy of Giji's. The only difference was Charmaine's animal print accessories and towels, the master bedroom had the same layout and dimensions as Giji's and it joined the master bath which also had the animal print décor and accessories. The guest bedroom was at the end of the hall and on first glance it appeared to be an office, the same as Giji planned for her room when she purchased a home computer. But Charmaine's guest room was more than a mere office.

Charmaine had a computer setup with a webcam focused on a round bed with leopard print covering and pillows. "You like?" Charmaine nodded toward the bed.

Giji nodded. "It's pretty incredible," she said sincerely. "I haven't seen a round bed in years. Does it rotate?"

Charmaine shook her head. "I wish it did," she admitted. "I'd love to own a round bed or heart-shaped bed that rotated."

"Me too," Giji said, staring at the webcam, which was a thin, dildo-shaped pen cam. "What's with the camera?"

"Oh, I have my own webpage, with webcam–or in this case– pen cam views for subscribers," she answered. "I have the pen cam positioned so that I can lay on the bed and my subscribers can watch me dress, or undress… or even get naughty on camera if I feel like it!"

"Really?" Giji couldn't believe what she was hearing.

"Yes, it's really fun to have people watch as you slowly undress, play with yourself or masturbate to your favorite song. You might say I really get off on it!"

They shared a quick laugh.

"Hey, you wanna go a stint on my webcam," Charmaine grinned. "You could warm up for what I have in mind later."

"Ummm," Giji pretended to hesitate. "That sounds great, but I have nothing to wear. I'd have to run back to my place and pick…"

Charmaine pushed open the sliding closet door. "Why don't you wear something of mine," she offered, running her hand along garments hanging in the closet. Giji saw a wide assortment of leisure wear of all types and lingerie in many colors and patterns – it even included animal prints!

"Are you sure?" Giji asked, excitement apparent in her voice.

Charmaine nodded. "I have just the thing, here's a pink teddy you can wear, with matching slip on heels with poofy feathers around the top that match the trim on the nightie."

"Oh, that sounds awesome," Giji said enthusiastically

Charmaine found the garment and held it up to Giji.

Giji looked down at the see-through teddy. "This is lovely," she cooed, then wondered, "What made you choose that one?"

"Well, it is your signature color," Charmaine glancing down at Giji's light colored blouse and hot pink faux leather skirt and matching heels. "But if you don't like it –"

"Oh, I love it," Giji quickly interrupted. "Where do I change?"

"There's the guest bath," Charmaine suggested, taking the matching heels from the rack on the closet floor, she placed them by the bed. "Or, you could undress here in front of the camera..."

"I've never been modest," she said, taking the teddy from Charmaine. She placed the outfit on the edge of the bed and sat on the bed where the camera was focused on her. Slowly, almost sensually, she unbuttoned her blouse, revealing her satiny pink bra that barely covered her round, full breasts.

"Nice," Charmaine commented as Giji unhooked her bra and her breasts bounced free. "Looks like we may have gone to the same plastic surgeon!"

"You too?" Giji grinned, pushing her huge breasts together.

Charmaine rolled her eyes. "I wanted to be able to see mine." She laughed self-consciously. "Mine were so small, like a little girl's."

"Mine too," Giji admitted, kicking off her heels. She stood and unzipped her skirt, which she slid down slowly and kicked it with her foot and it landed on the pen cam.

While the camera was blocked, Giji quickly slipped the teddy over her head and down over her breasts and stomach; the garment was see-through and so short it gave little coverage, but Giji knew that was the whole idea. She slipped on the matching heels Charmaine placed by the bed. Pleased with her appearance after a quick glance in the cheval mirror in the corner of the room, Giji tossed herself onto the bed, breathless.

Laughing at Giji's manic movements, Charmaine crossed the room and removed the skirt, folded it and placed it beside the computer monitor. She sat at the computer and removed the pen cam from its stand. Holding it on Giji's face, she said "Extreme close-up."

Feeling her pussy getting moist at the excitement of being watched, Giji pretended to suck her thumb and pout.

"We all know you're a naughty girl," Charmaine teased, pulling the pen cam back, "but play nice for the camera."

Giji rolled over on her back, kicked her legs up and slowly slipped off her pink silky panties, revealing her pussy, with its well-defined labia. As she opened her legs, Charmaine held the pen cam close to her pussy. Giji stared at the computer screen, her pussy looked enormous!

Suddenly, Charmaine shocked Giji! She placed the pen cam close to Giji's hairy crotch, teasing her pussy lips apart with the end of the camera, then she shoved it in just a bit and pulled it out, using the pen cam as a dildo. She giggled playfully and Giji joined her as she pushed the camera in again, deep between Giji's pouty pussy lips, farther inside, deeper into Giji's juicy pussy.

Giji wondered what the webcam viewers were seeing as the camera slid deeper and deeper into her hot cunt! It felt a little strange having a camera inside her pussy, but she had to admit in a weird way it was exciting and it made her pussy quiver. They both turned and stared at the computer; the image of the inside of Giji's pussy was out of focus, pink and splotchy.

Giji found it hard to think of anything except the heated friction Charmaine was creating with the pen cam. Charmaine pushed it in and out of Giji's juicy pussy until Giji started to moan. "Like that?" she asked.

"It's certainly stimulating!"

"And entertaining, among other things," Charmaine knew. "Online viewers love this sort of thing!"

"Will I get a shock?" Giji worried, looking down at the pen came sticking out of her wet pussy.

"Only if you cum too soon," Charmaine teased.

Charmaine pulled the pen from Giji's pussy and licked the tip. Giji watched her friend licking her pussy juices off the end of the camera. "Mmmm," she hummed and licked her lips. "Delicious!" She placed the pen cam on its stand. "I have another idea that might be fun."

Giji sighed appreciatively. "You have the most interesting and stimulating ideas."

"Gotta keep it interesting," Charmaine said, opening the top drawer of the desk and removed something that looked like a pen, only thicker. She looked at it, sniffed it, licked it and tossed it at Giji who caught it. There was a curious look on her face when she saw what it was.

"What's this for?" she asked, holding up the cigar. "You want me to smoke it?"

Charmaine shrugged. "Maybe later, silly," she said. "It's for play. Be creative. See what you can do with it."

Getting the idea, Giji removed the cellophane wrapper from the cigar with her teeth, then she placed the cigar between her lips as if she were smoking it. Taking the cigar from her mouth, she held it firmly between her fingers, Giji licked the length of the cigar like she would the shaft of the most perfect cock. Then she kissed the tip before placing it into her warm, wet mouth. She sucked it in and out, deeper and deeper until it was nice and wet.

Placing the wet cigar between her full, ripe breasts, she held it in place with her boobs and sucked it in and out of her mouth, up and down between her breasts, creating a friction that stimulated her smooth skin.

Finally, she pushed the sheer teddy up and she pressed the tip against her pussy lips teasing her pussy much as Charmaine had done earlier with the pen cam. Slowly she pushed the cigar into her wet, dripping pussy deeper and deeper, in and out, until she was close to orgasm.

Much to her surprise, Giji found that being watched by strangers, possibly thousands of eyes watching her every move, added to her growing sense of excitement. Being watched by others excited Giji in a way she never experienced before and soon she began to moan softly.

"Didn't you see that after school special about not stuffing things up your twat?" Charmaine teased.

"Oh. I missed that one," Giji quipped through clenched teeth, close to coming. "Obviously, I was busy shoving everything I could find up there!"

Giji saw Charmaine watching her and she continued to push the cigar in and out of her pussy, setting into a steady rhythm, deeper and deeper. She tilted the cigar back and rubbed the wet cigar to massage and stimulate her clit, slowly but steadily bringing her to a shuddering orgasm which was enhanced by being watched. Moaning loudly, Giji came in a heated rush, her head back, her red lips parted....

Exhausted and still breathing heavily, Giji lay back against one of Charmaine's animal print pillows and closed her eyes, enjoying the moment.

Charmaine moved to the bed and lay beside Giji who opened her eyes when Charmaine started to play with one of her nipples. "Nice, huh?" Charmaine asked, referring to masturbating in front of an audience.

Giji nodded. "I needed that," she said softly. "It was wonderful."

"Once you got into it, you were really good," Charmaine complimented. "I have something that will totally blow your mind!"

"What?" Giji wanted to know.

"It's a surprise," Charmaine said, grinning knowingly. "Let's just say its audience participation of another kind!"

"Up close and personal?" Giji prodded.

Charmaine shrugged. "In a way," she admitted, then she nodded, "Definitely a good description of what I have in mind."

"Well, it sounds like fun," Giji was intrigued.

"Trust me, it is!" She picked up Giji's blouse and threw it at her playfully. "Get dressed and let's go! We don't want to keep the audience waiting!"

Charmaine freshened up her makeup and Giji cleaned up quickly in the master bath, then returned to the guest room and dressed quickly. She was excited to see what Charmaine had planned, Giji had a feeling it was going to be fun and exciting!

Charmaine came to the door. "Ready?"

Before Giji could answer, the computer beeped. "What's that?" she thought the pen cam might be malfunctioning since Charmaine shoved it in places it probably wasn't designed to go.

Coming into the room, Charmaine went to the computer. She touched the mouse and the screensaver of a beautiful young woman disappeared. "Oh, it's nothing," she mumbled. "It's the message board on my website. Someone posted a message." She paused, reading, her lips moving silently. "Looks like it's for you."

"Someone left a message for me?"

"Yeah," Charmaine said.

"What's it say?"

"It says 'I've been watching you," Charmaine turned to Giji. "Hey, you have a fan!"

"Looks that way," Giji said uneasily, thinking of the person who had been calling her for months. "It's kind of creepy… the message, I mean."

"Well, it is a webcam," Charmaine pointed out. "Besides, it just says he's been watching."

"He?" Giji repeated. "How do you know it's a he?"

"Most of my subscribers are," Charmaine said matter-of-factly, "I don't know for sure. I just assumed the person who left the message was a man, most postings are…" her voice trailed off seeing Giji's reaction. "Are you okay?"

Giji nodded. "I'm fine," she said, deciding that the person who left the message was most likely not her caller. She gave Charmaine a reassuring smile. "Hey, let's get going. I'm ready to have some fun!"

29

Vixens!

Connie hesitated before knocking on the door of Real's apartment. When he called and asked her over, she'd hesitated, but he was insistent that he needed to see her. So, she gave in and said she would come over. The truth was she needed to see him. She had something she wanted to give him, something she needed to give him. It wouldn't be easy, but she reminded herself that she was a married woman. She couldn't continue to behave this way.

Real opened the door before she could even knock on the door He gave her a pleased smile. "Welcome to my humble abode." He gave her a quick, eager kiss and a little hug as she came in and he pushed the door closed.

"Nice," Connie said as she entered the living room, taking in the huge room with minimal furnishings and lots of uncluttered space. One entire wall was an expanse of glass windows and she could see the city below, small from here but bustling, chaotic. Quite a contrast to this room, she thought.

"Great view, huh?" Real asked, stood behind her, his hands on her shoulders. He kissed her neck, softly, his breath hot on her skin. She tried not to think about his touch, his smell.

"Yes," she said uneasily, "it's wonderful." The things she really wanted to say was that his apartment was overwhelming, just like her feelings for him. Looking around the room, she was perplexed by what she saw. Everywhere she looked there seemed to be another reminder of the difference before Real and herself. His style was modern, sleek, sophisticated glass and metal while she embraced the traditional lifestyle and surroundings. She knew, she had always known, even as a child that opposites attract. There was an attraction she couldn't deny. But she could hear her mother saying that would never be enough to overcome the differences between them.

Suddenly, she felt shaky and needed to get off her feet. Connie sank into one of the two large black, faux leather sofas.

"Are you tired?" Real asked, concerned.

Connie nodded wearily. "Just a bit," she didn't want to admit she was more apprehensive about what was to come than anything else.

"Poor baby. You rest a bit and I'll get us a bite to eat. Would you like some wine and cheese?"

"That'll be great." She nodded, thinking she could definitely use a glass of wine.

"Give me a minute, two." Real said and smiled. "I'll be right back."

Once he left the room, Connie sat up and placed her Aigner handbag on her lap. With nervous fingers she unsnapped her purse and fumbled through her things looking for the letter she wrote earlier. She hated saying goodbye this way. She placed the letter on the glass and chrome cocktail table, although she felt like a coward she couldn't say good bye to Real face to face. She wasn't sure she could, wasn't even sure she could summon the words or the strength. So, she wrote all the things she wanted to say to Real but wasn't sure she could. How could she say how much he meant to her without actually saying the word love, how she enjoyed every moment they had spent together. She stopped short of saying that if things were different... Instead, she wrote that there were too many differences to overlook. Seeing his apartment made her realize how right she had been. Maybe I'm just looking for the differences, she told herself.

Looking down at the letter and then quickly towards the kitchen, Connie got to her feet and started toward the door.

"Where are you going?" Real asked from the doorway that led to the kitchen.

Connie hesitated before she spoke, just like when she was a small girl and her mom caught her kissing her father on the lips while he napped on that ratty old couch after an exhausting day of working at the textile mill. "I... I," she stammered as she did as a child, caught. "I have to go." She paused, swallowing hard and choking back the tears. "I shouldn't be here."

She saw the hurt in his warm brown eyes. "I'm sorry you feel that way." He placed the plate of cheese and bread on the table, his eyes on the envelope that lay there. "I wish you could stay."

"I'm sorry," she apologized just like she did as a child. She took a deep breath , "It's better this way."

"For who? You?" He asked with a trace of anger in his voice. "Not for me," he added and came to her, taking her hands in his. "I have great news," he told her, excited. "I wanted to share my news with you, so we could celebrate."

She closed her eyes. "I can't."

"But, it could be good for both of us," he told her. "I just got news today that my cooking show is being picked up by the Food Network. It will be televised nationally. Don't you see how wonderful this could be for us? We could travel the world, Connie, together, enjoying a happy life."

"You want me to come with you?" Tears welled up in her eyes as she looked at him.

He nodded. "Yes, of course."

Connie thought of Lex, of their children, of her life here, and she knew she couldn't leave. "I am happy for you, Real," she spoke quietly. "You deserve this kind of success."

"We deserve it, the two of us?" he asked. "I could never have done this without you."

She shook her head slowly. "Of course, you could have." She remembered her clumsiness on camera and how they were caught having sex on live television. "You don't need me to succeed, or to have a great life. I can't be a part of it. I just can't." *No matter how much I wish I could,* she told herself.

"Just allow yourself to break free of the past." He insisted.

"I can't, Real," Connie told him. "You make me feel alive, spontaneous, free, but I can't let go of the past that easily. I'm a product of my past and I have to maintain some degree of control.... That's just who I am."

"That is not true, you can break free of the past," Real continued to insist. "You are perfect when you are just you."

"That's sweet, Real," Connie said gratefully, "but I am only comfortable when I am in control."

"You're afraid."

She nodded. "I'll always be afraid and I don't want that for you. You deserve better."

"So do you. If you would only let yourself –"

"I can't, I can't! Don't you see that?"

"You were abused..."

She sighed. "You make me sound like damaged goods."

"That's not my intention," he assured her. "At some point you have to stop blaming yourself –"

Connie put a hand on Real's cheek. "I can't," she said once more and gave him the softest of kisses on his lips. She looked into his eyes. "You've never been married," she added, more harshly than she intended.

"I hadn't met you," Real said, softly, almost a whisper.

The line melted Connie inside, affecting her in a way she hadn't felt in a long time. As corny as these words might seem to some, Connie knew that coming from Real the words were sincere, straight from his heart, and she felt herself hesitating. If only they had met sooner.... "I'm sorry," she said simply, afraid to say anything more.

"So this is goodbye then?" he asked in a defeated tone.

She nodded. "I came to tell you I couldn't be a part of the show..."her voice trailed off. "It's all in the letter."

"I see." He pulled her close and held her to him. "I'll always love you," he whispered softly in her ear.

She pulled away, wiping the tears from her eyes as she turned and left the apartment, never looking back....

***

Charmaine told Giji that her surprise was dancing at the Vixens Gentleman's Club. Giji thought she would be dancing on the floor of the club, but Charmaine had something else in mind: Giji doing an exotic dance onstage! Charmaine sometimes danced at the club on weekends to earn extra money and as a favor to the owner. He was a long-time friend, the first person to give her a chance and a job when she arrived in town. She thought Giji would enjoy dancing there, too–or she would enjoy trying it once. The thought was scary and at the same time very exciting, but Giji worried she might not be able to pull it off. She had never danced onstage in front of a large room full of people.

Charmaine assured her that she would be a natural. "I'll bet it's like second nature to you."

"I hope that's a compliment!" Giji had quipped, grinning.

"Of course, it is," Charmaine assured her. "Let's find something super for you to wear!"

Giji smiled. "Okay." She couldn't believe this was happening. In her teens and early twenties she dreamed of being a stripper, fantasizing about the glamorous life of an exotic dancer, but she never imagined she'd give it a try....

"Wow!" Charmaine gushed as Giji came out of the dressing area and did a twirl. "You look sensational, sweetie."

"I do," Giji agreed, checking herself out in the mirror on the back of Charmaine's dressing room door. She was wearing a deep blue bikini that Charmaine loaned her from the rack in her dressing room...with a thin white trim outlining the shape of the bikini. The light trim against her skin accentuated her tan beautifully and the thin spaghetti ties on the bikini top emphasized her full, ripe breasts. While the trim on the sides and rear of the thong, showed off her rear, the string in back disappearing between her round, well-toned ass cheeks. The bikini was made of a shiny satiny material almost like silk. "I love this outfit."

"Even better than the pink one you had your heart set on?" Charmaine teased.

"That one was hot, too," Giji said, turning to get a view of her rear in the mirror, "but this one fits all the right places!"

"It's slammin'," Charmaine agreed. "It doesn't miss a curve, that's for sure,"

When it was almost time for Giji to go on stage, she and Charmaine stood just behind the curtain waiting until the other girl finished her routine. Occasionally, Giji would catch a glimpse of her strutting her stuff in front of the cheering and whistling crowd

"She has them really energized," Charmaine observed.

"Is that good?" Giji wanted to know.

Charmaine nodded. "It's great," she replied. "Once the crowd is heated up, they'll respond to you better."

"I hope so," Giji worried.

"Don't be nervous," Charmaine told Giji, "just go out there and have a good time."

"Are you sure about this?" Giji bit her lip, nervous about dancing before an audience for the first time. She kept telling herself it was just like dancing at a nightclub with friends while others watched, but she couldn't totally convince herself that was really true. The last thing she wanted to do was make a fool of herself and embarrass Charmaine.

"You'll do fine," Charmaine gave her a little hug before

sending her onstage.

"If you're sure." Giji smiled uneasily as she turned to go onstage. She could see the audience, mostly male, cheering and applauding for the dance that just finished her routine. She passed Giji on her way backstage. "Good luck, sugar," she said in her southern drawl. "Knock 'em dead!"

Giji nodded, trying to smile, and started to dance as she went onstage, gyrating and swaying seductively to the steady thumping beat of Sex On the Beach's "Turn It On, Sock It to Me!" The song choice lent itself easily athletic movements, so she figured she'd just do some gymnastics she remembered from her days as a cheerleader at Chaddway High, but apparently Charmaine had other ideas. Almost as soon as Giji got onstage, swaying to the music, someone came up behind her and covered her eyes. It was so unexpected, Giji thought, and erotic. She half suspected it was Charmaine joining her onstage. When the person let go, she turned to see a stranger dancing with her. A gorgeous male dancer, dark-haired, with a smooth, muscular, his body tanned to perfection, swayed along with her to the music. He was wearing a deep blue bowtie and a thong that matched Giji's bikini and nothing else.

"Uh-hmmm, uh-hmmm, sock it, sock it, sock it to me!" Giji lip-synced the words. "Uh-hmmm, uh-hmmm, turn it on, sock it to me."

"Take you like a freight train," the male dancer's lips moved with the words to the male portion of the song," ah...ah...ah...I'll kick you like a bass drum!"

"Uh-hmmm, uh-hmmm," Giji's lips moved with the song. "Love love! Love love! Love love!"

"I'll kick you like a bass drum...ah...ah...ah!"

The male dancer licked Giji's neck, then down her chest between her breasts. His lips and tongue against the area between her breasts sent shivers of excitement through Giji, and she hoped she would not lose her footing. The dancer slid down on the dance floor behind Giji and she pumped her tight ass in his face, he kissed one of her ass cheeks, then he spun her around and put his face in the crotch of her bikini, his tongue licking the tight shiny fabric over her pussy. His strong tongue pressed against her pussy lips, and she felt herself respond, her pussy quivering at his touch. She was a little shaken by her body's response to his touch, but she managed to keep her mind on the dance and the pulsing rhythms of the music.

While the male dancer lay on the floor, facing the crowd, resting on one elbow, Giji gyrated to the music, dancing toward the edge of the stage, her body moving in quick but sensual movements. Her breasts jiggling despite the support of the bikini top as she sank to her knees at the edge of the stage. Several men near the stage slipped bills into the top of her throng. Nice, Giji thought, pleased. Giji thought she saw a couple of large bills, and she hoped she wouldn't have to share with her partner. When the men tried to grab her breasts, Giji started to slowly dance away, making her way back to her dance partner.

Giji took one of his hands in hers and helped him to his feet. He put his arms around her and held her firmly in his strong embrace as they twirled and pressed their bodies together, bumping and grinding to the music. In a move so quick that Giji did not see it coming, the dancer spun her out holding her by the hand and brought her back to him, positioning himself behind her, wrapping his arms around her waist, he started grind his bulging crotch into her rear, and Giji could have sworn she felt the beginnings of an erection. Sliding his hands up her smooth, flat stomach, the dancer cupped her breasts, one in either hand, and pinched her erect nipples between his fingers through the fabric of her bikini top. His strong hands on her breasts and nipples combined with the crowd watching and cheering was a powerful stimulant and Giji's pussy become moist; she hoped the wetness would not show on the front of her thong. *Maybe that's why dancers often wear shiny outfits,* she thought, hoping the shiny material would camouflage the wetness.

Giji used her teeth to untie the bowtie, pulling it off and

holding it between her teeth, until he took it from her using his teeth and tossed it aside playfully. He came to her and she licked down his broad chest, his skin damp with perspiration from the demanding movements of the dance, letting her tongue rest on one of his small brown nipples. She licked down his flat, six-pack stomach to the light patch of hair above his thong, she lingered there for a split second, then quickly kissed him right on the small piece of fabric that covered his bulging cock.

He took both her hands and helped her to her feet. They danced close, grinding into each other in time with the beat of the music. Suddenly he pulled away and licked one of Giji's large brown nipples, almost sucking it into his mouth. Giji put her hands on his tight, well-defined pecs and pretended to push him away roughly.

With quick, fluid movements, the dancer rebounded immediately and was back in her face as they danced to the thumping beat, their eyes locked in a passionate stare. By now even the audience could feel the sexual tension between these two, and most of the audience probably would never had guessed that they were strangers until they met just minutes before....

While the crowd cheered wildly, the male dancer used his teeth to unfasten Giji's bikini top, which had a center hook between her breasts. Her bikini top fell to the floor as her breasts sprang free, jiggling with the beat of the music. Seizing the opportunity, the male dancer kissed one of her firm, tight breasts and then sucked one of her lightly brown nipples into his mouth. The crowd cheered even louder, showing their approval.

For a finale, the male dance lifted Giji in his strong arms, she arched her back, and he pushed his face between her breasts. Again, she felt his warm, wet tongue against her sensitive skin, her body shuddered and her pussy quivered at his touch.

As the music faded and the dance ended, Giji thought she caught a glimpse of a familiar face in the audience. She couldn't place where she had seen him before. While she and her dance partner waved to the crowd, she searched the audience again for the man, but she did not see him. Deciding she was probably mistaken, she turned walked offstage just ahead of the male dancer.

"You were hot!" he whispered in her ear once they were offstage.

"Thank you," Giji said watching him walk away, his back broad and his ass perfectly rounded in his thong. "You're not bad yourself!"

Giji saw Charmaine walk up to the male dancer and they exchange a few words and a quick kiss on the lips. Giji was surprised by this, then she remembered that she had noticed many of the dancers kissing and hugging as they went on stage and off. It must be the way dancers show appreciation and support, she decided.

"You were great," one of the female dancers said as she walked pass Giji. "Looks like you cleaned up."

"Thanks," Giji said, pulling the bills from her throng. "I tried!" she added, beginning to count her tips.

Charmaine came up beside her. "Wow! You're like a pro!" she beamed happily. She raised her hand and they high-fived. "You were great!"

"You really think so?" Giji asked, excitedly as she finished gathering the bills from her throng. She would have to recount the tips later when she was less keyed up, but Giji guessed there were several hundred dollars in total. Great pay, she thought, and it was fun. Giji had thought nothing could top the excitement of having strangers watching her on Charmaine's webcam, but the having men watching her, applauding loudly and cheering her on was so much more intense than she had expected. The raw energy of the interaction between dancer and audience blew her away. It could easily become addictive, she decided. "I did my best."

"And you were awesome!" Charmaine said and gave Giji a little hug. "If you ever leave the real estate biz, you can always do well as an exotic dancer!"

Giji smiled, pleased by her friend's compliments.

"By the way, what'd you think of Chazz?" Charmaine wanted to know.

"Ooh la la!" Giji said, giggling.

"Just a little surprise for you," Charmaine told her, "for your first dance."

"Thanks." Giji smiled. "But he's hardly small!"

"Ain't that the truth!"

"I may need to borrow him later!"

Charmaine winked. "Sorry, Giji, he's all man–and he's all mine!"

***

Ariella parked her champagne-colored sports car in the parking lot at the rundown strip mall. Before getting out of her car, she slipped off her shades and quickly checked her look in the rearview mirror. *Nice,* she thought. *Every hair is in place.* She grabbed her designer bag and started toward the small, dimly lit shop, noticing the overpowering smell of rotting fish.

Once she was inside the shop, she looked around the small room, thinking it looked as rundown inside as it did outside. She was wondering if the dated red and gold wallpaper had been chic decades before, then she noticed a small Asian woman coming from an adjoining room.

"Yes?" the woman said.

"Oh, I'm here for a reading," Ariella told her.

"You follow me," the woman instructed.

Ariella did as instructed and entered the slightly larger but more dimly lit adjoining room.

"I Kimiko," the small woman introduced herself once they were seated at the table in the center of the room. She took a pen and a small pad from the pocket of her colorful kimono and started to scribble. "And you?"

"I'm Gabrielle. Gabrielle Garcia," Ariella lied, not wanting to give her real name. "My friends call me Gabby," she added then gave the older woman a phone number and email address that were also made-up. While Kimiko scribbled down the bogus information Ariella provided, she wondered how the older woman could see to write in the faint light from the candles scattered about the room.

"Okay." Kimiko looked up, finished writing and pushed the note and pen aside. She took a deck of cards from the other pocket of her kimono and began to shuffle them. Once she finished, she placed the cards on the table in front of Ariella. "Cut them," she instructed.

Ariella obliged and watched as Kimiko dealt the cards, one at a time, face up and began to study them intently.

"What do you see?' Ariella asked, concerned.

"Sssh!" Kimiko raised a hand to silence her.

"I need to know…"

"What you need to know?" Kimiko asked, irritated. "You tell me."

"I have been having a dream…"

"Handsome stranger accost you on train," Kimiko interrupted. "You give in…"

"No, no!" Ariella protested. "In my dream my husband catches me with another guy, and the guy keeps popping out from the closet, from under the bed, out of the hamper, and out of my lingerie drawer." She paused, unsure how much information she wanted to provide, she felt almost as if she were doing the psychic's work for her. "By the way, I'm not too sure about him, he was wearing my pink baby doll nightie!"

Kimiko chuckled, amused by this last revelation. "That funny."

"Yeah, okay," Ariella said, not amused, "but what does it mean?" Kimiko raises her eyes knowingly. "It sounds like you be a naughty, naughty girl," she said. "Maybe you 'fraid you get caught."

"Hmmm," Ariella thought it over, certain that she and Giji could have deduced this on their own. "Maybe. I'm won't get caught, will I?"

Kimiko shrugged. "Maybe yes. Maybe no."

"Well, that sure as hell doesn't help!" Ariella complained. "You enjoy sex?" Kimiko asked. Ariella nodded, her lips pushed out in a huge pout that reminded Kimiko of that hot actress, Angelina Jolie. That gave Kimiko an idea. "You no worry," the small Asian told her. "You enjoy sex. It all good. No problem!"

"Well, since you're so sure," Ariella said, relieved. "I have idea," Kimiko told her, her eyes lively now and excited. "How you like to be–how you say–character in my novel?" Ariella looked at the small Asian woman, interested. "Oh, wow, you mean like the star character or something?" she wanted to know. Kimiko shrugged her small shoulders. "Kind of," she said. "Star? Corpse? Beautiful pile of ashes? What the difference, you in book!"

Ariella had to admit it did sound appealing. "What is the book about?" she asked. "A love story? A naughty romance? Will I have sex scenes with a lot of sexy hunks?"

Kimiko nodded. "Oh, yes," she answered proudly. "You have sex with dozen men, maybe all at once! You be naughty, naughty girl sleep with sweaty muscle men on run from killer!"

"A murder mystery!" Ariella gasped. "That would be so CSI!" Kimiko nodded. "CSI, yes!"

"Wow, that is such a great idea!"

"Yes, yes, I have idea for 'Fear Factor' brand foods, too, but manufacturer felt real foods scary enough!"

Ariella looked thoughtful. "I could be like a forensics expert who solves crimes by having sex with people who knew the victim," she suggested. "That would be so cool!"

The small Asian woman shook her head. "You be naughty spy girl in novel, too hot to handle," she says.

Ariella smiles. "Ooh, I like the sound of that," she says.

Kimiko returned her smile, pleased. "You dangerous spy girl on mission to save the world or something like that," Kimiko further embellished. "You so hot you on fire like forest or something. Little bitch in heat you are, so hot you spontaneous combust, baffle everyone, but Sexual Psychic solve the case!"

"Gee, you make it all sound so glamorous," Ariella gushed. "Let's go with that. It sounds super." She looked into Kimiko's small, dark eyes. "I'll have to read manuscript, of course!"

"You do, you do," Kimiko agreed.

"Good, it's all settled then," Ariella told her, then turned to leave.

"Where you go?" Kimiko called to her.

Ariella paused and turned back to face the psychic. "Oh, I almost forgot," she apologized and took a fifty from her purse. "Here you go sweetie. Keep the change."

Kimiko took the bill and quickly ran the counterfeit pen over it. "You not go so fast," the little Asian woman told her. "I have surprise for you."

Ariella remained standing, unsure what was to come next.

Kimiko went quickly into the outer room and closed the shades, locked the door, then came back, motioning Ariella toward the ratty old sofa in the corner.

"You want me to sit on that?" Ariella asked incredulously.

Kimiko nodded her small head.

Reluctantly Ariella took a seat, taking a deep breath. She watched as Kimiko dropped to her knees in front of the sofa and pushed up Ariella's short, tight skit, working it up around her well-curved thighs. At first, Ariella was inclined to resist, but then she remembered Giji said the Sexual Psychic gave the best oral she'd ever had.

"No panties!" Kimiko observed excitedly. "You always ready for opportunity to get freak on!"

Ariella rolled her eyes. "Is this going to take long?" she asked, wanting less conversation and more action. "I have a hair appointment, and I think I broke a nail on the way over here."

"You get freaky with everybody, now you get freaky deaky with Kimiko!"

"Well, all right," Ariella agreed. "Giji says you're really

good."

"Good?" Kimiko repeated, offended. "I not good, I be the best! You watch. I show you!"

"Okay," Ariella agreed and giggled, "as long a I don't spontaneously combust!"

Kimiko smiled as she unbuttoned Ariella's crisp white blouse and freed her firm, young breasts. "Nice," she said, pleased. She pushed Ariella's breasts together, squeezing the soft flesh in her small hands and she pinched the well-defined brown nipples between her fingers.

"Mmmmm," Ariella moaned lightly.

"You like?" Kimiko asked.

Ariella nodded. "Ooooh yes," she moaned. "Oh, Kimiko, do that to me one more time! Work that spot. Work it! You go Asian girl!"

"You like this even more," Kimiko assured her as she started to kiss and lick the soft, sensitive area between Ariella's breasts.

Ariella began to breath heavily, then she lay back against the sofa and closed her eyes, moaning louder now. "That feels so fucking incredible!" she said through teeth that were almost chattering.

"I know you like," Kimiko told her and started to lick and kiss one of Ariella's breasts, letting her pointed tongue lick around the brown nipple before sucking it into her warm, wet mouth.

Without realizing it, Ariella put a hand behind the older woman's head and held her tightly to her breast while she sucked and nibbled.

Sliding down, with Ariella's hand still on her head, Kimiko settled her face into Ariella's dark crotch and began to kiss and lick around the younger woman's bulging pussy lips, then she used her small fingers and tongue to push Ariella's pussy lips apart. Ariella's pussy opened like a delicate flower, Kimiko licked and sucked the sweet folds, tasting Ariella's delicious juices as she pushed her tongue inside Ariella's tight cunt deeper and deeper. Kimiko's small, pointed tongue licked around her clit, making Ariella shiver with growing excitement. The louder Ariella moaned, the more intense the smaller woman worked, until finally she concentrated solely on Ariella's swollen, sensitive clit. All the while, she tongue-fucked Ariella's juicy pussy with such a force that Ariella could hardly believe the small woman could be so strong. The sensation of being tongue-fucked and having her clit licked vigorously with each thrust was so powerful that Ariella began to grind her pussy into Kimiko's small face while holding the woman's small, warm mouth tight to her wet pussy as she began to come with a force she'd never felt before....

She was hit by such a massive orgasm that she thought might swallow Kimiko's small head into her hot wet pussy.

"Ahhhhhhhh!" Ariella moaned so loud Kimiko was afraid the men in the fish market next door would hear her.

30

A Lie, A Promise & an Orgasm

SueAnn sat at the table in her dining room in the dark watching Nick's house, waiting for him and Giji to return from their date. It seemed, to her, that in the last week and a half Nick and Giji were seeing more and more of each other.

She had seen them leave together earlier in the evening, in Giji's enormous pink Cadillac, the top down. Smiling at each other and enjoying a laugh while Nick held the door for her. Giji wore a low-cut dress, almost completely revealing her firm, round breasts, her blonde hair swept back elegantly in contrast to Nick's crisp white shirt, sports coat and jeans.

SueAnn watched them drive away together for a wonderful, maybe even romantic, evening on the town. After eating leftover stroganoff, she turned off the lights and sat in the dark sipping the remainder of the wine left from dinner, waiting for Nick and Giji to return from their date.

Finding it hard to believe Nick was on another date with Giji, she wondered what Nick saw in the shallow blonde party girl? It was what all men saw. Easy. Hot. Sex. In a beautiful, clueless package. A beautifully wrapped gift that turns out to be an empty box!

Suddenly headlights flashed though the window as Giji's Cadillac pulled into Nick's driveway and came to a stop, lighting the interior of the dining room. Sitting there with the headlights in her face, SueAnn almost dropped her wine glass, afraid Nick and Giji might see her. She crouched hoping they couldn't see her as she peered over her dining table.

Yep, they were returning from their evening out, SueAnn observed, the top up now. After turning off the headlights, Nick got out and opened the door for Giji. For a few seconds SueAnn blinked as her eyes adjusted to the darkness again after the bright, blinding glare from the headlights.

In the light from the street lights, SueAnn could see Nick and Giji standing together. They lingered for a moment beside the car, sharing a laugh, perhaps over something amusing that had happened during dinner or over something they had seen on the drive home. Maybe they'd run down a homeless person or several for fun, SueAnn thought, then realized it was only the wine making her more bitter about Nick and Giji enjoying an evening together. Again. When she wished it had been her with Nick tonight instead of Giji. Why hadn't he asked her? Didn't he have any idea how much she cared about him? If not, he was as clueless as Giji. In that case, he and airhead Giji Brickhouse bimbo extraordinaire were perfect for each other!

SueAnn blinked as her eyes adjusted the darkness after the blinding light.

Expecting Nick and Giji would drop Nick off, say goodnight and be on her way, SueAnn noticed they were still beside Giji's car, only now they were embracing and enjoying what she would describe as a long, passionate kiss. Hoping her eyes were fooling her, SueAnn moved closer to the window, peeking through the blind and hoping no one saw her watching.

Yep, they were kissing...still kissing...would it never end? Finally the kiss broke and they chatted for a few moments.

Making the necessary small talk after the night out, SueAnn decided, the customary had a great time, see you later, we'll have to do this again. Then Nick would open the car door for Giji; she would get in, hiking the hem of her dress just a bit so Nick could see as much leg as possible. He would close the door for her, and she would start up the engine and, after a tiny wave of her hand, she would drive off. Nick would walk across up the walk way to his front door and go inside. Alone. But that's not what happened.

Much to SueAnn's dismay, Nick and Giji strode arm in arm towards his house and, after he fumbled for the key and unlocked the door, they went inside... together.

SueAnn went around her table, feeling her way in the dark, stumped her big toe on the leg of a chair. "Ouch, dammit!" she cursed out loud and sank back into her chair.

Tears welled up in her eyes, but not from the excruciating pain in her toe. There was a tightness in her chest and an agonizing pain in her stomach that left her feeling so sick, she wanted to puke. Wiping her eyes on the sleeves of her nightshirt, she sat there in the dark for what seemed like forever. Waiting for the door of Nick's house to swing open, for Giji to come out, briefly saying goodnight to Nick, giving him a kiss on the lips and then gliding home

But that's not what happened. Not exactly. The door of Nick's house did open. But Giji did not come out, Nick stood in the doorway with Giji by his side while they let Bismarck out to run around before bedtime. Bedtime. Nick stood there, bare-chested, wearing only his pajama bottoms, and Giji stood beside him, grinning, her hair down... wearing his pajama top!

Feeling sick to her stomach, SueAnn continued to watch. She couldn't tear her eyes away from the scene, but a part of her couldn't believe what she saw, could not accept it was actually happening. But it was. It was.

Waiting until Bismarck went back inside and the door closed, SueAnn crept through the dark into her dimly lit living room, up the stairs and into her bedroom, climbing into bed, feeling numb, defeated. Pulling the covers over her head, she settled into bed, her eyes damp as she tried to sleep. But, she kept thinking of Nick and Giji together, in his house, in his room, in his bed.... She tossed and turned, and some time before morning she finally drifted off to sleep. Giji has won, she thought as sleep engulfed her finally.

Her sleep was restless, filled with dreams. She dreamed about a wedding – but it wasn't hers. Giji walked down the isle in her gaudy pink lacy wedding dress to marry Nick who wore an equally tacky pink tux. And she–SueAnn Day–was Giji's maid of honor in a bridesmaid's dress that could only be described as a pink chiffon nightmare!

***

Connie lay in the dark listening to her husband's slow steady breathing. Occasionally Lex would grunt or make some vocal noise in his sleep. A couple of times she thought he said her name, but she realized the sound he made in his sleep sounded like her name. Staring into the darkness, she thought of Real. For the first time, she realized how much she missed him. She wondered what he was doing, if he was alone, if he was thinking of her.

Briefly she wondered what her life would be like with Real, if she threw away all the trappings of her unhappy life, let go of her marriage to Lex, and just threw caution to the wind to go away with Real. It could be heavenly. If only she could....

Lex stirred interrupting her thoughts. He shifted his body slightly and rolled over toward her. In the dark she could barely see his face as he raised himself up in bed and looked down at her. For a moment she worried he was still angry at her for her indiscretion on live TV and thought he might lash out at her again. But he didn't.

He caught her by surprise when he kissed her full on the lips, a gentle but promising kiss. "I have a surprise for you," he told her quietly.

"Okay," she said, hoping the surprise was one she would enjoy...or at least welcome. She'd had enough surprises that leave your life shattered while you try to pick up the scattered pieces, while you hope there's something worth rescuing, something worth saving....

"You'll enjoy this," Lex told her as if reading her thoughts.

She smiled in the darkness, not sure he could see her, hoping he was right.

Suddenly, his face was close to hers and he hesitated before kissing her. His breath brushed across her face as his lips drew close to hers. He kissed her again, their lips meeting in a more passionate, urgent kiss this time. She felt his tongue touch hers. *Nice,* she thought, *but not exactly surprising. Tonight of all nights, I really need to not be disappointed.* And she thought of Real...again.

When the kiss broke, she half expected him to say goodnight and roll over, his back to her and go back to sleep, back to making those noises. Instead he kissed her neck, then her shoulder as he made his way down to her soft breasts and sensitive nipples. He sucked on one of her nipples, nursing like a small child and she enjoyed his warm, wet mouth on her smooth skin.

Without even realizing it, she pressed herself closer to his body, pulled him tighter to her, one hand on the back of his neck and the other on the back of his head. Suddenly, he started to suck harder, his mouth engulfed her breast and he nibbled her breast, then he concentrated on her nipple, gently biting the tip until she was overcome with a heady blend of pleasure and pain. It was so intense that she wanted to scream out for him to stop and in the same instance she wanted him to continue. She moaned softly with each touch of Lex's cool lips and warm tongue. The intensity caused her pussy to become moist, twitching with anticipation of what was to come.

Lex raised his head, looked at her in the darkness, smiling.

"Good, huh?"

She smiled back at him for the first time...in so long. "Even better," she said softly, followed by what sounded like a quiet moan. "Don't...stop."

He lowered his head to continue pleasuring her.

She drew in her breath sharply as Lex slid down, his rough cheek brushing her smooth skin... kissing her stomach, her lower stomach.... He placed his head between her legs, nudging her legs apart slightly with his face, his breath was warm on her skin. Lex kissed her inner thighs, sending electric currents through her being and he placed his face closer to her pussy. She could feel his warm breath between her legs, on her crotch as he leaned in and began gently kissing the sensitive area around her labia, slowly moving, with each new kiss, closer and closer to her pussy.

Suddenly, he planted a series of soft, hot kisses on her bulging pussy lips, kissing and licking gently as he pushed her slit apart and continued kissing and licking her soft folds, tasting her sweet wetness. He pushed his tongue inside her, deeper and deeper inside her pussy, he began tongue-fucking her, his tongue moving in and out of her in a steady, pleasing rhythm. Connie closed her eyes, now moaning so loud she was afraid the kids would hear. She tried to control the loudness of her moan but the effort was futile. The sensation was more exciting and intense than anything she'd felt in her life. She would come soon...as she had never come before!

For so long, Connie had dreamed it could be this good, but she had never really believed it. In the past, when Lex had attempted to pleasure her orally, it either started out fine and ended badly or started roughly and ended up going nowhere. She wondered where had learned these new oral techniques, and the thought was a bit unsettling. Then she remembered...it must've been the Sexual Psychic. She felt a twinge of resentment at the thought of her husband and another woman. Still, she couldn't deny he had developed incredibly satisfying oral skills and her mounting pleasure was all that mattered at the moment....

   Connie heard herself moan so loudly, it was like hearing someone else, a stranger. It had been so long since she'd been so excited that she'd actually moaned out loud. Part of her worried the kids might hear her, but in the frenzied state of excitement, it didn't seem to matter.

   Lex's tongue seemed to be everywhere, all over her body, as if he were making love to her whole body at once. He was tongue-fucking her juicy pussy and licking with the tip of his tongue around her clit at the same time, stimulating the sensitive area in a way he never had before. At the same time, his nose occasionally rubbed against her clit, which increased the mounting excitement she was feeling. The more she moaned, the more urgently Lex's tongue worked, rhythmically stimulating her pussy until she was starting to climax.

   Although it has never happened in the twenty years she and Lex had been married, she started to experience small waves of orgasmic pleasure, each more powerful than the last. As the waves increased in intensity, she suddenly felt a deeper orgasmic wave sweep over her, leaving her tittering on the edge until a more powerful wave sent her to the edge and beyond. As she came again and again, her body shaking uncontrollably with each surge of orgasmic pleasure, she unknowingly dug her nails into Lex's back, clutching him, holding on to him tightly as if her life depended on it while her pussy juices flooded onto Lex's mouth and face. Again and again she came as she never dreamed she could. The orgasm was so pleasurable, powerful like the surf pounding a sandy beach, washing over her and leaving her quenched, refreshed and at the same time drained.

   "Hon, are you okay?" he asked, breathing heavily as he collapsed beside her.

   "Yes," she whispered, not looking at him.

   "Did you enjoy yourself?" he wanted to know.

   "I did," she answered, deciding that she would never tell him how much.

Laying in the darkness, exhausted, Lex's arm around her as he snuggled against her, Connie realized she had her husband back. There's still Real, she reminded herself. A part of her felt she was being unfaithful to him, but she told herself that was ridiculous. Lex was her husband; she was doing nothing wrong. Nothing. Yet the feeling persisted. It was the only thing, she decided, that kept her from enjoying her husband's surprise more than she had ever enjoyed a sexual experience in her life.

And yet it was enough...for tonight....

***

After unlocking the back door with the key SueAnn had given her to water the plants while she was away promoting her books, Wynette climbed the stairs and pushed open SueAnn's door, peering inside. The shades were drawn and in the semi-darkness she saw SueAnn sitting up in bed, back against her pillows, knees drawn up, arms hugging her legs. She rocked gently, lost in her own little world, oblivious to the fact that anyone was here except her. *It is as bad as I imagined,* Wynette thought as she entered the room.

She called earlier and SueAnn sounded terrible. When SueAnn refused her invitation to come over and have coffee, she knew her best friend was feeling bad. If SueAnn didn't want to talk, she must be feeling really low. She decided that when Steven left for the office and she had placed a call to the camp to make sure her kids hadn't burned the place down, she would go check on SueAnn.

"How are you, babe?" Wynette asked as if she were talking to one of her kids. Sometimes she felt like a mother, or an older sister, to her friend even though they were the same age. She felt SueAnn needed someone to lean on in order to help her get back on her feet when a crisis came along and left her temporarily disillusioned. "Feeling any better?" she added and noticed a glass with a tiny bit of Mandarin Cranberry on the beside table.

SueAnn shook her head slowly. "No, Wynette," she answered, her tone sounded agitated. "I'm not going to just snap out of this and be all better. I've lost the man I love to another woman."

"How can you be so sure?" Wynette wanted to know. "What's the proof, huh?'

"The proof is that Nick's with Giji." SueAnn sounded near tears. "I pushed him away. It's my fault. I practically threw him into Giji's arms."

"I've never seen you just give up this way," Wynette observed. "It's not like you."

"I'm tired of fighting a losing battle," SueAnn told her. "The harder I try, the closer Nick gets to Giji. I've lost. I admit it. Giji's the better woman. She has won and she's more than happy to gloat. Maybe I would too if I were her."

"Oh, SueAnn." Wynette sighed. "I hate to see you this way."

"I… I just have to get past Nick choosing Giji," she said in a shaky voice.

"Did he choose Giji?" Wynette asked, uncertain.

"Well, I don't know, maybe not exactly," SueAnn admitted, "but they were out –"

"It was just two friends going out to dinner, that's what Nick told you," Wynette reminded her.

"That's not what Giji says."

"And you believe her?" Wynette asked incredulously.

"I've seen them together several times," SueAnn reminded her, "and I haven't seen him since…well, it's been a while. We haven't been out, he hasn't called. It's like he's avoiding me."

"Maybe he has a guilty conscious," Wynette ventured.

"About what?"

Wynette shrugged. "I don't know," she admitted. "Maybe he thinks you're peeved at him for seeing Giji."

SueAnn frowned. "I am!" she snapped. "I just don't know what's going on with Nick. I don't. He was like a different person every time I saw him… when I saw him."

"Maybe he's in a street gang," Wynette said light, teasing. "It's a gang of Nicks, they all look alike, but their personalities and behaviors are different!"

SueAnn couldn't help smiling. "You're being ridiculous."

Wynette sat on the edge of the bed and patted SueAnn's hand. "You're not thinking clearly, SueAnn."

SueAnn closed her eyes and put a hand to her head as if for support. "I just need some time to sort things out and get my head together."

"I'm sorry I sounded pushy," Wynette apologized, truly sympathetic for what her friend was going through. "I know you need time to sort things out and feel better."

SueAnn rested her chin on her knees. "As if I couldn't feel any worse, Julie decided to stay with her dad," she said quietly.

"Really?" Wynette seemed surprised.

SueAnn nodded. "Yes, she called last night," she replied. "I wanted her to come home, but I felt that would be selfish. She shouldn't have to come home and baby-sit me." She glanced up at her friend. "She was so excited about staying on with her dad and..." her voice trailed off.

"I'm sorry."

"I wasn't too surprised," SueAnn admitted. "I saw it coming. She wants to be with her dad and his new wife."

"You haven't lost her," Wynette assured her.

"I know, I know." She closed her eyes. "I'm just feeling sorry for myself."

"You have too much going for yourself to wallow in self pity," Wynette told her.

"I just need some time," SueAnn explained. "I just need to think things through. There's so much I don't understand. About Nick. About us. About how something that was so good could go bad so quick. I just need to get over him."

"I know," Wynette assured her. "Like you said, it'll take time, but it'll be better soon."

SueAnn looked up at her friend. "Promise?" she asked in a childlike voice.

"Promise."

SueAnn reached down to pull the covers over her knees.

"Shouldn't you get up and get dressed?" Wynette asked, noticing SueAnn was still wearing her night gown. "It's almost noon. Don't you have things to do, places to –"

"Not really!" SueAnn interrupted helplessly. "I just thought I'd stay in bed and let time pass by, maybe watch a little TV."

Wynette came around the bed, lay down and started pulling up the covers.

"What are you doing?" SueAnn demanded.

"Well, if you're not going to get up," Wynette quipped, "I'll join you!"

"I'm really not up for company," SueAnn complained.

"Sure you are," Wynette disagreed. "We all need someone sometime. I'm that someone."

"Yes, you are," SueAnn said, smiling slightly. She had lost count of how many times Wynette had been there for her. "So, what does a person have to do to get a little peace and quiet around here?"

"Ummm," Wynette pretended to consider the question as she pushed down the covers and sat up. "I don't know. Get out of bed, get dressed, and go downstairs."

"Okay."

Wynette put a comforting arm around her friend's shoulder. "Is that a promise?" she asked, mirroring her friend's earlier question.

Reluctantly SueAnn nodded. "Yes, I promise."

But, SueAnn had no intention of getting out of bed–and they both knew it.

"I'll be by to check on you later," Wynette said, getting to her feet.

"Call first."

Wynette walked around the bed and paused at the door. "You know me better than that!"

31

The Mad Bomber

Wynette carried four glasses of iced tea on a small tray onto the brick patio and kicked the French door closed. "I hope everyone likes iced tea," she said, placing the tray on the table.

"My mom made it all the time, especially during hot summers in Georgia."

Giji shrugged. "Iced tea," she repeated, forcing a smile. "I can take it or leave it."

"As long as it's sweet tea, it'll be fine," Connie said coolly.

"I'm thirsty," Ariella chimed in, "You get no complaint from me!"

Wynette smiled at her appreciatively. "Thanks, Ariella."

After placing a glass of tea in front of each of the ladies, Wynette joined them at the table.

"How's SueAnn?" Connie asked and took a slow sip of her tea.

"Yes, how is SuSu?" Giji said, frowning. "Is she still sulking?"

Wynette sighed. "I'm afraid so."

"She should get over herself already–Nick has!" Giji sniffed.

"I guess she's just not a very good loser."

"We can't all be as good at it as you are," Wynette told her and grinned.

Giji knew she should be insulted, but she wasn't sure exactly why. "So, why'd you call us over?" she wanted to know.

"I was watching TV earlier today," Wynette began, "and I saw an ad for 'The Jerry Springer Show.'"

"Jerry Springer?" Ariella repeated, unsure where this was going. She and Giji exchanged quick glances.

"Really?" Giji's curiosity piqued. "I didn't picture you as a closet Jerry Springer fan?"

Wynette took a quick sip of her tea. "Oh, I'm not," she said. "I was watching...well," she hesitated to admit it, "I was watching Passions, and during a commercial break, there was an ad for an upcoming episode of 'The Jerry Springer Show' to be taped locally. In a couple of weeks Jerry and his crew will be in town to film the episode."

"Wow!" Giji sounded enthusiastic. "I had no idea Jerry Springer would ever come to our town."

"It's kind of exciting," Ariella chimed in.

"I thought so, too," Wynette agreed, pleased.

"We should go," Ariella said.

"Really?" Wynette asked.

"Sure," Giji agreed. "I've always thought about going to a taping of an episode of Jerry's show, but I never dreamed the show would come to here. We should definitely go."

"I agree," Ariella said, grinning at Giji. "It'll be fun."

"What do you think, Connie?" Wynette wanted to know.

Connie shrugged. "I don't know..." her voice trailed off uncertainly.

The woman who usually has an opinion on everything was suddenly speechless, Giji thought. "I can't wait to get my hands on Jerry Springer!" she gushed. "Hmmm. I bet he's better than chocolate!"

"I dunno," Ariella seemed unsure, "he seems kind of vanilla to me!"

"I heard Jerry is a closet homosexual," Connie said.

"Those are the worst kind," Ariella said.

"Well, I'm always up for a challenge," Giji announced excitedly.

"I guess I'll have to see if Jerry passes the Giji Brickhouse test!"

"Well, it can only go one of two ways," Ariella piped in, "since a person is either gay or straight."

"That's not really true, at least I don't think so," Wynette disagreed. "I believe there is a whole sexual spectrum."

"Like a rainbow?" Giji asked, thinking this sounded kind of gay so far.

Wynette nodded. "Yes, and people are straight, gay and lots of variations in between like bi-sexual, transsexual, –"

"Metrosexual?" Ariella offered with a smile.

Wynette nodded. "Absolutely."

"Good one!" Giji complimented Ariella and they did a quick high five.

"Do you believe a person's sexual tastes and possibly their sex drive is pre-determined either before or shortly after birth?" Giji asked, recalling an article she'd read on the subject years earlier while she was in college. "It's not necessarily normal or abnormal, it just varies depending on where the person falls along the sexual spectrum?"

"That's exactly what I'm saying," Wynette agreed.

Ariella looked across the table at Giji. "Wow, you really did go to college!" she commented, referring to Giji's impressive assumptions.

Giji smiled, pleased that she'd added something to the discussion.

"The gays add so many distasteful elements to society," Connie complained.

"Like what?" Wynette asked. "Crime? Sex crimes? Come on, Connie, they're only ten percent of the population, which means they can't be the majority in anything. That's pure bullshit, my friend, if not outright prejudice."

Connie gave a slight shrug as if she could not care less about Wynette's opinion.

"That's a good point, Wynette," Ariella agreed, "after all, you don't see too many lesbians out knocking off hardware stores or gay men stealing designer handbags!"

There was a slight chuckle among the ladies–only Connie seemed less than amused.

"Anyway the sexual spectrum is just my theory, I guess," Wynette admitted, not wanting the conversation to disintegrate into another argument.

"That's interesting, Wynette," Connie said dismissively.

Wynette smiled uneasily, sensing Connie's disinterest in the subject. She got an idea. "We can get SueAnn to go to 'The Jerry Springer Show' with us," she said. "She needs to get out, be around other people, lighten her mood, and I have a feeling 'The Jerry Springer Show' is just what the doctor ordered!"

"You mean set her up?" Ariella asked, almost choking on a sip of tea. "Using 'The Jerry Springer Show' as therapy of sorts?"

"I'll bet that's a first," Connie said under her breath.

"Well, yes, that's what I mean," Wynette told them, ignoring Connie's comment.

"Kind of a three-step program for SueAnn?" Giji said sarcastically. "Get out of bed, go to 'The Jerry Springer Show,' and get booed and heckled until you show your boobs!"

"Pretty much," Wynette agreed.

Ariella suppressed a giggle. "Maybe it'll lift her spirits," she hoped. "If not, at least she'll get her Jerry beads!"

"The show should be called the dysfunctional family hour," Connie said. "It should have a warning label."

"Haven't you ever watched?" Giji asked. "It does. At the beginning of each episode there's a disclaimer that watching the show can be hazardous to your health, devastating to people who live in trailer parks and it will frighten small children and animals." She paused, gave a little shrug. "Well, something like that."

"I've only seen the ads," Connie sniffed.

"Connie, you are coming with us?" Wynette worried.

Connie put a hand to her temple as if she were getting a headache. "I don't know," she said. "It doesn't sound all that exciting to me."

"Come one," Ariella urged. "It'll be fun. You'll have a great time. We all will."

Connie took a deep breath.

"Connie, you've got to come," Wynette told her, an urgency in her voice. "If you don't come, SueAnn won't come either."

"Fine, I'll go," Connie agreed reluctantly. "I wouldn't want to feel responsible for SueAnn's continued breakdown, but let it be known that I am going under protest."

Wynette smiled, pleased. "Well, as long as you're going."

"I'll get the tickets," Giji promised, thinking this was such a fabulous idea and wished she had thought of it herself.

"It's so close to the taping," Ariella worried, "are you sure –"

Giji sat up straight, pushed out her ample chest. "Trust me," she interrupted, "I'll get the tickets. We'll have the tickets in time for the show."

Ariella smiled, convinced.

"We'll have a great time if the local taping is anything like the TV show," Giji said knowingly.

"On the Internet I read that studies show watching the show is so hazardous it causes cancer in laboratory rats!" Ariella told them.

"Have you ever watched?" Giji wanted to know.

Ariella shrugged. "Me?" she asked, thinking fast. "I-I've seen a little of several episodes when Marco sneaks the remote and channel surfs. I watched. I admit it. It's like a car accident. You don't want to look, but for some reason you do. Marco seems to know when it's on and go right to the channel. It's like men are drawn to it."

"Yeah, I've caught Steven watching several times when he's supposed to be watching the kids," Wynette admitted and rolled her eyes. "He said he's trying to figure out where this place is with beautiful, young naive girls and dirty old men with homemade tattoos, one tooth and a chew of tobacco!"

"Has he," Ariella asked, seeming curious "found it?"

Wynette frowned. "If he does," she said loudly, "I'll kill him!"

"I think it's Jerryland." Giji laughed. "Also known as a trailer park!"

"That sounds about right," Connie agreed, surprised she actually agreed with Giji Brickhouse for the first time–ever!

Ariella put a finger to her lips. "Sssh," she said, giggling playfully. "We'd better not tell the guys!"

***

Wynette pushed open the door and frowned at SueAnn. "I see you're still in bed," she commented, entering the room and carrying a covered bowl of soup, a package of saltines and a spoon.

"Oh, it's you," SueAnn said, not taking her eyes off the television.

"Yeah, it's me," Wynette said sarcastically. As she placed the food on the night table, she noticed that there were now several partially empty glasses of Mandarin Cranberry on the night table. She hoped SueAnn wasn't becoming addicted, but she did not comment on it. "I told you I'd be back. Did you doubt me?"

SueAnn gave a half-hearted shrug. "I thought you'd forget," she said, then added under her breath, "at least I hoped you would."

"Well, I didn't, sorry to disappoint you," Wynette told her. "I brought you chicken soup. I got the recipe from an old episode of 'Mary Hartman, Mary Hartman!' "

"Need I remind you that Mary Hartman's chicken soup killed

someone?" SueAnn said, recalling the infamous chicken soup episode.

"Ah, I'm just trying to cheer you up," Wynette assured her. "If I really wanted to kill you I'd get Mrs. Hoover to make you one of her cheddar and cow brain casseroles. Now get your ass out of bed or next time that will be on the menu!"

"You really do want to kill me!" SueAnn said sarcastically.

"Well," Wynette said, "I'm glad to see you haven't lost your sense of humor." Then, sensing the edge of sarcasm in her friend's voice, she added, "I hope!"

SueAnn gave her a tight, forced smile.

"Are you feeling any better?" Wynette asked, patting her friend's hand as she seated herself on the edge of the bed.

SueAnn shook her head. "I-I need to get over you-know-who or just stop feeling anything," she said flatly. "On top of everything else, I feel like I'm getting a cold or something–"

"Then the soup will do you good," Wynette interrupted glancing around the room, her eyes coming to rest on the small TV inside the armoire. "Home shopping?" Wynette observed, frowning. She clicked off the TV using the remote from SueAnn's beside table. "Who are you becoming? Mrs. Hoover?"

SueAnn shrugged. "It relaxes me."

Wynette smiled. "If you start borrowing clothes from Mrs. Hoover, you and I will have a long talk!"

SueAnn gave her a blank stare.

"Hey, I'm only kidding," Wynette told her and gave a little laugh.

"I know you are," SueAnn said flatly. "I'm just not in much of a party mood."

"You'll feel better," Wynette assured her, sitting beside SueAnn on the bed. "It just takes time. That's all."

SueAnn actually managed a tiny smile, more for Wynette's benefit than her own. "Well, I have plenty of time. I'm only sleeping and watching television."

"I can tell," Wynette said.

"I don't know if it's what I'm watching on TV or what," SueAnn said weakly, "but lately I've been seeing a lot of those ads for assisted living. It has me thinking about retirement. After a while it starts to seem like a good idea."

"Retirement?" Wynette repeated. "You're not even forty! Besides, writers never retire, you know that. You were the one who told me writers die with the pages of their last manuscript clutched in their cold dead hands!"

"Yeah, I did say that," SueAnn admitted. "What was I thinking!"

"You were thinking clearly," Wynette told her. "The never say die SueAnn wouldn't just give up the way you have. I miss her."

"That was before I invested myself in a man whose personality can change from one second to the next," SueAnn told her. "I didn't know anyone could be a real 'Jekyll and Hyde!' But Nick sure is. I made a big mistake falling for him."

"Was it a mistake?" Wynette asked quietly. "You believed he was worth fighting for once. Why don't you feel he's still worth fighting for?"

SueAnn shrugged. "I want to," she answered quietly, "but I don't even know him, how can I trust him?"

"You have to trust yourself," Wynette told her. "Trust your feelings."

"I'm afraid I can't do that right now," SueAnn admitted. "I've been burned one time too many –"

"Haven't we all?" Wynette said and gave a self-conscious laugh. "You can't just give up."

SueAnn closed her eyes and said tightly, "It all comes down to one thing: Giji has won."

"Has not!"

"Has too!"

Wynette and SueAnn shared a laugh. "Now we sound like my kids."

SueAnn was quiet.

Wynette knew the easiest way to get her friend to see how

nonproductive her behavior was. "If I were Nick, I'd choose Giji too!"

"Well, that's a nice thing to say!" SueAnn snapped, then fell silent. "It's her boobs, isn't it?" she asked in a small voice, glancing down at her own chest, perky but small beneath the silky material of her gown.

Wynette slapped her playfully on the arm. "No! It's your attitude. It's like you're throwing in the towel, just giving up and letting Giji Brickhouse win!"

"You really think that?" SueAnn seemed hurt.

Wynette nodded. "I sure do." She frowned. "You're not putting up much of a fight."

"But, what can I do?" SueAnn wanted to know.

"You can fight for your man!" Wynette told her. "The first step is getting your ass out of this bed."

"I think there's a Judge Wapner marathon on later," SueAnn said weakly. "I think I'll just stay here."

"No, you're not," Wynette told her firmly, "you're coming with all of us."

"All of us?" SueAnn repeated.

Wynette nodded. "Yes,

"Giji's going?"

Wynette sighed. "Unfortunately, yes." She threw up her hands. "We kind of had to invite her, she got the tickets."

"That Judge Wapner marathon is sounding better all the time!"

"You're letting her win and worse, you're letting her dictate your life," Wynette said, using the reverse psychology she used on her kids, which in their case almost never worked. "You're not going to let that–that trampy little cunt run your life and keep you locked away up here in the dark, are you?"

"I can get out of here any time I want," SueAnn defiantly.

Wynette smiled, thinking her idea was working on SueAnn. "Okay, prove it," she challenged her friend. "Get out of that bed and go with me to see Jerry Springer!"

"What?" SueAnn asked incredulously. When Wynette

mentioned 'going with all of us,' SueAnn thought maybe going shopping or out to lunch or both but not what she'd just heard. "Jerry Springer?"

"The other wives and I have tickets to the local taping of 'The Jerry Springer Show.' I already told you about the show." Wynette told her. "We're all going, and we got you a ticket. It'll do you good to get out, be around other people and get your mind on other things."

"I am aware that my situation is bad," SueAnn admitted, "but I didn't think it was Jerry Springer bad. You don't get much more desperate than the women on 'The Jerry Springer Show.' Sad but true. That show isn't doing anything to help women's rights or improve our self-image!"

"I agree with you," Wynette said, pleased to see the old fighting SueAnn emerging.

SueAnn sighed. "So maybe going's not such a good idea," she said, sounding disinterested. "It's just going to make us look like a bunch of desperate housewives!"

"We're just going to see the taping of the show, not to be guests," Wynette reminded her. "Besides, anything's better than lying around here all day," her friend chided. "Let's do it. What do you say?"

"I say wake me when it's over," SueAnn said and attempted to pull the covers over her head.

Wynette threw up her hands.

"Okay, okay," SueAnn conceded and gave a small laugh. "I'll go if you promise to keep Giji Whorehouse as far away from me as possible–and you stop making those faces like a frustrated Chihuahua!"

"I don't do that!" She took a small pillow from a nearby chair and tossed it at her friend as they both laughed. "And I promise to keep Giji as far away from you as possible."

"Good." SueAnn caught the pillow. "Is Connie going to see Jerry?" she wanted to know.

Wynette smiled. "She sure is," she said enthusiastically. "Now that's definitely something you don't want to miss, right?"

SueAnn shrugged. "I guess not," she reluctantly agreed. "I never dreamed she'd agree to go! What'd you do, twist both her arms?"

Wynette grinned. "Something like that." She made another face and stuck out her tongue. "Rest up," Wynette urged as she paused in the doorway. "You'll need it for Jerry!" She took a deep breath and smiled. "So glad you're going with us."

"Thanks," SueAnn said and smiled back at her.

"Hey, you survived being kidnapped with Giji Brickhouse," Wynette reminded her. "You'll be fine."

"I hope you're right," SueAnn worried.

"Would I lie to you?" Wynette asked in a soothing voice as if she were speaking to a small child.

"I hope not," SueAnn quipped, her mood lightening now.

After Wynette left, SueAnn leaned back against her pillow and closed her eyes. She couldn't help wondering why Wynette had been so insistent that she joined her and the other wives at the taping of "The Jerry Springer Show."

***

In an old warehouse, several weeks before the scheduled taping of "The Jerry Springer Show" crew members for the show were busily wiring the soundstage while others setup the show's set.

At the end of the final day of preparations for the taping the following week, someone dressed in work clothes to blend in with the other crew members slipped quietly into the old warehouse. Carrying a small, metal toolbox, the person looked around cautiously to make sure no one was watching or paying any attention. Satisfied, the person kneels and carefully places the small toolbox beneath the edge of the soundstage.

After pushing the toolbox under the stage, well out of sight, the person stood and quietly left the building leaving only the promise of destruction in his wake....

32

Spank the Monkey!

Leave it to her sons to use their underwear to plug up toilets so they'd over flow! Camp high jinx, Wynette smiled to herself, as she drove to Camp Junaluska, her kids' summer camp. The kids would spend most of their summer at the camp, giving her a much needed break from their shenanigans.

Wynette was cutting it close to get their underwear to the camp which was almost a hundred miles away, and be on time to go with the other wives to the taping of "The Jerry Springer Show," but what choice did she have? Her kids had to have underwear. When she spoke to the camp counselor, he sounded like a heady mixture of anger and rage. She might need to do some serious convincing to persuade him and the other counselors to allow her 'little angels' to remain for the rest of the summer. She had enjoyed the three weeks they were at the camp and Wynette was prepared to give her best to keep her kids at the camp. If that failed, she would sulk, cry, beg and scream uncontrollably until the camp counselors agreed to keep her sons. She could bribe them with cash if necessary.

Wynette finally reached the camp after lunch. She parked her mini-van in front of the camp counselor's office. The building was small, shabby, in need of some repairs and a fresh coat of paint, she noticed. The office looked like a shed masquerading as a cabin. The gabled roof was covered with pine straw, which added to the rustic charm. She got out of the mini van and held the bag of new underwear she brought for her sons under one arm.

Knocking on the door as she thought how much the building looked like a hobbit's house. She imagined a short, bald guy with grotesque features opening the door. When Russell Brown opened the door, she was pleasantly surprised to see the camp counselor was even more sexy than he sounded on the phone. Tall and lean but with muscle, tanned like a sun-kissed god, sun streaked curly, blonde hair and his eyes were such a deep blue that she could get lost in, except that cliché was overused. She decided he was drop-dead gorgeous and not much older than a kid fresh out of college...how refreshing!

Standing just inches from him, Wynette could smell his earthy smell, natural but not unpleasant, she noted, his nature scent. So manly and appealing. It would be a pleasure to convince him to keep her angels for the remainder of the session. She took several deep breaths, feeling her pussy begin to respond, twitching and becoming moist.

"The fresh air up here is great, isn't it?" he asked, noticing her breathing deeply.

"Air, it is great," she agreed, "so refreshing. I could just take it all in!"

He held out his hand. "I'm Russell Brown, the camp counselor," he introduced himself.

"I'm Wynette Harris," she said, shaking his hand, feeling the coolness of his skin and the heated surge of electricity between them. "I'm the mother of the Harris twins–or the spawns of Satan as you probably know them. Good to meet you."

"It's good to meet you, Mrs. Harris," he said, ignoring her

comment about her sons.

"Call me Wynette," she encouraged as he let go of her hand.

His smile made him even more handsome. "Only if you call me Russ."

"Deal!" she agreed, then added, "I have to apologize for my kids." She paused, her voice breaking partly because of embarrassment and partly because his presence was overwhelming. "They're a handful, I know...."

He smiled again, genuine and warm. "Don't worry about it," he urged. "Boys will be boys, and at camp I've seen almost everything you can imagine and maybe a few things you can't!"

Wynette smiled at him. "I'll bet," she said lightly, thinking of the many misadventures her kids got her into over the years. "The lady who called told me that my kids and several other boys had stopped up the toilets using their underwear."

"I'm afraid so," he admitted.

"Well, at least they're original," she quipped, handing him the bag. "I brought replacement underwear."

"Good," he said, taking the bag. "After an afternoon of rope climbing, they'll appreciate these!"

"Ouch!" she said, pleased that he found the humor in the situation.

His phone rang and he excused himself to answer it.

Stepping inside to escape the heat, Wynette noticed the small office was dark and surprisingly cool. Once her eyes had adjusted to the darkness, she saw an old air conditioner in the rear window humming and shaking. Several times she thought the floor moved with it, which was a bit jolting.

Russ stood at a desk in the corner of the room, phone in hand. She wondered if he were talking to his girlfriend or wife. When she caught a few words about the scouts, she realized he was talking to someone who worked at the camp. She felt a sense of relief, but wasn't sure why, although she wanted Russ Brown to herself...for a little while.

"All done," he announced hanging up the phone. He turned to

face her. "Are you thirsty?" he asked, gesturing to a small refrigerator in the opposite corner of the room. "I have sodas, bottled water..."

Wynette shook her head. "Oh, no, thanks," she said, then wished she had accepted. It would have bought her a little more time in his company. "On second thought," she decided, "I'll take a bottle of water."

"Great." He walked to the small refrigerator. He turned and handed her the bottle. "It's a hot one out there today. I took the kids hiking along some of the trails earlier. Just after daybreak and it was already hot."

Wynette opened the bottle of water and took a quick, cool and refreshing sip. Almost as refreshing as Russ, she pondered. "Hmmm," she said aloud without realizing it.

"What?" he asked, looking at the bottle in her hand. "Did you say something?"

"Ah... ah," she stuttered, "this is really good water."

He smiled. "It's the only brand I buy."

She glanced at the foil label on the bottle then back at him. "I'll have to get some for myself," she said softly, looking into his eyes, "from the grocery."

She held the cool bottle against her neck, enjoying the cooling sensation but enjoying his reaction even more. His eyes were on her neck, watching her moving the bottle against her moist skin. Unable to take his eyes from her, he licked his lips and tiny beads of perspiration formed on his forehead and upper lip.

Wynette took a sip of water, sipping slowly, placing the bottle against her neck. She lowered the bottle from her lips and let the bottom of the bottle press against her breasts, nuzzling against her cleavage. Again, he watched her, unable to pull his eyes from her.

Wynette noticed his eyes were on her breasts–and there was a bulge in his jeans that she hadn't noticed before! She decided to take a chance and reached out her hand and started to massage his erection, feeling his hard, throbbing cock beneath her fingers. His cock was thick, long and had a distinctively huge mushroom head.

"Ahh," he moaned aloud.

"You like that?" she asked in a low sexy voice.

"Oh, yessss!" His was almost a whisper. "That feels sooo good."

Wynette smiled, pleased. "I can make you feel even better." She stepped into his strong arms, her knees were weak because he was so close and she was engulfed by his manly presence. Their lips met in a hot, wet kiss. She broke the kiss, surprised by the freshness of his breath. For a few seconds, they stared into each other's eyes, then once more they were overcome by a rising wave of passion.

In a heated rush, they undressed each other, Wynette could not believe his muscular body was so toned, much more than she'd even realized while his clothes were on. Self-consciously she hoped he wasn't disappointed in her appearance, which she didn't think was too terrible given she'd given birth to three sons. Maybe chasing her three little terrors kept her in much better shape than she would have been otherwise. Of course, if she was honest, the frequent "work outs" with the rent a hubby men, delivery men and others, helped her stay in shape as well.

Russ reached out and pulled her into his powerful arms, holding her close to his muscular chest as their lips met again in a heated kiss that was deep and passionate, tongue-to-tongue. Their naked bodies became entwined as they embraced, and fell onto the small cot along one wall of the small room. The cot gave way under their weight and movement, but they didn't pay attention as her back hit the floor. He lay on top of her, kissing her neck, then taking her breasts in his mouth, first one and then the other. His warm, wet mouth was exhilarating against her cool skin.

Wynette loved the feel of his strong, calloused hands on her body, caressing the soft, fullness of her breasts. His fingers massaged her nipples as the large head of his shaft teased her clit. She felt the moisture between her legs as she throbbed, wanting to feel him between inside him.

Anticipation of how that large mushroom head would feel made her wetter. He teased her, but hesitated to enter her warmth. She couldn't stand it anymore and she pushed her hands against his chest, catching him off guard. He rolled off of her and she pushed him back against the rough floor of the cabin and straddled his legs. Surprise and pleasure blended in his eyes as his passion grew.

Wynette thought about her sons and their friends playing in the forest outside, but it was much too late to stop. Lifting her hips, she dropped onto his long, hard cock and drove it deep within in. His shaft pulsed deep inside of her, the base rubbing against her clit and the sensation drove her closer and closer to orgasm. She was in control and rocked against his hips with a fever pitch. The excitement built inside her and she was on the verge as he shoved his hips against her in several hard thrusts. They each came in an explosion and she collapsed onto his chest.

She loved the sensation of little Kimiko skillful tongue performing oral sex on her, but sometimes nothing satisfied her like having a good stiff cock inside her warm, wet pussy pounding her. That pounding seemed right in the small rustic cabin in the woods, with the old air conditioner banging along, the rickety floor seeming to move, and the remains of the old cot beneath them made the whole experience daring and exciting.

Later she would let him show his oral talents, if there was time...if there was time...

Afterward, they lay together on the floor with broken pieces of the small cot around them. They were spent and still breathing heavily. Suddenly, Wynette remembered she was supposed to be at 'The Jerry Springer Show.' She kissed his rugged chest as if she were kissing him goodbye. "I've got to go," she announced, scrambling to her feet.

"What's the rush?" he asked, lounging on the floor, resting on one elbow. "Can't you stay a while longer? Let me catch my breath, and we can go again!"

Wynette shook her head. "No offense," she said and started to dress. "You were great…"

He grinned. "But…"

She paused for a moment, looked at him. "I need to be somewhere."

"Mind if I ask...?" He lay on the floor and lazily traced her thigh with his calloused fingertip.

Wynette finished dressing and paused at the door. "You will never believe it." she told him. "But, I'm late for 'The Jerry Springer Show!' "

He frowned as she closed the door behind her, feeling as if she had just blew him off. But, he had to admit, it was the most original excuse he'd ever heard!

***

On her way to the taping of "The Jerry Springer Show," Ariella had a little spare time and decided to make a quick stop to see the Sexual Psychic. *It might be a fun way to get in the mood for the show,* she thought as she entered the shop. She glanced around and seeing no one, went through the silk curtain into the adjoining room. "Oh, Kimiko," she said, seeing the small Asian woman seated at the card table in the center of the room. "Here you are."

The older woman looked up and frowned. "Here you are," she said flatly. "What I do for you today?"

Ariella pursed her lips. "How about a quick reading?"

Kimiko shrugged. "Why not?" She began to shuffle the tarot cards. "Sit, sit."

Ariella seated herself while Kimiko dealt the cards, placing them face up in front of her.

"What do you see?" Ariella asked.

"It going to rain tomorrow," Kimiko said with a slight, knowing smile, "but you not get wet. You nice, dry, but change be coming." She paused and looked directly into Ariella's amber eyes. "Soon."

"A good change, I hope?"

"Eh," Kimiko said, not looking up as she continued to study the cards. "Sexy stranger, bald head, muscular."

Ariella thought for a minute. "Oh," she said, thinking of "The Jerry Springer Show" and Jerry's head of security, Steve. "I believe I know what you mean. What else do you see?"

"Just a change," the Sexual Psychic said evasively.

"Oh, okay," Ariella said, thinking this wasn't heading anywhere. But, she remembered seeing the words Celebrity Gossip on the sign in the window and she decided it might be fun to ask a few questions about her favorite celebrities to pass some time. "What is the deal with Whitney Houston and her husband Bobby Brown?" she asked. "They had an awful TV series where they repeatedly mention bodily functions–and Whitney spazzes around like a broken down old lady on crack."

"Bobby Brown a bad man. He scare small children and make strange body noises."

"Ok, what about Whitney? Did they lock her away somewhere and replace her with her grandmother?"

"No, no, Kimiko say Whitney Houston either crazy like a loony tune or very smart cookie!" She shrugged. "Whitney in her own little world, or maybe she been replaced by her grandmother!"

Ariella checked her watch. "I've got a little time to kill." She sighed. "Okay, forget Whitney and Bobby Brown," Ariella said, sounding frustrated. "Are Brad and Jennifer ever going to get back together?"

Kimiko's eye lit up. "Ah, I say about time hell freeze over." She paused, studied the cards. "Or, could be when blizzard hit Caribbean. Cards not clear."

"Will Britney Spears ever be a good mother?" Ariella asked quickly.

Kimiko rolled her eyes. "She not even a good singer, so…."

Ariella glanced at her watch again. "Okay, I gotta go."

"Where you go like panties on fire?" Kimiko asked, curious.

"I thought I was supposed to be asking the questions," Ariella complained. "Oh well! I'm headed to a taping of 'The Jerry Springer Show,' and I have to go. I don't want to be late."

"No, no, you wait. You listen Kimiko. I tell you about Jerry Springer!"

Ariella huffed. "Okay, Kimiko," she agreed impatiently, "but make it fast, okay? What about Jerry Springer?"

"Jerry Springer not black or fat like Oprah used to be. He not have friendly smile like Rikki Lake. He not off the air like Jenny Jones or Geraldo. He not funny lesbian like Ellen –"

"Can you get to the point, Kimiko? I don't have all day!"

"Jerry Springer sucks!" the small Asian woman suddenly spat.

"He doesn't seem so bad. He was the governor of Peoria or something."

"He was mayor of Cleveland, I think. Cleveland rocks, so what? The guy like some kind of Donald Trump of trash TV without the crazy comb over!"

"Hurry, okay," Ariella urged, again glancing at her watch. "I have to go. I do have a life, you know!"

"Oh, you get smart with Kimiko." The small woman frowned, then said firmly, "No, you listen to Kimiko warning. At start of reality TV show craze, Kimiko get role on new show called 'Spank the Monkey!' Kimiko think 'Spank the Monkey' about discipling simians. No! I go on 'Spank the Monkey!' and get spanked. Kimiko get monkey spanked again and again and hard! Kimiko never the same. Before that Kimiko almost Miss America. Kimiko was Miss Compton twice. Twice!" She pointed a bony finger for emphasis. "Now I Sexual Psychic. I see into future. Kimiko not get fooled again!"

"Spanking, huh?" Ariella said, pleased. "I guess I have nothing to worry about then." She handed Kimiko a fifty and smiled. "I could use a little spanking!"

Kimiko quickly ran the counterfeit detecting pen across the wrinkled fifty and smiled.

Unable to take Kimiko's rambling any longer, Ariella left the Sexual Psychic and headed to 'The Jerry Springer Show,' blissfully unaware that her life was about to change... forever.

***

Kimiko watched Ariella get in her small sports car and drive away. She got an idea from Ariella's visit and she was about to pull the shade down on the door so she could lock up when she saw someone she recognized heading toward the shop.

"I saw Miss High and Mighty leave in a rush as usual," Sun Li told her almost as soon as she opened the door to enter. "Did you get anything on her?"

"Not yet," Kimiko admitted as she closed the blinds.

"I believe she is having affairs with men, but so far I can only catch her in strangest positions ever with blonde trollop!" Sun Li sighed heavily. "Ummm, maybe she's just too smart for us," she worried.

"Pulleeze!" Kimiko rolled her eyes. "We talking 'bout same bimbo!"

They shared a hearty laugh.

"Oh, she get hers," Kimiko assured Sun Li. "It just a matter of time." She paused, smiled, thinking of 'The Jerry Springer Show.' "Maybe sooner than she think!"

"You're a good sister, Kimiko," Sun Li told her, pleased.

Kimiko sighed. "I know," she said in her regular speaking voice. "Hey, Sun, I'm headed to the taping of 'The Jerry Springer Show,' want to come?"

Sun Li shrugged. "Nah! I watch 'Judge Judy!'"

33

Meet Jerry Springer!

The lights were low. The stage was barely visible. The five wives sat among a cheering crowd of strangers. Suddenly the lights came up, getting brighter and brighter, and the crowd leapt to their feet and started chanting "Jerrrrry! Jerrrrry!" over and over again while pounding their fists in the air to the beat of pounding rock music.

"Hello, everyone," Jerry greeted the audience as he came onstage. "It's great to be here in your fair city. We've found lots of sexy and sordid stories. Some of these stories you have to hear to believe!"

Jerry Springer, a fair-haired likeable man with a thin face, a bulbulous nose, and large glasses, appeared to be a cross between Ichabod Crane and a disoriented garden gnome. At times he seemed to have a bewildered expression as if he were wondering "What the hell am I doing here!"

After the introduction, he went off stage to confer with his staff about upcoming segments.

***

SueAnn could not believe she was sitting in the audience at 'The Jerry Springer Show.' Although she had seen the show a few times, she never imagined she would be in the audience for a show.

Sometimes when she was at a rough spot in one of her children's stories, she would take a break and watch TV for a while. While flipping through the channels occasionally she would see Jerry and paused to see what the show was about. Jerry's not so glamorous guests usually participated in stories like *Hairdressers and the Women Who Love Them* or *My Stepmother Ran Off with My Twelve-Year-Old Son* or worse.

What little she had seen of Jerry's show made SueAnn glad she was in the audience and not onstage! Suddenly, SueAnn noticed something that she had been totally oblivious to. *Hmmm, she mused, a stripper pole, Jerry must have put that in just for Giji!*

***

Giji glanced past Wynette and Connie to SueAnn's seat. *Well, SueAnn,* she thought, *if you're going to spill your boobs as usual there's no better place to do it than 'The Jerry Springer Show'! You could lift your blouse and give Jerry, his crew and the audience an eyeful, but that's more my style than yours!*

***

Ariella looked around the studio audience. *So many unattractive people in one place,* she thought, *like diners for an all you can eat buffet at a cattle show!*

People were chattering among themselves, creating a buzz of excitement. But, Ariella wasn't interested in Jerry Springer or even interested in his assortment of sideshow freaks masquerading as guests. She was interested in spanking… or, more accurately, being spanked.

Okay, she thought impatiently, *bring on the spanking! I'll even volunteer to go first!*

***

Restless and worried her legs would go to sleep sitting in the uncomfortable folding chair, Connie shifted in her seat like the lady in the TV commercial. She wondered if people would think she had hemorrhoids. *Probably half of them did,* she thought with disgust. Then she found herself wondering why she even cared what total strangers would think. They were people whose opinions meant nothing to her and people she would probably never see again. She made a mental note to care less what others thought.

I have to block this out, Connie told herself. *According to Giji "The Jerry Springer Show" built a thriving franchise, including pay-per view, no holds barred specials, degrading people for entertainment. I'm trying not to look at less fortunate people so harshly,* she reminded herself. *I'm trying not to be too judgmental of people who are...less perfect than me! I should never have been persuaded to come to this taping,* Connie decided, *but my defenses were down. I'm trying to be more spontaneous!*

***

What am I doing here? Wynette wondered, already bored. I could be someplace having sex. She found her mind wandering back to her latest sexual encounter with the earthy camp counselor....

Then Wynette remembered the main reason she was here... for SueAnn. She glanced over at SueAnn sitting next to her. *So clueless,* she thought. Hoping SueAnn would forgive her, she noticed Connie shifting in her seat and wondered if she had hemorrhoids.

***

The stage suddenly grew bright and again the music started, slow at first, then faster and louder and louder until you could not hear your own thoughts. The audience pumped their fists and chanted "Jerrrrry!" in sync with the pumping metal music as the talk show host Jerry Springer came back on stage.

Jerry Springer again greeted the wildly cheering audience, then he was handed a handful of small, just larger than credit card sized, cards. Quickly he flipped through the cards until he found the one he sought. "Okay, here we go," Jerry said, looking out at the audience and then back at the card. "Is there a SueAnn Day in our audience?"

SueAnn could not believe what she was hearing, nor could she hide the surprise on her face, her eyes were wide and she was sure her jaw was on the studio floor though she was too nervous to move.

"Go ahead," Wynette urged. "Get up!"

Reluctantly, SueAnn stood up, forcing a smile to her thin lips as she looked around at the staring eyes of all the strangers looking at her.

"Come on down, SueAnn!" Jerry called in a light voice. "Don't be shy." He looked directly into the camera and gave a sly smile. "That's not what this show is about!"

At the urging of her friends, SueAnn started toward the stage, pushed along by the crowd more than by her own freewill. Several times she felt a hand on her ass, but she was too worried about what was to come when she reached the stage to worry about being felt up.

Once she reached the area in front of the stage, SueAnn came to a stop beside the king of sleaze TV, talk show host Jerry Springer. Jerry helped her on stage.

"Welcome, SueAnn," Jerry said brightly once they were standing center stage.

"Thanks." SueAnn was petrified. "Wha-what am I doing here?" she stammered through teeth that were almost chattering.

Jerry grinned. "Ah, shucks," he said, "I was hoping you were here to see me!"

SueAnn tried to smile.

Jerry frowned at her lack of response. "I'm going to take that as a no," he teased. "You want to know why you're here?"

SueAnn nodded.

"Sure, you do," Jerry said looking at his next card. "Oh, we'll get to that, but first we have a surprise for you."

SueAnn stood on the huge stage, alone, looking uneasy and uncertain of what was to come next. As it turned out, she didn't have to wait long.

"Let's have your friends come down and join you," Jerry suggested, glancing at SueAnn, who seemed almost frozen in place on the stage.

SueAnn cringed. Something told her this was going to get worse. She found herself looking out into the audience, a sea of unfamiliar faces, except for the other wives who had come with her. She found her friends and looked at each one. The looks on their faces ranged from shock to surprise to elation.

The only one who seemed genuinely thrilled to be coming on down on "The Jerry Springer Show" was Giji. She was on her feet and walking toward the stage before Jerry got the words out of his mouth. Giji was smiling and grinning, her eyes twinkling with mischief as she made her way to the stage, hi-fiving people on her way down, her breasts jiggling, her ass shaking to Jerry's pounding metal anthem.

The other wives made their way down, a bit more reserved, although Ariella seemed to have taken a cue from Giji and was strutting her stuff with a whole Latina vibe of hot tamale with a saucy wiggle. SueAnn had to admit that her spicy, sexy moves were a definite hit with the audience–especially the men.

While she watched her friends making their way to the stage, SueAnn couldn't shake a queasy feeling that was slowly coming over her. She wasn't sure why, but the whole situation gave her a sick feeling in the pit of her stomach. She felt as if she were about to hurl, the way she'd felt that time Mrs. Hoover brought over her cabbage and liver casserole and insisted she take a few bites while Mrs. Hoover watched. She remembered chewing and swallowing– and nothing going down. The taste. The taste. She recalled it was worse than bile. Her stomach was churning and she could almost taste the bile burning its way along her throat. Knowing the audience would just be more frenzied if she threw up, SueAnn willed herself to keep it down, just as she did with Mrs. Hoover's casserole... Once she got it to go down, of course!

As they approached the stage, Connie and Wynette gave SueAnn uneasy glances with more than a hint of shock, while Giji and Ariella danced their way onto stage and went directly to the stripper pole where they danced around, lifting their blouses just enough to reveal their smooth, flat stomachs and drive the audience into a frenzy. While they danced, the audience stood and cheered.

"Show your boobs!" the audience chanted. "Show your boobs!"

Taking a cue from the audience, Giji and Ariella stopped dancing around the pole and stood close together, then in unison they lifted their tops revealing their beautiful, firm breasts.

The audience cheered.

One of the stage hands threw Giji and Ariella their Jerry Beads, and they put them on each other.

"Dance around the pole! Dance around the pole!" the audience chanted.

Wynette turned to SueAnn and Connie. "Now they want us to do it," she told them.

"Not even when hell freezes over!" Connie said loudly over the chanting.

"Dance around the pole," Wynette repeated, smiling as she looked at SueAnn. "Let's do it!"

SueAnn shook her head. "No! No, let's not."

Wynette caught SueAnn by the arm and dragged her to the pole. Together they started to dance, one on either side of the stripper pole, they danced slow and really bad. SueAnn barely moved and Wynette gyrated obscenely against the metal pole, while the audience cheered.

"Show your boobs! Show your boobs!" the audience chanted.

"Do it!" Wynette urged SueAnn.

"I will not!" SueAnn refused.

Wynette looked at the disappointed audience and shrugged as if to say "I tried!"

Together they made their way back toward center stage, and as they neared Jerry, SueAnn's heel got caught on a cable running across the stage. She staggered and then just as it appeared she would get her footing back, she started to fall toward Jerry. The host seemed to be trying to catch her and at the same time get out of the way. While the audience watched and gasped, SueAnn fell on top of Jerry. As she fell her low-cut blouse slipped down and her breasts slipped out. While SueAnn closed her eyes and hoped to die of embarrassment, a helpless Jerry Springer lay beneath her, her boobs resting on his face!

Almost instantly two of Jerry's security guys freed Jerry by lifting SueAnn off of the talk show host while she held her arms across her breasts.

SueAnn reluctantly accepted her Jerry Beads and slipped them on.

Jerry smiled as he was helped to his feet. "Gee, I just about got the wind knocked out of me!" he quipped, taking a deep breath.

"Jerry, she does this kind of thing all the time," Giji told him, disgusted.

"Need I remind you, Giji, that you've had your own series of accidents in recent weeks?" SueAnn taunted. "Some you probably think we don't even know about?"

"This woman has the emotional stability of Jell-o!"

"This comes from the woman who needs a zip code for her thong!"

"Are you trying to say my ass is huge?" Giji tried to look around at her own ass. "I won't deny that I have a lot of junk in my trunk, but –"

"Butt is right. Like a couple of spare tires!" SueAnn jabbed. "And a few spare parts!"

"At least I have an ass, sweetie!" Giji said quickly. "You look like a toothpick on a Slim-Fast diet!"

SueAnn pursed her lips in a pout. "Some guys like it," she said quietly, "one guy even said I have the all-American girl next door look!"

The guys in the audience went through a series of whistles, "Yeah, baby" and cat calls.

Wow, SueAnn thought, *this isn't so bad!*

***

"Let's not forget Giji," Jerry said and looked deadpan into the audience. "Who could forget Giji!"

Giji stood up, jumping up and down with excitement, her body bumping into the talk show host and his microphone

"You're humping...er...riding my microphone like a stripper's pole. Can your pussy talk?"

"You wouldn't believe the things it says," Giji assured him.

"What's it saying right now?" the talk show host wanted to know.

"Jerrrrry! Jerrrrry!" Giji shouted and the audience joined her.

"Gee, I guess I stepped into that one," Jerry said, grinning.

"Giji, we have a blast from the past," Jerry said. "Well, not the distant past apparently since you just moved out of her home where you had been a houseguest after living under a bridge where she was kind enough to rescue you."

"I did not," Giji protested, enthusiasm waning as she sank back into her seat. "I did not live under a bridge. Martha Hoover will tell you anything to make her self look good."

"Whatever the truth is," Jerry said, "here's Martha Hoover!"

Mrs. Hoover waddled out in her best plaid polyester pantsuit, waving and smiling at Jerry's audience. Quickly, she embraced the talk show host and gave him a peck on the cheek. "Even more handsome in real life," she cooed.

"Thank you, Mrs. Hoover." Jerry smiled. "Welcome to the show."

Mrs. Hoover seated herself beside Giji. "Thank you, Jerry"

"What do you do, Mrs. Hoover?" he wanted to know. "Are you a lady of leisure? Do you do a lot of charitable work?"

Giji almost choked and then pretended she was clearing her throat.

Mrs. Hoover gave Giji a cold stare. "I believe charity starts at home," she said.

"And should stay at home!" someone in the audience yelled.

"I'd like to work with shut-ins," Mrs. Hoover explained, "but I don't get out much."

The audience laughed.

"Okay, well," Jerry said as soon as the laughter died down, "you made it here. That's the important thing."

"Thank you, Jerry," Mrs. Hoover said and smiled.

Jerry looked at his notes after taking a cue from his director, a short, stout man with salt-and-pepper hair. "Well, we have another guest with her own special outlook on things," Jerry announced. "Something tells me she's going to be a most insightful guest. Let's bring her out!"

The audience applauded.

Each of the wives turned and looked toward the stage entrance, wondering who was going to step on stage.

The audience applauded as Kimiko, the Sexual Psychic, came out smiling, waving and blowing kisses at the audience.

The glances the wives exchanged made a clear statement–"This can't be good!"

As the small Asian woman seated herself besides Mrs. Hoover, Giji gave her a quick glance, her eyes questioning why the psychic was here.

"Welcome, Kimiko," Jerry greeted. "It's good to have you here."

"I glad to be with you, too, Jerry," Kimiko said. "I big fan of show. I watch you all the time. Watch you almost as much as Dr. Phil."

"Well, I'm flattered," Jerry said. "I'm sure Dr. Phil is pleased, too."

"No need to suck up," Mrs. Hoover said under her breath, wishing she'd thought of it first.

"Kimiko," Jerry said, glancing again at his notes. "I see here that you're a psychic, actually a sexual psychic. What exactly does that involve?"

"I see future, Jerry," Kimiko answered. "I read Tarot card, but I offer, too, sexual counsel. The spirit need sexual healing!"

"Amen!" someone yelled in the audience.

Mrs. Hoover rolled her eyes heavenward.

"Good for you, Kimiko," Jerry told the small Asian woman, but he still seemed unsure of what exactly being s sexual psychic entailed. "Now, Mrs. Hoover –"

"Jerry, please call me Martha," Mrs. Hoover said and batted her eyes at the talk show host.

"Okay, Martha," the talk show host said, "you recently had a traumatic event in your life, right?"

Mrs. Hoover frowned, looking on the verge of tears, then dabbed at her eyes with a handkerchief embroidered with roses that she pulled from the pocket of pantsuit. "Yes, Jerry," she said in a weak voice. "My home was burglarized just two weeks ago."

"Oh, I'm so sorry."

"Thank you, Jerry."

"Was anything taken?"

Mrs. Hoover nodded slowly, still dabbing at her eyes. "Just my sense of security and well-being –"

"Well, I'm sorry to hear–"

"And my little red book," Mrs. Hoover went on. "My diary that I have been keeping since I was a schoolgirl."

"You did say little red book?" Jerry asked, thinking that she had either had a really uneventful life or she didn't write very much—or both!

There was sporadic laughter in the audience.

"Yes, Jerry," Mrs. Hoover answered, missing the point. "My diary was stolen. It contained all my inner most thoughts, dreams, wishes, sexual fantasies –"

Jerry tried not to cringe, unsuccessfully. "Okay, I wish you the best of luck in getting your diary back." He paused. "Any leads?"

Mrs. Hoover looked down the row of wives seated on the stage and her eyes came to rest on Kimiko. "Nothing concrete," she said firmly and put her handkerchief away. "Just suspicions!"

"Oh, enough about her little book," Kimiko interjected. "Her book old news. I work on my book, Jerry. You be character in my book. You handsome, dashing talk show host who solves crimes on side. You have affair with beautiful, exotic geisha called Sexual Psychic but–poof! It all a bad dream and Jerry caught with his pants down!"

"Gee, I'm almost flattered, I think," Jerry said when the audience stopped laughing and chanting his name. "But, I don't want to go from a well-known, highly respected talk show host-slash-country western singer to a footnote character in your book!"

"Good, Jerry!" Ariella called out. "Don't fall for her bullshit! She used the same line on me, only I was supposed to be a gorgeous, glamorous spy. Instead I ended up as a freaking pile of ashes at the end of chapter one!"

Kimiko frowned at Ariella, then she turned back to Jerry. "Okay, Jerry," she persisted. "You be average Joe talk show host who come to trailer park to solve murders of young ladies with freakish good looks but no taste in men!"

Jerry shook his head. "Oh, Kimiko," he said, sounding amused. "So very tempting, but except for the murders, I do that every day on my talk show." He sighed. "Hmmm, sorry, I'm going to have to pass."

Kimiko threw up her hands. "What I gonna do!" she said. "You pass up opportunity to be star!"

Jerry gave a deadpan look into the camera, a look not unlike a sad puppy. "Who? Me? What can I say?" he said flatly. "I'm just a humble talk show host with his own show."

"Your loss, Jerry," Kimiko said, disappointed. "Someday you regret not being big star and potential sex symbol!"

"Don't fret, Jerry," Mrs. Hoover soothed, "I'll write about you in my diary, if I ever get it back."

Jerry nodded, wishing that were comforting.

"I baked you one of my special casseroles," Mrs. Hoover told him proudly. "I left it backstage in the green room for you to eat later."

"You might want to eat it in the emergency room," Giji suggested, "with the paramedics on call. I can offer the names of a couple who are very good at mouth to mouth."

"Thanks, Martha," Jerry said, pretending not to hear Giji's comments, as one of his security guys, Todd, came from backstage clutching his stomach.

Todd, a stout, somewhat nerdy fellow with small eyes and thinning hair, seemed somewhat unkempt to put it nicely. Todd was often referred to as "Toad" by other staff members and was the butt of jokes by Jerry and his staff about his lack of a life, especially his lack of a sex life! In one episode of "The Jerry Springer Show," Todd's life had been ridiculed in ongoing segments titled "24 Hours In the Life of a Loser." Worse still, on several occasions Jerry had let everyone know that Todd was a virgin by circumstance, not choice.

In truth, Todd didn't seem to have game when it came to charming the ladies. Ariella cringed on several occasions when Todd was in close proximity to her, and Giji refused to even acknowledge his existence. The other wives just kind of nodded and smiled at him as if he were some scary stranger they were passing on the street.

"Todd, what's wrong?" a concerned Jerry asked.

Todd stood, wavering as if he were about to collapse, then stumbled around the stage. "I ate a bowl of scraps someone left in the green room," he replied weakly. He seemed to be foaming at the mouth, his eyes sunken and rolling around in his head.

"Well!" Mrs. Hoover sniffed but chose not to comment further given the young man's condition.

"Looks like you've claimed another victim, Martha," Giji said under her breath.

"Shhhh," Mrs. Hoover hissed.

"Are there any paramedics in the house?" Jerry asked, looking at the audience, who were unusually quiet for a change.

A young lady on Jerry's staff helped Todd to a chair and he sat slightly bent forward, a hand across his stomach. "I'll be okay," he said weakly, "as soon as the room stops spinning!"

"Oh, he'll be fine," Mrs. Hoover assured Jerry. "Now let's discuss you coming home with me!"

"Jerry, not good idea to tempt fate with crazy casserole lady," Kimiko said ominously. "This one, she kill husband. You go home with her, you be next."

"Oh, Kimiko," Mrs. Hoover admonished, lightly laughing. "You exaggerate. Everyone knows my husband died of pneumonia!"

"And deadly codfish casserole!" Kimiko added.

"Oh, stop now, Kimiko," Mrs. Hoover pleaded, her voice sounding playful. "You're going to make Jerry and the people who watch his show in the trailer parks across America think I'm some kind of casserole-baking black widow-slash-domestic sex goddess!"

"Slasher, maybe," Kimiko said under her breath. "Sex goddess, never! No vaccine for this one. She deadly like plague wipe out San Francisco."

"Aids?" Jerry asked, confused.

"No, no, Jerry," Kimiko said urgently, "Mrs. Hoover. She like suburban Dr. Kevorkian!"

Jerry bit his lower lip. "Well, okay, we've been warned. Let's move on."

Everyone watched as the female stage hand led Todd off stage, still clutching his stomach.

"I'm sure she'll have a medic look after Todd," Jerry assured everyone. "Now, Mrs. Hoover, what do you think of all this? The show today and the discussions we have each day here on 'The Jerry Springer Show.' "

Martha Hoover rolled her eyes heavenward. "Oh, I'm in agreement with the ladies at my church." Mrs. Hoover said with a serious tone in her voice. "I'm in favor of wholesome violence, but not all this sexual hanky panky that young people are into these days." She sighed deeply. "Well, Jerry, I am so appalled at the lack of morality in our society right now."

"Boy, are you at the right place!" Jerry said sarcastically.

"Fishy woman! Fishy woman!" the audience chanted.

"Go kick your own ass!" Mrs. Hoover bellowed and she turned to a woman who was standing in the audience calling her a hypocrite. "Watch it, sister," she yelled at the woman, "I'll go trailer park on your ass!"

Jerry sighed. "So much for those family values, Martha."

"Oh, I'm sorry, Jerry," Mrs. Hoover apologized in a softer tone. "They just… really get to you, don't they?"

"Only when they're right, Martha," Jerry said sadly, "only when they're right."

Mrs. Hoover shrugged as if she couldn't care less. "Jerry, I'm headed to Charleston for a leisurely trip," she announced and winked at the talk how host, "and I would love to take you with me, you… you cutie pie!"

"For the first time in my life," Jerry began, "I'm happy to say I have to work."

"Jerry, you don't have to play hard to get with me!"

"Who's playing?" Jerry asked. "I really do have to work."

"You don't know what you're missing," Mrs. Hoover said and lifted her blouse, exposing her enormous sagging breasts. She definitely had not defied gravity.

"I do now," Jerry told her.

"Well, if you're not going to give me the old stiff microphone routine," Mrs. Hoover said, disappointed, "then I want my Jerry beads!" A stage hand gave Mrs. Hoover her beads, which she placed inside her ample cleavage.

"Ewwww!" the audience said. Jerry cringed... again.

***

"Wynette," Jerry began, "now that all your friends are on stage along with Mrs. Hoover and Kimiko, we may as well start with you."

Wynette laughed foolishly, a nervous, out-of-control laugh. "If we have to," she said, "but I'll be glad to pass my turn to anyone who would like to go ahead of me."

She glanced around. The other wives sat still, a fearful look in their eyes, and no one volunteered. "Okay, well," Wynette said, "I guess you can start with me."

"Thanks, Wynette," Jerry said, looking at his notes. "Would it be safe to say you're a sex addict?"

Wynette froze. She was afraid that was coming. Seeing no point in denying it when it was obvious that Jerry already knew she was addicted to sex, she nodded. "Yes, I have been addicted to sex for several year... months," she babbled on and on, trying to convince Jerry and his audience that was no longer the case. "I should say was because I am a recovering sex addict now, really I am. I have put that behind me. I am seeing a therapist."

"Would that be a sex therapist?" Jerry inquired.

"Yes, yes, a sex therapist who is helping me overcome my addiction. In fact, I have already made great strides in just a few weeks. I almost never think of sex anymore. It's certainly not the main focus of life now."

"That's good to hear," Jerry commended her, "but didn't I see you checking out the rears of several of male crew members and possibly a couple of females?"

Wynette shrugged, guilty as charged. "What can I say?" she gushed. "They have cute asses!"

"Speaking of asses," Jerry began, "cute ones, that is. Let's meet your husband, Steven."

Steven came from backstage, gave his wife a quick peck on the lips, and took a seat beside her.

"Steven, did you know your wife was addicted to sex?" Jerry asked.

"I didn't right away," he admitted. "At the time I was doing quite a bit of traveling for my job, and I had no idea she was sleeping with anyone else. When I came home, she was always ready to get busy– if you know what I mean!"

"I'm sure there are a lot of fellows around who know firsthand, we'll meet some of them later," Jerry said. "What do you think now that you know?"

Steven shrugged. "I keep thinking about all the money we could've made if she'd been charging for it!"

The audience booed.

Wynette gave Steven a sharp look.

"Hey, fella," Jerry drawled, "we're not that kind of show!" He paused, smiled and added, "Okay, we are that kind of show! Go ahead, let it all hang out. We're all willing to listen, look, point and discuss it afterwards!"

"For my own safety and peace of mind," Steven said, "I will refrain from making any further comments of that nature."

"Okay, wise man." Jerry looked at his notes. "Here are three of Wynette's victim...I mean...lovers," he announced. "From Rent-A-Hubby. Welcome Greg, Mort and Cameron." He paused, took a second look at his notes, pushed his off his nose, then up, then back in place. "Yep, I read that right, Greg, Mort and Cameron!"

Three guys dressed in olive green uniforms, with name tags sewn on the right front pocket of their shirts, came out and stood behind the guests on stage. "Hi, Wynette," the short, stout guy in the center, Mort, said and gave a little wave. The two taller guys, one blond and the other dark-haired, just stood to attention, looking straight ahead.

Wynette glanced at the guys and did not say anything.

"Recognize these guys?" Jerry asked Wynette.

"Vaguely," Wynette lied.

"Well," Jerry taunted, "they do have their clothes on!"

The audience roared with laughter.

"Wynette, sounds like you were keeping yourself pretty busy," Jerry commented, glancing at his notes. "It says here you're the mother of three boys. How did you have time to raise your kids?"

Wynette shrugged. "I manage somehow," she babbled. "I found the time."

"Wynette's a great wife and a wonderful mother," Steven spoke, coming to his wife's defense.

"And apparently a hell of a lover!" Jerry quipped.

The audience chanted: "Jerrrrry! Jerrrrry!"

"I admitted I was addicted to sex," Wynette said when things quieted down, "but–" She paused winked at Kimiko. "I think I've found a solution. My friends staged an intervention, and I agreed to work with a therapist. I'm making progress already."

"And you haven't had sex since this show started!" Jerry interjected. "Are you sure you're making excellent progress? After all, I felt you grab my ass a couple of times since you came on the stage, and I'm pretty sure you molested most of my staff. Can I see a showing of hands?"

Steve, Todd and the other guys on Jerry's staff raised their hands as did some of the other men and women on Jerry's staff.

"Well, like my therapist says these things do take time, Jerry," Wynette countered. "It takes several months, if not years, of sessions to get to a point where you control the addiction instead of having it control you!"

"Hon, we all understand that, but you have to stop touching people inappropriately," Steven warned. "That's not right, you know."

Wynette nodded like a meek child who had been caught

swiping candy. "I know and I apologize to everyone. Just remember, recovery doesn't happen overnight, and I've only had the first of my many sessions."

"Sounds like a lot of money for those sessions," Jerry observed.

"Oh, 'bout fifty buck a session," Kimiko told him.

"Ummm," Jerry said, "that sounds very reasonable."

"The important thing is that I have faced my addiction," Wynette said. "I'm well on my way to recovery."

"That is the important thing," Steven agreed quickly, thinking he saw Kendra lurking in the rear of the audience. But, surely her father had sent her to that camp for troubled teens in the boondocks by now, he decided. "I am so proud of you, sweetheart," he added and gave her a quick kiss. "You should have confided in me. I could have helped you."

Wynette smiled. "You still can," she told him. "The therapist says I need you to be there for me and to help fulfill my sexual needs on a regular basis so I don't get tempted to revert back to my addiction."

"Maybe we could see the therapist together," Steven offered, hugging his wife.

Kimiko smiled. "That sound like excellent idea," she said quickly, thinking Wynette was not bad, but her husband was a real hottie!

"Well, I don't know," Wynette hesitated. "Maybe after I've had a few more sessions and feel more comfortable with the idea."

"Okay, hon," Steven told her, "but I'm looking forward to being apart of your recovery and your sessions."

"Me, too," Kimiko said loudly. "Me, too!"

"Kimiko, is there something you're not telling us?" Jerry wanted to know.

Kimiko's small eyes grew wide. "I sex therapist and give sessions to... whore," she admitted. "I very ashamed, but she trick me with money and sad story. I want to help. No man safe with this one pinching booty."

The audience's laughter was deafening.

Wynette turned on the small Asian woman. "I thought you told me what happens in Sexual Psychic's shop, stays in Sexual Psychic's shop!"

Kimiko shrugged. "I lie."

A guy on Jerry's staff leaned in and whispered in his ear. "Oh, okay, we have a caller," Jerry announced. "This call is for Wynette. Go ahead caller."

"Hello, Jerry. This is Angela from Rent-A-Hubby," the caller introduced herself.

Wynette looked uneasy, like she was the guest of honor at an unusually hostile roast.

"Wynette was one of our best customers," the caller explained. "She was a repeat customer over several weeks, often requesting different repair guys. Well, at first we thought nothing of it, just good business."

"It certainly sounds that way," Jerry interjected.

"Don't be fooled, Jerry," Angela urged. "This woman slept with so many of our Rent-A-Hubbies, we may have to change our company name! If all our customers were like dear sweet Wynette, we'd have to become Rent-A-Gigolo or maybe even Rent-A-Ho!"

The audience gasped and then there was a chorus of sporadic laughter.

"Oh, Wynette, what do you have to say for yourself?" Jerry wanted to know once things had quieted down.

Wynette shrugged. "Busted!"

"I'm sure my wife regrets her behavior," Steven quickly came to Wynette's rescue, "and she's seeking help to overcome her addiction. So let's cut her some slack."

"She like little train that could," Kimiko observed. "Toot! Toot!"

Wynette looked at her husband, smiled and he pulled her into his arms. "You owe me big time," he whispered in her ear.

Suddenly a young woman way up in the audience stood and

started making her way toward the stage. She was wearing what appeared to b a Catholic schoolgirl uniform, with a skirt that was so short you could see her crisp white cotton panties as she raised her long legs to walk. When she was about half way down, Steven recognized her: Kendra!

Jerry went to meet the young woman. He met her just as she was about to step onstage. "Do you have a comment, miss?"

"I still love you, Steven!" Kendra said so loudly into Jerry's mic. "My dad sent me away to Aunt Betty's Camp for Wayward Girls, but I ran away! I won't let my dad come between us, Steven. We have something wonderful! We're like Romeo and Juliet."

"It looks like Wynette isn't the only one who's been getting busy!" Jerry observed. "What do you say, Steven?"

Steven shrugged, speechless.

"I guess we're even," Wynette told her husband and gave him a sharp jab to the ribs with her elbow.

Steven started to speak but thought better of it. He found it interesting how the men in the audience could not take their eyes off Kendra and how they seemed to drool when she lifted her way too small blouse and revealed her young, perky breasts and their fleshy pink nipples. "Bead me, Jerry!" she squealed.

"If only I remembered how..." Jerry drawled.

"It's just like riding a bike, Jerry," Kendra said and caught his mike in her hands, pressing it and his hand between her still exposed breasts.

Jerry grinned. "Nope, my memory's not that bad," Jerry told her. "I happen to remember it's nothing at all like riding a bike!"

***

Jerry Springer looked at the group of wives now seated on the stage. Each wife seemed fearful that she would be called upon, their faces wooden but their eyes lively. Their expressions were not unlike kids in school when the teacher asked a question. The children's eyes would dart around the room to other students, hoping that someone had raised his or her hand. They hesitated to raise their own hands, but they knew the teacher might call on them anyway.

"Now, Connie," Jerry said, looking at his notes.

Connie tensed up even more visibly, face paler than normal, chiseled features more defined and standing out clearly, hands at her side, knuckles white, fingers shaking ever so slightly, eyes fixed on something in the distance. For once she looked like an ice princess, the very thing she'd been accused of being all her life. Like ice, Connie looked as if she could shatter into a million tiny pieces at any moment, without warning.

"I can't believe I'm here at 'The Jerry Springer Show,' " Connie said stiffly as if she were thinking out loud. "This is so not me!"

"Martha Stewart! Martha Stewart!" the audience roared again and again, louder and louder.

Connie blushed visibly. "I'm nothing like that domestic jailbird!" she protested loudly, her green eyes now alive and flashing with rising anger. "So what if I presoak before I do the wash? It helps get out stains that could be set in!"

"Domestic diva! Domestic diva!" the audience chanted.

In frustration, Connie threw up her hands.

"Connie was caught doing it Jerry Springer-style on live TV!" Giji told everyone.

"Hey! Hey!" Jerry protested. "Don't go blaming me. I wasn't even there!"

"Jerry, she was really cooking!" Giji told him. "And I don't mean she was preparing food!"

"She's right, Jerry," Mrs. Hoover chimed in. "I saw it myself. Right in the middle of an info-mercial for increased sexual stamina! here she comes with her cooking partner–and they were really hot to trot if you know what I mean." She winked at Jerry. "She and Chef Boyardee were spiraling around like human pastries and covering themselves with food. They were a naughty, nasty mess entwined in unspeakable sexual acts right on live TV!"

"Unbelievable!" Jerry gasped.

"I wouldn't have believed it myself," Mrs. Hoover admitted, giving Connie a distasteful glance, "if I hadn't seen it with my own eyes. I certainly would have expected that from most of my neighbors." Mrs. Hoover sniffed and glanced over at Giji. "But, I never expected such an outlandish display from quiet little Connie. Like I always say, it's the quiet ones you have to watch."

"On live TV, apparently," Jerry interjected.

"That not all, Jerry," Kimiko beamed knowingly. "I Sexual Psychic, I see all." She placed a hand on either side of her small head, fingers at her temples, then she closed her eyes as if for added emphasis. "I see Connie. She masturbating with cooking utensils!" she added accusingly.

"Oh, really?" Jerry sounded doubtful.

"Yes, yes, Jerry." Kimiko opened her eyes now. "Oh, she caught masturbating with cooking utensils and she not even cooking. She whipping up a storm...tenderize herself, maybe, she like being watched." She sighed. "I say Julia Child roll over in grave if she see how Connie use that big spatula and where she put poor whisk! It kinda... obscene!"

"Really, no!" Jerry couldn't believe what he was hearing. "Surely not! Really? Well, this may be a first even for 'The Jerry Springer Show'! You heard it here first, folks." Jerry turned to Connie. "Were you trying out for the Sex-a-lympics?" the talk show host wanted to know.

Connie was shocked. *How could she know?* "I was dreaming," Connie said, then wished she had said nothing. Deny, her mother had always stressed, spare your reputation at all costs!

"You mean you were sleepwalking?" Jerry asked.

"No, I was dreaming," Connie explained. "This didn't happen, not really. I was dreaming that I was trying to be more spontaneous, more creative."

"I'll say you were," Jerry agreed. "Were you trying to

tenderize yourself? That's a whole new way to beat your meat!"

The audience "oohed" and "ahhhhed," then went hysterical with uncontrollable laughter.

Connie's usually pale skin took on a pink tone just a few shades lighter than her red hair as she blushed. "I won't dignify that with a response," she choked out, unable to believe what was happening. Afraid it would get worse, she had to fight the urge to get up and run out. The only thing that stopped her was that she couldn't imagine how it could get worse–and she wasn't sure she could get her legs to carry her, they suddenly felt like two shaking, limp noodles.

"Okay, well," Jerry said, sighing, "we have a surprise for you."

Connie gave Jerry a look so cold it could chill the soul.

Jerry made an exaggerated shiver. "Ooh, I felt that," he said, smiling. "Let's get on with the show. We only have an hour, folks. Here's your husband, Dr. Lex Vanderkellen!"

Lex came out, smiling and waving to the audience. He took a seat beside Connie.

"Lex, did you know your wife was fooling around with cooking utensils?" Jerry asked.

Lex shrugged, grinning. "Hey, I didn't know she could even be that spontaneous let alone creative!" he said proudly.

"It was a dream," Connie said frustrated. Lex reached over and patted her hand. "Of course it was, honey," he said soothingly, "and not a bad one at that!"

"Well, if you like that," Jerry told him knowingly, "then let's hope you like the other creative pursuits your wife has been up to."

Lex and Connie exchanged uneasy glances, neither certain of what was to come.

"Here's one of the men in your wife's life!" Jerry announced.

Connie tried to get up and flee, but Lex was holding her hand so tight it felt like he was cutting off her circulation. Together they watched as Real came from backstage. He was dressed in a blue-gray tuxedo, with a white ruffled shirt and a red bow tie. He looked as if he were going to a wedding–or at least his high school prom! The fact that he was carrying a bouquet of red roses only added to the illusion.

There were snickers in the audience, mostly directed at his attire.

Smiling at Connie, Real took a seat beside Connie, opposite her husband.

"Let's see," Jerry said, glancing at his notes, "Real, you're a chef, correct?"

Real nodded, glancing at Connie. "Yes."

Jerry looked at Connie. "I'll say one thing, you certainly have a thing for food."

"Well, food can be very sexy," Connie said, trying to defend herself, then wished she hadn't.

"Real, why are you here?" Jerry asked.

"I'm here to woo the woman I love, Jerry," Real said, glancing at Connie.

"Go ahead and tell her."

Lex tried to stare Real down, but the beefy chef ignored his glare. "Connie –'

"Get on your knees!" the audience chanted. "Get on your knees!"

Real handed the bouquet to Connie, then he slowly kneeled in front of her.

Lex watched as if he could not believe this was happening.

Real took Connie's hand in his and looked deeply into her eyes. "Connie," he began, "I am here for you, because I love you, and I would like nothing more than to spend the rest of my life with you."

Connie closed her eyes. "Real, you're a wonderful person," she spoke, opening her eyes and looking directly into his. "You're a good man with a kind heart, but I cannot be with you. My heart tells me I belong with someone else." She glanced over at Lex who sat stone-faced. "No matter how much we wish things could be different, we can't change how they are."

Real nodded. "I know," he said quietly. "Just know that I love you and that I'll always be here if things change and even if they don't."

Connie expected no less from Real than being sincere and caring. The audience "Ohhhed" and "Ahhhed", apparently touched by Real's words.

"Well, if she doesn't want you, Chef Hunk," Mrs. Hoover quipped and smiled sweetly at Real, "you can cook in my kitchen anytime! Hmmm, we could make delicious casseroles together!"

"I don't care for casseroles," Real said quickly, not looking at her.

"Don't knock it till you've tried it," Mrs. Hoover told him.

"No, no," Kimiko chimed in, shaking her head vigorously. "You eat, you die!"

Real got to his feet, kissed Connie on the cheek and strode off the stage without looking back. Connie looked after him, wondering if she had just seen Real for the last time.

For a moment, Jerry was speechless, looking after the chef. "That was one of our most dramatic exits–ever," he said.

Connie brushed away a tear.

"That was truly touching," Jerry observed, "but, in true Jerry Springer fashion, we're not done yet."

Connie put a hand to her temple as if she were getting a headache, but she was really wracking her brain trying to figure out what else there could be. It had dawned on her just about the time the next guest walked out onto stage.

Jimmy!

Sitting with the other wives, moving only occasionally when stage hands brought out additional chairs, SueAnn watched what was happening to Connie. She still didn't know why she was on stage at "The Jerry Springer Show," she reminded herself. Unable to shake a sense of dread that had settled over her, she had a feeling things would get a lot worse before they got better. All she could do was wait–and watch what was happening to Connie.

"Welcome Jimmy, everyone," Jerry said in a lively voice.

Connie covered her eyes with her hand. She could not believe what was happening. *It's my worse nightmare,* she thought, feeling a sense of helplessness to stop what was coming. If only I could wake up, she wished, and all this would be over.

"You slept with Jimmy?" Lex asked incredulously. "Are you addicted to sex, too?"

Connie shook her head. "No, it was an accident!" she said pleadingly.

"Gee, where have I heard that open before?" Jerry asked, then added. "Usually, it's the guy pleading hit-and-run!"

The audience screamed: "Jerrrrry! Jerrrrry!"

"Let's hear about this so-called accident," Lex urged when he audience had quieted down.

"It was all a bit mistake," Connie said. "I thought it was you. I had planned a surprise for you in your office, with the lights low and me in..." her voice trailed off as soon as she realized what she had just said.

"Go on," Jerry encouraged. "You were in...?"

"My husband's office," Connie said weakly. "I heard someone come in. I thought it was Lex, but it was Jimmy."

"And you let him have sex with you?" Lex asked as if he could not believe what he was hearing.

"Not once I knew who it was," Connie answered. "But, by then it was... too late."

"Well, at least your husband is getting his surprise," Jerry observed, "even though it's a bit delayed, you might say!"

"Dr. Vanderkellen, I'm sorry," Jimmy apologized. "Your wife was my first. I lost my virginity to her, and. I haven't been able to think of anything since."

"So, that's why your work is suffering?" Lex assumed.

Jimmy shrugged. "My work is suffering?" he said as if he had no clue this was happening. "I - I just haven't been able to concentrate. I'm almost thirty. I had never had sex before that day in your office. I planned to save myself for marriage. Now I'm here..." his voice trailed off.

"Why are you here?" Lex wanted to know.

Connie closed her eyes tightly. She was trying to will herself to be somewhere else, it wasn't working. When she opened her eyes she was still seated on stage at "The Jerry Springer Show" – and Jimmy's head wasn't spinning around till it popped off like that girl on "The Exorcist!"

"I-I'm here," Jimmy stuttered, "because I want to be with your wife again."

"What?" Lex asked incredulously.

"Absolutely not!" Connie erupted. She could hold it in no longer. "I didn't intend for it to happen the first time–and it certainly will not happen again!"

Jimmy smiled uneasily. "Well, truthfully it already happened twice. Remember, you said something about being spontaneous. That time was just as good as the first. I'm sure the next time will be even better. So, why are you saying no to me now?" he asked cluelessly.

Connie stuttered and Lex looked between her and Jimmy. "I just spelled it out for you! NO! NO! NO!"

"I thought it was just foreplay," Jimmy said quietly. "Or, that you were playing hard to get." He gave Connie one last pleading look. "Are you sure you don't want to –"

Connie looked at him, shocked at what she'd just heard. "When hell freezes over!" she said, her voice tight.

Jimmy nodded. "Ooh, gotcha," he assured her with a deep frown. "I'll be the one shivering!"

Connie closed her eyes and wished he would just disappear.

"Wow, you don't want to get her riled up anymore than you have," Jerry warned Jimmy, then turned looked at Connie. "So, I take it that's a no?"

Connie gave Jerry a soul scorching look.

"Okay," Jerry backed off. "I just got a glimpse of hell. It's hot down there–and scary, too. Connie, I take it you have other ideas than what young Jimmy proposes?"

"I want to stay with my husband," Connie said quietly, composing herself, "and try to work things out."

"Lex?" Jerry asked.

"I'm willing to try," Lex agreed, "especially if Connie will show me how to masturbate with silverware!"

The audience erupted in laughter and applause.

Lex turned toward his wife, Connie turned away, a disgusted look on her face. She hoped she was making the right decision, but she had been totally honest with Real, she had to follow her heart.

34

Jerry Springer Take Two

"Ariella, you have no idea why you're here, right?" Jerry asked.

Ariella smiled, her shiny red lips as beautiful as her perfect face, olive skin and dark and mysterious amber eyes. "Jerry, I just came here to have a good time!" she announced with enthusiasm and pumped her fist in the air.

The audience cheered her on.

"Well, that's always a good reason to be here," Jerry said when the audience had quieted down, "but someone also wanted you to be here. Actually, several people–and all these people, too!" Jerry gestured toward the audience.

The audience chanted. "Jerrrrry! Jerrrrry!"

Ariella smiled, but she wasn't quite as confident. She knew the other wives weren't the only ones getting 'surprises.' It appeared she was about to get a surprise of her own. Her mind was a blur as she wondered who could have wanted her here–and why. She wondered if she should have listened closer to that damned Kimiko. Maybe there was some cryptic message in the psychic's message that she'd missed?

"Are you ready?" Jerry asked her.

Glancing around at the other wives, Ariella took a deep breath and nodded.

"Come on out," Jerry invited.

Ariella looked back at the stage entrance, her heart pounding. She truly did not know who was going to step onto the stage. Her heart fell to her feet when her young gardener, John, came on stage and came over. He stopped a few steps away and stared at her as if trying to gauge her reaction. She gave him a cold 'what the hell are you thinking?' look, her full lips pouty and unresponsive as he tried to kiss her. She turned her head and his lips planted a kiss somewhere between her upper neck and ear.

The stage hands placed a chair beside Ariella and John seated himself. He glanced nervously Ariella and then at Jerry, who was discussing something with the short, stout man, who was the series' director.

"Welcome, John," Jerry greeted the handsome, dark-haired young man. "Good to have you here."

"Speak for yourself," Ariella said under her breath.

"John, you say that you and Ariella have been fooling around for a while now," Jerry said. "How did you meet?"

"I cut her grass," John answered uneasily.

"I've never heard it called that!" Jerry joked.

The audience erupted in laughter.

"I'm her gardener," John added.

"Oh, I see," Jerry said. "So, how did this start?"

"Well, we started talking when her husband wasn't there," John explained. "She was nice and friendly. She offered me cookies and milk –"

"If she tucked you in," Jerry teased, "we have another Jerry Springer first!"

Sporadic audience laughter.

"No, no," John protested. "We talked and became friends, and she started telling me that her husband wasn't turning her on the way he did when they were first married. She said he was mostly interested in work and that he wasn't interested in doing anything new or trying anything different."

"Sexually?" Jerry pressed.

"Yes."

"So you, and Ariella tried new things together," Jerry pressed on, "new positions?"

"Yeah we tried new positions in new places. We've done it in places she said her husband would never do it."

"You didn't do it in the dirt?" Jerry teased.

John nodded. "Yeah, Jerry." He swallowed hard and gave a little nervous smile. "We did it in their flower beds right next to the next to the azaleas under the wisteria."

The audience cheered and laughed.

"You're having sex with your gardener?" Jerry asked Ariella once the noise had quieted.

"It was just a fling," Ariella said flatly. "That's all."

"That's all," John repeated. "Ariella, I love you. I want us to have a life together, build a future and start a family."

The audience "Ohhhed."

"You can roll around in my grass anytime!" a woman yelled excitedly at John.

Ariella rolled her eyes. "Start a family?" she repeated "John, what we had was fun, but that's all it was. It was never anything serious. You're going to have lots of women your age chasing after you. I belong with my husband."

"Does your husband know you've been getting down and dirty with the young gardener?" Jerry asked, curious.

"I have a feeling he will now!" Ariella answered in a worried voice.

"Obviously, you've seen our show," Jerry quipped and then sounded apologetic. "I don't want to get personal, but how are things between you and your husband now?"

"If by things you mean sex," Ariella responded, glancing at John, "the answer is much better. We have great sex several times a week and it's great!"

John looked at her, his face hard with anger. "So, you've been cheating on me with your husband?" he asked.

Ariella gave him an incredulous look. "That's not even possible," she told him.

"I do believe she's right," Jerry agreed with Ariella. "I'm not sure exactly what the official rules are, but I'm not sure you can cheat on the other person." He shrugged. "Well... I guess she's right."

Marco came storming onto stage, putting his finger in John's face. "You're damned right she's right!" Marco piped in loudly, then he turned his anger on John. "When I'm done with you, you little pecker-pumpin' twerp, you won't be planting anything anywhere for a long, long time!"

John got to his feet. "Hey, don't make threats," he said, ripping his shirt open to reveal his hard, smooth chest and washboard abs.

Giji took one look and started to fan herself.

"Giji, are you okay?" Jerry asked, concerned.

"Oh, Jerry, I'm fine," she assured the talk show host. "Whew! It's getting hot in here!"

The audience applauded and cheered.

"What can I say," Giji said, grinning. "From where I sit, a lawn does a body good!"

As if in a macho response to John's actions, Marco ripped open his own shirt, revealing his well-toned, muscular chest which was covered with dark hair but still appeared tanned and muscular.

The boxing bell dinged and Marco and John sparred a little and shoved each other as the security guards moved into break them up.

"You were supposed to be cutting my lawn, not screwing my wife!" Marco told him, breathing hard.

John raised his hands as if surrendering. "Hey, she gave it up," he pleaded, also winded, "it's not like I had to take it!"

Marco leapt at John again and the younger man fled backstage and did not return.

"What were you thinking?" Marco demanded standing over Ariella.

"You don't own me," Ariella shot back. "As I recall, you've had some indiscretions of your own!"

Hanging his head, Marco sank into the chair beside his wife.

"Is that true, Marco?" Jerry asked.

Marco looked up at Jerry. "I'm afraid so, Jerry," he admitted and glanced at is wife who sat very still and did not return his gaze.

"Isn't it also true that you also have a surprise for Ariella?"

Marco nodded. "I do, Jerry."

Ariella turned and looked at him, her fiery eyes searching his handsome face for any clue.

"Well, let's not keep Ariella in suspense any longer," Jerry said.

"What is this about?" Ariella asked, already sounding a bit angry.

"Well, Ariella," Marco said nervously, "I have someone here, too."

"Let me guess," Ariella said, thinking back to the few episodes of 'The Jerry Springer Show,' "you have a male lover? A transvestite hooker or some drag queen –"

"No, no," Marco told her. "It's nothing like that."

Tia came from backstage, holding a baby bundled in a baby blue blanket.

Ariella looked at Tia and the baby then at her husband, an incredulous look on her face as if she couldn't believe what she was seeing. "You got Tia pregnant?" she said angrily, then slapped her husband across the face. "You horny Latino pig!" she spat angrily.

"Listen to me," Marco pleaded.

Ariella ignored her husband, raised her short skirt revealing her nice round ass, young and tight, smooth olive skin. She swiveled her hips, grinding her ass seductively as she turned to face the audience. With her skirt up and one hand in her panties and the other holding up her blouse, she played with one nipple while she fingered her pussy.

The men in the audience cheered and whistled.

"Hey, you can stop that!" Marco yelled at her.

"Why?" Ariella asked defiantly. "None of this, ain't none of yours!"

"You can bring that over here!" a guy in the audience yelled.

A heavyset guy with a beard and a beer belly hanging over the front of his jeans suddenly leapt to his feet and called for Jerry who held the mike for the guy.

"Yeah, doll," the heavyset guy said, "come be my Latina princess!"

"As a Latina Queen," Ariella said and pretended to pout, "I'm insulted!"

"Ariella, I would have your children!" a guy in the audience yelled.

"As soon as you can ovulate and carry a child to term, give me a call!" Ariella yelled back, her hands on her curvy hips. "I'll use my ex-husband's generous alimony to pay for your maternity wear, sweetie!"

Marco gave the guy a stern look of warning, then turned back to his wife. "Would you just listen, please?"

"I've enjoyed a certain Latin hunk myself," Mrs. Hoover interjected, licking her lips. "He's easy on the eyes and sweet on the tongue!"

The audience cheered, laughed and made howling sounds like a dog.

Ariella turned on Marco again. "You horndog!" she shrieked. "You and...ah...I can't even say it, Mrs.-Mrs. Hoover? What the hell were you thinking!"

Marco shrugged. "She knew about Tia," he explained. "She was going to tell you... everything!"

"That's your excuse? You should have told me," she told him, "but let's not talk it anymore. The images flashing before my eyes are more than a little disturbing!"

"Please listen to what I have to say," Marco pleaded.

Ariella looked at him coldly as she smoothed her clothing, and then, without any warning, she slapped him again. "I'm not sure I want to hear anything you have to say!"

"Just listen, please," Marco continued. "Hear me out. I want us to be a family and raise the baby together."

"What do you think about all this, Ariella?" Jerry asked. "I'll step back and let you tell Marco what you really think."

"Well," Ariella began, looking directly at Marco, "it doesn't look like you need me. Looks like you've already gotten the little family you always wanted. I hope you will all be happy together."

"I want you," Marco told her in a tight voice. "I want us to be a family."

"Us?" Ariella repeated, glancing at Tia and the baby then back at her husband. "I'm not sure what you're getting at, but I'm not sharing you with Tia!"

"Looks like you've been doing that already," Jerry pointed out. "What exactly do you mean, Marco?"

Ariella slapped him again. "That is so sick," she said loudly, her voice tight with anger. "You, me and Tia raising your love child!"

"No, it's not like that," Marco assured her. "Tia will give us the baby to raise as ours together. You and me, baby. We can be a family."

"Is that what you want, Tia?" Jerry asked.

Tia smiled sweetly. "I want what Marco wants," she said quietly.

"I want Ariella and I to raise my son," Marco said and almost as soon as he got the words out of his mouth Tia's mother, a small Latina woman with fire in her eyes, came racing from backstage and began slapping and hitting Marco while he cowered.

"Mama, no!" Tia pleaded.

Ariella started to walk away, then paused and said, "I'm done with this shit. C'mon, Steve. Let's go party, baby!"

"You go girlfriend!" Giji called.

Marco watched as Ariella put her dainty arm inside Steve's muscular arm. After she blew the audience a kiss, she and Jerry's head of security strode off the stage together, while the audience chanted: "Steve! Steve! Steve! Steve! Steve!"

***

"SueAnn," Jerry began, "You've been waiting patiently for quite a while, and I take it you still have no idea why you're here?"

SueAnn shook her head. "No, Jerry. I don't have a clue, really." There was sporadic laughter in the audience and even among those seated onstage. Jerry grinned. "Ah, shucks," he said, "I was hoping you were here to see me!"

"That's why I came," SueAnn assured him, "to see you, I mean."

"Ah, you're sweet," Jerry said, taking her hand and helping her to her feet.

"Now, SueAnn, you were recently kidnapped by bank robbers in addition to the whole fruit salad thing and others." Jerry read from his note card. "It sounds like you lead a very adventurous life. It may be even more outrageous than Giji's."

"Now, Jerry, don't get carried away," Giji protested.

"Yes, don't," SueAnn said, "I'm nothing like her."

Getting an idea, she quickly added, "She sleeps with clients to close deals!"

The audience gasped.

"She exposed herself to the whole neighborhood when she wore a dress that became invisible when she fell into the pool!" Giji spat.

The audience laughed.

"I had to rescue her from the trunk of her car where she got locked inside while having sex with a stranger she picked up on the freeway!"

The audience burst into uncontrollable laughter.

Deciding that last one would be tough to top, Giji wisely chose not to continue to pursue retaliation. Instead she smiled and smoothed her blouse, her hands sliding up and down over her huge breasts and obviously erect nipples! As an added bonus, she twirled around and quickly lifted her short-short skirt revealing her perfectly round ass and letting everyone know she wasn't wearing panties! The audience loved the visual.

"Okay, let's pull ourselves away from the lovely Miss Brickhouse and get back to SueAnn," Jerry urged. Some members of the audience, mostly male, booed. "SueAnn," Jerry began knowingly, "someone is here to see you. We've kept you waiting long enough. I promised you would eventually know why you're here."

Standing beside the talk show host, SueAnn gave her sexiest 'girl next door' smile. "Yes, you did, Jerry," she said so sweetly some of the other wives almost cringed.

"Well, I'm not going to keep you waiting any longer," Jerry said. "Someone has a secret to reveal to you today on our show."

SueAnn could not speak, she just bit her lower lip, wondering who could have wanted her here–and what the secret could be. She had a sinking feeling inside after seeing what the other wives had just endured, she had a feeling it wouldn't be anything good.

"Are you ready?" Jerry asked.

SueAnn's lips moved, but, again, no words came out.

Jerry frowned at her lack of response. "I'm going to take that as a no," he teased, "but the show must go on. Let's bring out the person who's here to reveal a secret to SueAnn."

The last person SueAnn expected to see step onstage was Nick, especially after it was apparent he and Giji were involved. Yet there he was coming from backstage toward her, smiling. Once he reached her, he gave her a kiss on the cheek and took her hand in his. For a brief time she searched his eyes, trying to get a clue what he was doing here and what he was about to reveal, but his eyes gave nothing away, except a tinge of concern. That made her even more worried.

Briefly, she glanced at Giji who was watching them closely as if she were also wondering what the hell was going on.

Kimiko patted Giji's hand offering comfort. "I am Sexual Psychic," she said, "but I not see this coming!"

"That makes two of us," SueAnn said flatly.

Jerry turned and grinned at the audience. "I know. He's not as handsome as I am," he said in a sly voice, "but whatcha gonna do, huh?" He winked. "Now Nick, are you ready to come clean with SueAnn?"

Nick glanced uneasily at SueAnn, then looked at Jerry and nodded. "I'm as ready as I'll ever be."

SueAnn looked puzzled. "What's going on?" she asked in a weak voice. "Nick?"

"SueAnn," Nick began, then he went on to explain how he and his twin brother had come up with the idea to date her and Giji without telling either of them that they were twins. "When Nate suggested it, it seemed like an interesting idea, maybe even fun. We had to plan how we would keep from being seen together, who would stay at my house which night of the week, and who would date who on any given night so we wouldn't be out at the same time on different dates."

Jerry gave the audience a quick look. "Yeah, that would have been like deja vu or something!"

"More like deja voodoo!" Kimiko quipped.

SueAnn gave Nick a sobering look. "How could you do this?"

"At the time we didn't know how we would feel about either of you," Nick tried to explain. "We figured we might end up as friends or that we might never date again after that first date. If we ended up as friends or more, I figured we'd have a good laugh over it when you and Giji figured it out."

SueAnn looked at Nick on the verge of tears. "So you played with my feels and Giji's," she said quietly.

"I'm sorry, SueAnn," Nick apologized. "I realized it was a mistake and wanted to come clean with you, but as it went on it became more complicated. The big problem was Nate developed feelings for Giji, and I developed feelings for you. When it was obvious we would continue seeing each other again and were developing feelings for each other, it became more complicated and obvious to us that we had made a huge mistake. It was a mistake that would not be easy to explain." He took a deep breath. "The last thing I ever wanted to do was hurt you."

SueAnn brushed a tear from her eye, determined not to cry. "Well, you did, and I don't know that I would ever want to be seriously involved with someone who takes the feelings of others for granted this way," she said a bit more forcefully now.

Nick shrugged. "I was afraid you'd feel this way," he admitted.

"I do." She gave him a cold stare.

He tried to pull her to him and hug her tightly, but she quickly pulled away.

The audience "Ahhhed."

"I know," Jerry agreed with the audience. "I'm tempted to hug the guy! But we have another guest to welcome. Here's Nick's twin brother Nate!"

Nick's identical twin came out, dressed exactly as Nick, in jeans and a tight T-shirt

"It give me double-vision!" Kimiko said loudly.

"Nate's kind of like a male Giji," Mrs. Hoover observed. "I can see why they would be attracted to each other."

"It won't last," Kimiko warned. "They be like two flames but– no good–they burn each other out!"

"We've already burned out!" Giji piped in.

"It's almost like having sex with themselves!" Mrs. Hoover added.

"Now that's just sick," Connie noted, cutting her eyes toward Giji.

Nate said hello to Jerry, gave his brother a supportive pat on the back and went directly to Giji. She seemed oblivious to his presence at first, then he took her hand in his and pulled her to her feet. He tried to kiss her, but she raised her hand as a warning for him to back off.

"She's a spitfire!" he said to Jerry and the audience. "See why

I love her?"

Jerry gave Giji a quick look from head to toe. "Oh, yeah, we can definitely see why you love her," he told Nate. "What do you want to say to Giji?"

He looked at Giji. "Just that I am crazy about her," he began. "I've never felt this way about a woman before! I think we have something special, and I want to see where it takes us."

"And, Giji, what do you think of that?" Jerry asked.

"Hmmm, it's a chance for SuSu and I to have matching boyfriends and maybe someday identical husbands!" Giji said sarcastically. "Sorry, Nate," Giji told him. "I really like you and I enjoyed our time together. But, it's time to move on. Besides, the whole twin thing has me feeling deceived, lied to and used. What else can I say now that you reduced our relationship to silly putty!"

A few members of the audience laughed at the last remark.

"I never meant to hurt you, Giji," Nate said pleadingly. "I really feel we have something special that we could build on."

Giji sighed, disinterested. "It was pretty much over before we came here," she told him. "I'm not looking for a long-term relationship right now. All I wanna do is have some fun!"

Nate nodded, his face drawn showing his disappointment. "I have to accept that," he agreed. "Good luck, Giji. I wish you the best."

After kissing Giji on the cheek, Nate turned and went back stage.

SueAnn seemed to be hyperventilating.

"SueAnn, are you okay?" Jerry asked.

"I... I think so," SueAnn stammered.

"Bring her some water," Jerry ordered.

Quickly a member of Jerry's staff brought a small paper cup of water. SueAnn drank a couple of sips and seemed to be better.

"I'm fine now, Jerry," SueAnn spoke. "I have something to say to Nick."

"The floor is yours!" Jerry told her.

"Thank you, Jerry." SueAnn smiled then turned to Nick. "I'm shocked by what you've said here, by what you did. I thought we had something between us."

"We do, we do," Nick assured her. "Just give me a chance to prove it to you."

"I can't right now," SueAnn said softly. "I have been trying so hard to believe in you and trust you, and now all of this has been revealed, finally. I don't know if we can ever go back and pick up what we had or if we can move forward and work on what we share."

"Please," Nick pleaded.

"Get down on your knees!" the audience chanted. "Get down on your knees!"

Nick got up from his chair and sank to his knees in front of SueAnn. "I'll do anything to make it up to you, SueAnn, honest I will. Please give me a chance to show you how much you mean to me."

SueAnn looked into Nick's eyes. "I wish I could," she began. "I hope I can eventually, but I can't right now." She drew in her breath, "I can't promise anything, maybe eventually we can get past this and see where things go from there."

Nick kissed her hand and then he returned to his seat.

"Are you okay with waiting, Nick?" Jerry asked.

"I'll wait as long as it takes," Nick told him and reached over and took SueAnn's hand in his. "I'm sorry, SueAnn," he apologized again. "So many times I wanted to come clean, explain everything to you, but there never seemed to be a right time. Then when 'The Jerry Springer Show' came to town and Wynette told me you were going –"

"Wynette, you knew this," SueAnn asked incredulously, "and you didn't tell me?"

Wynette smiled sheepishly. "I knew Nick was going to be here," she admitted quietly, "but I didn't know the whole story. I had no idea Nick has a twin brother!"

"How did you keep from being seen together?" SueAnn

wanted to know. "And being found out?"

"It was very tricky," Nick admitted. "We had to be very careful not to be in the area at the same time."

"And, of course, we both had to drive Nick's pickup," Nate said. "That helped keep us both from being in the neighborhood at the same time."

An idea occurred to SueAnn. "Wh-who did I kiss and...?"

Nick knew this was coming. He looked at her uneasily, apologetically. "Unfortunately, both," he answered simply. "You kissed both of us and... more."

"Oh, great," SueAnn cried, then in a calmer voice, admitted, "That explains a lot."

"That doesn't explain why you chose that whiny bitch over me!" Giji said under her breath.

"Giji, did you want to say something?" Jerry asked.

"Congratulations to you both!" Giji lied and put on her best faux smile.

"SueAnn didn't forgive him yet," Jerry pointed out.

"True," Giji agreed. "I'm getting ahead of myself!"

"Okay, well, we have another surprise guest!" Jerry announced.

SueAnn closed her eyes. It was hard to believe this was really happening, she decided, feeling a bit nauseous as she wondered who this new guest could possibly be.

"Here he is!"

SueAnn nearly passed out as Nick and Nate's dad came from backstage. All she could think of was the day he walked in on her naked and covered with fresh fruit!

"Well, there's someone else who wants a crack at SueAnn," Jerry announced and winked. "My, my, you're a very popular girl!"

Nick and Nate's father came from backstage. "My name is Mac, and I'm the Mac Daddy!" he announced in a loud, proud voice, waving his arms about spastically as he joined the others on stage.

"Dad?" Nick exclaimed. "What are you doing here?"

"I'm here to claim my prize," his dad announced. "Sweet SueAnn!" He looked at SueAnn. "What do you say, darling? Lose these clowns and come with me, the old ball that started everything rolling!"

The crowd roared with laughter.

SueAnn was speechless.

"Come on, sweetheart," he pleaded. "I've already seen you naked!"

Giji rolled her eyes. "Who hasn't?" she quipped.

The audience broke into a long burst of laughter.

"So," Jerry said when the audience had quieted down, "how'd it happen that Nick's dad saw you naked, SueAnn?"

"I was trying to surprise Nick," SueAnn explained weakly. "His dad came in instead... and that's pretty much what happened."

"It was love at first sight for me," the old guy announced. "I haven't been able to get her out of my head since!"

SueAnn closed her eyes and tried to wish herself away. Right now she wanted to be anywhere else but here.

"Sweetie, we can make beautiful noise together," he persisted.

"Mac Daddy," the audience chanted. "Mac Daddy!"

The older man pounded his fist in time with the audience chants.

"Be careful, Dad," Nick warned. "You know the doctor warned you not to get too excited. He said your pace maker could short out!"

The crowd let go with another outburst of laughter.

"Well, okay," Jerry said as the laughter again subsided. "Does this mean you're not choosing dear ole dad?"

"As tempted as I am, I'm afraid I'll have to say no," SueAnn told him. "I'm not sure I'm prepared to choose anyone." She closed her eyes, trying to remain calm. "This has to be a dream," she whispered to herself. "No, a nightmare. This has to be a nightmare."

"Speak up!" Jerry told her. "We can't hear you."

"I choose," SueAnn said in a monotone voice, "to remain on my own."

As she spoke those words, she looked at Nick and she could see the deep lines of disappointment on his handsome face. She wanted to reach out to him, comfort him, but she couldn't... not after what she'd just learned. Knowing that Nick had deceived her, violated the trust she had been trying to build in him while she had been dating not only him but also his twin brother. She had wondered why he seemed to change from one date to the next, and then the Sexual Psychic had said Nick had two faces. Now she knew why! It all made sense now. She had been dating two men...and she did not really know either of them! Her eyes blurry with tears despite her resolve, SueAnn ran off stage....

35

The Explosion

"As you may have noticed," Jerry addressed the audience. "Giji has gone backstage. She has a surprise for us." He winked at the audience. "Gee, I can't wait to see what it is."

"Yes," Mrs. Hoover said flatly, "I thought we had seen everything! It's not like she's been saving much for the imagination."

"Well, we don't have to wait much longer," Jerry announced. "Here's Giji!"

Giji came back onstage hand in hand with a companion, Charmaine. Dressed identical, they wore black shiny vinyl dominatrix outfits that clung to their shapely bodies, skin tight, and that lifted their impressive boobs to best advantage and were wearing matching black stiletto heels and each carrying a whip in her free hand.

Mrs. Hoover rolled her eyes. "Pinch me, I think I've gone to hell!"

"Not more twins!" Kimiko wailed. "Please god no!"

"Wow!" Jerry gasped at the sight of the two blonde beauties.

"Amazing! You two are so hot!"

"Thank you, Jerry," they said in unison. "We wore these just for you!"

"In that case, thank you," Jerry said, still smiling. "So, Giji, introduce us to your sexy friend."

"Okay, Jerry," Giji began, "this is my friend and neighbor Charmaine."

"Welcome, Charmaine, everyone!"

"Hi, everyone," Charmaine said sweetly and swiveled her slim hips.

"So, Giji," Jerry observed, "you said you were considering changing your line of work from being a real estate agent to... a dominatrix?"

Giji shook her blonde tresses. "No, Jerry, I'm thinking of becoming a stripper!"

The audience chanted. "Giji! Giji!"

"Really?" Jerry asked.

"Yes, Jerry, I'm thinking about dancing with Charmaine at Vixens Gentleman's Club."

"Well, I guess that's okay for career advancement!" Jerry quipped. "Wanna give us a preview?"

"Just for you, Jerry," Giji said and winked.

"It like watching porno movie," Kimiko decided. "Ooh, I like! Shiny go-go girls crazy fun!"

As the music came up, pounding drums and screaming guitars, the two young women started dancing together, gyrating their hips while they cracked their whips on the stage. The two entwined their bodies, the shiny, smooth outfits pressing together, their boobs coming together, then apart and their pussies also touching as their hands explored each other, sliding across a thigh here and a round, firm hip there.

The guitar-driven music faded and the softer hip hop beats and acoustic guitar of Sex On the Beach's "Burning for You" came up with each of the women lip-syncing the words: "Always want you, babe. You're the only one. Ah yeah! Oooh! Can't you feel the desire...Can't you see I'm on fire. Can't you see I'm on fire. Can't you see I'm on fire. I'm burning for you! Move your hips and I'll move mine. I'm burning for you."

The sensual movements of the two women drove the audience, especially the male portion, into a frenzy of excited cheers, applause and cat calls.

Suddenly, Giji dropped her whip, fell to her knees and hugged Charmaine's legs. Quickly, she gave her friend a kiss between her legs on the area of her outfit that covered her pussy.

The audience cheered even louder.

Charmaine tossed her whip aside and sank to her knees and the two women embraced, kissing each other's necks, then Charmaine started to caress Giji's ample breasts, pushing them even closer together until they looked like they would explode out of the top of her outfit.

Their dance climaxed with the two women sharing a lingering lip-to-lip kiss that left the audience cheering and applauding.

"Man, I haven't seen a kiss like that since Madonna laid one on Britney!" Jerry said as the dancing ceased and the music quieted. "Steve is gonna whip himself for missing this!"

"Jerrrrry! Jerrrrry!" the audience chanted.

"Whew!" Jerry wiped his brow. "Is it hot in here or what? That's so damned hot I should have saved it for pay-per-view! You girls give me fever!"

***

"Giji," Jerry began, "there's someone here to see you."

"Really?" Giji said, thinking Nick was here to surprise her. Could he be planning to propose to her on 'The Jerry Springer Show'? she wondered, almost unable to control her excitement. She felt a little faint just thinking about it!

"Yes, really," Jerry assured her, "but first, Giji, we have a little surprise for you, too. Do these cute kids look familiar?"

Giji turned and looked at the large flat-panel TV screen on the wall behind the stage. She seemed shocked when the picture of a mousy brown haired girl with narrow cat-eye glasses and a slight over bite appeared on the screen. Beside the first picture another of a nerdy guy with a crew cut, buckteeth and huge Adam's apple appeared.

"Tha-that's me and my ex-husband Darrell," Giji admitted reluctantly. "We were a couple of crazy kids, barely out of high school when we met, and –"

Listening backstage, Ariella came back out with Steve close behind her. "You were married before?" Ariella asked, surprised. For months she thought she was becoming intimate friends with Giji and now to learn something this important on "The Jerry Springer Show." She felt hurt and slighted.

"Yes, I was married once," Giji admitted, sounding uncomfortable talking about it. "We were married in Vegas at the Love Me Tender Wedding Chapel. He was an Elvis impersonator I met while cruising the strip and I was a would-be Marilyn Monroe looking for work. Not exactly a match made in Heaven." She paused as if remembering. "I believe he left me for a waitress from the hotel lounge while I was changing out of my wedding dress!"

"You, Marilyn...?" Ariella repeated, still upset. "Gee, this is pretty funny, but I don't know whether to laugh or cry!"

"Are you ready, Giji?" Jerry asked, sounding concerned.

Giji shrugged. "Aside from the fact that I never want to see my ex-husband again," Giji started, "I guess so."

"Well, here he is!" Jerry announced. "Giji's ex-husband, Darrell."

A tall, lanky guy with the same huge Adam's apple came rushing out from backstage. "Hey everybody!" he said in a weaselily voice. "Hey Jerry!" He leaned toward Giji like he wanted a kiss. "Hey hot stuff!"

"Hey," Giji managed to say.

"So what'dya got to say for yourself?" he demanded of Giji.

She shrugged.

"What is this about?" Jerry asked him.

"Well, hell, man, I woke up after a night of drinking and playing poker with the guys," he began. "Once I recovered from my hangover, I realized it was just me and ole Rover in the trailer house."

"You mean Giji was gone?" Jerry asked.

"Hell, yes, man," Darrell told him. "The sweetest piece of pussy I ever did have was gone. Not even a note. She just left like that."

"Giji, you left...?" Jerry asked.

Giji nodded. "Okay, I made up the part about him taking off with that waitress," Giji admitted. "It was me who left, but Jerry, I warned him. He just wouldn't listen. I told him I'd leave if he didn't stop, but he repeatedly did the Cabbage Patch after we had sex!"

The crowded roared.

Jerry frowned. "Surely, there was more to your marriage ending than that."

"It was just so annoying."

"Like celebrating a touchdown in the middle of the game?" Ariella ventured.

"Exactly!" Giji exclaimed. "To be honest, I never understood the need for celebrating, the sex certainly wasn't that good."

Again, the crowd roared.

"Jerry," Giji said when the audience had settled down, "if Darrell was any dumber, he'd be on life support!"

The audience laughed.

Darrell frowned. "Okay, Giji good one, you got me there," he stuttered, "but you're still my girl. Always keep you right here." He put a hand over his heart. "You always gonna be PDA!"

"PDA?" Jerry repeated uncertainly.

"Pretty damned terrific, Jerry." He did a simulated toke, slow exhale. "Giji is one hot bitch!" he drawled. "Freaking PDA!"

"There were so many annoying things. Like when he slept with my friend Monique. Then to get even I slept with his best friend Shawn."

"And Pete. And Mark. And Joe –"

"Who's keeping score here?" Giji interrupted. "I figured our marriage was over at Monique!"

"I figured the same thing at Shawn!"

Giji batted her eyes. "Okay, so we're both right," she told him. "Monique! Shawn! Whatever! End of marriage."

Jerry adjusted his glasses, looking at his notes. "Giji, there is something else," he said.

"Yes, Jerry," Giji said quietly, a thought occurring to her. Could her ex-husband be the person who had been calling her for months? If anyone were capable of such rotten behavior, she decided, it was Darrell.

"Someone has been calling you for months, harassing you and even making threats, is that right?"

Giji nodded, looking closely at Darrell to see his reaction. The surprised look on his face made her believe he genuinely did not know.

"Someone has been stalking you?" Darrell repeated as if unsure to believe what he had just heard.

"Yes," Giji said. "Calling me, anyway." She paused, looking into his eyes. "Darrell, was it you?"

Darrell shook his head. "No, no way," he denied. "I wouldn't do that. I care too much about you for that. Deep down you know it, too. If I was the one who had been calling you, would I be here now on 'The Jerry Springer Show' in front of all these people asking you for another chance?"

"I don't know," Giji said simply. "I don't...know."

"I wouldn't, Gi," he assured her. "I'm here to win you back, you're my girl," he added, trying to take her hand in his but she pulled away.

"Save it, Darrell," she said quickly, remembering her past with Darrell, a past she wanted to forget...forever. "It was over between us almost before we finished saying I do!"

"You're breaking my heart, girl," Darrell said, putting a hand on his chest.

"Too bad, Darrell," Giji said, defiantly. "It's too little, too late."

"So, Giji, who are you gonna chose?" Jerry wanted to know.

"Choose me, Giji," Darrell pleaded. "Girl, you don't know what you're missing. I have a good job now in the manufactured housing industry. I can get you that double-wide you always dreamed of!"

The audience snickered.

"Don't forget Nick," Jerry said, then corrected himself. "Ah, I meant Nate. He's pretty smitten with you I'd say."

"I've made a decision," Giji announced and paused for dramatic effect. "I choose...Jerrrrry! Jerrrrry!"

The crowd cheered Jerry with her, then they started chanting: "Kiss that cunt! Kiss that cunt!"

Jerry gave her a small kiss on her cheek. He turned away just as a stage hand slipped a slip of paper into his hand. "I've just been handed a note," Jerry said, his voice now hardened with concern. "It says a bomb has been hidden beneath the soundstage, and that we're all about... to die!"

Giji seemed to be the first person who reacted to what Jerry had read. She wrapped herself around the talk show host as if seeking protection.

For a few awkward moments there was a disbelieving silence from the guests onstage and the audience as if no one was sure if the note was real or a cruel prank. Suddenly, everyone seemed to realize it could be true, especially when Jerry's security personnel whisked him off stage. Jerry headed backstage with Giji clinging to his side, his staff closely in tow.

"Let's clear the building," the head of Jerry's security told the audience. "There's been a bomb threat!"

"Is this a publicity stunt?" several people were asking as people scurried about in a frantic effort to get to the exits as quickly as possible. "Is this for real?"

***

Giji stayed close to Jerry and his bodyguards as they left the warehouse where the episode of "The Jerry Springer Show" was being taped. They exited out a side door and hurried toward a waiting limo.

Jerry had his arm around Giji's waist as they approached the limo. He helped Giji into the back and then slid into the seat beside her. One of the bodyguards got into the back with them, and the other, after closing the door, got into the passenger side in the front with the driver.

Giji closed her eyes and put her head on Jerry's shoulder, trying to calm down. Shortly she heard the engine start, and then she felt the car move forward. Jerry took her hand in his and she opened her eyes.

"Are you okay?" he asked, concerned.

Giji nodded slowly. "I'm better now," she said, relieved to be out of the building just in case the madman made good on his threat. She suddenly shivered at the thought and wondered where Charmaine had gone. She hoped her friend had gotten out of the building. After their dance, Charmaine had gone backstage to change and gather her things. That was the last time Giji had seen her...

"Are you cold?" Jerry asked, feeling her shaking.

Giji nodded. "A little."

Jerry motioned for his bodyguard to hand his trench coat from the other seat. Jerry placed it across Giji's lap to warm her. "Is that better?"

She smiled, appreciative. "Thanks."

"You're safe now," he told her, putting his arm around her shoulders. "It's going to be okay. This was probably just some wacko pulling a prank. The good news is that in most cases that's all these kinds of situations are...."

The quiet was suddenly broken by the sound of her cell phone ringing. She started to reach for it, but Jerry held her hand firmly.

"It can wait," he said in a calm voice.

Giji nodded, then lay her head back against Jerry's shoulder, feeling the reassuring warmth of him against her cheek. She felt safe, but she couldn't help thinking it was him calling. He was calling to taunt her, to threaten her, to... Suddenly, there was a loud boom. They were a couple of blocks from the warehouse when they heard the explosion...

***

"Have you guys seen SueAnn?" Nick asked Wynette and Steven as they exited the warehouse, mostly being pushed along by the frantic crowd exiting with them, heading toward the parking area.

"No," Steven said over the noisy crowd, "we thought she was with you."

"She must be here somewhere," Wynette told him, her eyes quickly searching the crowd ahead of them. She saw Ariella near the front of the crowd and Marco a bit behind her; Connie and Lex were walking together just ahead. "I don't see SueAnn," she said, suddenly worried.

Nick looked around him at people nearby, searching for a familiar face. "I have to find her," Nick said, turning back toward the building. "I'm going back inside."

"That's not a good idea," Steven said loudly, but Nick was already headed back toward the building entrance, people looking at him incredulously as he passed them headed in the opposite direction.

Steven caught Wynette by the forearm and pulled her aside so the crowd could pass them. "Go with Connie and Lex," Steven told her, looking in the direction Nick was headed then back at her. "I have to stop him."

Wynette caught his arm. "No, you can't –" But before she could get the words out of her mouth, there was a loud boom as the building exploded. She and Steven fell to the ground along with other people nearby as the impact swept into them with a force so strong it was like hitting a wall. Their ears were filled by the sound of the explosion, followed by hysterical screams. As they fell, Wynette and Steven saw Nick being pelted by dust and debris, then quickly being buried under falling brick and mortar. Suddenly the dust was so thick that they could no longer see the area where Nick was, in fact, they could barely see each other as Steven pulled Wynette close to him.

Following the explosion, time seemed suspended as if it were standing still, and they lay together for what seemed like forever, Steven holding her close, their eyes closed against the stinging dust, trying to breathe while all around them people coughed and choked on the dust-filled air.

After a while, the dust thinning, people started to move about around them. Occasionally they heard someone cry out in pain or call someone's name, and in the distance, they heard sirens blaring louder and louder, coming closer and closer....

Steven held her in the safety of his arms, Wynette thought of Nick and wondered how anyone could survive being buried under all that falling rubble. For SueAnn's sake...then she remembered, SueAnn.... Could she have been inside? She buried her face against her husband's chest and wept softly, wondering, *What has happened to SueAnn? Where is she?*

36

Jerry's First Nude Scene

In her sleep, Giji heard Mrs. Hoover singing "I Touch Myself" in the shower as she stirred from sleep and she sat up in bed with a start. It took her a few minutes to realize where she was; she was still getting used to her new place. It also took her a while to realize that it wasn't Mrs. Hoover singing in her shower. Who was it? she wondered, still half asleep. Who...? She tried to remember what she had done last night. There was a party, drinking, people dancing, hands....

She closed her eyes. It was all a blur.

Yawning, she started to get out of bed, deciding she would see who was showering, but just as she pushed the covers down, her cell phone rang. It seemed louder than normal, she thought, as she took it from the bedside table and answered. "Hello?" she said weakly, dryly, with a half-yawn.

"Hello, cunt," the caller said and Giji recognized the voice as that of her obscene caller. "I'm glad you survived my little talk show blast. You're quite the cunning bitch. I've just been reading all about you in Mrs. Hoover's diary!"

Giji paused, trying to wrap her brain around what she had just heard. "You... you planted the bomb?" she asked, her heart racing.

"That's right," the caller told her, laughing a deep, throaty laugh. "Now be a good girl and do exactly what I tell you and no one will get hurt."

Giji didn't say a word at first. She couldn't shake the shock–and fear–she was feeling. She knew she had heard the voice before. *Recently!* She had heard the voice at the taping of 'The Jerry Springer Show'!

"Darrell?" she screamed into the phone. "Oh my god, Darrell, what have you done?"

Again the laughter, only now it was louder and even more exaggerated like the laughter of clowns at a circus...

Giji could still hear his maniacal laugh as she stirred and awakened, sitting up in bed with a start, her heart pounding. Opening her eyes, she looked around the room. For a few seconds she was half asleep and did not recognize her surroundings and then she realized she was in her new apartment, in her bedroom, in her bed.

Relieved, she breathed deeply, almost a sigh of relief. It had all been a dream, she realized. The obscene caller! "The Jerry Springer Show"! Mrs. Hoover's little red...

Suddenly she could hear the water running in the adjoining master bath. Slipping out of bed, Giji realized for the first time that she was completely nude. Taking her robe from a chair, she slipped it on and fought the urge to run. What if it was him in her shower? Barefoot and shaking just a bit, she started toward the master bath. With a shaky hand she reached out and turned the door knob, slowly opening the door. Just as she stepped inside, bare feet on cold tile, the shower door swung open.

"Good morning, sleepyhead," a very wet Jerry Springer said, wearing nothing but a smile.

Behind Giji the phone started to ring.

Looking back toward the bedroom where the phone rang and rang and then at a nude Jerry Springer, Giji collapsed...

***

When Nick came out of surgery, the doctor came to the waiting room and told her and Wynette that Nick had come through the surgery fine, but he had not yet woken up. A while later a nurse came to the waiting room to get SueAnn.

Wynette caught her hand as she stood to leave. "Are you going to be okay?"

SueAnn nodded, then she followed the nurse. The nurse lead SueAnn to a small, darkened room, then left. Alone, SueAnn stood in the door way. She could see Nick lying on the bed. He looked so helpless lying there under the sterile white sheet, with machines blinking and beeping all around him. It was all at once overwhelming, especially knowing Nick was attached to those machines. *Those machines could be keeping Nick alive*, she thought, feeling a slight panic inside. Fighting to steady herself, she took several deep breaths. *He's going to be fine,* she told herself. *He has to be. He has to be!*

Slowly SueAnn made her way to the side of the bed. She stood, looking down at Nick. He had cuts and scratches on his handsome face, along with a few bruises, she noticed, and a bandage across his forehead. *But he was alive,* she told herself, *and he would be fine. That's all that mattered.*

He blinked several times, letting his eyes focus, then he slowly opened his eyes, looking up at her. For a few moments, he did not speak. Finally he said, "You're okay."

She nodded. "I am, I'm fine," she assured him, trying to smile, "and you're going to be fine, too."

He swallowed hard, closed his eyes and asked, "You forgive me?"

SueAnn nodded when he opened his eyes again. "Of course, I do," she said softly. "If I hadn't run off – "

He swallowed hard and put his hand on hers. "It-it's not your fault," he told her weakly. "I should have been honest…ah…from the beginning."

"I would never have forgiven myself if anything had…" she choked up for a second… "had happened to you. When I…well… during this I realized how much I love you."

He managed a little smile. "Me too," he said quietly, drifting off…. "I love you."

For the first time in so long, SueAnn felt at ease. She took Nick's hand in hers, holding it tightly as if she were holding on for dear life. *He looks so fragile,* she told herself, *but he's a fighter, he's strong.* She lightly kissed him on the lips, thinking of all the happiness that lay ahead of them. *That's so much more than others have to look forward to,* she reminded herself, thinking of the explosion….

Epilogue

The Aftermath

Dressed in black, the wives watched as the coffin was lowered into the ground...

to be continued...

About the Author

Tamarias Tyree is an International best-selling author and editor. Her erotic best-sellers include **Sex You Up!** and **Sizzling Hot Erotica -** Volumes I & II. **Delicious Housewives!** is Ms. Tyree's first novel.

www.fireflyerotica.com

LaVergne, TN USA
02 December 2010
207134LV00001B/113/A